A Lasting Spring

A Lasting Spring

Jean Stubbs

St. Martin's Press
New York

Library of Congress Cataloging-in-Publication Data

Stubbs, Jean, 1926–
    A lasting spring.

    I. Title.
PR6069.T78L3   1987   823'.914   87-16271
ISBN 0-312-01154-7

First published in Great Britain by Macmillan London Limited.

First U.S. Edition

10 9 8 7 6 5 4 3 2 1

To star-farers and wayfarers

Acknowledgements

Manchester and Blackstone shared the same weekend of the blitz and a performance of Handel's *Messiah*, but my city is not that city. I have lived these years and they are not mine. I have known the Fawleys and Schofields throughout my life, and they do not exist. But I am beholden to all the people who made this book possible, and yet again I thank Ian Atlee and the staff of Helston Branch Library, and D. G. Willcocks of Longs Booksellers, Pouton-le-Fylde, Lancashire, for finding books relevant to the period and place. Especially do I owe a debt of gratitude to my editor James Hale for persuading me to change *she* into *I*, capturing an elusive title, and being generally terrific; to Tess Sacco for spiriting up the idea; to Hilary Hale for hospitality in times of stress; and to my husband Roy Oliver for both kinds of dedication.

'Orpheus with his lute made trees,
And the mountain tops that freeze,
Bow themselves when he did sing:
To his music plants and flowers
Ever sprung; as sun and showers
There had made a lasting spring.'

SONG
'King Henry VIII'

William Shakespeare

A Lasting Spring

1945

Peeble's tea-shop is beginning to fill at this time of a May afternoon, but I have chosen a table for two in a niche, from which I can see anyone who enters but will not immediately be seen myself, and have hung my coat over the chair opposite, as if my companion has just left it there and will soon be back. So the room is filling with shoppers and idlers and those who have nowhere in particular to go, and I am allowed to sit on by myself.

The war is over and we are all a little lost, prisoners walking out uncertainly into the sunlight after six years of confinement, now finding liberty too great a concept to grasp, finding we have grown used to our cell.

Cigarette smoke and disjointed conversation drift across from nearby tables. In this recent state of peace, people are totting up their wartime profit and loss. Some of it is my own.

'. . . but now there's nothing to worry about I feel as if something was missing!'

'. . . haven't seen him for five years. The two older children have grown up, and of course Shirley was a baby when he left. Imagine, she starts primary school in September! Naturally, we're longing for him to get back home, but — we'll be strangers, won't we?'

'. . . and I did want to look nice for him, but I hadn't enough clothing coupons to buy anything new, so I put a new collar and cuffs on a dress he used to be fond of.'

'. . . and Mummy's offered to look after the children so we can have a week in Rhyl. A second honeymoon. Well, the first one was only for twenty-four hours!'

'. . . the time? Almost four o'clock.'

We'd arranged to meet here at half past.

'Don't come to the station,' he'd said. 'Wait for me in Peeble's tea-shop. I want to walk in and see you sitting there as if we'd never had a war. Oh, and if I look thin or strange or different, don't take any notice. I'll soon pick up again. Prison camps aren't health resorts and it's been a long time.'

From fear of being late I have come far too early. I order a pot of tea, pour a cup immediately, curl my fingers round the handle and sip. My body occupies its share of space. My mind wanders elsewhere. Gradually, the tea grows cold.

I find myself rubbing the toe of my right court shoe on the calf of my left leg, and stop. It's an old habit, signalling excitement or apprehension, but by the age of twenty-four I should have conquered it. Besides, I only possess one pair of nylon stockings. The alternatives are substantial lisle or a solution called Liquid Stockings, on top of which I draw a seam with an eyebrow pencil.

Peeble's, formerly the tea-palace of Blackstone, is now as drab as most of its customers. My outfit is far too smart and attracts glances of admiration, envy and suspicion. The glances ask if I am the mistress of a wartime profiteer? A better-class prostitute?

No, I answer silently, this was my wedding costume, provided by my stepmother who could survive anything and manipulate anybody. Too late, I realise that its quiet opulence is out of place here as well as out of season, being wool and the colour of autumn leaves. I hope that his sense of humour has remained intact.

In a little flurry of panic I play with the idea of getting up that moment, putting on my coat, giving my saucer of a hat an extra tilt over one eye, drawing on my fresh white gloves, picking up my patent-leather handbag, and simply walking away. Walking away in my glossy court shoes, which cost Dorothy a pound of butter for the clothing coupons on top of their shop price.

And how much did she pay for the rest of this handsome outfit, I ask myself. How many tins of American ham, Canadian pack apple, and honest old English Tate & Lyle sugar? Not forgetting the joint of beef for Miss Chadderton so that she should sew it all and never enquire where Dorothy found a bolt of pure new tweed.

The round clock on the wall says ten past four.

Opposite me, that woman's face is old and sad. She is speaking of someone who died. She is not alone in her trouble. Most of us have been afraid and watched young men march away into the dark.

The sun is shining on Peeble's famous cream cakes. The menu tells me sadly, stiffly, that the cream is artificial and our allowance is one per person. He can have mine as well. Oh, I want to see him more than anything in the world and yet I want to run away and never see him again. Because I have lived on the thought of him and the memories of him for nearly two years, but both of us must have changed. Suppose that our beginning was an end, and we can never be the same again?

The sun comes round like a searchlight, illuminating the wall behind me and the table in front of me, spilling over people's hands and faces with unrationed extravagance.

'Oh, look!' says the woman opposite, and her face is suddenly younger and radiant. 'Isn't that lovely?'

The winter of war is over and gone. Peace and spring are with us. We are going to create a wonderful new world. I know it, I believe it. All shall be well, and all manner of thing shall be well.

And though that part of me which knows how much experience costs, which knows how high a price we pay for love, whispers, 'Suppose that it isn't?', still I must hope for a lasting spring.

Part One

1928–1931

I

May 1928

All at once the sun shone through the classroom window and illuminated the page on which I wrote. I paused, smiled at the shaft of light, and touched it delicately with the nib of my pen. Around me, fifteen obedient little girls bent over their books, perhaps unaware of beauty, possibly knowing better than to attract attention by daydreaming. Unmindful of my surroundings, I lifted my face to trace the beam to its source and was most wonderfully dazzled.

Mrs Tate's voice sounded a muted warning.

'Evelyn! Get on with your weekly news, if you please.'

Fifteen pairs of eyes slid smugly round to gaze at me, and as smugly returned to their tasks.

The sun had given me false hope, which brought forth sheaves of words, and I began to write at top speed. Mrs Tate now spoke with some exasperation.

'Evelyn! How often do I have to tell you that it is better to do a little work well than a great deal of work badly? Take your time. I don't want to see pages of blots and spelling mistakes.'

The sun hid behind a cloud, and inspiration was gone. Worse still, the state of what it left behind filled me with apprehension. And now I came to think about it I had not written my weekly news at all. I read it through uncertainly, hoping that the meaning would still shine for me, in spite of errors.

Mrs Tate said sternly, 'Evelyn, bring your exercise book to me!'

I was then small and thin for my age, and solemn of face and soul: a dark-haired Alice, banished from Wonderland. While the teacher read, I stood twisting my arms behind my back, looking up into her large white face, hoping. Unpopularity at school was new to me, and I could not understand it. My fellow pupils had stopped writing in order to watch. She slapped the book shut, and the sound of disapproval made me jump.

'If,' said Mrs Tate in soft reproach, 'I saw this work without knowing who did it, I should judge it to be that of a backward child, Evelyn. As it is I can only come to the conclusion that you have grown careless and lazy. Perhaps you feel that it doesn't matter, since you are leaving us at the end of this term?'

I shook my head, murmuring truthfully, 'Oh no, Mrs Tate.'

'Then let us hope that you do better work than this at . . .' and she paused lightly, cruelly '. . . Moss Lane Elementary School.'

All the girls, even Marianne who had been my best friend, tittered. And though Mrs Tate had created and encouraged this reaction she silenced them instantly with a disapproving stare.

'I should not like to think that a pupil of Townley's was going to disgrace herself and us in this fashion.' She paused again, and said, 'Put this on your desk and stand in the corner, please.'

I had been shamed, but would not accept her verdict as final. I rubbed one white sock with the toe of my Clark's sandal, thinking.

'Did you not hear what I said, Evelyn?'

The desire to make all right with my world made me brave.

'But, please, Mrs Tate, did you like my news?'

The teacher began at last to lose patience.

'I should have thought my opinion was plain enough. You ignored the subject I set, and scribbled a lot of nonsense very badly. And stop fidgeting. Someone has to wash those socks, remember.'

I found that exercise book in the bottom of a toy cupboard when we were packing up the family home last autumn. The spelling was eccentric, the handwriting straggly, the page blotted, and to me the hopes were underlined with a certain despair. I marvel, looking back, at Mrs Tate's lack of perception and charity.

> *At the beginning of the summer holidays my father is geting maried agen becors my mother died when I was litle. He is a widoh and so is she and I call her Arnt Dorothy. She has a son called Mickal. He is two yeers older than me. She will be my new mother and he will be my brother and we shall be a reel family and they are lukking for a big howse so we can all live in it together*

At this point inspiration had proved too much for my spelling and handwriting, both of which grew wild.

> *Granmuthe's sowing ladi Mis Mafuws is making me a long frok of pail lilak voyal to ware at the weding and they are going to the Laak Distrik for a holida by themselfs and Mikal and I are staing with his grandmutha hoo lives in Hathasol . . .*

But Mrs Tate was made in an iron mould, for all that she looked like a large white soft sack of flour.

She cried, 'And I *said*, stand in the corner. At once!'

The teachers at this small private school prided themselves on never raising a voice in anger. That rule had been broken. We all stared at her, shocked and silent.

She made a great show of dipping her pen in the inkwell.

I picked up my exercise book, placed it with elaborate care on my desk, walked stiffly to the back of the room and stood very upright. We were expected to face the class rather than the wall, to increase our shame. I clutched my hands behind my back to stop them from shaking, and stared haughtily at the ceiling.

Mrs Tate communed with herself for another minute or so. Then said very brightly, 'Now who would like to read out their news? Barbara?'

A tall girl with thick corn-coloured plaits stood up smiling, and was eventually acclaimed.

The second reader was my best friend Marianne Nash. Perhaps in memory of our numerous dolls' tea parties she ventured to draw attention to my plight before she covered herself with glory.

'Excuse me, Mrs Tate, but Evelyn's crying without making a noise.'

'Thank you for telling me, dear.'

She addressed the oldest girl in the class.

'Barbara, take Evelyn to the cloakroom to wash her face. She is deliberately working herself into hysteria.' To me she said sternly, 'I shall have to write a letter to your grandmother and send you home early. Barbara will see you safely to the top of Church Street.'

As my wardress closed the door behind us, I heard Mrs Tate say, 'And now, perhaps, we can continue in a civilised fashion?'

Standing up and away from Church Street, only partly screened by the black bay trees which gave it the name of The Laurels, my grandmother's house was a gloomy one. On a dark winter afternoon its aspect was enough to cow the most unimaginative spirit, but even on a fine blue day the sight of it oppressed me.

Satchel strapped across my chest, I clambered up the nine stone steps, ran round the side of the house and entered by the back door. And there in the kitchen were both my aunts talking to Ada the general servant, who was preparing Grandma's afternoon tea-tray.

'You're home early, Evelyn,' said Aunt Kate, grinning. 'What is it this time? Teacher's birthday or feeling ill? If my two limbs of Satan came home early I wouldn't need to ask!'

For the house would be quiet until four o'clock when Alex and Leo would charge in, demanding bread and jam and flinging their caps and blazers down on Ada's clean floor.

Aunt Maud had seen the envelope in my hand, and clucked forward to take it.

'Oh dear! Have you had one of your sick turns, lovie?'

Her large blue eyes were awash, her mouth quivered in easy sympathy. She could have been vital and pretty, but all her colour and strength seemed to have gone to her fiery crown of hair. Forever sweet and anxious, she was a spinster daughter shaped by a strong-minded mother into a suitable companion.

The contents of the note made the corners of her mouth droop.

'Oh dear!' she said, quite fallen. 'This *will* upset Grandma.'

Still, she nerved herself to post the bad tidings between the china teapot and milk jug.

'Then why give it to her?' Aunt Kate asked, eyebrows raised.

'Because it's addressed to her, lovie. See? Mrs H. Fawley.'

'Well I'm Mrs H. Fawley, too. Here, let me take a gander!'

Aunt Kate was admirable. Tall and heroically slim, with shining brown plaits of hair coiled round her ears and a handsome reckless face. She leaned against the table edge, one hand in the pocket of her long fawn cardigan, the other disdainfully holding the sheet of paper

'H'm . . . *highly-strung of late*. Why of late? Evelyn's always been highly-strung! . . . *perhaps the impending changes at home and school etc.* I do detest people who hint! . . . *formerly obedient and anxious to please*. Well, thank God that's changed! . . . *lack of self-discipline*. Tommyrot! Mrs Tate's just fed up because Gilbert's taking Evelyn away from the school. They don't want to lose the fees and can't be rude to him, so they're taking it out on his daughter. We never had anything but golden reports and treacly sentiments previously. What a set of hypocrites they are! Well, that's that. And this is what *I* think of it!'

And she dropped the note into the kitchen fire.

Aunt Maud turned first white and then scarlet, and clapped two freckled hands to her freckled cheeks.

'If we say nothing we save trouble,' Aunt Kate advised. 'We don't want the merry widow up all night with palpitations.'

Ada, taking not the slightest notice of anything or anybody, walked past us, carrying the tea-tray upstairs.

'Oh, Katie!' said Aunt Maud in a voice reminiscent of the sandwich-board man calling her to repentance.

'Oh, stuff!' said Aunt Kate robustly. 'Let's have a cup of tea before the pirates of Penzance board us.'

Aunt Maud giggled. Her two nephews both horrified and delighted her. She drifted back to her bland and pleasant self again after the little drama of the burned note.

Aunt Kate's championship had somewhat restored me. I took my sketch book and crayon box from one drawer of the big deal table, sat at one end out of everyone's way, wrote THE WEDING in careful capitals, and began to draw and listen at the same time.

'Those boys of yours are just like their father. Just like our Harold,' said Maud fondly, warming the large brown teapot. 'Harold was always in trouble, and yet he's always been mother's favourite.'

'Yes,' said Kate drily, 'and she'll never let him go. Harold and I have been married for fourteen years, Maud, and I still haven't got a home of my own.'

'This *is* your home, lovie,' said Maud reproachfully, and placed a glass of Robinson's lemon barley water and two digestive biscuits in front of me.

Kate folded her arms and stared ahead of her.

'Fourteen years,' said Kate. 'Two-thirds of a life sentence! I'll say this for Gilbert,' she went on. 'He fights the old girl tooth and nail. He got away from her once with Clara, and this time I think he'll manage it for good with Dorothy.'

Her voice changed. She grinned.

'I like Dorothy, I must say. She's more . . .'

'My sort' would have been the words. But this implied that Maud was not, which was true but inadmissible. Her tact, however, was wasted on Maud who had found a happy ending fit for a nice little girl.

'Who's going to have a lovely new Mummy, chuckie?'

'Me, Aunt Maud,' I replied automatically.

'And who's going to have a nice big brother to look after her?'

But Kate laughed aloud at this sentiment.

'I should think she's had enough big brothers to last a lifetime. Besides, young Michael's no angel.'

'No,' said Maud reflectively. 'He's nearly as bad as your two.'

I glanced up and met Kate's amused eyes. We smiled at each other.

'Let's have a look at this work of art, shall we?' said Kate.

I put down the crayon and rubbed my wrists. As usual there was an abyss between intention and execution. A diminishing row of dropsical figures, with famished limbs and startled hair, marched above their names from one side of the page to the other.

'I wish there weren't quite so many people coming to Daddy's wedding,' I said, in excuse. 'This is only our family, and now I've got all Aunt Dorothy's family to draw and there simply isn't room. I shall just have to do them on another sheet.'

Kate discussed the drawing seriously, and agreed to the absolute necessity of a separate sheet of paper for the Schofields.

'You can see it too, if you like, Aunt Maud,' I offered, being fair to both aunts.

'Drink your barley water, lovie. It'll settle your tummy,' said Maud, not listening. 'Here's a cup of tea for you, Kate.'

Ada came downstairs and sat down in her rocking-chair by the kitchen range. She poured tea for herself, dipped a digestive biscuit into it, and ate and drank composedly.

I began to draw the Schofields, whom Grandma despised.

'It's a good thing,' I observed, 'that Aunt Dorothy's other family aren't coming. I should run out of paper if I had to draw those Harlands as well?

Aunt Kate twisted round from the waist and regarded me with affectionate mockery. She held herself beautifully.

'We couldn't expect the Harlands to come to a daughter-in-law's second wedding, Evelyn. Besides, they're much too grand.'

Maud raised her eyebrows and looked significantly at Kate.

Then she said in a lowered voice, 'When you think of it, Katie, Somebody-not-too-far-from-here has done very nicely for herself twice over. I mean, she comes of respectable people, but they're not quite . . .'

'Out of the top drawer,' I supplied wordlessly. She was talking about Aunt Dorothy and the Schofields.

'My God, you are a snob, Maud,' said Aunt Kate forcefully. 'And who might the Fawleys be when they're at home? Royalty? What's so wonderful about marrying into a family of grocers?'

Maud was shocked.

'Not just grocers, lovie. High-class grocers. The Honourable Mrs Newton wouldn't have her weekly order from anyone else in the district.'

'Only because Walter and Harold let her have it on everlasting tick, and nobody else would deliver it up that long drive of hers.'

'*My* father's not a grocer!' I said, forgetting I should not be listening.

'No, he's a headmaster, and a very fine one,' Kate replied sincerely.

A teacher herself, before she married Harold, she respected him.

To Maud she added, 'And the best thing he's done so far is to find Dorothy and get out of this funeral parlour.'

'Oh, lovie, do you think you should . . . ?'

'Speak the truth now and again? Yes, I do. What's more, I'm going out into the garden to have a gasper.'

'Not under mother's window, lovie. Smoke makes her feel faint.'

'If I thought that old witch would lose her senses for five minutes,' said Kate, 'I'd blow it up her nostrils.'

She took a packet of Kensitas out of her cardigan pocket, shook one out, lit it with a spill from the box on the mantelpiece, gave a rich giggle, and sauntered out into the back garden.

Now Aunt Maud's going to try and explain that Aunt

Kate didn't mean what she said, I thought. But I knew she did. I knew she hated Grandma. I didn't like her much either. A new thought occurred to me.

I asked, interested, 'Did Mummy hate Grandma, too?'

Maud was diverted from one dangerous topic to another.

'Of course she didn't. They loved each other dearly.'

I was puzzled to make sense of this remark.

'Besides, you know very well that we don't want to upset your poor Daddy by talking about your poor Mummy,' said Maud, concerned. 'I should have thought we understood that by now, chuckie.'

Her lack of logic annoyed me.

'But Daddy isn't here!' I cried.

Kate's two sons spared me a reprimand by hurling themselves into the kitchen, casting aside striped caps, blazers and satchels, and thundering upstairs before anyone could stop them.

Behind them came Kate, swearing under her breath and stubbing out her cigarette in a saucer as she passed. She paused to snatch up an old leather slipper, and followed them swiftly.

We listened, biscuits poised.

Kate's voice cried, 'I'll give you what for, you wicked boys!'

'Mrs Kate's got them penned in,' said Ada, as though Alex and Leo were sheep. 'And that means no tea as far as them lads are concerned!'

Slaps and shouts were followed by theatrical cries for mercy. A series of sharp raps on the ceiling diverted our attention. Over the tattoo a voice called feebly, and yet with perfect clarity.

'Maud! Katherine! Ada! What's wrong? What is it?'

Maud leaped up crying, 'There now. They've disturbed Mother!'

She stood awkwardly, hand to mouth, an adolescent girl in her middle years.

'I'd better see to her,' she said, harassed.

She tucked three fiery wisps of hair into place, put on a soothing expression, and departed.

Left alone, Ada and I maintained an amicable silence. Ada stacked the cups and saucers, poured out a final cup of stewed tea for herself, and stood it on the wooden draining-board while she peeled potatoes. I drew a sheet full of staring Schofields.

'I think I might be quite glad to stay with Grannie Schofield while Daddy and Aunt Dorothy are on holiday,' I said at last.

'I should think you might, love,' Ada answered drily.

'And quite glad to live with Michael and Daddy and Aunt Dorothy instead of here.'

'I'm not surprised to hear that, neither.'

'Oh, but I shall miss Aunt Kate. And I shall miss you, Ada.'

'I shall miss you, too, love.'

'Because you've always been very kind to me.'

Ada pursed her lips and shook her head.

I supplied her inward comment, silently. 'Eh, she's a right old-fashioned little lass!'

'And even though you won't be coming to the wedding,' I said, 'I've drawn you in with our family in your best black Sunday dress.'

'Well, that's very kind, I'm sure.'

'And I've drawn Aunt Dorothy in a long white wedding dress and a veil, even though she isn't going to wear one. Ada, why aren't they having a proper wedding in church?'

'Well, they've both been married afore. Folks don't make such a fuss the second time.'

I crayoned the bride's hair in bright yellow curls.

'Aunt Dorothy isn't like my Mummy at all, is she?'

Ada considered this question cautiously.

'No. Neither in looks nor nature. But she's a very nice kind lady as'll be a good mother to you and make you a good home.'

'Would she let me have a kitten, do you think?'

'I should wait and see,' Ada advised. 'She'll have enough on her plate without kittens.'

A spurt of laughter escaped me.

I cried scornfully, 'Ada! You don't have kittens on plates!'

'Now then, don't be cheeky! And what about your piano practice? The teacher'll be vexed if you're no better than last time.'

A weight descended on my chest and stayed there.

'I don't want to practise the piano.'

'What? And poor Grandma paying Miss Hibbert sixpence a lesson?'

'Miss Hibbert hits my knuckles with a ruler when I make mistakes.'

'But your mam used to play the pianner lovely. A lovely singing, playing lady she were. Don't you want to be like her?'

Blackmailed, I put away my sketch book and crayon box and trailed disconsolately into the front parlour where green blinds were drawn against the sun.

The room smelled of Mansion polish. The chairs and sofa were upholstered in horse-hair and slippery to sit on. An upright Waldemar piano stood against the far wall. Before it sat an ornate music-stool. An assortment of albums and sheets in its tray bore witness to the musical tastes of the Fawley household: hymn tunes, a selection of popular light classics, and my two piano exercise books.

I had looked in vain for any of my mother's music, but though they paid tribute to her graces and talents there was no evidence of her there or anywhere else in the house. My father had taken her death badly, they said. He had sold up the home they had made together and brought me here to live. Since she was an only child, brought up by an elderly aunt in the south of England, he lost touch with her family too. His silence on the subject was total. When anyone mentioned her he politely turned the conversation aside or closed it. His loss had gone too deep.

Grandma accepted me out of duty. Aunt Maud cried a lot. But it was Aunt Kate who comforted my first grief and gave me my mother's silk shawl to hold until I fell asleep. A shawl of ivory silk, embroidered with birds. I kept this wrapped in tissue paper nowadays, for it was showing signs of wear, but its beauty brought her alive again, and as I buried my face in its shimmering folds I believed I could still smell the scent she used to wear.

Aunt Kate made sure that I had a photograph of her, too, taken only a few weeks before her death. She was tall and slim and dark, wearing her hair caught loosely up in a Grecian knot. She stood under a horse chestnut tree in full blossom, holding me up to face the camera. And whoever took the snapshot had caught us before we could pose, and she was laughing at me and I was laughing back and patting her cheek. I looked fatter and happier then.

I began to render the scale of C major in uneven runs.

2

August 1928

At first, Grandma Fawley had declined to attend my father's wedding, on the grounds that it would take place in a registry office and therefore be unconsecrated. Nor should her three grandchildren, she said, be allowed to witness a heathen ceremony. In any case Evelyn tended to be sick when she was excited, and Leo and Alex always misbehaved. Also, she needed her eldest son Walter to hold her arm and Maud to carry her smelling salts. She acknowledged that Harold, as a witness, must accompany his brother to Hathersall registry office, but the rest of us must go straight to Parbold House for the reception.

Then, public appearances being rare, her toilette was so prolonged, and involved so many changes of mood and mind, that my aunts had scarcely time to dress themselves and oversee the three of us. By the time she was ready, dressed entirely in glistening black, and reeking of camphor and lavender water, our neighbours were peeping between long lace curtains at the waiting taxis.

And what a spectacle it was, to see Grandma in her finery, supported by Uncle Walter and Aunt Maud, negotiating the nine steps down to the pavement, and stopping for breath every step of the way. Finally they hoisted her into the first cab, where she sat with her black-gloved hands on the knob of her ebony walking-stick.

We three children were automatically assigned to the

other cab because, Grandma said, our presence caused a curious singing noise in her ears. This left Aunt Kate to deal with us single-handed and keep my stomach on an even keel. First she addressed her sons.

'Just one word from either of you two villains, and I'll lock you up in Mrs Schofield's cellar and make sure you have nothing to eat.'

The boys' fair young faces became solemn. They pulled up their grey knee socks and sat, legs dangling, shoes shining. They were dressed in their best grey flannel suits, and wore identical pale blue shirts and dark blue ties. Only the purple bruises on their knees, and their fearless blue eyes, made them recognisable.

As well as my suitcase, packed for a fortnight's stay at Parbold House, a brown paper carrier bag stood by Aunt Kate's side. Into this, as on any journey long or short, she had thrown last-minute essentials. From it, closely watched by the three of us, she brought two comics. *Chums* for Alex and *Tiger Tim's Weekly* for Leo.

'I've got *The Rainbow* for you, Evelyn, but hold on a minute!'

She took a hair-brush and a silk handkerchief from the carrier bag, and brushed and polished my long straight brown hair, and retied my lilac satin ribbon.

'Why didn't I have a daughter?' she asked the universe.

On the edge of tears, I said, 'Oh, I shall miss you, Aunt Kate!' and hugged her.

'Mind my hat!' she said briskly. 'And don't start crying down the front of your new frock. How do I look?'

'Like that lady in the advertisement for Mansion polish.'

'Who could ask for more?' said Aunt Kate, and giggled.

She found her packet of Kensitas, and lit one.

'Nobody tell!' she cautioned us all.

And blew a circle of smoke into the air and sat back, contented.

This was not the first time that I had visited the Schofields, but visiting is not belonging. They could not necessarily be trusted to behave nicely to me when I was a member of their family. Only my father's presence could guarantee fair treatment. Still, I would rather stay with them than with Grandma Fawley, and so far neither their hospitality nor their home could be faulted.

From an adult point of view I can see that Parbold House must have been highly inconvenient. A century ago Hathersall had been farming country, and Parbold one of the biggest farms in the district. But its land had been sold and built on, and only the tall brick house remained on an island of cobbled yard and back garden, facing the main road to Blackstone. The rooms stepped up and down and into one another. The kitchen floor was stone-flagged and uneven. There was no hot-water system and no electricity. But to me it was a magical place full of unexpected corners and treasures, with window-seats broad enough to sit in, bounteous fires and food, and a ceremonious lighting of oil lamps on winter evenings.

A quiet and solitary child, lingering on the edges of adult conversations, I picked up the family gossip parrot-fashion, for much of it was beyond my understanding. From my aunts I gathered that the Schofields were an offence to Grandma in every way: working-class as compared to middle-class, devout Methodists rather than Church of England and, worst of all, Socialists instead of Conservatives. From my father and Dorothy I overheard that they were teetotallers, the nearest article to alcohol in their household being a sweet dark liquid bearing the misleading title of *Oporto-type Wine*, which might prove a stumbling-block at the reception.

Dorothy, though devoted to her parents, was of a more worldly frame of mind. She wanted her second marriage, like her first, to be launched with wine and toasted in champagne. My father had offered to provide this, as his predecessor had done. The Schofields' hospitality ran broad and deep. Once more they sacrificed a principle for their daughter's sake, and wine both white and red, sparkling and still, was to grace the buffet table. Grandad Schofield had only one stipulation to make. He said that those who drank alcohol should pour it. For his part he would offer only temperate beverages.

So on this warm August morning some thirty newly-related, ill-assorted guests collected in the front parlour of Parbold House, about to be united by a Schofield banquet.

Grandma Fawley was a careful housekeeper, and Ada's cuisine was of the stewed mutton and rice pudding sort, but the Schofield women had a natural talent for cooking, to which they had given reckless rein. Only the wedding cake had been professionally baked and iced by Peeble's of Blackstone.

There was a cold salmon as the centrepiece, cut into steaks, with a leg of boiled ham on one side and a cold jellied tongue on the other. These were flanked by bottles of Heinz mayonnaise, artistic gardens of mixed salad, and paper-thin triangles of white and brown bread and butter with the crusts cut off. On a side-table stood bowls of strawberries, a variety of cold fruit tarts, a jug of thick fresh cream and another of custard, a red jelly and a pink blancmange, a glistening chocolate layer cake, and an assortment of fancy biscuits.

Our family was deeply impressed. My uncles looked frankly greedy, my aunts smiled at each other in anticipation, my father became very affable, and we children gaped until we were nudged.

Cautioned to behave, Alex and Leo and I held out our plates and received what was thought best for us. Due to my temperamental stomach I came off worst, but Michael surreptitiously stuffed the pockets of his best blue suit with chocolate biscuits.

'You be a little gentleman!' said Grannie Schofield, tapping his shoulder as she passed. 'And look after Evleen and Alick and Leah!'

'Yes, Grannie!' he said promptly and politely, but winked at us.

The three boys had already established a fellowship. Michael, at ten, was a year younger than Alex and a year older than Leo: a tall lad for his age, with dark-blond silky hair, cool grey eyes and a tendency to freckles. In appearance and temperament he might well have been brother to Alex and Leo, but there were subtle differences. Where they were reckless, he was daring. Where they looked for mischief, he looked for adventure. Now he beckoned us to follow him into the kitchen, where Grannie Schofield was keeping reinforcements.

'Come on, you lot!' he said, in lordly fashion. 'Take your pick!'

And he began to pile his plate with richer delicacies.

We were following his example when a laconic male voice from the kitchen doorway froze our hands.

'And what are you four musketeers up to?'

An incredibly thin man lounged there, grinning. His ears jutted out from the sides of his bony head. His clothes hung from his lanky frame. His face was plain and kind, his expression droll.

'It's okay!' said Michael, relaxing. 'It's Uncle Arthur. He's a good egg. You won't tell on us, will you, Uncle?'

The thin man put a long finger to his lips and smiled.

'But you'd best scarper while you can,' he advised.

'Just off, Sergeant! Come on, you lot, and we'll hide!'

The thin man said, 'Try the work-shed outside. It's the only place without a bed in it!'

We scarpered.

'Your uncle's just about the thinnest man I've ever seen,' said Alex, who had never met him before. 'Is he really a sergeant?'

'He was, but he got gassed at Wipers in the war.'

'Where's that?'

'Some place in France. He can't work. He stays at home. On bad days he stays in bed. Today's a good day. On a good day he's a good egg. The best egg in the world.'

Michael's word was sufficient recommendation for Alex and Leo. They accepted Uncle Arthur without further question.

I held my tongue and followed them, holding up the long skirt of my lilac voile dress in one hand and carrying my spoils in the other. They shinned up the wall of the cobbled yard without a backward glance, and my appeal for help was answered grudgingly by Michael. He looked down on me

23

haughtily as he straddled the wall, and hesitated, but he had orders to take care of me.

'Okay then, but give us your plate first!' he commanded.

Trustfully I handed it up. I like to think that he meant me to join them, but Grannie Schofield called me from the kitchen at that moment, and Michael disappeared, taking my plate with him. So I went back into the house, attaching myself unnoticed to first one group and then another, eating plain bread and butter and listening.

Grandad Schofield paused in front of the bride and groom.

'Well, our Dollie, there's summat to be said for second weddings. Your mother and me have got us-selves a new granddaughter already!'

My new stepmother answered him vivaciously.

'Yes, I can tell you're pleased about that. You'll be set up with her while I'm away, I can see!'

Dorothy must have been an exceptionally pretty girl and at thirty was a very handsome woman. Fashion, even in the late nineteen-twenties, had not persuaded her to shingle. Her hair was abundant, ash-blonde and naturally curly, worn in a bun at the nape of her neck.

Both she and my father, being in their maturity, had kept the wedding as informal as possible. The discreet stripe in his grey suit was evoked in his plum-coloured silk tie. She had chosen a long crêpe-de-chine gown and wide-brimmed hat in eau de Nil. Her bouquet was a spray of pink roses, gypsophila and asparagus fern.

'You needn't give that little lass a second thought while she's here, Dr Fawley,' said Grandad. 'She'll be as right as ninepence.'

My father was quite the most distinguished-looking man present. A lean, dark dandy in his late thirties, his stance was easy but his eyes wary. A sardonic little smile turned down the corners of his mouth. Unlike Dorothy, who was loving every minute of her day, he was going through a necessary ritual, but his answer was warm.

'Thank you, Mr Schofield,' my father said. 'You're very kind.'

Grandad nodded and walked on, and I shadowed him at a distance, until he bumped into Grannie. They paused for mutual refreshment.

'Well, Mother, we've done us best, and they seem to be enjoying theirselves – except for t'owd lady. What's up wi' her? She's getten a face like a wet weekend.'

'Oh, take no notice of her! Our Dollie's got no time for her.'

'And where have them three lads gone?'

'Over t'backyard wall!' she answered tartly. 'And taken a mort of our Dollie's petty-fours off the kitchen table!'

'Ah well, lads'll be lads. Is little lass with them?'

'Nay, I saw her round here not long since.'

The exchange was commonplace. His words were not tender and her tone was dry, yet they seemed to derive strength and comfort from the encounter. Grannie was pondering a more immediate problem.

'I'st never manage to call him *Gilbert*! she said, worried. 'And our Dollie says as I should, now we're related.'

'Aye, I daresay she does, but he'll be *Dr Fawley* to me,' Grandad Schofield replied. 'It'd seem a liberty to say *Gilbert*, and I canna call him nowt!'

I thought it tactful to crawl along, underneath the table, and reappear at a safe distance. I accepted a glass of homemade lemonade.

Up came their younger son Eric, fresh-faced and important. A future student at Blackstone University, a former head prefect at Blackstone Grammar School, he was the Schofields' pride and their most polished representative, already popular with everyone except Grandma.

'I say, Harold wants to know if it's time for the toasts?'

'Aye, I daresay it is. They've eaten enough to keep them going for a month o' Sundays!' said Grannie Schofield censoriously. She had been watching my uncles enjoy their food. 'And high-class grocers or not,' she added, 'they've never had their legs under a table as good as this afore, I can tell you! Gormandising!'

'Now, Mother, you know you'd be vexed if they left it!'

Grandad observed peaceably, 'And we'd only have to eat it up us-selves.'

Eric hurried away, and in another moment was calling for silence.

'Ladies and gentlemen. Lend us your ears, if you please!'

Grandma Fawley, seeing everyone's attention focused on him, asked Aunt Maud loudly and querulously to find her spectacles. But she looked proudly around as Harold gave his brief and humorous speech, and was quiet and attentive when my father replied to the toast, though she shook her head when he thanked the Schofields for 'this splendid feast' and sighed heavily when he referred to Dorothy as 'my dear wife'.

Once the speeches were over, and the cake cut and distributed, a definite mellowness set in.

Uncle Harold was flushed with wine and bonhomie. He sat by Grandma and made her smile, albeit unwillingly. He slapped Aunt Kate's neat bottom, and pronounced her a queen among women. He kissed the bride yet again.

'I'll be damned glad to leave Harold behind, I can tell you,' my father said to Dorothy, who was laughing at this gallantry. 'And if he thinks he's coming to supper with us he's very much mistaken!'

'Well, we can't very well ask Kate without him,' said my stepmother sensibly, 'and I've promised her an invitation as soon as we're settled in!'

And she waved across the heads of the company to her new sister-in-law, who waved cheerfully back and, seeing me hovering unnoticed in the background, called me over to her.

For once, Aunt Kate had enjoyed a family assembly. Warmed by wine, freed of impediments, she had found interesting company in Eric. By the time I reached her she had forgotten me and had pitched into a controversial discussion about the plight of women teachers, who were not allowed to work once they were married unless, of course, they became widows.

'It's an infamous rule!' she cried, incensed. 'I got a first in history at Blackstone University and I was a good teacher. My sons are at school. My mother-in-law and Ada run the house between them. And I'm reduced to arguing with Maud over who should arrange the flowers! Why should I waste my abilities simply because I'm married? I'd be a better teacher and a better person, I can tell you, if I were allowed to work again – and so would lots of other women who have nothing to do with their time.'

The company had spread through the ground floor of Parbold House, leaving Grandma Fawley isolated in the front parlour amid the ruins of the banquet, where she shortly fell asleep out of chagrin.

In the hall, my father and stepmother paused for a private word. They had been making the rounds of their guests, smiling much and eating little, doing their duty by those who had attended and wished them well, thanking them for presents of varying use and beauty. The reception had been a success. My father consulted his gold fob-watch, lifted his eyebrows and nodded. Dorothy turned and began to make her way to the stairs.

A murmur ran through the throng.

'She's going up to change!'

There was a flurry to catch the bride's bouquet of pink roses.

Now Grannie Schofield's sisters began to collect the best plates ready for washing up at the stone sink. In the kitchen, Grannie had put the kettle on the black-leaded range. She looked tired, as if she needed to be alone for a while, to rest and collect herself, but her guests were coming through in ones and twos and standing in the doorway asking questions.

Aunt Kate asked, 'Has anybody seen my two young beasts?'

Grannie was busy counting cups and heads. Under her breath she muttered, 'Thirty. That means we'll have to use the kitchen ones as well.' Then, 'The disgrace!'

The three boys were tracked down, herded in and scolded. Their hands and faces were cleaned briskly with the end of a wetted towel, their clothes tweaked, shaken and brushed into place. Finally, in a fair semblance of their original state of purity, they were pushed into the hall to await the bride.

Heavy with the knowledge that my father's departure

would leave me among strangers, I pressed against his side and clutched his hand, staring mutely up at him. He swung me to his shoulder and kissed me. People said he was a remote man, an undemonstrative man, but in my childhood I never found him so. He could not take the place of the mother I had lost, but he was a loving father.

'Now, Evie, Evie,' he coaxed, 'you're going to enjoy yourself here. Grannie Annie is very kind and a very good cook, and Grandad was telling me how much he liked you.'

Even this unwonted popularity could not assuage my fears.

'Please let me come with you. I wouldn't be a nuisance.'

He stroked my hair, saying, 'But you've had your holiday already, my lass. A fortnight at the seaside with Aunt Kate and Uncle Harold and the boys.'

While preparations for the wedding went on in peace without me, I added silently.

I remained uncomforted.

'I tell you what we'll do,' he said. 'We'll see what the Lake District is like and then we can all go there together next year.'

Kissing him again and again, I said, 'And when you come back we'll be going to our very own home, shan't we?'

We were tender with each other, old allies in our common loss.

'Not right away, Evie. We're renting a furnished house in Kersley for a few months while we look round. But we'll be together in a home of sorts, and we shall be on our own.'

He was frowning slightly with the effort of making me happy. I strove not to disappoint him.

'And Aunt Dorothy is very kind and a very good cook, too.'

'Yes, she is indeed! In fact, between you and me,' and he whispered in my ear, 'she cooks even better than Grannie Annie!' Then he looked seriously at me, and said, 'Have you thought about what you'll call her? You can't go on saying *Aunt Dorothy* now we're married. And I'm hoping that Michael will acknowledge me as a father.'

I tried the precious name over in my mind. 'Mummy!

Mummy! Mummy!' The name I called out in black or restless nights. But it would not come at will, and never for Aunt Dorothy. Perhaps Michael suffered from the same difficulty, though his father had been killed before he was born.

'I could call her *Mother*,' I said helpfully.

There was no intimacy in *Mother* at all. *Mother* was a title, a role, a state of being.

'That would be splendid, and she'd be very pleased. She wants to do her best by you – by all of us. And see if you can't persuade Michael to see matters from that point of view. We want to be a proper family, don't we? There's only been you and me, the past four years.'

I nodded emphatically. To be a proper family was the ultimate happiness.

'Do you get on quite well with Michael?'

'Oh yes. It's just that he doesn't take any notice of me.'

'That will come. We all have adjustments to make.'

Michael stood shyly on one leg and then the other, keeping well away from us, back against the wall. The whole company, with the exception of Grandma Fawley, who still slept soundly, now pressed into the narrow hall or as near to it as they could get. And down the stairs came Dorothy, abundant with life and promise, radiant in a powder-blue costume and matching cloche.

My father set me down and moved towards his wife. The newly-wed couple linked arms, resplendent, remote. And we two children stared at them dumbly. Our lives lay in their hands. Swooping to earth before flying away, Dorothy left my father and bent down and hugged us both.

'We're going to have such jolly times together!' she promised.

My father joined her, kissing my cheek and patting Michael's shoulder. It was a moment only, but the dream was reborn, the four of us seemed as one. The moment was enough, was over. The rest of the company came forward to say their farewells.

'Handkerchiefs at the ready!' said Uncle Arthur, grinning.

Dorothy, flushed and tearful, broke away from the group.

Once more she linked arms with her new husband. They moved towards the waiting taxi, and smiled and waved.

'Goodbye, everybody, goodbye!' And last of all, and most meaningfully, 'Goodbye, children!'

Michael and I exchanged glances.

Then I waved vigorously, and cried, 'Goodbye, Daddy. Goodbye, Mother. Goodbye!'

'Goodbye, Mum!' cried Michael, waving. And then, 'Goodbye, Father!'

We were brother and sister now. Our lack of choice in the matter formed some sort of bond. We moved closer together, watching the taxi drive away from us.

3

In deference to my nerves, on which subject Aunt Maud had been eloquent, Grannie Schofield decided that I should sleep with her. So Grandad had been banished temporarily from the marital bed, and was sharing Uncle Eric's room at the back of Parbold House.

Used to a private cubby-hole at The Laurels, I was lost in the big front bedroom. My summer coat and straw bonnet hung timidly in the cavernous wardrobe. One drawer of the tallboy swallowed the contents of my suitcase at a gulp. Mahogany armchairs sat like aldermen, legs spraddled, carved hands upon their knees, in two separate corners. A carpet of Eastern design covered most of the floor. Round it glittered brown borders of linoleum patterned to resemble parquet. The room was dominated by a big brass bedstead from which, when I sat up, I saw myself reflected in the dressing-table mirror on the far wall.

The marble-topped wash-stand by the window held a blue-and-white flowered jug, basin and soap dish.

'You can wash you in here,' said Grannie. 'I'll fetch you a jug of hot and a jug of cold in the morning. Grandad shaves downstairs in the kitchen. I tell him, I say, "We've got a bathroom in t'house, tha knows!" And he says, "Aye, I know, but it's allus got one of them lads in it!" Which is nobbut the truth, when all's said and done!'

She opened the centre cupboard of the wash-stand, reveal-ing two chamberpots garlanded with roses.

'I'll put one o' these under the bed on your side,' she said delicately. 'And there's summat else. You might not be used to so much traffic. We're right on t'main road and the trams don't half rattle and flash. Shall you be feared?'

'Not unless it's dark,' I said diffidently.

'Well, it's light until gone ten o'clock. I'st be in bed myself by then, and I'll put a night-light in a saucer o' water on the wash-stand in case you wake up afore morning. How about that?'

I thanked her very much.

'Say thi prayers, then,' Grannie commanded. 'No gabbling, mind!'

She sat on the side of the bed, hands folded in her apron, while I knelt beside her and went through the ritual, remembering to include the Schofields on my nightly roster.

She was a small brisk woman who always wore black, as if to mark the fact that life had caused her a great deal of grief, which indeed it had. She grieved also over her lack of height, saying that she should have to stand on a box before she could peg the washing out. But lack of inches did not mean lack of dignity. Hardship had strengthened her. Perhaps it had also robbed her of humour for she seldom laughed and never made a joke. And she loved deeply and loyally but, in a sense, narrowly. For she was interested in no one outside her family and the daily round. Parbold House was her universe.

I hesitated a moment, wondering whether it would be accounted bad manners to include my real mother, but it seemed treacherous to leave her out, particularly as my father had now officially replaced her and she might be feeling usurped.

'And keep Mummy safe,' I whispered into my fingers. Then loud and clear. 'Amen.' And on to the prayer of protection. 'Matthew, Mark, Luke and John, the bed be blest that I lie upon. Four angels to my bed. Four angels round my head. One to watch and one to pray, and two to bear my soul away.'

And please let it not be for a very long time, I added mentally. For the idea of being whisked away in my sleep was disquieting.

'In you get,' Grannie ordered. 'Give us a hug and a kiss, then.'

The hug was friendly and tight. The kiss had a grand smack to it. She paused at the door. The Schofield evening ceremonies were evidently not yet over.

'Night night. Sleep tight. Sweet dreams. God bless. See you in the morning.' For the benefit of any evil thing that might be listening, she added, 'All being well.'

I did not hear her come to bed but the trams made me dream of dragons, and the last one, on its way to the city depot in Blackstone, bared its teeth and poured flames into the room and hissed and rattled its metallic scales. I woke to find that the night-light kept nothing at bay but was vaulting shadows on the walls, and they were all elders sitting in judgement. As I sat up in bed, quivering, a little ghost rose also and quivered in the looking-glass opposite.

In terror, I forgot where I was and shrieked for the lost guardian of my childhood.

'Mummy! Mummy! Mummy!'

A warm rough voice, sleepy but alert, replied, 'It's all right, love, I'm here. Grannie's here, love.'

But I was hysterical in a house of strangers.

'Now then, that's enough!' said Grannie, chiding kindly, hugging me closely, patting my back.

After a minute or two I stopped sobbing and explained, 'I dreamed the trams were dragons, you see.'

'Did you, love? Then next time you'd best dream about St George and all, and get him to chase them off.'

'I never thought of that,' I said, impressed.

Grandma Fawley would have used the dragons against me.

'There you are, then. Sleep on, now.'

So I slept, while St George kept the dragons at bay, and woke only once more to ask, 'Where's Mummy?' and was answered, 'She'll be home presently, love. Never fear.' And so went back to sleep again and didn't stir until morning.

I was a shy little oddity, full of unexpected knowledge and unexpected innocence, and the Schofields made much of me then and afterwards. Their admiration encouraged me. For the first time in my life I felt myself to be a person of importance.

Each August morning I woke with the feeling that great events were at hand, and I the centre of them. The sun, abetting this imperial fantasy, transformed the old crimson plush curtains into a stage, with footlights beneath their faded folds and a subdued glow above and beside them, waiting to open on the day's performance.

Each morning Grannie aroused me at half past seven, placing on the wash-stand a copper jug of hot water and an earthenware jug of cold, which I could mix to my liking in the flowered basin. And while I washed, the sounds and smells of early day were all about me. From the bathroom came male voices, from the kitchen an aroma of bread and bacon frying. Outside, the trams were clattering to and fro with their cargoes of workers.

And each morning came the ritual of saying goodbye to Grandad Schofield before he set off to work. Sometimes I thought I liked him best of all, but Grannie's nightly company was precious, Uncle Arthur made me laugh and Uncle Eric made me feel agreeably shy. My feelings for Michael were confused as yet. Our enforced relationship hampered both of us.

Hearing the parlour clock begin to chime, I ran to the top of the staircase, mounted the handrail as Michael had taught me, and slid slowly and timorously down to the newel post.

Grandad was waiting by the back door, white-haired, blue-eyed, rosy-cheeked, spruce and freshly-shaven.

'There, Mother,' he said to Grannie, with some satisfaction. 'I towd thee she'd be down in time to see me off.'

His short white moustache bristled against my cheek.

'You kiss like a toothbrush,' I said, and he laughed.

'And what are you and our Mick doing today?' he asked. 'It's a grand morning. Not to be wasted. He should take thee fishing.'

'And suppose she falls in?' said Grannie sharply. 'What then?'

'Well, then, take a few jam butties with thee and a bottle of ginger beer, and have a picnic.'

'Where?' said Grannie grimly. 'I'm not having them traipsing miles and endways.'

'They could go to Hathersall Park. That's safe enough.'

I cried, 'Oh, I should like that!'

Michael said nothing.

Grannie hesitated. She was responsible for my safety and happiness, and the burden lay heavily upon her.

'Think on, Mother. You canna pen them in t'back garden for ever,' said Grandad good-humouredly.

'It's ten to eight,' Grannie cried, exasperated. 'Why don't you get on wi' your job and let me look after mine!'

His own temper rose, swift and hot and brief.

'You should try a spoon o' sugar wi' that tongue, instead o' so much vinegar. I'll see thee at dinner-time.'

And he went off in a huff.

'He'll be as right as ninepence by the time he turns the street corner,' said Grannie, unperturbed. 'And now I can get on.'

She cooked breakfast in relays. Grandad first of all, then us and Uncle Eric, with Uncle Arthur coming last. Finally, around nine o'clock, she toasted two slices of bread, brewed a small brown pot of tea, and sat down in peace to read the *Hathersall Weekly Advertiser*.

'Here's a cup o' tea while you're waiting,' she said, pouring, 'and I'll just take a cup to our Arthur afore I start frying again.'

So she could discover the climate of his day.

As soon as the door closed, Michael whispered, 'She'll let us take sandwiches and go to Hathersall Park.'

'How do you know?'

'She always takes notice of Grandad. And if Uncle Arthur's having a good day he might take us fishing as well.'

'Good-ho!' I said, anxious to be the perfect companion.

Michael was planning something. He sat quite still in his chair, staring ahead of him with a half smile. He was everything that I would have liked to be: confident, handsome, brave and a boy.

The door opened again, and Uncle Arthur's day was reflected in his mother's face.

'Not so good, Gran?' Michael asked directly, sympathetically.

She shook her head. She kept her back to us, trimming rinds off the bacon, and by tacit consent we did not speak to her or each other. Once, she lifted her apron to wipe her eyes, then turned round to speak in her usual brisk tone.

'You'd best eat a good breakfast if you're picnicking at Hathersall Park. I never thought much o' jam butties for dinner!'

We had fed the ducks on the pond, taken turns to push each other higher and higher on the iron swings, sipped water from a tin cup hanging by a chain from the drinking fountain, consulted the sundial and admired the ornamental flower clock. Now we sat on a bald hillock near the empty bandstand, all pleasures spent. From this promontory we could see beyond the park gates and mill chimneys to the hills on the horizon. Michael took the grass stalk from his mouth and pointed.

'That's the Pennine Range. Where *you* live!' he said.

The statement divided us, and I did not answer.

'That's where we're *all* going to live soon,' said Michael, amending his statement.

I cheered up, and asked, 'Are you looking forward to it?'

He shrugged.

'I expect it'll be all right. Mum wants her own home, anyway.'

'Daddy and I want our own home, too. It wasn't very nice at Grandma's house, except for Aunt Kate. They were always telling me what not to do.'

We sat in silence for another minute.

'How much money have you got with you?' Michael asked.

My purse hung from one shoulder by a long strap. I had no need to consult its contents. I was a natural financier.

'One shilling and tenpence ha'penny.'

'How come you're so rich?'

'Daddy gave me the shilling, and your mother gave me the sixpence, and Grandad gave me a threepenny bit, and the rest is what's left of my pocket money. How much have you got?'

He emptied all his pockets, and found sevenpence ha'penny.

'Between us we've got half-a-crown,' he said. 'You can do a lot with half-a-crown.'

'Why, what do you want to do with it?' I asked, discomfited.

'I was thinking that the tram fare to Kersley Town Hall is only a penny, and I can treat us to that. Then we can go to your grandma's house and play with Alex and Leo, and get back in time for tea.'

He did not mention my possible contribution to the cause, which made me suspicious. Three boys of similar tastes and temperament were likely to ignore me until refreshment time, when my one and tenpence ha'penny would be coaxed or bullied from its purse and squandered on aniseed balls, fizzy lemonade and ice-cream. Still, I could hardly say this. I put forward a reasonable objection.

'Grandma doesn't like children to visit the house unless they're invited. It makes her ears sing.'

'Your Aunt Kate seemed a decent sort. I bet she wouldn't mind.'

But I did not see why I should finance an idea which I disliked.

'You go then,' I said slowly. 'I can find my own way home.'

He frowned and stood up.

'You know very well that I'd get a telling-off if I let you!'

By this stage of an argument Alex and Leo usually moved in on me, one either side, and began thumping and arm-twisting and pinching me into submission. I had no idea how Michael would react, but there was something cool and tough about him and I was very much afraid of rousing his wrath.

'Then see me safe to the corner of Parbold Street first, and go to Kersley afterwards. I'll tell Grannie that you looked after me.'

37

'And what happens when I get home, stupid? I'll be in hot water for leaving you *and* for going to Kersley.'

'Why? Aren't you allowed?'

'Course not.'

I answered, with devastating logic, 'Then if we *both* went, we'd *both* be in trouble.'

He said quickly, 'They wouldn't be cross with you. They'd blame me. Because you're a girl, and you're younger.'

My scanty stock of confidence was fast waning. I stared down at the grass and plucked its short blunt blades.

'Look,' said Michael frankly, 'I've been stuck at home because of you all week. Why can't we do something I want to, for a change?'

'But you *can*! Only you've got to do it by yourself, because I don't like playing with Alex and Leo.'

He thought this over, then said with persuasive grace, 'It'd be more fun if we were together though, wouldn't it?'

But I knew why he needed me. Anger gave me courage. I jumped up and flung the purse contemptuously at his feet.

'Here, take it, if that's what you want!' I cried. 'And spend every penny for all I care. I don't like Alex and Leo, and they don't like me. And I'm not a baby. I can find my own way home.'

I ran down the mound and away from him towards the park entrance, heart thundering in my chest as I listened for the following feet.

They did not come. Outside the gates I paused and peeped back through the iron railings. He was nowhere to be seen.

In my haste and distress I longed to sob and cry, but knew that I must keep my wits about me, and in fairness to Michael should not reach Parbold House in tears. So I looked carefully to right and left, trying to remember the way we had come, and began to walk as fast as I could up Park Street by Chorley's Paper Mill, and across the market.

As I stood waiting for the traffic lights to change, Michael's voice behind me said, 'How about an ice-cream, Miss Fireworks?' And he grabbed my arm before I could run panicking into the traffic.

'You blooming old squib, you!' he said, grinning.

He handed my purse back.

'I don't want your rotten old money,' he said, steering me towards the ice-cream cart. More honestly, he added, 'Not unless you're there to spend it, anyway.'

I was so shocked and delighted that I began to cry.

He coloured up in shame, turned his back on me and said very loudly, 'Two penny cornets, please.'

Spinelli's homemade ice-cream was sold from a cart of many colours which stood permanently on the outskirts of the market. Dorothy had once taken us to their ice-cream parlour further up the street, and told us they churned their wares in the back kitchen.

'Why does the little girl cry?' Mrs Spinelli asked accusingly.

'It's all right. She's my sister. She'll stop in a minute,' said Michael. He nudged me hard. 'Here, skinny-legs, get this inside you!'

I ate the ice-cream, sniffling, and watched the trams go by.

'Would you like to go to Kersley if we *didn't* see Alex and Leo?' Michael asked. 'Just for an adventure.'

I could not oppose another scheme, so I nodded.

'We could go and explore back o' beyond,' he offered.

'Where's that?'

'Oh, it's Grannie's name for anywhere that's a long way away. But when I was a little boy I thought it meant that long hill with the funny crag on top like a toppling wave, just beyond Kersley.'

I cheered up and became a fount of information.

'The long hill is Tarn Fell, and the crag on top of it is called Tarn How. Daddy and I used to go for walks there on a Sunday afternoon when it was fine.'

Until he met Dorothy.

'Tarn How? I've never been there. Let's go and explore it.'

I had been betrayed so often, both openly and subtly, that I could not help extacting a promise from him.

'Are we truly not going to Grandma's house at all. Truly?'

'Cross my heart and hope to die. Did you hate it that much?'

I nodded emphatically, and licked up a dribble of ice-cream from the side of the cone. I wiped my eyes and fingers.

'Funny!' said Michael, 'I always *liked* living with my Grannie.'

'I'm not surprised!' I replied, in Aunt Kate's driest tone.

'Quick! There's a number nineteen to Kersley just stopping on the other side of the road, and the lights are green!'

We scrambled aboard, Michael pushing me ahead of him up the stairs. I had never been frightened so often in one day, but clutched and swayed my way to the top, and we sat in the circular seat at the very front of the tram. And it was wonderful.

We surged up Market Street and over the brow, saw Hathersall sink away in the distance behind us and open country stretch ahead of us. Here, at the end of a long chain of towns from the city of Blackstone, were remnants of the original agricultural community. Islanded farms overlooked by mill chimneys. Streams polluted with froth and chemical dyes. Cattle grazing only a few hundred yards from the main road.

'Do you know what Parbold means?' Michael said. 'Grandad told me. It's "the place where pear trees grow". There's still one sooty old pear tree left, but it doesn't grow pears any more.'

'Was Grandad ever a farmer?'

'No. He's always been a toolmaker. He's the foreman of a workshop in Hathersall which makes machine tools. It's a good job. Grannie says they've never been as well off in their lives, and if only Grandad can keep his mouth shut he'll retire with a pension.'

'Why must he keep his mouth shut?' I asked, interested.

'He's lost his job before now, for speaking to the workmen about politics. He believes in trade unions. Some managers don't want a trade union. But old Mr Dewsbury, who owns the factory, likes Grandad. Grandad says he's a good boss, and knows every man by name.'

The finer points of this were beyond me, but I grasped one fact.

'Your Grandad talks to you as if you were grown up, doesn't he?'

'Yep. He talks to me about politics. And Uncle Arthur talks about the war. Uncle Eric doesn't say much because he's studying for his exams. Besides he's courting – but you mustn't tell anybody.'

I drew a deep breath and sat up straighter. He had told me a secret. The tram was gathering speed on the straight, preparatory to clashing up a steep incline. I reciprocated as best I could.

'This is Broom Hill. When Daddy and I have been Christmas shopping in Blackstone, and we come back late and it's dark, we can see it all lit up from as far away as Hathersall Brow. And the two rows of streetlights look like a big hairslide with diamonds in it.'

Michael paused politely before changing the subject.

He said surprisingly. 'Do you know what a mongrel is?'

I answered promptly, 'Yes, it's a dog that the gipsy had when she came selling clothes' pegs, and Ada said, "Be off with you! And take that thieving mongrel with you!" But it wasn't thieving anything. Just shivering. And Ada said that the gipsy must have left a mark on our front gate, because somebody stole our underclothes off the washing line the next Monday.'

Again he heard me through politely, picking up the conversation where he had left off.

'Being a mongrel means your breeding's mixed. I'm a mongrel. Mum comes from the working-class, and my dad came from the middle-class.'

Remembering Grandma's scorn, I felt I was on delicate ground.

'It doesn't show,' I said diplomatically.

'Oh, I think it's a good thing. I can live two lives, that way.'

'A cat has *nine* lives! Would you like nine lives?'

'I'd like as many as I could get. I could use them all.'

The tram threw us about, and shuddered to a halt in front of Kersley Town Hall. A familiar weight sat on my chest. I followed Michael cautiously down the iron staircase, still afraid of treachery.

But he said, 'Okay, Squib, how do we get to Tarn How?'

In my relief, and my anxiety to get out of a part of town in which I could be recognised and somehow recaptured, I made a gesture.

'It's a long way. I'll treat us to a ride on the Shawcross tram. That'll take us to the foot of the Fell, and then we'll have to walk.'

This time I was the leader. I sat up importantly and did not speak during the journey, watching the streets go by, anxious lest I miss the right place. But my memory did not play me false. There were the landmarks: a five-barred gate hooked back against the wall, a lane which led to the Fell, and the redbrick chimneys of a tall house almost hidden in its own trees.

'Quick!' I cried. 'This is our stop!'

Here on the outskirts of Kersley the countryside was unspoiled. A row of very old stone cottages faced the road. A letter box was set crookedly into the wall by the gate. The tram stop was simply an iron pole without a shelter. In the valley below us, a haze of smoke hung over crowded streets and factory chimneys. Ahead of us lay only hills and sky, outlying farms and arthritic trees. And far away rose the dark spur of rock, so fantastically shaped by wind and weather that it looked like a great wave about to topple over.

'Tarn How!' I cried, pointing. 'That means "the hill where the lake is". Daddy told me. And there is a lake on the other side. The lane to Dowson-under-Fell goes round it.'

For once I had impressed Michael.

'It'll take us more than an hour to get there, I should think,' he said. 'We'd better have our picnic first. What time is it?'

No public clock of any description could be seen or heard.

'Oh well, never mind,' he said, undaunted. 'I'm hungry, so it must be about dinner-time. Where shall we eat?'

'There's a nice field over there – if it hasn't got cows in it.'

'I suppose you're frightened of cows, too?'

I nodded, ashamed but truthful.

42

'You're frightened of a lot of things, aren't you?'

I could not refute that.

'I'm not frightened of anything,' said Michael.

I had no answer to this. We walked through the gateway together and down the lane. Behind a wire fence, hens humbly bobbed and pecked, and the cock strutted in the midday sun.

The field was full of cows.

'Never mind,' said Michael charitably, 'we'll hop over this wall and have a picnic here instead.'

Always, his concessions to me were followed by greater demands.

'We can't. It's private property.'

'But it's empty. Look, there's a notice-board saying where enquiries should be made.'

'Yes, and underneath it says *Trespassers will be prosecuted*!'

Ignoring that remark, Michael climbed the high stone wall effortlessly and sat on top, grinning down at me. He unhitched his rucksack and dropped it into the garden below.

'Come on. I'll give you a hand up, Evie!'

It was the first time he had called me by name, and a pet name at that. In a state of euphoria I managed to scale the wall, scratching my palms and knees in the process, and found myself confronted by a six-foot drop on the other side.

'Everything always gets worse when I'm with you!' I wailed.

'You'll be all right. I'm going down first, and I'll help you.'

Humiliated by the expanse of knickers I must be showing, I slid and clutched my way down, scraping one elbow and snaring my dress on a twig as I landed. I rubbed my wounds and surveyed the garden, while Michael stood by me, as silent as myself.

This was a different world again to the village outside. A hushed retreat in which even the birds sounded subdued and the stillness was one of tranquillity.

'Shall we hunt around a bit?' Michael whispered, and I nodded.

The wood was small but thickly planted with trees. Oaks

and elms, sycamores and beeches, and a horse chestnut which must be glorious in May. There were rhododendron and holly bushes, too, and slender young silver birches, and the grass was new-green and silky. Then the bushes thinned out and we were on the edge of a neglected lawn looking towards the front of a house.

My heart beat so furiously that my gingham bodice shivered in sympathy. The long windows were blank and uncurtained. Grass grew in humps over former flower-beds. A few straggling roses bloomed above the mounds.

Michael put one finger to his lips and motioned me to stay there. He ran rapidly, lightly, through the jungle of lawn, and disappeared round the side of the house.

Past fear by this time, I sat down in quiet despair to wait for him. I wondered what my father would say when I was prosecuted. I pictured prison bars, files in loaves, and messages in bottles bobbing on a grey sea. I was tunnelling through the wall of my cell with the help of a dinner-knife, like the Count of Monte Cristo, when Michael strolled back, whistling.

'It's empty, and there's a side window unlocked. Come on!'

I did not even protest as he picked up the rucksack, but followed him stoically. If we were going to be prosecuted we might as well commit every sin in the book.

The garden had been a delight to us but the house was more so. It had been conceived by someone with a dream of grandeur. The carved oak staircase was particularly fine. Three vast stained-glass windows, comprising two panels of crimson roses either side of a coat of arms, and bearing the date 1895 on a blue scroll, were positioned directly above it. Shafts of coloured light dappled the stairs and the parquet floor. The climbing rose pattern was repeated in the glass swing doors which opened from hall to vestibule. And the hall itself had a high carved fireplace, stretching from floor to ceiling, with a beaten copper hood over the firebasket, and was big enough to hold a party.

Strangers to pretension, we sensed only the splendour of

this princely place, so mysteriously deserted and fallen into decay. Entranced, we wandered from room to room, up the curving staircase and along both corridors, and down again into a warren of cellars where fungus grew. A chill and musty breath issued from the kitchen larder when we opened the door. Its marble slab was clammy to the touch. Thick soft shawls of cobwebs shivered on the pantry shelves. Patches of rust showed through the kitchen range, and mice scuttled in a wallful of mahogany cupboards long since bare of food.

'You choose where we eat,' Michael whispered.

I decided on a ground-floor room facing the lawn, through whose windows the sun was beginning to enter. It was a place in which to sit and take tea on a summer afternoon. The oak boards had been highly polished at one time. Ceremoniously, I dusted them with my handkerchief and laid out our sandwiches and bottles of ginger beer.

'We'd better save the biscuits and some of the ginger beer,' I said. 'Because by the time we get to the top of Tarn How we shall be jolly hungry and thirsty, I can tell you. But when we come down the other side, to Dowson-under-Fell, there's a little shop that sells Fry's chocolate cream bars. I'll buy us one each.'

'Is that what you do when you walk with your father?'

'No. There's a Hovis tea-shop next door to that, and we have a big pot of tea, and brown bread and butter and jam, and homemade cakes. But it costs him about two shillings and he gives the lady twopence. So we can't afford it.'

We sat cross-legged on the floor and ate everything but the biscuits. And no one burst in with truncheons and arrested us. No one grabbed our legs and cried, 'Gotcha!', as we slid down the garden wall into the ordinary world. In one sense we went free. In another we were forever captured.

For a moment in the lane we both stopped and looked behind us, to glimpse the house through the trees one last time. Overhead a little aeroplane flew, scribbling an advertisement on the billboard of sky.

Then we set out at a good pace up Tarn Fell.

It was a late August afternoon, hot, drowsy and silent, but up on the fells a little breeze riffled the grass. Higher and higher we went, walking more slowly as the track grew steeper. The sense of space and solitude was awesome, immense. Time was suspended, was a perpetual present. And Tarn How played a dark and dignified game of hide and seek with us. For no sooner did we think we were almost there, than he retreated higher and further away.

I had a blister on my heel and Michael was growing more freckled by the minute, but we toiled on remorselessly. And so we scrambled up the final incline and stood breathless beneath the towering wave of rock, seeing Lancashire spread below us like a counterpane. On one side the spires of Blackstone were visible in the distance. On the other the shining lake, and the fashionable market town of Dowson-under-Fell.

We smiled at each other in mutual triumph. Without words, or need of words, we sat down and divided the rest of our picnic, absorbing landscape, sun, breeze and the beauty of the day.

'Look! There's our hidden house!' I cried.

We could see it clearly, the size of a doll's house, surrounded by its little wood, with a garden back and front.

'Oh, I'm glad we had an adventure,' I said in gratitude.

'Yep. It's worth a row,' said Michael philosophically.

I thought back over past misdemeanours at home and school, the shame as well as the pain of retribution. Flesh and spirit shrank.

'What will they do to us? Smack us? Shut us in a dark cupboard? Make us go to bed early for a week?'

'Oh, *you* won't be blamed. They'll take it out on me. Grandad'll probably thrash me. Grannie will row me and tell Mum. I shan't be allowed out for ages, and they'll probably stop my pocket money.'

I thought this a trifle excessive.

'It seems a lot of punishment just for one naughty thing.'

He shrugged.

'I've done what I liked, so it's fair enough. I expect they think that being punished will change me, but it won't. I don't like being bottled up and told what to do. I like to feel there's space and air all round me. I'd like – I'd like to live on this hill forever.'

It was the most personal confession he had yet made to me. I tried to meet him halfway.

'*I'd* like to live in that house down there forever, and be able to come up here whenever I wanted to,' I said. Being practical, I added, 'But I think you might find it rather cold living up here in the winter. Tarn How gets the first snow.'

'I could live in a tent. I want to go all round the world, living in a tent and cooking baked beans on a camp fire . . .' He checked himself then. To cover his tracks he asked, 'What do you want to do?'

I hesitated, but he had confided in me and I must reciprocate.

'I want to be grown up, and wear a bright red coat and high-heeled shoes and have a handbag full of money. I don't like being a child.'

'Me neither,' said Michael. 'I'm going to grow up as fast as I can, and leave home.'

We were caught up in a tide of freedom. I stammered slightly, as I tried to convey my truths.

'S-s-sometimes I d-dream that something n-nasty is happening, and I p-press my arms down – like this – and I lift up into the air like a bird, and I fly away. Right, right away.'

I fluttered to earth, remembering not to trust.

'But promise you won't tell,' I begged. 'Not anyone. Ever.'

He spat on his finger and crossed his throat. I thanked him.

The heat of the day was waning. The light turned a deeper gold.

'Time we were off!' said Michael, picking up the empty rucksack. 'How long do you reckon it'll take us to get back, Evie?'

'It's an hour from here to Dowson-under-Fell. Daddy times it so that we get there by four o'clock. Then we catch the five o'clock tram to Kersley, and walk into Grandma's house at a quarter to six.'

'Crikey! And we've got to get back to Hathersall from

47

Kersley on top of that! We'll have to leg it.' He took command. His tone was firm but friendly. 'Now listen to me, Evie, and do what I say. When we get back you must leave all the talking to me. You're likely to tell them anything they ask you. I know how much to say to keep them quiet, and when to keep my mouth shut. Okay?'

'Okay, Mick,' I said. And then, 'I wonder what the time is?'

In the stillness of that hot late Saturday afternoon a chime as faint as a harebell answered me.

'Listen!' I said, holding up a finger.

We were silent, counting.

'It can't be five o'clock, can it?' Michael asked, aghast.

'I counted five, too.'

'Heck!' said Michael. 'Let's scram!'

We scrammed.

Late that night, when the Schofields were still holding a family conference in the kitchen downstairs, I slipped out of bed and tiptoed along the corridor to Michael's room. The wrath of the adult gods had descended upon him and him alone, as he had prophesied. Only Grannie had tried to divide the blame. She supposed, she said, that Evleen had a tongue and a pair of legs, and could have said 'No!' and come home!

But Grandad would have none of it. His chivalry towards the female sex, his fondness for me, made him blame Michael entirely. He took his grandson into the scullery and thrashed him despite my pleas.

I tapped on the door and whispered through the keyhole.

'It's me, Micky. Are you all right?'

I heard him getting carefully off the bed, and winced in sympathy. He came to the keyhole and whispered from the other side.

'Not bad!' And then, 'Grandad fairly laid about him, this time.'

'Does it hurt?' I asked, awed.

'A bit. How's your blister?'

'Grannie burst it with a pin and bandaged it.'

I felt that he deserved commendation.

48

'You're a lot braver than Alex and Leo. They shout and sob and scream and yell when Aunt Kate goes for them.'

'I expect they're bluffing, so's she'll stop. They're pretty tough actually.'

'I didn't know Grandad could get so angry.'

Temporarily his shining image had been tarnished, but I would burnish it up in another day or so.

Michael had accepted the anger.

'You can't blame him. What with Uncle Eric scouring the countryside on his motorbike, and the police looking for us.'

'I suppose so. Anyway, they did give us something to eat. Grandma Fawley would have sent us to bed without supper.'

There was a pause.

'I'll tell you something,' Michael whispered. 'When we're living in Kersley, and this row's blown over, we'll go to Tarn How again. And we'll have another picnic in the hidden house.'

'By ourselves, though,' I begged. 'Not with Alex and Leo.'

He was silent, thinking this over, but it had been our day. His whisper strengthened.

'Cut my throat and hope to die! But let's get one thing clear, Evie. I'm not going to stick around with you all the time, even when we're living in the same house. I shall go off by myself, or bring other chaps home, and you mustn't hang around. Understand?'

For a moment I was annihilated, but had been disappointed too often to make a fuss. I whispered very loudly to convince him of my own popularity.

'Oh, I've got lots of friends, too!'

I tried to remember one, since Marianne had deserted me. I glimpsed the wilderness before me. My pride slunk away.

I asked humbly, 'But just now and again we'll have an adventure on our own, won't we?'

'Lots of times,' said Michael graciously. 'Lots of times. Buzz off now, Evie, or they'll hear you. And this time it might be your turn to get spanked!'

I crawled back into bed in ecstasy. And every tram that trundled by chattered 'lots of times LOTS OF TIMES lots of times', and lit the ceiling in its joy.

4

January 1928

Michael's destiny and mine had been decided six months earlier, when my father and Dorothy Harland officially announced their engagement in the *Manchester Guardian*.

On a wintry Saturday, following the announcement, the four of us went out together for the first time as a future family. And as the weather was not fine enough for a country walk our prospective parents took us on an expedition to Blackstone, where we saw a Laurel and Hardy film at the Hippodrome and afterwards had tea at Peeble's as a special treat.

We all looked very smart. Aunt Kate had sent me off in my fawn coat and hat trimmed with rabbit fur, and my dark brown gaiters buttoned from ankle to thigh. Michael wore his Milton Lodge school uniform, navy-blue and gold. My father was always immaculate, but Dorothy outdid us all with her high-collared crimson coat, and a clover-pink velvet cloche ornamented by a single rose.

My father was not a man to waste opportunities, so as soon as we had eaten our fill of Peeble's famous cream cakes he came to the serious business of the afternoon. And at once we children became one of his educational experiments.

Conversationally, he said, 'I think this is a good time to tell Michael and Evelyn our future plans, don't you, Dorothy?'

He spoke as though it were a joint decision, and she leaned forward as if in true accord with him, hands clasped on the white damask cloth so that her engagement ring shone uppermost. I was to discover that Dorothy played many parts in her life. At that moment she was being the head-master's wife.

'In our opinion, neither of the schools which you children attend at the moment is a satisfactory educational establish-ment,' my father said. 'Milton Lodge has a wider curriculum and a good sports' master, but Townley's is no more than a pleasant place in which to pass the time. So you will both be leaving in July.'

I felt I had entered suddenly upon unknown territory. Townley's at that time was still a haven for me and contained my best friend.

My father digressed for a moment, reading my expression.

'I know you've been happy there, Evie, and Townley's has served its purpose, but now you need an educational challenge.'

Michael looked directly at his mother, who looked down in guilt.

He spoke up for himself.

'Excuse me, Uncle Gilbert, but Grandfather Harland chose Milton Lodge for me because it was my father's old school. And all I'm really good at is sport, and you said we had a good sports' master. So I'd rather stay, if you don't mind.'

My father's reply was equally direct.

'You can't make a future of playing games, and I can't afford to pay Milton Lodge's fees.' He added, having a strict regard for truth, 'To be frank, I wouldn't even if I could!'

Michael looked again at his mother and said, 'But you needn't pay my fees. Grandfather Harland pays them for me.'

Dorothy intervened, trying to sound cheerful and natural.

'I hadn't thought of that, Gil. I could have a word with Grandfather Harland. I'm sure he'll be only too pleased to continue paying the fees. Micky is his grandson, after all.'

'That's quite out of the question,' my father said. 'I intend to make myself fully responsible for Michael in every way, and I have no time for expensive private schools such as Milton Lodge.'

Dorothy twisted her engagement ring, troubled. My father took out a silver case and selected a cigarette. Michael had not yet given in.

'Excuse me, Uncle Gilbert, but I don't see the difference between Milton Lodge and your school,' he said, as politely as possible.

'There are very great differences,' said my father, lighting his cigarette. 'Grizedale's was founded as a grammar school in the time of Queen Elizabeth. Milton Lodge was built by nineteenth-century cotton merchants who needed somewhere to send their sons. Our education is broadly based, and aims at producing young men with a sense of public duty and a lively social conscience. Milton Lodge simply gives them an exterior polish. I would say briefly that we aim to educate in the highest sense of the word, whereas Milton Lodge only covers the ground without cultivating it.'

Michael's freckles stood out against his pallor.

Dorothy said timidly to him, 'Grandad never thought much of the education at Milton Lodge, you know, Micky.'

'I know,' Michael replied, and his jaw jutted with the effort to keep it steady, 'but he never tried to take me away from it.'

'A change of school will benefit you, Michael,' my father went on, in his reasonable, even tone. 'You're an intelligent lad, but you lack self-discipline and a sense of purpose at the moment. This is not your fault,' he added fairly. 'I think you show promise, and I shall do everything within my power to help you.'

Michael said, still very polite, 'I suppose, as Grizedale's is so good, you want me to go there instead?'

'Oh no,' said my father, and drew his brows together. 'It surely follows that if I can't afford fees for Milton Lodge I certainly can't afford them for Grizedale's?'

The silence that followed was faintly chilled. I stared round at Peeble's in its splendour. The pink and white walls, the long mirrors reflecting tiers of exquisite cakes, the spindly gold chairs, the white and gold china on white tables.

Michael said doggedly, 'Where am I going, then?'

My father cleared his throat. He saw that my attention was wandering, and recalled it with a touch of his hand.

'I intend to send both you and Evelyn to Moss Lane Elementary School in Kersley.'

Michael remained puzzled but I thought it was a joke. I began to giggle, and then stopped. My father spoke stiffly.

'That's where *I* went – and I haven't done too badly.'

No one answered. He hurried on.

'I know that Moss Lane hasn't the kudos of Townley's or Milton Lodge. But it does possess a remarkable scholarship record, and I have the highest opinion of its headmaster.'

'If both of us are going, then it must be a *mixed* school,' said Michael, his masculinity threatened.

'There's no harm in a mixed school for younger children,' said my father, unexpectedly at bay. 'You'll be segregated at grammar school.'

Dorothy was abdicating from a conversation which had gone badly.

'I know nothing about Moss Lane,' she said. 'Nothing at all.'

'Well, I know it!' I cried. 'It's full of nasty children who shout rude things at me when I run past on my way home. Daddy, why are you sending me there? Why do I have to go there?'

'That's enough, Evelyn!' said my father. 'You must take my word for it that I know exactly what I'm doing.'

I did, and was silent, though my afternoon was spoiled and probably my life for all I knew.

Encouraged by our reaction, Dorothy ventured to say, 'Gil, dear, I did suggest that they wouldn't be used to that sort of school. It's like throwing them in the deep end before they've learned to swim!'

But he was riding some educational hobby-horse of his own.

'My dear girl, one of my strongest convictions is that it does youngsters good to struggle, so long as help is at hand and they have a sense of purpose. Instead of taking their education for granted, and moving from one easy option to

53

another, Michael and Evelyn will be given the incentive to work hard. They'll see another side of life. Moss Lane will provide a good basic education and I shall coach them privately. I expect them both to win good scholarships.'

Dorothy said, more to herself than us, 'I don't know anything about Evelyn, but wherever would Micky win a scholarship to?'

My father said, 'Blackstone Grammar School, of course. And Evelyn will go to Blackstone High School.'

My imagination was immediately caught. I was a cloistered child. At the thought of travelling to such a metropolis as Blackstone, and becoming a member of its most exclusive girls' day school, I cleared the hurdles of Moss Lane in a twinkling.

He saw he had a convert, and brilliantly made sure of me.

'Only two girls have won a Blackstone High School scholarship from Moss Lane in forty years. I know you can be the third, Evie.'

The winter afternoon was growing dim. A waiter switched on the concealed lighting, and Peeble's, like myself, was most wonderfully illuminated. But Dorothy and Michael remained in total darkness.

'Blackstone Grammar?' said Dorothy, appalled. 'Four hundred boys competing for twenty free places?'

My father was impatient of her astonishment. He had said Michael could do it. His judgement did not allow of doubt.

'I won a scholarship there, and so did your brother, Eric. And both of us came from local elementary schools.'

'But you and Eric are exceptionally clever,' said Dorothy, now showing signs of irritation as well as despair, 'and Eric does nothing but swot. Michael's not like that.'

'Well, what did you expect him to do?' my father replied, with some asperity. 'Play games at Milton Lodge until he was eighteen?'

She answered with some spirit, now on Michael's side.

'Grandfather Harland intended to take him into one of the family mills, to be trained as a manager.'

Unimpressed, he stubbed out his cigarette.

'I shouldn't have thought Michael wanted to be a

businessman. Should you?' he remarked, and summoned the waitress.

We sat in silence until the bill came. My father put on his reading glasses, checked every item, and settled it. He gave the waitress a good tip and he looked round his new family with a gentler expression. He helped Dorothy on with her coat, and brushed his fingers along the great fur collar.

'This is pretty stuff!' he said, courting her again.

'Dyed rabbit!' said Dorothy, managing a smile.

He smiled back, sorry that they had come so near to quarrelling.

'Shall we look at some furniture?' he asked, holding out his arm.

Outside, the day was dull and cold. A fine drizzle of rain had begun to fall. My father opened his umbrella to protect Dorothy's velvet cloche and they walked ahead of us, arm in arm, from the precincts of St Anne's Gate towards the main shopping centre. Blackstone was a great adventure to me in those days. That afternoon, coupled to my new dream of the high school, it became an earthly paradise. Michael was thinking dark thoughts to a wet pavement, but I hummed under my breath, walking quickly to keep up with all those longer and older legs.

On this, the busiest shopping day of the week, the city was at its exciting best. Stallholders shouted their wares on every corner. A dray-horse pulled its heavy cart over the cobbles of a side street. A man roasted chestnuts on a glowing brazier, and popped them piping hot into paper bags.

'I'll treat us!' cried Dorothy, recovering her spirits.

And she bought us a bag each.

An old woman sat beneath the statue of Queen Victoria selling violets from a basket. My father presented his future bride with a nosegay of bunches, and kissed her cheek.

Newsboys cried the late edition of the evening paper. A hurdy-gurdy man was playing 'Roses in Picardy', while his monkey shuddered in its little red cloth coat and held out a shrivelled paw for our pennies.

The Palace Cinema was showing *Flesh and the Devil*, with

55

Greta Garbo and John Gilbert. Blackstone Repertory Company were giving *The Passing of the Third Floor Back*. Marie Lloyd headed the music hall bill at the Alhambra. A Clara Butt song recital was on at the Concert Hall, a Noel Coward play at the Prince's Theatre.

For those with full purses, hoardings advertised Reckitt's Blue for whiter washdays, Horlicks for night starvation, and Skegness for being so bracing. The Bisto Kids lifted snub noses in appreciation. One and a half glasses of milk poured into every bar of Cadbury's Milk Chocolate. Sunny Jim was leaping the fence because he had eaten Force cereal for breakfast.

And along the gutter, at intervals, stood the heroes of the previous decade: selling matches, balloons or gimmicky toys, singing or playing musical instruments, or simply begging. Driftwood, cast up by the sea of war, they wore their medals and their placards of woe.

Blinded in the Service of My Country.
Spare a copper.
Thank you, friend.

5

September 1928

Moss Lane Elementary School had been built during the 1880s, when education became compulsory and even the poorest children must be accommodated. So Kersley Council erected a gaunt Gothic edifice, and endowed it with the minimum of facilities. The price of land being high, they also economised on space. And, duty done, no doubt opened the school premises with pomp, bunting and self-congratulation.

Mr Wadsworth, the headmaster, was a remarkable man. Given the right opportunities he could have bettered himself. Instead, he bettered Moss Lane School. And in this he was inheritor of a long tradition, since all its headmasters were noted for achieving much with little.

'I welcome all our new boys and girls!' he cried, on that first day of the autumn term. 'And I want them all to take a look at this noble board on the wall behind me.'

The board was big and black and glossy, and the names of scholarship pupils shone upon it in ranks of shining gold.

His voice and chest swelled as he delivered his annual message.

'This board is our claim to fame over the last forty years! It begins with the name of a lad who is now a grandfather – and I know him, and have shaken him by the hand! – and he won our first scholarship to Blackstone Grammar School. That's one of the biggest plums on the tree, and we've picked quite a few over the years. But as you'll see, we've only won two scholarships to Blackstone High School – some of you girls might get more for us! We reckon to pick up at least a dozen places every year to Kersley County, and a few to Stansfield Girls' and Stansfield Boys' schools. Now every single scholar and school on that board is an honour to Moss Lane School. And while you're reading those illustrious names you should say to yourself "I'm going up there!" And if you work hard then you will do. And we'll do everything we can to help you.'

He was such an orator in his homely fashion that we all clapped and cheered and stamped our feet, and he let us have our way for a minute before holding up his hand for silence.

'I'm going to do *my* best,' he said. 'So you do *yours*!'

We gave him another clap for that. Then the senior mistress poised her hands above the old piano, and attacked the keyboard with a march by Sousa while we all filed out.

Exalted, I drifted with the current of children into Form Three. Miss Todd was an excellent teacher, noted for hammering laggards into shape, and consequently somewhat difficult to bear. Pupils well-versed in school ways were all crowding to the back of the room. Ignorant of this, I slid into one of the front desks. The headmaster's words still rang in my head. In my daydream glistened a legend.

Evelyn Fawley Blackstone High School 1932

Monitors were being chosen and dragooned into service. New blue exercise books, old battered textbooks, and sputtering school pens were given out. And Miss Todd, grasping a piece of chalk as if it were the neck of an enemy, threatened the blackboard with cruel fractions.

Arithmetic being a strong subject, I fell to musing over my first real wristwatch, presented by my father that morning. He had given Michael one, as well, saying to us jokingly, 'Make the most of your time with these!'

Miss Todd's voice, and the piece of chalk she threw with stinging accuracy at my right cheek, made me jump.

'You. The new girl. Twenty lines. To be written in your own time at home, and brought in first thing tomorrow morning. Write out "I must always pay attention in class"!

58

Well, what are you waiting for? Copy the line down in your exercise book so that you'll remember it!'

Some wag had stuffed blotting paper in the bottom of my inkwell, and though I cleaned the nib with spit and blotting paper and polished it with my handkerchief, it would blur, and I gained another twenty lines for untidiness before the playbell rang.

My prospects continued to be dismal, even in moments of leisure.

The schoolyard was not large enough to contain all the pupils at once, so they were divided into groups and let out at different times. The youngest ones trotted forth and tumbled down regularly on the concrete, spending most of their playtime whimpering over bleeding knees. The older ones ran out, shouting with freedom, like convicts escaping prison. Indeed it was rather like a prison, though having spiked iron railings instead of a high wall. A teacher with a handbell did her best to supervise us, but it was not possible to impose good manners on such a multitude. At best we could be prevented from injuring each other.

I stood with my back against the school wall, along with the other social lepers. I had never seen so many children in one place in my entire life. The schoolyard was full of them, and they were full of themselves. Shouting, fighting, pushing, thumping, skipping, hopping, gossiping and plotting in little groups. Seeing that I was a misfit, they ignored me ostentatiously. Whereas Michael, by dint of punching one boy on the nose and climbing the school railings, had already been accepted as one of them.

Toilet facilities were another problem. Cloakrooms were inside the building, each offering fifty hooks and two chipped washbasins, but lavatories stood outside in the centre of the yard. One was for the boys, the other for girls. The sexually advanced prowled between the two. I had peeped into the girls' block already, but its damp wooden seats and crazed bowls, waiting spiders, unravelled toilet rolls, and doors which would not bolt, had driven me out again. In a dilemma of fear and discomfort, I twined one leg round the other.

It was all very different from Townley's.

A smell of hot pastry greeted us on the threshold of our temporary home, and there was Dorothy, cooking abundantly in her temporary kitchen and issuing orders to her temporary charwoman, Mrs Inchmore, who was washing up in the scullery. Mrs Inchmore was doing us all a great favour, as Dorothy frequently said in her hearing.

'Along of not knowing how long you'll be here, nor where you might be going,' Mrs Inchmore would interpose mournfully, 'and me legs being bad, and me not able to walk far.'

'But we can't do without Mrs Inchmore,' Dorothy continued playfully, 'so we must just find a house near her, mustn't we?'

'I hope not,' Michael whispered to me, 'because she lives down near the canal and it smells.'

I smothered a giggle.

'Where are your manners? What do you both say to kind Mrs Inchmore?' Dorothy asked, ignoring both whisper and giggle.

We chorused a polite greeting.

Already I was finding that I had exchanged one set of family rules for another. Dorothy's household gods were different from Grandma's but just as sacred. Inexplicably, Mrs Inchmore was one of them. Dorothy flattered her so obviously, so atrociously, that I wondered how the charwoman could swallow it. But she always did, and sang a dreary hymn or two afterwards while she washed up. 'Rock of Ages' was her favourite.

'Now hang up your coats and wash your hands, children. Dinner won't be a minute. We're eating in the kitchen.'

The kitchen table was covered with brown-checked oilcloth. The evening meal would be served up on white linen in the front room.

'And how was the first morning at Moss Lane School?' Dorothy asked, setting down a deep brown pie dish.

'They made me drink school milk and I was sick,' I said.

Dorothy paused, hand on hip. Her own appetite was

healthy and her digestion sound. She found my wayward stomach a trial.

'What happened to the orange juice I gave you?'

'They wouldn't let me drink it unless I brought a note.'

'Ridiculous! Can't you eat this pie, then?'

'What is it, please?'

'Meat and potato! Try a bit! If you don't like it you can have bread and butter instead.'

I would have preferred bread and butter, but she and I were doing our best to get on together and I did not want to offend her.

'I'll try a bit,' I said reluctantly, and returned to the Moss Lane fray. 'Oh, and the teacher, Miss Todd, says I've got to have my hair plaited because it's unhygienic flying about my face. And she asked if we knew what "unhygienic" meant, and I was the only one who did, and then she called me a know-all! Not fair!'

'Unhygienic?' Dorothy said, knife poised on the pie crust. 'I don't like the sound of that! Have those children got nits? Did the teacher say anything about head inspections?'

'Yes. The district nurse is coming on Friday afternoon.'

Dorothy frowned and spoke to some invisible arbiter.

'I knew it!' she said. 'I told him what it would be like. He wouldn't listen. Theory isn't the same as practice.'

Seeing her reaction, I heaped on the agony.

'And we're going to have a medical inspection next Monday, and Miss Todd said particularly that we were to have a bath the night before, and wear a clean vest and knickers.'

Dorothy was outraged.

'She's wasting her breath telling *me* that. You're clean every day of the week, underneath and on top!'

'Mum, I'm starving!' said Michael, impatient with the pair of us.

Dorothy's brow cleared. Lips pursed judiciously, she cut generous helpings of pie for herself and Michael and Mrs Inchmore, and a small piece for me. Her tone and face softened as she watched her son eat.

'And what have *you* been up to, Tricky Mick?' she asked, with dry indulgence.

Michael said, smiling and watching to gauge the exact effect of his words, 'I can pee higher than any other boy, Mum.'

Her mouth quivered momentarily, and then behaved itself.

'Never let me hear you say anything like that again!' said Dorothy sternly. 'Particularly in front of your little sister. Now get on with your dinner and try to act like a gentleman.'

But we saw her trying not to smile, and when she carried Mrs Inchmore's dinner into the scullery we heard her talking and laughing and saying something about boys being boys.

The pie was very hot and good and soothing. I ate my sliver and had a baked apple and custard. Dorothy watched me appraisingly.

'That's better,' she remarked. 'I'll put some flesh on your bones if it's the last thing I do! You must have been half-starved at The Laurels! Well, Harold said they put too much water in everything!'

Already the knives were out between Dorothy and Grandma. Doughty fighters, they relished the weekly visits which had become contests.

'Now come here while I plait your hair,' said Dorothy kindly.

She was the sort of woman who prefers boys, but she was trying to build a good mother-and-daughter relationship.

'Do you want one plait or two?'

'I should give her two,' Michael advised shrewdly, 'because she can keep them in front of her. If she has one hanging down behind some boy can dip it in his inkwell.'

'I hope you don't do naughty things like that!' said Dorothy, more out of habit than hope. She added, plaiting away, 'And then I must write a note about the milk. What's your teacher's name, again?'

'Miss Todd. Oh, and she says I can't wear a fancy red ribbon like this. She wants it to be black or dark brown or navy-blue, and plain.'

'She wants a lot, considering you've only been there five

minutes!' said Dorothy crisply. 'Oh well, I might have a dark ribbon in my sewing box.' She rummaged in a wicker basket that looked like a magpie's nest. 'I haven't got everything to rights yet,' she would explain. And then, cheerfully, 'Never mind. It'll all be the same in a hundred years' time!'

We had been in this furnished house for six weeks now, long enough for Dorothy's priorities to become evident. Her pride in her new and distinguished husband was mingled with awe, so she created an oasis of peace and plenty around him.

She was his guardian. The front room in which we dined and sat together of an evening, and the box room which acted as his study, were always orderly and dusted. So he could choose whether to be sociable with us or to work alone.

She was his valet. Whenever he opened the chest of drawers or his half of the wardrobe, he found clean shirts, pristine handkerchiefs, well-brushed suits and highly-polished shoes.

She was his chef. He had, as he often said, never eaten as well in all his life.

She was his companion when he wanted one. And even in this cramped and temporary accommodation she was already giving dinner parties for members of his staff and their wives. Entertaining had been difficult for him at Grandma's house. Even Aunt Kate acting as hostess could not counteract the atmosphere of gloom, nor the dullness of Ada's food, and this was a definite drawback. A headmaster without a wife who can cook and talk is a poor creature, socially speaking. Now to find himself the owner of a first-class private restaurant run by a handsome and vivacious helpmeet, was to crown his married bliss.

So my father was Dorothy's chief concern. After him came we two children, who were kept clean, clothed, fed and supervised. But once our immediate needs were met she lost patience with housekeeping, and would tidy up a room by hiding newspapers behind cushions, sweeping dust under carpets, and stuffing odds and ends into whichever drawer she opened first.

Mrs Inchmore was an absolute necessity. Without her

63

help three mornings a week no job would ever have been finished. There were always saucepans left to soak, ironing to be done tomorrow, washing which could wait. And Michael referred to Dorothy's handbag as 'Mum's dustbin' because it held such an incredible amount of junk. When it became too full to close she emptied the contents on to the kitchen table and sorted it out.

We children did not mind. Michael made himself at home wherever he happened to be, and I found it relaxing after the barren tidiness of Grandma's house. And if my father, for all his pleasure in this new life, occasionally objected to seeing last night's supper dishes still in the sink at breakfast, or last Sunday's gravy growing a soft white beard at the back of the larder shelf, Dorothy had one answer.

'It'll be different when we get a home of our own. I can't settle in here properly.'

She was a good nurse, too. As soon as the first winds of autumn scoured down from the north I was taken ill with bronchitis and Dorothy went into action with zest. She sent Michael off to school with a note for Miss Todd, saw my father off to Grizedale's with instructions to telephone the family doctor as soon as he arrived there, and ordered Mrs Inchmore to light a fire in my bedroom.

Wheezing contentedly, sitting up in bed in my new blue wool dressing-gown, with a stack of drawing paper and a box of waxy crayons, I entered the haven of myself. A small handbell had been installed on my bedside table, enabling me to communicate with the household downstairs, but I had everything I wanted.

The morning passed delightfully. Dorothy made an instant conquest of Dr Gould, and when she ushered him into my presence they were both laughing. He was in his forties, a big aggressively healthy man with an eye for a pretty woman. The rough wind pleased him. He battled against it joyfully, and brought a gust of cold air into the heated room.

'Ah, you and I have met before, young lady,' he said to me, and apologised for his chill hands and chillier stethoscope. 'Yes, as I thought. Same old complaint. Can't you think of a new one for me? All right then, I'll let you off this time. One bottle of nice red medicine, and one bottle of nasty brown stuff – which entitles you to a barley sugar afterwards.' He turned to Dorothy, saying, 'If you send somebody down to my surgery at two o'clock I'll have them ready,' for he made up his own prescriptions.

He winked at me, and said as he always did, 'Well, you look jolly comfortable here. I think you should stay in bed until that cough clears up, don't you?'

Then he pinched my cheek, and followed Dorothy out. I heard his rich bass voice booming down the stairs.

'I'll call again at the end of the week. Keep her in bed until then. Plenty of fluids. Light diet. Wrap her up well.'

In the hall his voice, though still audible, became more intimate. He talked like this to Aunt Kate, whom he admired greatly.

'I'm the second generation in our family practice, Dorothy. I may call you Dorothy, mayn't I? My name is Neville. So I know all the inherited weaknesses of my private patients. The Fawleys have a history of dodgy lungs. One of their girls went off with consumption in her teens.'

That was Aunt Jane. Grandma often said I reminded her of Aunt Jane, and then sighed and shook her head.

'But old Mrs Fawley was a Hibbert before she married, and the Hibberts are an apoplectic lot. She suffers from high blood pressure. Didn't you know? Oh, yes! She prefers to call it heart trouble, but it isn't her heart that'll carry her off. She'll drop dead with a stroke, like her father did. You mark my words!'

I began to draw Grandma Fawley lying on the floor, with a wild-eyed God lifting an axe marked STROKE just above her.

'I didn't have much to do with Evelyn's mother. She came from the south so I didn't know her family, and she went into a Blackstone Nursing Home to have Evelyn. She was a good-looker, like you – Gilbert knows how to pick 'em! – but you've got a first-class constitution. Clara was too thin for my liking.'

Dorothy said something about my weak stomach, but he pshawed.

65

'Nothing wrong with the child that a good table won't cure. Old Mrs Fawley's too fond of slops, and Mrs Kate's always dieting! No, I think you can put that down to nerves. Clara Fawley was the nervous type. Up in the air one minute and down in the dumps the next. Highly strung. Over-sensitive. And that's Evelyn's inheritance.'

Mentally I added that information to my dossier on Clara.

They were walking towards the front door and I could only just distinguish his final sentences.

'You're doing a grand job with Gilbert. He looks a different man these days. And young Tinkerbell upstairs seems happy enough. Make sure you take care of your own health.'

Then the conversation passed beyond my ken.

'Shall I be seeing you one of these days? Or are you a follower of the infamous Marie Stopes?'

'Oh, there's time yet,' said Dorothy.

'That Stopes woman is a menace to public morality,' said Neville Gould loudly and emphatically. 'Birth control indeed! Having babies is good for a woman. Right and natural. My mother had ten, and none the worse for it. Fine old lady. Women should have as many as possible, and when they don't want any more their husbands should exercise restraint. Why, before we've finished, everyone in the country will be having sexual relations for the hell of it.'

Then I heard a sound like a little slap and he laughed heartily.

'Mind you, with a good-looking lass like you around, you couldn't blame 'em!'

I decided that Dorothy was enjoying my illness. In ten minutes she was back again, looking pink and pleased with herself, and bearing a jug of hot homemade lemonade, glycerine and honey.

'I'll be glad when we move,' she confided. 'And glad to get rid of that old humbug in the kitchen. Bad legs indeed! Just an excuse.'

'But I thought you liked Mrs Inchmore a lot.'

'No, I've never had any time for her,' said Dorothy,

straining the lemons. 'She's a hypocrite. Here, get this down you.'

'What's a hypocrite?'

'A person who says one thing and means another.'

I opened my mouth to comment. And shut it again. Evidently, Dorothy did not recognise hypocrisy close to home. She chattered on.

'Grannie Annie will be coming over this afternoon. And Aunt Kate drops in for coffee most mornings. So you'll see them both. What do you want for your dinner? Boiled egg and toast soldiers?'

'Yes, please!' I said, astonished by good fortune. 'What fun you have at home, don't you?'

'I like a bit of company,' Dorothy admitted. 'It can be lonely during the day. I had lots of friends when I was Mr Murchison's private secretary in Blackstone. And I used to pop out in the lunch-hour and look at the big shops. It was the top job in the firm. For a woman that is. And quite well paid. Of course, I had to give it up when I married your father. He wouldn't allow me to work – a man in his position. Naturally. And I'd sooner be married to your father and have a home of my own, instead of working in an office and living with Mother and Father.

'There's a lot of life in a city. Nothing much happens in a small town. Still, I enjoyed being in Hathersall Dramatic Society. People said I ought to have been a professional actress. I played leading roles there for years, until I met your father. I'd have loved to go on the stage in London. But, of course, Grandad would never have let me. And talking of London, I'll never forget seeing it for the first time. Never! That was an experience, I can tell you.'

She seemed to have led a very exciting life.

'When did you go to London?' I asked, fascinated.

'Oh, a long time ago. Twelve years ago, when I married Michael's father. We spent our honeymoon in London.'

And she sat smiling, hands clasped loosely in her lap. She looked like a picture in my *Tales of Greece and Rome*, Ceres the earth goddess. Her inward self flowed with milk and honey.

67

'What was Mr Harland like?' I asked very softly, so that I should not waken her from this reverie.

'Oh, if you know Michael you know Harry Harland!' she said, and laughed. 'He loved life and he knew how to live it. He loved life.'

I did not break her silence, but watched her smiling back at Harry, who had loved life so much and lost it so soon. The smile could not make up its mind whether to be happy or sad. Then, briskly, she recalled herself to the present.

'Oh well, I must be getting on. Ring when you want anything, but not too often, if you can help it. Dozy Daisy says she can't manage the stairs!'

'Oh, I shan't be any trouble to you,' I assured her. 'Ask Aunt Kate. She says she wishes Grandma was half such a good invalid.'

Dorothy laughed, made up the bedroom fire until it began to climb the chimney, fixed the fireguard firmly to its hooks, and departed.

'Dozy Daisy indeed!' I said to myself, selecting a bright orange crayon. 'Mrs Inchmore doesn't seem to be very popular this morning.'

Through the window I could see the long grey shoulder of the Pennine range, and three lone farms. The wind had polished the air to the brilliance of diamonds. From the trees at the side of the house leaves fled before it, some scuttling along the sill or clinging for a moment to the wall in vain hope of shelter. A robin peeped in on me, cocked his head and departed. I ate and dozed and read and drew pictures, and the household revolved delightfully around me.

At noon, Grannie Annie arrived. And, on hearing I was in bed with bronchitis, turned round again directly and went out to the shops to buy a small bunch of black grapes, a quarter of dolly mixtures and a copy of *Little Folks*.

At four o'clock Michael came home from school and sat on my bed, sharing afternoon tea. He admired my drawings, listened to my news, and gave the deceased Grandma Fawley a brown moustache which made us both laugh a lot.

At six o'clock something wonderful happened. My father

68

walked in smiling, and dropped a fat black kitten on my bed.

'I know you always wanted one when we were at Grandma's,' he explained, as I kissed the kitten passionately and thanked him over and over again, 'and Michael wants a dog for his next birthday, and your mother seems to think children need animals . . . .'

He was caught up, as I was, in Dorothy's domestic tide. Already his thin dark face was fuller, his stance more relaxed.

'Is it a girl or a boy?' I asked, inviting the kitten to bite my forefinger.

'He's a tom cat. Comes from a litter belonging to Mrs Archer, the school cook. Do you remember meeting her at Grizedale's fête?'

'Yes. She's a nice large smiling lady. Please thank her for me.'

'I will. And you should write her a letter when you're feeling up to it. What are you going to call him?'

'Oh – what you called him. Tom Cat.'

The hour before my bed-time had always belonged to my father and myself. Typically, he used it to extend my general knowledge, but he was an excellent teacher who made learning a pleasure and sweetened it by reading a chapter from a book of his choice. Though he edited skilfully, to hold my interest, his choice was sophisticated and sometimes hard on my nerves. Aunt Kate had to stop him from reading *Treasure Island* because Pew proved too much for me, tapping through my dreams, but generally I shared his taste for dark adventure, and recently we had embarked on *Wuthering Heights*.

This was going well. I thought Mr Lockwood a poor fish, but Heathcliff thrilled me. I lay against a hill of pillows, the kitten asleep in the crook of my arm, and listened to my father in utter contentment. He read very well, with fine emphasis on the descriptive passages, and used a different voice for every character.

My own eyes were closing when the branch knocked furiously against the casement window, and my father echoed it on the wood of my bed. Then Mr Lockwood's fingers closed on a little ice-cold hand, and Catherine Linton's ghost sobbed and begged to be let in.

'I've been a waif for twenty years . . .'

I sat up wide awake, heart hammering. I could have shrieked aloud with Mr Lockwood. My father stopped, and looked at me questioningly over his reading glasses.

'It's all right!' I said, shivering. 'I'm not really frightened. I know it's only a story.'

I had to know what happened.

But when Heathcliff wrenched open the lattice and called for the ghost to come in, come in. I sobbed aloud. And after my father had closed the book and kissed me, and kindly left a night-light burning on the chest of drawers, tears rolled thick and fast down my cheeks. For terror had turned to pity, and I mourned for my mother lying alone in Kersley churchyard, and wondered whether her ghost peered through our windows and grieved that we could be happy without her.

6

Aunt Kate said, 'If you don't move before Christmas, Dollie, you'll be here until Easter. Now Harold says why doesn't Gilbert ask our solicitor about Hartley's old place. It's been empty for donkey's years now.'

'If it's anything like the others we've seen so far, I'm not surprised!' said Dorothy drily. 'What's wrong with it?'

We had been hunting for our permanent home all round Kersley and its environs every Saturday and Sunday afternoon for three months. At first it had been fun to visit so many unknown houses, and afterwards to regale ourselves at a local tea-shop, but as the weather grew colder the fun began to pall.

Aunt Kate sat by the front-room fire that blustery day, smoking. She had refused biscuits and was drinking tea with lemon. She was on a new diet. I knelt on the hearthrug, drawing and listening.

'Oh, you can't have seen this one, Dollie. It isn't on the agent's books yet, but it soon will be. Apparently our solicitor has been sorting out the will. Josh Hartley left the house to a niece in Australia, who hadn't been in touch with him for years. When they finally tracked the niece down she couldn't make up her mind whether to come back and live in it, or stay where she was and make money out of it. Anyway, yesterday someone in the shop told Harold that they'd heard everything was settled. Now what the rent will be I don't know, but it's worth asking.'

'What's it like?' Dorothy asked curiously.

'Big. Not too big. Ten rooms. Harold was telling me it

caused a furore in its day. Old Hartley was a bookie with ideas above his station. When he made his pile he wanted to build a baronial hall. He went all over Lancashire buying up parts of old mansions that were being pulled down. Then halfway through he lost a lot of money and had to compromise. They say that the minstrel's gallery isn't complete. It stops short at a wall! Mind you, when Josh Hartley built it there were plenty of cheap servants. It might not be convenient for a modern family. There's no electricity. You'll have to put that in yourselves. And it's a bit off the beaten track, too. Up near Tarn Fell Farm. All anyone can see of it from the road are the chimneys poking up above the trees.'

'It's too big!' said my father, staring up into the icy splendour of the hall ceiling. 'And it's too damned cold!' Staring down into the empty fireplace, which a considerate house agent had filled with crumpled red crêpe paper. 'However would we heat the place?' he accused Dorothy.

'It's very well built,' she said defensively. 'Good thick walls like these will retain the heat.'

'H'mph. You'll need a lot of domestic help here. Somebody will have to come every day of the week. That Mrs Inchmore of yours won't manage. Too many stairs. And a long walk round to the wash-house.'

'Oh, Mrs Inchmore wouldn't even manage the walk up from the tram stop! I'll get someone local. These are hard times,' said Dorothy. 'There are plenty of poor women glad of a job.'

My father ignored this, saying, 'And I've counted sixteen windows already, long and small panes, apart from those stained-glass efforts. *They'll* take some cleaning!'

'We're a fair way from the town, up here. They wouldn't need cleaning often.'

He strode through to the drawing room, where Michael and I had eaten our picnic in the summer, and stared through the window at the neglected flower-beds.

'I should have to get a man to work in the garden. I can mow the lawn, and the children will help me to sweep up the

72

leaves, but look at the rest of it! There must be well on an acre of ground.'

'A lot of that is just woodland.'

'Pruning!' said my father gloomily. 'Decorating!' He glared at a strip of paper which was gradually uncoiling down the wall. 'Look at the height of the ceilings. It'll cost a fortune!'

'But there are so many men out of work nowadays. That shouldn't be a problem. Besides, I can decorate the smaller rooms. And when Arthur has a good day he'll come over and help me out.'

Michael and I communed with each other in silence.

'Evelyn, put your scarf over your mouth,' Dorothy whispered. 'You're only just better. You don't want to start coughing again.'

She meant, 'Don't distract your father while he's thinking!'

'Shall we look upstairs?' she asked brightly.

The staircase branched to left and right. She hurried ahead of us to the left, knowing what to look for first.

'Well, fancy that! Here's your study!' she cried, opening the door to a secluded little room at the end of the landing.

'H'mph.'

'You'll be nice and quiet, tucked away here. And it looks over the kitchen garden at the back. We can grow our own vegetables. We'll keep the room next door to that for occasional guests. And the bathroom and lavatory are on this landing as well.'

We children were so quiet that we could hear ourselves breathe.

'And what's up here?' my father asked abruptly, turning right.

The master bedroom had huge windows like the drawing room below, which gave a long vista of frozen lawn, bordered by rose beds, with the little wood beyond. And beyond that lay Tarn Fell hugging a brood of small farms and wind-blown trees to its winter bosom, and over all hung the carved wave of Tarn How.

My father strode across the echoing boards and lifted his

73

eyes to the hills. He said nothing, but I came up to him silently and put my gloved hand in his, because this was our old walking country.

'There are three smaller bedrooms beyond ours, besides the one next to your study. The children can choose which ones they like,' Dorothy's voice was saying at the far end of the landing. 'Oh, and there's the wall. I see what Kate meant. Like a cul-de-sac. It is peculiar. You expect it to go on. Still, small beer's better than no beer! Oh, and talking of beer reminds me. The solicitor said there used to be a medieval malt-house on this site. So Josh Hartley named this place the Malt-house!'

I was wearing a new scarlet tam o'shanter, and now felt my father's hand rest lightly upon it. I smiled up at him and he smiled down on me.

'Would *you* like to live here, Evie?' he asked, as if no one else mattered.

I nodded emphatically, and swathed my mouth with the plaid scarf again, so that I should not cough and upset the delicate balance of his decision.

'I tell you what I like best,' Dorothy's voice said, coming nearer, 'the kitchen downstairs. It's big enough to have a table in the middle of the room, and my mother always says that's the mark of a good family kitchen, because you can eat in it when you're by yourselves. And wait until she sees that wall of mahogany cupboards, and the kitchen range! *I've* never seen a range like it, I can tell you! I could cook for a hundred in that. A bit of black lead and a good fire, and it'll come up like, like . . . I don't know what.'

My father winked at me.

He raised his voice and said with dry good-humour, 'I suppose it's no use saying anything if you've made up your mind to have it?'

Dorothy gave a little shriek, rushed in, and hugged him.

'Oh, Gil, I knew you'd love it as much as I did. It's all I've ever dreamed about. Oh, you don't know what it means to me!'

'I know what it will mean to me,' he replied factually. 'A pile of damned big bills!'

But he was only protesting to cover his own pleasure.

Michael gave me a triumphant look, ran down the gallery and slid along the smooth boards, leaving a track in the dust. I copied him.

'That's enough of that nonsense!' said my father indulgently.

'Just behave yourselves!' Dorothy added, trying to sound stern.

The decision had been made. There was much to be done. Down the stairs they went, arm-in-arm, chatting. Puffs of conversation floated up in shapes on the cold air.

'Like those balloons out of people's mouths in comics,' I said bending over the stair rail, watching them.

We listened raptly.

'Dorothy, don't be ridiculous. There is no way we can move house before Christmas.'

'But we're having our Christmas dinner with mother, Gil.'

'I don't entirely follow your line of reasoning.'

'Well, we don't have to bother about entertaining. It gives us a breathing space.'

'Really, Dorothy. There's more to a removal than cooking the Christmas dinner. And Christmas is only six weeks away. I've got all the end of term work to cope with at school. Besides, you'd never get this place cleaned up in time!'

'Oh yes, I would. I'll find two good charwomen and supervise them. We can start next week. Mrs Inchmore will look after things at home for me.'

They disappeared, still arguing.

Michael took a run from the far end of the gallery and skidded to a halt at my side.

'How now, good Puck?' he asked.

'It sounds to me,' I said contemplatively, 'as if we're moving in before Christmas.'

'Cripes!'

'Which room do you want?' I asked, and added quickly, 'I'll tell you which room I want. The one next to Daddy and Mother, that looks out at Tarn How.'

'You would. You're Tarn How mad! I'll have the one

furthest away from everybody, round the corner. Hey, Evie, watch!'

He swarmed round the newel post and hung in peril over the floor twelve feet below, but I was growing used to such exhibitions.

'Drop dead, then, and see if I care!' I cried.

And pulled my tam o'shanter dashingly over one eye, and walked with dignity down the great staircase, imagining myself ten years older and clothed in velvet and silk.

The Malt-house was a presence of a magnitude unknown to me so far, rather like Clara who lived but was not alive. It sheltered us, invested us with dignity, and yet stood alone and apart. And that which was genuinely old within it, saved or wheedled from other men's mansions by the grandiose bookie, possessed certain powers.

If I were sad I could peer through different panes of the broad stained-glass window in the hall, and see the outside world in five different colours, which altered my mood wonderfully. If I needed comfort I sat on the stairs and rested my head against the oak banisters, or hugged the carved newel post. The mere sight of those long brick chimneys standing above the trees, as I stepped off the tram at Tarn Brow, restored me. When I closed the gate I shut out the ordinary world, and the little wood afforded immediate sanctuary.

The staircase, my father had to admit, was beautiful. Being a truthful man he must also remark that the hall was out of proportion to the size of the house, and part of the gallery was certainly missing. There should have been a back staircase leading to another wing, and an upper staircase giving access to the servants' quarters.

I wished he were not so exacting. He destroyed illusions much as he swatted flies in summer: efficiently and un-emotionally. I preferred to ignore defects in those things and people I loved.

Dorothy revelled in the distinction conferred upon her by living in the Malt-house. The civility of Kersley shopkeepers increased, their credit extended, when she gave our new address. Nor did the reactions of the Schofields disappoint her.

'A big house is a big mouth!' Grannie said sententiously. 'Just you wait until the bills come in for cleaning the guttering, my lady!'

But her disparagement was a form of pride. In Hathersall market she boasted about her daughter's residence, and Dorothy knew it.

Eric, now in his first year at Blackstone University, liked to bring friends over to meet this superior sister, but she did not encourage him too much because my father objected to casual visitors dropping in at the weekend.

On one of his good days Arthur would sometimes catch the Kersley tram and come for his dinner. He and Dorothy had no means of instant communication so he had to take pot luck, but she always cooked enough to feed an extra mouth or two. His unexpected presence was a treat for Michael and me when we ran in from school, and perhaps a greater treat for himself and his sister because they understood one another. With consummate tact he always went back well before my father came home, leaving his respects to this distinguished brother-in-law.

And Mrs Inchmore's legs found themselves vastly improved at the prospect of being employed at such a distinguished residence. They had allowed outside helpers while the first awful invasion of dust and dirt was laid low, but once the place was habitable they felt they could manage. So they boarded the Shawcross tram, and walked up Tarn Brow without faltering, five days a week, supporting Mrs Inchmore while she maintained the house in that state of polish to which she felt God had been pleased to call it.

'It's no more than I expected,' cried Dorothy, when my father remarked upon this extraordinary turn of events. 'I always said that woman was worth her weight in gold. And she'd do anything for me. Anything!'

Which made us all exchange glances of amused disbelief.

Michael was not inclined to express his emotions. Outwardly he was laconic about the Malt-house, and his praise was for its practical aspects. The climbing facilities were cried up to his schoolmates at Moss Lane, and he regularly traded a Saturday afternoon's visit for sweets. He had soon scaled every tree and wall and was working out a route up the drainpipe, via the front bedroom balcony and on to the roof. Only I knew how he had responded to the house initially, and by mutual consent we did not tell our elders that it had been ours before it became theirs. This was our secret.

Even more secret was my personal sympathy with the spirit of the place, with what it was meant to be. To me the gallery ran on and met its appointed newel post, and turned into a back staircase which led to another wing. I opened up the servants' quarters. In my dreams I haunted rooms which might have existed in Josh Hartley's imagination. I sensed other presences in house and garden, stray wanderers between earth and heaven. Out of respect I did not mention them, for once they had been people and their shades should not be feared or mocked.

7

1929

Four seasons had come and gone. As a family we were a year older, and though united by good intentions and the Malthouse, our honeymoon waned as we began to know each other too well.

Michael was faring badly on the scholastic side. He had only eighteen months in which to prove his worth, but neither his teacher nor my father could kindle in him the desire to pass examinations. And yet he was quick to learn anything which caught his interest. Moss Lane had no private facilities for games, and did not expect to do well, but Michael won medals for them in both junior and senior swimming teams. Their rough-and-tumble football team, under his captaincy, began to win local matches. As a scout he accumulated badges without difficulty. His range of skills was wide, his knowledge of certain subjects profound, but he could not please my father. Indeed, he did not try, feeling that a mistake had been made and it was no use pretending otherwise. And as my father, like God, was a jealous God, Michael suffered.

Dorothy suffered too. She suffered because she loved him deeply, and because he was flesh not only of her flesh, but of Harry Harland's also. She suffered because, as a good wife, she must support her husband even against her own wishes. Finally she suffered because I tried hard and by comparison made her son seem stupid. And then I suffered because she would vent her sorrow and resentment on me.

However gloomy and nay-saying life had been at The Laurels, I was never punished physically. Aunt Kate, who would slipper her boys without compunction, never laid a finger on me. My father believed in the efficacy of a quiet rebuke. But I sensed that in some situations Dorothy's hands itched to push and slap me, and this was disquieting. I kept out of her way as best I could, to avoid conflict.

Our first crisis began with a row about Michael's homework at breakfast, and ended with Dorothy attacking my fickle appetite at lunch-time.

'I'm tired of cooking a hot meal and watching you push and pick at it. I might as well cut you a slice of bread and butter.'

In my anxiety to placate her, I said, 'But I'd rather you didn't cook a dinner for me. I'd rather have bread and butter.'

The tirade which followed robbed me of what appetite I had, and I returned to school feeling sick and shaken. Then Miss Todd was in a martial mood, reducing my confidence to untidiness and blots. Finally she decided to make an example of me.

'Come up here!' she commanded, and reached for the cane which lay across her desk. 'Hold out your hand!'

I saw my palm spread out obediently. I saw the cane swish down like a guillotine.

The first blow seemed to land in the pit of my stomach. The other two compounded the offence. I was too stunned to cry.

'Let that be a lesson to you,' said Miss Todd. 'Go back to your seat. Now I want tidy work, no crossing out, no blots, from everyone in this class. Is that understood?'

The other children were very quiet. I sat and looked at my exercise book, trying not to cry, but injustice and emotion were choking me. When the bell rang for play-time I packed my satchel, put on my hat, coat and scarf, and walked out of the school gates.

I was afraid to go to the Malt-house lest I rouse Dorothy's

wrath. I would not go to The Laurels because that meant trouble with Grandma. But I had to go somewhere, so I set off for Parbold House. And as my savings were at home, and I had no money on me, I had to walk to Hathersall.

Grannie was lifting loaves from the long oven when I arrived at tea-time. I tempered Dorothy's part in my story by saying she had a headache and I didn't want to upset her, but what Grannie did not know she could evidently guess. Lips compressed, she examined my hand, bathed and bandaged it and said what she thought of Miss Todd. Then she brewed a pot of tea and cut me a crust from the new loaf, and sat, arms folded, waiting for Grandad to come home.

There followed the biggest family conference since our Tarn How adventure. The Schofields sitting in judgement were formidable. They did not even fear my father in deciding their course of action. At six o'clock, Eric was given a slice of new bread and jam to ward off hunger, and sent on his motorbike to Kersley to say that I was safe.

'And tell them exactly what happened to her,' said Grandad sternly, 'and tell them what we think on it!'

'And tell our Dollie that it's best for the child if I keep her overnight!' was Grannie's parting comment.

I had been asleep on the parlour sofa, full of beef stew and sympathy, and woke out of a warm well to hear the sound of a taxi drawing up outside, and then voices in the hall.

Dorothy was on the defensive: breathless, intimate, apologetic.

'Oh, Mother. Thank God. We've been nearly out of our minds. I can't think what she must have told you, but . . .'

Grannie's reply was scathing.

'She told me nowt. She didn't have to. You should be ashamed of yourself. A grown woman like you. Why don't you take your temper out on somebody your own size instead of bullying a child?'

I marvelled at her championship of me.

'You don't know how difficult it is, Mother, with Michael doing badly at school . . .'

'That's not Evleen's fault, is it?'

'There's no pleasing her. She picks and pecks at her food . . .'

'She eats my food all right. And it were me she turned to when she were in trouble. I'll not forget that in a hurry. And nor should you. You're supposed to be the one who's looking after her.'

Dorothy's silence was heavy, and she answered heavily.

'Well, perhaps I was hasty. I know my faults. But I've got to take her home, Mother. Gilbert sent me in a taxi, and it's waiting.'

But Grannie would not let me go without assurance.

'What are you doing about that teacher?'

'You needn't worry. That should never have happened. And it won't happen again.'

'I should think not indeed. And don't you start on that child, neither, the minute I'm out of sight. Just behave yourself!'

Dorothy and I were embarrassed, meeting again after so much had happened. In the taxi, on our way home, she made only one reference to the events of the day, and her tone was hurt rather than reproachful.

'You could have come home to me, you know, Evie. You could have trusted me to take your side against the teacher. I may be hasty but I'm not a pirate.'

She was sincere in this, and I nodded to show that I understood.

On the following morning she came with me to school, and brought a letter from my father to Mr Wadsworth, who interviewed Miss Todd and me separately, and looked through the offending exercise book.

'You'll have to be a bit neater than this, Evelyn, to get to Blackstone High School,' he said mildly, 'but the work itself is of an excellent standard. Try thinking before you write. Don't be so anxious to get it down on paper.'

No one apologised to me but I was never caned again. Miss Todd dealt with me cautiously thereafter, and I learned to set out my work to the best advantage.

With no friends to distract me I did well at Moss Lane

School, and by the end of the first year I was regarded as a bright hope for the Blackstone scholarship. In my father's eyes this was proof that his educational experiment worked.

I paid the price with social exile, but it was a fruitful exile, passed in the realms of the mind and the imagination. It nurtured a stoicism which has often stood me in good stead. Perhaps its worst effect was a sense of smugness, of being above the common herd, and since life is a great leveller I had to learn humility later.

The December day began sullenly and ended early. By the time I jumped off the tram at Tarn Brow the lamplighter was already going his rounds. I lingered on the pavement while he lifted up his long pole and illuminated the gas-jet of the lamp overlooking the lane, before walking on. Smoke, rising from our chimneys, mingled with the fog. The trees wore veils. The glow from our hall window was blurred, the outlines hazy. And though I respected the watchers in the wood I did not want to glimpse them at dusk, and ran down the path between the trees careful to look neither left nor right, and round to the back door, and burst in on Mrs Inchmore, who was sitting in Dorothy's rocking-chair by the kitchen fire drinking strong tea.

'Good afternoon, Mrs Inchmore. Where's Mother, please?'

'Gone to poor Grandma Fawley's funeral, ain't she?' said Mrs Inchmore. 'And I'm to get tea and cake for you, and she'll cook your proper tea when they both get back.'

'I'd forgotten about the funeral.'

'Forgotten about poor Grandma? Oh, that's very nice!' said Mrs Inchmore sarcastically, rising reluctantly from the rocking-chair.

'Well, I never liked her very much, you see,' I called over my shoulder, hanging up my hat and coat in the cloakroom. 'So I couldn't be truly sorry, could I?'

Mrs Inchmore drew on her imagination, which was lurid.

'Poor Mam and Dad was sobbing their eyes out, I can tell you!'

I did not believe her. She watered the leaves in her teapot.

'Mrs Inchmore,' I said politely, 'I don't mean to be rude, but I'd rather have fresh tea if it's not too much trouble. I can't drink it when it's been standing a long time. It tastes stewed.'

Mrs Inchmore popped a piece of biscuit in her mouth, chewing and ruminating. Then she fetched out the small aluminium teapot.

'Likes and dislikes!' she grumbled. She instilled a moral. 'If you was in starving China you'd be glad o' stewed tea, I can tell you! And where's that Michael o' yours got to?'

'He won't be in for another half-hour. He plays football on Friday afternoons in the county playing fields.'

'He's better at playing than working, that one! Like our lads. And my mester!'

'Oh, how is Mr Inchmore keeping?' I asked. Though I knew.

'He's keeping out o' work!' said the charwoman testily. 'And keeping me in it. Here's your cake. Twelve childer to feed. They've got no likes and dislikes, I can tell you. They're glad of owt!'

I endeavoured to make amends, warming my hands on the cup.

'The kitchen looks so bright and warm,' I said truthfully, 'You polish everything so beautifully, Mrs Inchmore.'

'A good fire,' said the charwoman, scarlet from its attentions, 'is better than a good meal. Not that I don't like both.'

She either killed a topic or distorted it. I tried again.

'Mrs Inchmore, do you know how to make fire without matches or paper or firelighters? I do. Michael showed me. Shall I tell you?'

'There's a little girl died in a fire not long since,' said Mrs Inchmore mournfully. 'It were in the paper. Screeching for help from t'top window, but they couldn't save her. Burned to a frazzle, she were. Same age as you. That's what comes o' playing with matches.'

I sipped my tea and nibbled the cake.

'I think perhaps I'd better do some mental arithmetic

before Daddy comes back,' I said, paving the way to escape.

'Aye, get on wi' your book-learning. Else you'll be working in t'mill from morn to night, like our poor Norah.'

I asked dutifully, 'Oh, how is Norah these days?'

'Badly. She's getten a cough on her chest from the cotton fluff.'

'I'm very sorry to hear that.' I could not help adding, 'You seem to have a lot of trouble in your family, don't you, Mrs Inchmore?'

'Nowt *but* trouble.'

I attempted to round off the talk sympathetically.

'I used to have trouble when I was living at Grandma's . . .'

'Poor Grandma. Dead and buried.'

'Yes, poor Grandma.'

I held suitable silence for a moment and then began again.

'Well, when I was living with her I had to practise the piano. And one of the things I liked about moving here was that we hadn't got a piano. So I don't have to play it any more.'

'Oh! You'll be learning the pianner again afore you're very much older!' Mrs Inchmore remarked, suddenly and unkindly animated.

'Not until Daddy's saved up some more money to buy one, and he says that won't be for a long time yet.'

'You've got a pianner this very minute! God's truth!' Triumphant.

'Where is it?' I asked uncertainly, looking round.

'Grandma's left you hers. Your Mam told me this morning.'

Disgusted, I set out my exercise book and text book.

'That's just the mean sort of thing she *would* do!' I said.

'But don't go saying I towd thee,' Mrs Inchmore warned me, 'on account of your Mam wanting it to be a nice surprise.'

I sighed, and opened the arithmetic book. It was not worth my while to betray an informer.

'No, I won't say anything, Mrs Inchmore!' But to myself I

said, 'Nice surprise, indeed! Whatever next? Back to blooming old Miss Hibbert and having my knuckles rapped every five minutes!'

'You're getting a new teacher, and all, to make you work!' said Mrs Inchmore, enjoying herself. 'A lady as charges two shilling a lesson and lives at Dowson-under-Fell. So they'll have your tram fares to pay on top of the two shilling. Talk about pianner practice! At that price you won't have a knuckle left, my girl!'

The sound of the front door bell brought me to my feet. I was running through the hall before Mrs Inchmore could get up, hastening to unfasten the heavy door.

'You're back!' I cried to the dim figures in the porch.

They were dressed from head to foot in solemn black: Dorothy subdued, my father chilled in body and spirit. I clasped his waist and kissed the middle button of his sombre overcoat.

'I got ten out of ten for my mental arithmetic test!' I cried.

'Don't worry your father!' Dorothy cautioned, and to him she said, 'I'll make us both some tea. You go into the front room, Gil. You're frozen to the marrow.'

I studied his face. Something was gnawing him inwardly. He removed his overcoat, hung up the top hat. His flesh was the colour of old ivory. His hands were cold.

'Was it all very sad?' I asked, finding the way to his trouble.

'It was a damned long miserable business. I detest funerals.'

I raised my arms and smiled at him.

'You're growing too heavy to lift up!' he said, but spoke a little more cheerfully and swung me to his shoulder.

Face to face, I was suddenly enlightened.

'I never thought of it before,' I said, 'but Grandma was *your* mummy, wasn't she?'

'Yes,' he said reluctantly.

'What was she like when you were a little boy. Just as cross?'

'No. I remember her as being young and handsome and full of life. She taught me to read and write. I was the one most like her. She was very proud when I went to the university. She used to be a teacher before she married my father – I never had much time for *him*!'

And he slid me down again, saying, 'There, that's enough.'

A thought occurred to me.

'Does everybody always die?' I asked curiously.

His answer was honest.

'Yes. Some sooner than others. In the end we all come to it.'

'Even me?' For I had been certain of a dispensation.

He never ducked a question, whatever it cost him or the questioner. It was one of the characteristics that made him both respected and feared.

'I'm afraid so.'

He must have seen the shadow on me, and held out his hand, saying gently, 'Let's go in by the fire, shall we?'

8

The maid wore her afternoon uniform: a silky brown dress
with cream lawn cuffs, a frilly cream cap and apron threaded
with narrow brown ribbon. Confronted by this superior type
of servant Dorothy adopted a superior mode of behaviour.

'Good afternoon,' she said condescendingly. 'We have an
appointment with Miss Lacey. Kindly tell your mistress that
Mrs Gilbert Fawley and Miss Evelyn Fawley have arrived.'

I noted that the maid was more at ease than Dorothy.

'Certainly, madam. Should you like to wait in here,
please?'

She ushered us into a pretty sitting room, which Dorothy
explored with unbridled interest. This house, built early in
Queen Victoria's reign, was smaller and older than ours and
did not strive to impress. The woodwork was painted white,
an unusual choice for a county which preferred dark brown
paint or varnish. The pale wallpaper contained a subtle
silver stripe. Ornaments and pictures were few and restrained. An air of tranquillity prevailed. From the bow
window we had a cloudless view of the other side of the
Fell and Tarn How, which at once aroused my private
passion.

'Oh look! We're through the looking-glass!' I cried,
pointing.

For the tables had turned, and I was reading *Alice* to my
father at the end of our evening sessions.

But Dorothy, not being interested, was not listening.

'Fancy employing a maid, when you live alone in a little
place.'

88

'I should think it must be very nice!' I replied coolly.

'You know nothing about it!'

I recognised her note of discontent, and guessed that my father had been angry about Michael's school report. I swung my legs, thinking. Michael must feel the same way about my father teaching him mathematics as I felt about learning to play the piano: miserable beforehand, stupid during the lesson, and sick at heart afterwards.

'Now don't tell Miss Lacey that you're no good and you don't like music,' Dorothy warned, 'because you're very lucky to get the chance of an interview with her.'

'It won't matter what I *say*. As soon as she asks me to play the piano she'll *know* I'm no good!' I replied logically.

'Don't argue the point with me, my lady! Tell her you'll do your best.' Then Dorothy made one of her about-turns, and added, 'She might not take you anyway. She's very particular.'

Hope sprang in my heart and evidently showed in my eyes.

'It's no use looking like that,' said Dorothy, with some asperity, 'because you've got to learn the piano! If not with Miss Lacey then with someone else. Every girl has to play the piano. Even my parents managed to pay for music lessons, and we were poor.'

She strove to draw a moral from this sacrifice.

'And now I can rattle off any tune. Almost.'

My reply was unchildlike in its irony.

'I know. I've heard you,' I said.

Dorothy lost her temper.

'And don't be cheeky or I'll give you a shake!'

As if I was a sauce bottle, I thought. But I put on a more suitable expression and swung my legs again.

'I wonder where she is,' Dorothy mused, looking at her wristwatch. 'She said four o'clock, and it's almost quarter past!'

The lady who came towards us smiling, one hand outstretched, resembled the sepia image of Clara in the only

89

photograph I possessed. Her eyes were a wonderful soft rich black. Her black hair was fashionably short, parted at one side and cut to form points which touched her cheeks. Her figure was boyish and long-legged. She wore her brief checked skirt and long-waisted jersey well. The jersey was the colour of chocolate. Against it glowed a long string of amber beads.

In her early thirties, Lilian Lacey's reputation as a music teacher was becoming notable, and explained in part why she remained a spinster. With her good looks, her small private income and desirable private residence, she was an undoubted catch. That she declined to be caught was annoying, inexplicable. Married women could only conclude that she had not yet found Mr Right. Her own explanation was unacceptable. She said she preferred not to marry at all.

Her voice was light, quick and pleasant. She sounded very much in command of herself.

'Mrs Fawley, I do apologise. I should have finished half an hour ago, but my pupil is taking an examination in Blackstone on Monday and we were working so hard that neither of us noticed the time!'

'I *quite* understand!' said Dorothy confidentially, as if she had taught music for years. 'How do you do? So pleased to meet you at last. This is my daughter Evelyn.'

I had been unable to take my eyes off this vision. I answered automatically, 'How do you do, Miss Lacey?'

But she smiled formalities away, and said, 'Hello, Evelyn!' as if we had known each other for a lifetime.

'Evelyn has brought her music-case, and the pieces upon which she was engaged with her former instructor,' Dorothy explained, still in superior mode.

'Oh, that's very thoughtful, but we shan't need them at this stage, Mrs Fawley.' She rang a little bell on the side table. 'Perhaps you would like some tea while you're waiting?'

'Most kind,' Dorothy murmured, puzzled.

'I want to borrow Evelyn for perhaps a quarter of an hour, so we can become acquainted. May I?'

'Of course, of course!' cried Dorothy, waving her gloves.

The maid appeared, carrying a tray of tea and biscuits, which she set down, smiling.

Obviously feeling that the situation was slipping from her grasp, Dorothy said, 'I quite understand that the audition should take place in private.'

'Oh, I'm not planning anything as grand as that!' said Lilian Lacey, amused. 'We shall just have a chat. You can leave your case here, Evelyn. Do make yourself comfortable, Mrs Fawley. If you'd like to smoke there are cigarettes in the box by your side. Mary, will you make sure that Mrs Fawley has everything she needs?'

I had never seen Dorothy vanquished before. It was an awesome and highly satisfying spectacle.

In a room which was the twin of the one we had just left, Miss Lacey and I sat opposite one another. A glossy Broadwood piano straddled the flowered carpet, a bust of Mozart gazed thoughtfully beyond me, and a metronome stood mercifully still.

Miss Lacey clasped her hands round her knees and leaned forward. Even when she did not smile her eyes smiled. She began in a bright and forthright fashion.

'Are you fond of music, Evelyn?'

I hesitated, for I longed to please this goddess, but my father's influence forbade me to lie.

I said, 'I like listening to music, Miss Lacey, but I'm not very good at playing it.'

Her eyes gleamed with inner amusement.

'What kind of music do you like to listen to? What makes you feel happy – or sad in a happy sort of way?'

I consulted an extremely limited repertoire, none of which sounded right for Miss Lacey. Again I compromised.

'Lots of things. I can't remember them all.'

'Oh, I don't want a list. Just a few favourites. What about Christmas carols, for instance?'

My mind cleared. I could cope with carols.

' "In the bleak mid-winter . . ." ' I began.

She interrupted me with, 'And why do you like that?'

I realised that she wanted me to talk to her properly, to say what I thought rather than what I was expected to say. I answered somewhat self-consciously.

'I can feel the cold and the hardship, but the baby's safe from cruel King Herod, and everybody will be glad when they see him lying in the manger, wrapped up nice and safe.'

There was a slight pause before Lilian Lacey said, 'Hymns?'

I was warming to this interview.

'"Jerusalem". Because they say, "Bring me my bow of burning gold, bring me my arrows of desire", and I feel like Achilles. I like Achilles, except that he shouldn't have dragged Hector's body round the walls of Troy because Hector was a brave man.'

Lilian Lacey's gleam was now intent rather than amused.

'Have you ever been to a music concert?'

I shook my head.

'Do your parents play records of concert music on the gramophone? No? Do they play any musical instrument themselves?'

'My father played the banjo when he was a student, but that was mostly in fun at parties. . . .'

For some reason I could not have specified, I did not want Lilian Lacey to associate me with Dorothy, whose maternal sun had already set as far as I was concerned.

'. . . and my stepmother plays the piano.'

I stressed the *step* lightly but definitely.

'And what does she play?' Lilian asked, seemingly unmoved.

'Selections from the *Community Song Book* – and when Grannie and Grandad come over we all sing together. And an album called *Popular Light Classics*. And lots of song sheets. "Charmaine" and "Glad-Rag Doll" and "Among My Souvenirs" and things like that.'

'And do you enjoy the singing and the tunes?'

'Yes,' I said, but reluctantly.

The bust of Mozart disturbed me. Although I did not know who it was supposed to be, and had not heard his name anyway, I guessed that he belonged to a more superior realm of music than 'Glad-Rag Doll'.

92

'Do you have any music instruction at school?'

'They teach us to sing "Cherry Ripe" and "God Save the King".'

With a frankness that my father would have admired, she said, 'Not a strong musical background.'

I was cast down in an instant.

Lilian said kindly, 'I can only take a certain number of pupils, you see, Evelyn, and I care very much about music. So I must be sure that my pupils care about it, too. Why do *you* want to learn?'

I had known that this woman would be too clever for me, but I made one last effort for my parents' sake.

'My father believes in a broad education. And my step-mother says that girls should be able to play the piano.'

'A form of good manners?' Lilian suggested, eyebrows raised. 'And what do *you* feel about that?'

The battle was lost. Honesty could not damage my chances now.

'It doesn't matter what I feel if they've made up their minds,' I said, resigned. 'If you don't teach me then some-body else will have to. Grandma Fawley died and left me her piano, you see.'

Lilian Lacey rocked back in her chair and laughed aloud.

'I shouldn't laugh!' she said, seeing that I was hurt, 'but you *are* a funny little girl!'

I managed a polite smile.

'Now you've been so good, answering all those questions,' said Lilian unexpectedly, 'that I feel it's my turn. Instead of asking you to play for me, why don't I play for you?'

'Oh yes, please,' I said, relieved at this unorthodox suggestion.

Then Lilian Lacey became another person, who removed her rings and placed them in a little china dish on top of the piano, sat down on the plush stool, concentrated for a few moments, poised both hands above the glistening teeth of the keyboard, and began to play.

The music came forth as if she were thinking it aloud. In my mind's eye I saw a host of pictures, old and infinitely precious and full of meaning. The music became a reflection of myself. I remembered things I had long forgotten. I had glimpses of what was to come. Then the music stopped, and I found myself standing by Lilian Lacey's side, smiling and crying at the same time.

'Now that's what I call true appreciation,' said Lilian quietly, making no fuss over the tears.

I found a handkerchief tucked just under the elastic of my navy blue knickers, pulled it out and dried my eyes.

'Mummy used to play like that,' I said.

Lilian swung round on the piano stool, hands on knees, and looked at me in quite a different way.

'Did she indeed? Why didn't you tell me about her when we were talking just now?'

'I don't talk about her to anyone. I knew she played the piano, but I'd forgotten how she played.'

'How old were you when you lost your mother?'

'I was almost four. They didn't like me to talk about her in case I upset Daddy. She died in a road accident and he wouldn't keep anything that reminded him of her. So I've had to piece bits together, like a jigsaw. Her name was Clara. She had a pretty laugh. She was a daydreamer like me. She was tall and slim and dark. Dr Gould said she was the nervous type. I've got a photograph, but it's a bit brown and blurry. I don't look like her yet, but I hope I will someday. So far, I take after my Aunt Jane who died when she was young.'

'What a mine of information you are, once we start digging!'

I, who had been about to cry again, now laughed instead. I felt light of heart. I knew I could trust her absolutely.

'Mummy used to play like you do, as if she was listening to herself. Sometimes she sat me on the piano stool and picked out a tune with my fingers, as if I was playing it. Her music made pictures, like yours does. It said something for me. I can't explain what.'

'You explain very well. And did your father enjoy her playing?'

'Oh yes. She used to play to him in the evenings when I was in bed. I always tried to stay awake until she'd finished, but I never managed it. She played different kinds of music.

With my fingers she picked out tunes I knew like "Baa baa black sheep". But when she and Daddy were by themselves she played music that was like Andrews Liver Salts. All fizzy and full of bubbles.'

'Something like this?' asked Lilian Lacey, and she turned round again, and her fingers moved nimbly over the keys.

'Yes. Yes. Not quite the same, but like that.'

'That's Chopin,' said Lilian, thinking.

She was drawing all the threads together in her mind, as I was.

'So your mother played Chopin, and your father listened?'

'Yes. And she used to play the other kind, too. The music like moving water, that you played first.'

'Schubert? You mean this one?'

'Yes.'

We smiled at each other in complete understanding.

'It's a wonderful thing,' I said, 'to have something given back again that I thought I'd lost.'

'I can understand that.'

With infinite tact she said, 'We know that your stepmother sees music as a social accomplishment – and, of course, she's quite right in her way – but had you thought that perhaps your father wanted you to learn the piano because he'd lost something, too?'

I considered this, hands clasped behind my back, one black lace-up shoe rubbing one black stocking. I nodded, too moved to speak.

Lilian said, 'I think there's quite a lot of music in you, waiting to be let out. Are you sure you don't want me to teach you?'

I had asked, and been answered, and knew I was not worthy.

'But I've never been any good at it,' I cried. 'Nobody thought I was any good. Including Miss Hibbert.'

A covert smile lit Lilian's face.

'Well, never mind Miss Hibbert for now,' she advised. 'Suppose you and I start again? Right at the very beginning as if you'd never learned a single scale.'

I said hesitantly, glancing at the metronome, 'You see, I

always lose my place when that thing tocks at me, and then my fingers trip up, and the pennies fall off the back of my hands.'

'I believe we can manage without the metronome and the pennies.'

I said shyly, 'And I don't like having my knuckles rapped with a ruler when I make mistakes.'

'Oh dear, oh dear,' said Lilian, laughing outright. 'Music, what crimes have been committed in thy name! Let's forget the horrors, shall we? Where's my appointment book? We can begin next week, I think. Bring your music-case with you, but bring it empty. . . .'

Then she clapped one hand to her mouth and cried, 'Oh, Lor'! I had totally forgotten your poor stepmother. What time is it? We must have been chatting away in here for nearly an hour!'

Dorothy said, on the way home, in a tram which trundled from star to star, 'I suppose all these artistic people are the same. Head in the air and no idea of time. Your father will be waiting for his evening meal.'

Still, she was pleased with the outcome.

'You see what happens,' she said, 'when you take notice of what I say, and do as I tell you?'

I could find no way of breaching the wall of my father's defences without hurting him, so I left a message outside it instead.

As I said good night, I whispered in his ear, 'I'm going to practise very hard, Daddy, until I can play as beautifully as Miss Lacey. And then I'll play just for *you*.'

9

1930

'I think Michael's scholarship results have come,' said Dorothy.

She had been sorting through the morning's post at breakfast, and now sat immobilised, holding the official communication as if it were about to explode.

Michael and I stopped eating. My father set down his cup and accepted the time-bomb calmly. The three of us would have ripped the envelope open, but he inserted a clean knife into one corner and slit it neatly. He read the letter through, drew a long breath through his nose, and handed it back to his wife without a tremor. Afraid to look at it, she beseeched him.

'What does it say? What does it say?'

'He hasn't even passed the first half of the examination,' said my father coldly.

Michael's head was bent over his plate. He did not look up. 'Well, it's not the end of the world,' said Dorothy helplessly. 'I'm sure he did his best. Can't he try again?'

My father gave his unalterable judgement in four sentences.

'He did *not do* his best, which is why he has failed. No, he *can't* try again because he'll be too old. And *I* wouldn't lift a finger to help him if he did.'

Dorothy's eyes filled.

'Oh don't, Mum,' said Michael between his teeth. 'Please don't.'

My father said impatiently, 'Tears are useless, Dorothy. We must think what can be done for Michael's future.'

'Daddy . . .' I began, attempting to mediate.

His expression silenced me.

He said, 'Your mother is upset, Evelyn, perhaps *you* would be kind enough to pour me another cup of tea?'

Receiving it, he disappeared behind his newspaper without a further word.

Dorothy dried her eyes, and whispered to us, 'If you've finished breakfast you'd better go to school.'

She looked at the letter. She nerved herself to speak.

'I don't know whether he has to take this to show his teacher or not,' she said tremulously to the *Manchester Guardian*.

It did not answer her.

'I'd better take it,' said Michael.

He had difficulty pushing the envelope into his satchel. His movements were unusually clumsy. He was so pale that the freckles stood out on his skin like a rash.

'Are you all right, Micky?' Dorothy whispered.

He did not answer, keeping his head down so we should not see his expression.

'I'll just see the children off to school!' said Dorothy to the newspaper, which took not the slightest notice.

But in the hall, as if my father's absence released her, she put her arms round Michael and began to cry in earnest. The sound and sight of her adult grief awoke a sense of shame in me, as if I had caught her naked. Michael's mouth trembled.

He said, 'Mum, I'm sorry. Mum, I just . . . I can't . . .'

'I know, I know. I don't care one way or the other,' she said passionately. 'What does it matter? You should have stayed at Milton Lodge where they understood you. All I want is for you to be happy.'

Hurriedly, because I must not be there when Dorothy lost complete control, I whispered, 'I'll go on ahead, Mick.'

He was stroking his mother's hair and trying not to cry himself. He nodded, and the nod conveyed that he did not blame me because of my father, but Dorothy was cast in a less charitable mould.

'Yes, you mince off to school, Miss Fawley!' she cried, lifting a face ravaged with tears and trouble. 'You're just what your father ordered. A regular little know-all, forever sticking your nose into a book. No wonder you can't make friends. And don't imagine that you're a teacher's favourite. They think you're a bit odd. . . .'

'Mum, that's not fair! Evie, why don't you go?' Michael urged, divided in his loyalties. 'I'll catch you up when I can.'

I walked quickly away, feeling as if Dorothy had slapped me, and reaching the lane I ran as fast as I could. I was trying to escape the words she had thrown at me. But however fast I fled they kept pace.

What she said about my lack of friends was true, but what hurt most was the knowledge that people had been disparaging me behind my back, and that she had listened and then used the information against me. My own mother would have been incapable of such disloyalty.

I avoided Michael, who also avoided me, and did not return home with him at twelve o'clock to eat her food. In self-exile, I bought a pennyworth of biscuits and hung on the outskirts of other children's groups in the playground. The hour and a half seemed long.

At four o'clock I decided to come home rather than cause another scene, and this was the right decision. Dorothy was relieved to see me and anxious to make amends. She had produced a culinary apology in the shape of chocolate blancmange. In the evening we all ate in silence. No one mentioned my absence from the midday meal or Michael's failure. But my father did not coach me as usual, and directly he had drunk his coffee he retreated to his study to work.

Left to ourselves, we made the best of a bad day. Dorothy brought out a pack of playing cards and a box of liquorice allsorts, and we played rummy on the kitchen table until nine o'clock, using the sweets as stakes. We had all been bruised and were restrained with one another for quite a while afterwards.

And yet spring came, and the horse chestnut flowered.

Unlike my father, who could remain dumb for twenty years if need be, Dorothy was quite incapable of keeping a secret. So a number of confidantes were sworn in over morning coffee and afternoon tea. And finally, when the three of us were sitting in the kitchen one evening, and my father was working in his study, she shared it with us.

'Now I know you and Gil haven't always seen eye to eye, Micky,' she began, in her most judicious manner, 'but when I tell you – in strictest confidence, mind! – what he's going to do for you, you'll wish you'd tried harder to understand and please him.'

Michael was making a model galleon out of balsa wood, frowning slightly with concentration. His frown deepened. She now addressed both of us.

'Promise that neither of you will tell, because it's a secret.'

'I promise!' I said promptly, for I loved secrets, and unlike Dorothy I could keep them.

Michael said drily, 'If it's about him paying for me to go to Blackstone Grammar School I know that already.'

Dorothy's disappointment sharpened her tone.

'And where did you hear that, might I ask?'

'You told Aunt Kate, and she told Uncle Harold, and Alex overheard them and told me.'

'Well, I'm blessed! Oh, well, as you know, what do you think about it?'

'Not much,' said Michael briefly. 'Mum, I'm making rigging, and it's very tricky. Please can I get on with it?'

To save Dorothy's fallen face, and satisfy my own curiosity, I said, 'You can tell me, if you like. I'd love to know. Where's Daddy getting the money from?'

'Grandma Fawley's legacy,' said Dorothy, pleased as a child to talk. 'Only you mustn't ever say I told you.'

I swore a great oath.

'Not even if I'm branded with hot irons!'

Michael, annoyed with the pair of us, laid the rigging down for a moment, to interrupt.

'Liar!' he said to me. 'You'd tell anybody anything if they so much as waved a lighted match at you!'

He tackled his mother next.

'Mum, I don't want him to spend his money on me. It'll be wasted. I want you to back me up. If you won't then *I* shall tell him.'

But the kudos of Blackstone Grammar School had quite won Dorothy over. She was up in arms in an instant.

'The nicest thing you can do, Michael Fawley, is to thank your kind father for his generosity!'

'Oh no, Mum! Oh no! He just wants to take me over. Like having my name changed from Harland to Fawley. And that's another thing. You persuaded me to agree to that Fawley business in a weak moment, and I'm sorry I gave in. But let me tell you this. Inside me I'm a Harland and I always shall be! And when I'm twenty-one I'll change my surname back again!'

I sat appalled and fascinated. That mother and son should battle as equals always astonished me. Even in the nether-most depths of hell my father and I always respected his status and his dignity.

Dorothy became aware of a delicate situation.

'Fancy talking about Evelyn's father like that, in front of her!' she said, shocked.

But Michael would not let her escape in this fashion.

'No offence meant to you or him, Evie,' he said instantly, 'but he is not, and never will be, my father. So there.'

Mother and son returned to battle.

'You should be grateful he puts your interests first . . .'

'But he doesn't. He's sending me to Blackstone Grammar because *he* wants me to go there, not because *I* want to go, or because it would do me any good – because it won't! I'm not the type, Mum, and I thought you understood that. Mum, they don't nickname that place the "Old Crammer" for nothing. If a chap can't swot himself silly they've got no time for him! They're going to push me harder than he's ever done – and in a direction I don't want to go!'

Dorothy said weakly, 'I hope you won't say things like that to him, Micky, after all he's done for you.'

'I shan't be rude, but I shall be straight. If you won't stick up for me then I must stick up for myself. It probably won't make any difference, but at least he and I will know where we stand.'

Dorothy was wavering, saying, 'I'm sorry I ever told you . . .'

'You didn't tell me. Alex did.'

And Michael concentrated on the galleon's rigging.

For a minute or so silence reigned in the hot light kitchen. Then the insistent tick of the clock on the mantelpiece brought Dorothy to herself again.

'Just look at the time. Your father will be wanting a cup of tea. You can take it up for him, Evie.'

Evie. That meant I was in favour for the moment, or simply that Michael was out of it. I took advantage of her mood to put in a word for myself.

'Mother, is Daddy spending all of Grandma's legacy on Michael?'

Flattered by a title I seldom used, Dorothy returned to her gossip with zest.

'Oh no. That wouldn't be fair, and you know how fair he is. In fact – Michael, I hope you're listening to this! – in fact he had no need to spend any of it on Michael. Grandma left the money entirely to him. But he chose – are you listening, Michael? – to set aside a certain sum for each of you children, to be spent as you need it most. That's why he's decided to spend Michael's now. On his education.'

'So if I don't get a scholarship to Blackstone High School, might he use mine to pay fees there?'

My logical conclusions always surprised her.

'I hadn't thought about that. Yes, I suppose so. He's a just man. He won't make fish of one child and flesh of the other.'

An unworthy thought naturally occurred to her.

'But that doesn't mean you stop working for it!' she warned me.

I despised her, and resolved to leave her at the earliest opportunity. Michael was not the only one to resent a step-parent. But I replied enigmatically, and with seeming obedience.

'Oh no. I shall work even harder now.'

She recognised the ring of sincerity but did not understand

the reason. Nor did I enlighten her, for she was capable of using the information against me. But it had occurred to me that if the legacy was not needed for fees, and I won my scholarship, I could probably persuade my father to buy me a good piano.

Something was delighting them. I could tell, from the way Michael and I were excluded, that the adults were rejoicing in a secret of their own. The exclusion was not unkind, just absent-minded. Dorothy kept saying amiably, 'So there you are!' whenever she saw us, and my father would ask pleasantly, 'So what have you two been up to?' and, like Jesting Pilate, did not stay for an answer.

That summer we rented a house for a month in the Lake District, and took Grannie Schofield with us to help Dorothy. The air of secrecy had not dispersed. Rather did it grow and thicken, as Dorothy herself was growing and thickening. Though slapdash, she had never been lazy. Now she slowed down quite noticeably.

Observing her lie on the beach for the whole of one long hot afternoon, I looked round for a confidante of my own.

'Grannie Annie, don't think I'm being rude, but isn't Mother getting a little bit fat?'

Grannie's colour and temper rose unexpectedly.

'I'm surprised at you, Evleen. I thought better of you than that! Here, throw these peelings away for me and make yourself useful.'

I had been trained to accept adult mysteries. Nor was I curious enough about the animal world to have gained knowledge by observation and enquiry. Yet something was afoot and I sought to discover what. Instinctively I did not ask any of the men in our family. Of the women, Aunt Maud chose never to know anything and Lilian Lacey inhabited a different world. There was always Aunt Kate, of course.

'Aunt Kate, why is Mother getting fat?'

'Is she?' Kate asked warily. 'Hasn't she said anything to you? Oh!' Then, rather lamely, 'I must tell her about my new diet.'

The answer came from Moss Lane School in the autumn,

when Dorothy came to collect me in the morning for a dental appointment and returned me that afternoon with a metal filling.

As I nursed an aching jaw in the school playground the most nubile girl in the class approached me, trailing giggling cronies. By this time I had grown used to being an outsider, and expected nothing.

'Eh, you! Fancy Nancy! You didn't tell us you was having a new kid at your 'ouse!'

'A new what?'

The girl patted her flat little belly.

'Your Mam's got summat inside there!' she said derisively. 'Unless she's like barber's cat – all piss and wind!'

The circle of jeering children closed in. None of them had ever hurt me, but the threat and the humiliation was always sickening. And Michael, in his first term at Blackstone Grammar School, was no longer there to protect me.

'Didn't you know?' one boy asked. 'Are you daft or summat?'

I was totally bewildered.

'She knows nowt!' said one wise old woman of ten. 'She thinks you find 'em under t'goozeberry bush!' Loudly, as if to an idiot, she cried, 'Your Mam's going to have a babby. Ask her. See if I'm right.'

Dorothy was resting on the drawing-room sofa when I got home, and I could not help thinking that she resembled the picture of a beached whale in our *Children's Newspaper*. I decided to approach the question obliquely.

'Muriel Shaw's mother has had a new little baby.'

'Ridiculous. They can't feed the ones they've got!' said Dorothy crossly, avoiding my eyes.

I felt my way round the problem. 'I've often wondered,' I said casually, though I had not, 'how babies were born.'

Dorothy's reaction was astonishing. She hauled herself into a sitting position, loud, flushed and dishevelled.

'Never say anything as rude as that again!' she cried. 'I know where you get those nasty ideas from!'

To her invisible arbiter she said, 'He wouldn't listen!' and to me, who was stunned and uncomprehending, 'If you'd stayed at Townley's you'd never have dreamed of saying such a thing!'

The reprimand was out of all proportion to the offence. From the moment that she ceased speaking, Dorothy was obviously sorry. She adopted a conciliatory tone.

'It's not your fault, Evie. It's those rough children you have to play with. Don't talk to them. They've got nasty minds. Go and ask Mrs Inchmore to make your tea.'

My embarrassment was so great that I withdrew into myself for the rest of the evening, and resolved to keep silent on the subject forever. But evidently my father's common-sense over-rode his wife's modesty, for at the weekend he told us the news while she was out shopping. He rattled the change in his pocket as he spoke: a sure sign that he was ill at ease.

'I expect you know you're going to have a brother or sister?'

'I've known for ages,' said Michael, offhand.

Doubly betrayed, I answered stoutly, 'So have I.'

My father was plainly relieved.

'Good. It's expected some time at the end of December, so we shall be having a quiet Christmas at home this year. We must do what we can to help your mother before and after the baby arrives. She'll have a lot of extra work to do, and she'll get tired easily.'

Then he came, as far as he was concerned, to the crux of the conversation.

'You're growing up now. It's time you became more independent. Starting from Monday, you should both make your own beds each morning and tidy your rooms before you go to school. And as Mrs Inchmore isn't here in the evenings, and your mother has to cook a big meal, you must do the washing-up before you begin your homework.'

I accepted his edict without question, but Michaël was disgusted, and grumbled to me in private.

'It's his baby, too. Why doesn't he do something, as well as us? He doesn't even clean his own shoes!'

*

105

It was the last day of the year, and we two children had been marooned in the front parlour of Parbold House all afternoon, with orders to amuse ourselves in a clean and orderly fashion. I was allowed to sit in the window-seat and read one of the Sunday School Prize Books won by Dorothy in her youth. Michael's choice of occupation proved more difficult. He was making a balsa wood battleship, which involved the use of a razor-blade and threatened the carpet with sawdust and chippings. Grannie finally solved the problem by surrounding him with single sheets of the *Hathersall Weekly Advertiser*, protecting the table top with a thick wad of them, and putting his building tray on top of it.

We had been sitting in harmonious silence for more than an hour while she prepared a steak and kidney pie in the kitchen. Then I put down my copy of *Nellie, or The Noble Way* and communed with the atmosphere of Parbold House.

'It feels just the same as their wedding day!' I announced.

I had picked up the air of apprehension and delight.

Michael did not answer, and I understood that he was dealing with a tricky bit of cutting.

'What excitement this morning!' I went on. 'I thought the baby was never coming. We've had our bags packed for days. And this time Grannie Annie has given me my own bedroom.'

Now Michael could talk while he glued.

'That's because you're not a cry-baby any more.'

I came over to see how the battleship was doing.

'Micky, what do you hope it will be? A brother or a sister?'

'It makes no odds,' said Michael. 'I'm not interested in babies. And by the time it grows up I shall have left home.'

There was no answer to that. I changed the subject.

'Why has Grannie put us in the front parlour? It isn't Sunday.'

'I expect it's because she lit the fire early and didn't want to waste it.' He added, with a wry smile, 'Your father will come over to tell us when the baby's born, and Grannie feels that he can't be asked to sit in the kitchen!'

'Is that why she's making steak and kidney pie?'

'Yep. Mum told her he liked it.'

'Goodness, how thoughtful everyone is!'

Michael said, keeping his eyes on the battleship so that I should not be embarrassed, 'Do you know how babies are born?'

The memory of that shameful question made me colour up.

'Oh yes,' I said hurriedly.

Michael said, glueing with exquisite precision, 'Because if you didn't I was going to tell you. I thought you ought to know.'

I changed my mind. This kind of information was hard to come by, and I had wondered how Dorothy would rid herself of that grotesque lump. It seemed too big to cough up, for instance.

'I know in a sort of a way. But not exactly.'

'They come out of a special hole in the lady's bottom,' said Michael succinctly, and reached for his instruction leaflet.

I said incredulously, reproachfully, 'You know your mother doesn't like you to say rude things like that!'

'It might be rude, but it's true.'

I rubbed my shoe on my sock. He was probably teasing me.

'There wouldn't be a hole big enough,' I said at length, thinking of the size of Dorothy's belly.

'It stretches. Like elastic.'

Now I knew he was joking.

'It doesn't!' I said, and giggled.

'It does. That's why the kid takes so long to get out. It takes hours. I mean, we've been here since breakfast time, haven't we?'

I could tell by his tone that he was perfectly serious.

'If you want to know how it's done Mum hides a book at the bottom of the blanket drawer in their wardrobe, called *The Family's Own Home Doctor*.' He added, 'I knew you hadn't the faintest idea. Dumb-bell!'

Humiliated, I cried, 'How could I when nobody told me?'

'Nobody told *me*. I just found out. You must learn to rely on yourself, Squib. Use your initiative – as your father always says!'

I retreated to the window-seat and picked up the book. Some minutes ago I had read the final page with innocent joy. Soiled with knowledge, I read it again.

'Dearest Cyril, I have something special to tell you,' Nellie whispered, blushing as red as the roses over their cottage door.

'What is it, sweetheart?' asked her young husband tenderly. .

'If I told you that I could love someone else as deeply as I love you,' she faltered, 'and that this love would enrich our own. . . .'

She could not go on, but hid her rosy face in her pretty hands.

'Sweetheart, you cannot mean . . . ?' he cried.

'Yes, dearest, yes. Before the snows of winter come, God will have entrusted a new and precious soul to our loving care.'

It was the seal on their happiness.

There appeared to be some discrepancy between these transports and Michael's information. Perhaps no one had told them, either.

I heard my father's voice, young and excited as never before.

'What? Once in a while, and on New Year's Eve of all times? No, Grannie! Let's get them up and tell them the news.'

I drifted to the surface through fathoms of sleep to see him materialise in the doorway, exalted.

'Is it the baby?' I asked, fuddled.

'A little brother!' he cried. 'What about that as a start to nineteen thirty-one? And they're both fighting fit. Your mother's sitting up in bed, drinking tea and eating toast.'

Amiable but puzzled, I mumbled, 'Who made the toast? Who's there now? Have you left them all alone?'

'Oh, they're all right. Aunt Kate's staying the night, and she and Mrs Inchmore have been there all day. Come on. Up you get. We'll see the New Year in together.'

I scrambled out of bed willingly, and reached for my blue wool dressing-gown, which was now skimpy and short in the sleeves.

'You've outgrown this!' said my father, helping me into it.

His dark face was aglow with joy and relief. I could hear Michael being woken by Grannie Annie, and hoped he would join in the celebrations with a good heart.

I hugged my father and said, 'Oh, I am glad. We've been waiting all day for news. Grannie cooked a special meal for you, but you didn't come. Still, you seem to have had quite a party!'

'We're going to have another party right now!' he cried. 'I've brought a bottle of wine with me, to celebrate.'

Mindful that there was no wife to caution him, I whispered, 'Don't forget that the Schofields are teetotal!'

'Good God, so they are! Well, I'm sure Eric isn't, after two years of Blackstone University! And I should think a drop of something strong would do poor Arthur good!'

He was laughing, and I loved him even more than Michael.

'Did you want a son so much?' I asked wistfully.

He understood me in an instant.

'I didn't need another daughter,' he said, 'and I hadn't a son.'

I hugged him. I remembered my responsibilities.

'Don't say that to Micky, will you?'

'No, no. Of course not. Poor old Mick. He's going to get his nose pushed out! Dorothy's over the moon about this little chap!'

He was fiercely, childishly glad about that. He and Michael had been competing for Dorothy's attention since the wedding. Now they were both relegated to second place by my father's own son.

I looked fondly into the face I had never seen before. It was the face my mother must have known. Young and dark and eager.

'I'm glad you got what you wanted,' I said.

It was almost midnight. Neither Michael nor I had ever been up so late before, and we relished every broken rule that came our way, including a sip of wine when Grandad Schofield wasn't looking. Eric the undergraduate, and Arthur the invalid, proved to be as weak in teetotal principles as my father had predicted, and helped him to finish the bottle. And for the first time they were all easy in each other's company, joined together by their delight in this common bond of the new child.

'And have you made up your mind what to call him, then?' asked Grannie, refilling the glasses of those who drank ginger beer.

'Yes, Grannie, we have. We've decided on *Julian*.'

The Schofields tried it on their tongues, finding it exotic but very acceptable.

'Julian Fawley,' said Grandad. 'That's a fine name. A noble name. That's a name as'll count in high places. We shall hear that name in future years.'

I saw by the humility and reverence in his face that he was pondering on how far he had come in life, to be given a grandson called Julian Fawley with all the world before him.

'Nearly midnight!' Uncle Eric reminded us. 'Shall I open the door, so we can hear the chimes?'

'Wait a bit!' cried Grannie. 'I'm forgetting. We've got a dark gentleman with us for once. Dr Fawley, will you let the New Year in for us?'

He was ready to do anything for anybody. He listened courteously to instructions which would formerly have aroused his instant derision.

'Take this piece o' coal with you,' Grannie advised, 'and wait at t'front door until you hear the first stroke o' the clock. Then knock, and we'll let you in, and you say "A Happy New Year to all beneath this roof". Then go over to t'parlour fire and put the coal on it. You'll see a shilling on the mantelpiece. Pick it up, and put it in your pocket, and take it away with you. Right?'

'Right!' said my father.

He had fulfilled his obligations with grace and tenderness. The wine bottle was empty. We children were yawning. 1931 had begun.

'I must try to get a taxi home,' he said lazily.

'Not a bit of it!' said Eric. 'Why don't I run you home to Kersley on the back of my motorbike?'

The Schofields' chorus of disapproval was waved away.

'Haven't been on a motorbike for years,' said my father. 'I

had one myself in South Africa, when I was a young man. Yes, I should enjoy that.'

None of them had ever seen this Gilbert Fawley before, and would never see him again. Only I had always known he existed.

The whole family stood on the front door steps to watch him go.

'Goodbye, everyone! Happy New Year!' cried my father, mounting the pillion like a veteran.

'Be careful of them tram-lines, Eric!' cried Grannie.

'Stop mithering, Mother!' said Grandad. 'You know nowt about it!'

Eric opened the throttle.

A smile, glance, a wave.

The meaning of life was in those moments.

His motorbike roared off to Kersley down the empty road.

Part Two

1933–1939

10

February 1933

In the next two years, as I grew in stature and achievement, life became easier. The acquisition of a baby brother made me seem more human to the pupils of Moss Lane School, all of whom had siblings in abundance. And though they could not befriend someone whom they regarded as both a snob and a swot, they were pleased to accept a half-holiday when I became the third girl in Moss Lane's history to win a scholarship to Blackstone High School. Some of them even congratulated me, but I did not need them then, and like Dr Johnson I regarded their patronage with contempt.

As in my dreams, I had flown above their hostile heads and out of their hostile reach, and when I came to earth again it was to find myself a very small nautilus in a very great educational ocean. At Moss Lane I had no rivals. At Blackstone High School I was only one of many bright girls. I retreated into my shell there, and spent my first term cautiously testing these new waters, with no idea that my body as well as my mind was due for a sea-change.

I was twelve years old when I crossed the dividing-line between childhood and womanhood, in the changing-room of the school gymnasium. Probably I had entered maturity somewhat earlier, swarming up the ropes or vaulting the wooden horse, and simply found the evidence as I undressed, but the shock was profound, because I had no idea what was happening to me. Worst of all, the problem was extremely intimate.

Brought up to regard any bodily function below the waist as an indecent necessity, I would have found it difficult to speak of this even to Aunt Kate, who was still my closest confidante. Among strangers, for I was only in my second term at Blackstone High School, it was impossible to ask anyone. So I resolved to consult the index of *The Family's Own Home Doctor* under *Bleeding*, as soon as I reached home, and to manage the rest of the school day as best I could.

As a precautionary measure I went into the lavatory and made a wad of toilet paper, but as well as feeling uncomfortable, it crackled when I moved. So I discarded it and used a folded handkerchief instead. Fear and my mysterious physical condition numbed my spirit.

In class I stared down at my books and up at the blackboard without seeing them. I heard but did not understand what the Latin teacher said, and was given an extra verb to decline with my homework as a punishment for lack of attention. At twelve o'clock I sat in the cloakroom, unable to face the prospect of school dinner.

The discharge, slight at first, had now increased. The dull ache in my groins became a grinding pain. As I shifted position on the wooden bench beneath the row of navy blue coats, trying to ease myself, a prefect on corridor duty looked in, and ordered me off.

'. . . because you know jolly well that you're not allowed to hang about here during the lunch-hour! I won't report you this time, seeing you're a first year, but hop it!'

I dragged my wretched body down the corridor, and pushed open one swing-door of the dining room. A combined smell of Irish stew, prunes and tapioca pudding drove me to find another shelter. There was nowhere in the playground to sit, and sit I must, or die. So I crept back to the form room and crouched over my desk, head on arms, until my classmates began to drift back for afternoon lessons.

We were still new to each other and though friendly with several I was close to none. I heard them whispering among themselves. Then a girl with auburn plaits called Jill

Babbage came from the knot of whisperers, and put her arm round my shoulders and asked me what was wrong. I had admired her vivacity and self-possession from a distance, and on any other occasion her interest would have delighted me, but there was no way of making friends over this unladylike problem. So I shook my head and sobbed aloud on both counts.

Jill turned to the waiting group and spoke with authority. 'Someone should fetch Miss Anderson!'

The form captain was chosen for this mission, and Jill stayed with me and kept her arm round my shoulders. She asked me no more questions, simply wrapped me in the kindness of her silence. And when Miss Anderson said I should be taken to the sick room she offered to escort me, and left me with one final comforting squeeze of the hand.

A brisk and sensible woman who taught biology, Miss Penrose extracted the shameful details like so many milk teeth, informed me that I had embarked on puberty, and would henceforth be plagued in this unseemly fashion once a month for the next thirty years or so. She then gave me a sanitary belt, a sanitary towel, a hot-water bottle, a hot drink and an aspirin.

Tucked up on a hard high bed, wrapped in a rough grey blanket marked B.H.S.G. in red wool, I cried myself to sleep.

I woke, feeling strange and weak but healed. The clock on the wall had ticked its way through two afternoon lessons. From the office next door came a murmured conversation. Miss Anderson was chatting to Miss Penrose. They called each other 'Andy' and 'Pen'. I lay listening and drowsing, watching a pale sun cast slats on the glossy green wall.

'. . . so I've left them all writing essays, like good little mice, and come up with Evelyn Fawley's particulars. How is the child?'

'Still sleeping it off! I've been sitting here marking exercise books, and popping my head round the door from time to time. She should be feeling well enough to tackle the journey by half past three, but of course someone must take her home.'

'Yes. Well. That's our problem, Pen. She lives in the wilds

of South Lancashire. I've been checking up, and though we have a dozen pupils of different ages who travel in that direction, no one lives nearer than Apethorn.'

'Have you contacted her family?'

'In a roundabout way. A word in Mummy's ear would have been best, but unfortunately they haven't a telephone. So I got through to her father at Grizedale's and told him that Evelyn wasn't very well, nothing serious, but I thought that she would need her mother when she got home. He understood me perfectly, and we then tried to sort out something between us. He hadn't got a car, he said, or he would have come and collected her. There's an older brother at Blackstone Grammar School, but of course an adolescent youth is hardly a good choice in these circumstances, and Papa didn't like the idea of her coming home on trams and buses anyway. So he suggested a taxi, and if all else fails we must do that. But it really is so expensive that I asked him to leave it with me while I made further enquiries. I'm to ring him back before he sends a message to Mrs Fawley.'

Miss Penrose made an impatient sound.

'I have a very poor opinion of mothers who don't prepare their daughters for such an event! That poor child hadn't the faintest idea what was going on. What's wrong with the woman?'

Miss Anderson spoke with dry tolerance. 'I think it may well be a case of middle-class prudishness! She's one of these talkative, jolly ladies who can't stick to any point in the conversation except their own. By the way, she's not Evelyn's mother but her stepmother. We met at the first parents' evening to discuss Evelyn's progress and I found her a teeny bit condescending. You know, the fulfilled woman talking to the spinster teacher. And she would keep on saying what a happy and united family they were, which made me think that there were quite a number of underlying strains.'

Miss Penrose replied, 'I really do wonder sometimes if emancipation has made any difference at all to most members of our sex. A well-to-do married woman, far from being superior to a working spinster, is entirely dependent on a man for emotional and financial support. And though I don't wish to sound uncharitable, I find too many women of that sort are smug and mentally lazy!'

'But you and I would also have been dependent on our own husbands, if the war hadn't decided otherwise,' said Miss Anderson, being fair-minded.

'Perhaps,' Miss Penrose conceded.

A brief silence spoke for them.

Then briskly, brusquely, Miss Penrose said, 'But never mentally lazy, Andy! And always able to earn a living if necessary!'

They both laughed.

'If I were allowed,' Miss Penrose went on, returning to the original subject, 'I should give a regular talk about menstruation to first-year girls in the first week of term. But when this was mooted a few years ago we had a crowd of mothers objecting, on the grounds that it was their business and not ours! Some of them are sensible, of course, but far too many – like our Mrs Fawley – are ostriches.'

'No doubt the day will come. In the meantime, we must get Evelyn home. Can you think of something?'

'Try members of staff. Patricia McKinley lives in North Cheshire, and she comes in by car. It might not be too far out of her way.'

'Bless you, Pen! I'll have a word with her. Lord above! Is that the time? I must get back to my class. By the by, would you say that *Sally in our Alley* is permissible viewing for a High School girl?'

'The Gracie Fields' film? Certainly not.'

'It's sentimental, of course, but perfectly harmless and moral. And she has a remarkable singing voice.'

'You could hardly call it an educational film, now could you?'

'One can't forbid them to go, of course. Only indicate . . .'

'Stuff and nonsense, Andy! When I caught one of my girls reading a twopenny film magazine, *Picture Show*, in the cloakroom the other week, I confiscated it and gave her fifty lines for being stupid. We must keep up our standards!'

*

Miss McKinley, who enjoyed comparative youth, undoubted glamour and a first-class degree in Modern Languages, lived out at Shawcross. She made a detour for my sake, and kindly lifted the burden of conversation by suggesting that I might like to lie down on the back seat and rest. The stage was set for a domestic drama which I feared that Dorothy would be unable to resist, and I was quite right.

By the time we arrived at the Malt-house she had dumped my two-year-old brother on Aunt Kate, laid a sumptuous afternoon tea in the drawing room, and changed into her best blue costume. The birth of Julian, and five years of good living, had increased Dorothy's girth. She was handsome still, but over-ripe. And she still played roles and was inclined to over-act. Attracted by the sound of Miss McKinley's name she had adopted a faintly Scottish accent, though the teacher spoke impeccable English.

'*Offly* kind of you!' Dorothy cried, holding out a gracious hand. 'Come your ways in!'

Then she embraced me tearfully, and in quite a different voice said, 'My little girl has grown up!'

Touching her eyes delicately with a handkerchief to indicate maternal tears, she led the way to the drawing room, where Patricia McKinley stared at the tea-table in undisguised astonishment, saying faintly, 'What a wonderful spread!'

I saw that it was too much, and feeling that Dorothy's conduct reflected on myself I hung my head in shame.

'Poor Evelyn really has had quite a day,' said Miss McKinley, with a hint of reproach.

'Oh, I do understand,' said Dorothy deeply, 'but we'll soon set the lassie to rights. Off to bed, my wee girlie! You shall have your tea on a tray.' To Miss McKinley she added winningly, 'And you and I will have a nice long talk, the whiles.'

She was to be disappointed.

'It's very sweet of you, Mrs Fawley, but I really must get home,' said Miss McKinley quickly. 'I have an aged mother who will already be worrying and watching the clock, and it would be unfair of me to take up time which Evelyn needs.

So I'll just dash away, if you will excuse me . . . so very kind.'

Dorothy's smile remained fixed and pleasant, though I could tell she felt snubbed. As she escorted the retreating teacher out, I disappeared upstairs to the sanctuary of my bedroom, sore in body and spirit. She had let me down once too often. Anger was beginning to take the place of self-pity. I waited for her.

She began Act Two with a subdued knocking on the door, and entered softly. Her expression regretted a childhood gone and yet looked proudly on a womanhood to come.

Fat old ham, I thought savagely.

She sighed, sat on the side of the bed, and tried to hold my hand. I twitched it away. She asked me in a low voice how I felt. For once I declined to reassure her.

'I feel miserable!' I said passionately. 'And I feel dirty! Physically, emotionally and spiritually *dirty*!'

Dorothy looked lost. She tried another tack.

'Didn't Miss Anderson explain things to you?'

'It was Miss Penrose who explained. She said I was menstruating.'

Dorothy was shocked, but under the circumstances could not scold a semi-invalid, and of this I took full advantage.

'That's a medical term,' she said as kindly as possible. 'Ladies don't use words like that. It would be nicer, between ourselves, to refer to it as your "poorly time".'

'Well, you may think so but I don't,' I replied curtly. 'And what's more, I shan't say it, either! I detest euphemisms!'

Intellectual snob that I was, I suspected she did not know the meaning of the word. She swallowed and tried again.

'You can stay in bed tomorrow. They won't expect you back at school until the end of the week. And in the morning, when I'm shopping in Kersley, I'll buy you a nice packet of thingummies and hide them beneath your undies in the top drawer here.'

'If you mean sanitary towels I prefer to call them that. And there's no need to hide them under anything, either. I don't suppose anybody will be searching my room!'

'I tell you what I'll do,' said Dorothy, to pacify me. 'I'll make you a little allowance every month so you can buy your own.'

'Thank you,' I said ungraciously.

Mistaking my grudging politeness for a change of attitude, Dorothy attempted a woman-to-woman conversation.

'We must tell Grannie and the aunties that you're a big girl now,' she said coyly, confidentially, 'but of course we don't mention this sort of thing to the men.'

Then I lost my temper.

'What makes you suppose that I want it to be mentioned to *anybody*?' I cried. 'How would *you* like to be whispered about, like some kind of social leper?'

'It's natural enough. It happens to all us women,' said Dorothy, trying to be reasonable. 'There's no need to talk about lepers.'

'But I feel as if it's only happening to *me*!' I said. 'And it's a horrible thing. And I loathe it. And I loathe myself. And I loathe *you* for letting it happen to me, and not warning me. Why didn't you say anything about it? I thought I was dying!'

Dorothy's hands moved as if they itched to slap. But to give her credit, which I did not at the time, she sat there for another few minutes attempting to put our relationship on a new and more intimate footing. She was unsuccessful. I had inherited my father's ability to sever himself from humanity at will. I turned my face to the wall.

Dorothy got up and closed the door behind her with excessive care, though I'm sure she would have loved to slam it.

Isolated, I cried myself to sleep again, returning to the world at seven o'clock to find my father standing by the bed, hands in pockets, smiling down on me.

I did not speak for a few moments, watching him closely for signs of disgust or regret, but he only stretched out one fine hand and stroked the damp hair away from my forehead.

'Feeling a bit better now, Evie?' he asked.

I nodded awkwardly, very much aware of the wadding between my thighs, a sensation of unusual warmth, and an earthy scent. Passages in Leviticus, which in my innocence I had put down to tribal rites, were now explained. In biblical terms I was unclean.

'Your mother says you haven't eaten anything yet. Would you like anything?'

'I could eat something, but I don't know what.'

I remembered that I had dared to be rude to Dorothy, and this revived me momentarily, but I was not fit enough to sustain a running battle. I decided to call a truce.

'I don't want to cause any trouble,' I said unwillingly.

I wondered if I had to be set apart while this thing happened to me, sit on my own chair, sup from my own dishes.

'You're no trouble to anyone, my love. You're never any trouble,' my father said gently. 'What would you *like* to eat?'

I gave a child's answer.

'Bread and milk, please.'

Food meant to Dorothy what music meant to Lilian Lacey. Its preparation called forth her craft, its presentation her art. She laid my tray with a blue linen cloth embroidered in white. She plunged out into the February night with a torch to find yellow and purple crocuses, and slipped them into a silver egg-cup of water. She laid my silver christening spoon beside the bright blue bowl. She chopped the bread into bite-sized pieces and sprinkled it with demerara sugar. She scalded the milk and skimmed it. Finally she scraped a bit of nutmeg on top, so that the rising steam smelled spicy and sweet.

The Fawleys were rallying round their wounded member. Aunt Kate brought Julian in, freshly-bathed and lovable in his sleeping-suit, so that he and his teddy bear could kiss me good night. Then she kissed me too, most warmly, and said, 'Let's go off shopping in Blackstone on Saturday, shall we? Just the two of us – and tea at Peeble's!'

My father fetched two extra pillows from the guest room. Dorothy punched them soft and slipped them neatly behind my back. And Michael brought up my tray, followed by his golden labrador, Flora. Tom Cat padded after them, winking green and greedy eyes, waving a predatory tail.

I felt shy with Michael. No one would tell him, of course, but he always guessed right. He would know about this revolting female disorder, just as he had known how babies were born and probably knew how they got there in the first place. I sensed that this final piece of sexual knowledge might be revolting too, and drew back from it. But he was his most delightful self this evening, judging exactly what to say and how long to talk. And when we were on easy terms with one another he left me in peace, to savour the food of childhood and the company of my cat.

My status improved. I returned to school at the end of the week to enjoy a modest popularity. I was now able to divine who had crossed this female Rubicon and who had not. The former simply said they were glad I was better, the latter enquired what had been wrong. Stomach trouble, I said airily. Miss Penrose gave me a brusque but friendly nod as we filed out after prayers, and Miss McKinley smiled kindly in recognition. Best of all Jill Babbage was pleased to see me and said so.

'I knew what was wrong with you, because it happened to me, but I didn't know what to say.'

'Did your mother warn you about it?' I asked.

'Oh yes. She told me about six months beforehand. She's a doctor, you see. So's Daddy.'

Mentally, I hammered another nail in Dorothy's coffin.

I was miserably ill again the following month, but this had its compensations. Dorothy, always an excellent domestic nurse, kept me in bed the first day, though the worst was over in a few hours, and made me rest on the drawing-room sofa the second day. As this became a regular event she consulted Dr Gould.

He smacked his thick brown leather gloves against his thigh and grinned, staring down at me with bright black shallow eyes.

'I hear you're a young lady now!' he remarked.

Then treated me like a little girl by asking his questions of Dorothy.

'Yes, she's one of the unlucky ones,' he said, when the last painful detail had been recounted. 'Are the periods regular? Well that's something. All you can do is to anticipate them, and keep her off her feet that first day. If the loss is heavy let her stay at home the second day as well. I'll give you some tablets to ease her, but I can't work miracles.'

He patted my cheek and said, 'You're going to have to put up with this until you've got yourself a husband, miss! He'll sort your troubles out – and probably give you a few more in the process!'

And he laughed loudly all the way to the door.

I hated him then, with a trembling, cringing hatred, and hated Dorothy who was laughing with him in the hall. They were joined in an adult conspiracy, and I wanted no part of it.

Yet after a while I began to look forward to this regular interval of recuperation, and to reap benefits from my lost childhood. Dorothy saw to my needs but otherwise left me to heal or amuse myself in peace and privacy.

She was a voracious reader of modern novels, and fed her mental appetite as generously as her physical one, borrowing from both the Public Library and Boot's Library and belonging to a Book Club. To her way of thinking I was a young adult, though she had done nothing to assist me in the process and could not have guessed how much or little sexual knowledge I possessed, and she never did tell me any single fact of life. But whereas she would have hidden more explicit novels only a few months ago, she now handed most of them on.

I read those. I read through my father's varied and extensive library. I discovered my own rich and strange fictional worlds which, by the grace of my sex, I could inhabit once a month. So I became Anna Karenina, Tess of the D'Urbevilles, Joan of Arc and a hundred other tragic, noble and beautiful heroines, all day and far into the night, until I fell asleep over the pages.

A few hours' discomfort seemed a small penalty to pay for such magnificent metamorphoses.

*

I had had no friend since Marianne Nash at Townley's, and I was very proud to bring Jill Babbage home to spend a Saturday at the Malt-house. She was a great success. My father liked her intelligence, Michael liked her sense of humour, Dorothy liked her background, and my baby brother liked yet another female lap to sit on.

I had felt a little shy of Jill seeing me at home, for I was a different person under my parent's dominion. So I was relieved to see a different Jill, smiling demurely, behaving impeccably, emerging in recognisable form only with Michael.

Alone in my bedroom we exchanged confidences about the adult world which made me see it in a new light.

'While they're in charge,' said Jill, 'you've got to do as they say unless you want a row, and they always win rows anyway. And when we're at school it's the same with the teachers. But by ourselves we can do what we like.'

'By ourselves – and inside our heads,' I ventured cautiously, because our friendship was new and I was not completely sure of her.

'I'm a boatload of pirates inside my head!' she cried.

And she laughed, and tossed her auburn plaits over her shoulders.

I thought her wonderful. She absorbed my admiration, smiling.

'What are you inside your head, Evie?' she asked.

'Lots of people,' I said. 'I keep finding different ones I want to be. But Michael lives as he likes *outside* his head!'

'Boys can,' said Jill. 'My brothers do that. But we can't. Not unless we want a lot of trouble. We can't. Because we're girls.'

Then she looked around her and said, 'I do like your room. Aren't you lucky to have a room to yourself? I've got to share mine with my sister. And I'd love to have a baby brother like Julian. I'm the youngest, you see, and there are so many of us. Five altogether. And Mummy runs the family practice with Daddy, so we don't see much of our parents. We call ourselves The Orphans, sometimes, for fun!'

'Then who looks after you?' I asked, enthralled.

'We have a housekeeper who lives in, and a charwoman to do the rough work, and we have girl students from abroad. A different girl each year, who comes to learn the language and teach us some of hers. My parents know a lot of people abroad, and we travel for a month in the summer while a couple of locums take over the practice.'

'Where have you been?' I asked, who had travelled no further than the Lake District.

'France. Germany. Italy. Spain.'

'And can you speak all those languages?'

'Not properly,' said Jill, 'but I know bits of them.'

'Aren't you lucky?'

Travel had not as yet entered my head. I resolved to travel widely in future. As yet I had only the advantages of a room to myself and a baby brother, advantages which must be pressed if I were to keep up appearances.

'It's lovely to be an elder sister,' I said with truth, 'and I simply adore Julian, but sometimes I must be on my own, and then this room,' spoken grandly, 'is my sanctuary.'

Mrs Inchmore's husband, when he chose to work, was an odd job man, and he had decorated it. With Lilian Lacey's little parlour in mind I had chosen white paintwork, over whose cleaning both Dorothy and Mrs Inchmore grumbled constantly. The wallpaper and curtains were light and flowery, and the whole place resembled an illustration I had found in my *Girls' Own Paper*, entitled *A Room of Your Own*. I could picture myself growing up gracefully here.

I took Jill on a tour of my treasures.

'That's my window-box. I read an article on window-boxes in the *GOP* called "Flowers Beneath Your Window". Of course, it doesn't look much now, but in the summer it's blissful. And at any time of the year I have a marvellous view. That's Tarn How. Next time you come we'll take a picnic and go there . . .'

We laughed over my cupboard full of dolls and the elaborate names I had given them, because of course we were too old for dolls. Still, as Jill said, one kept them for old times' sake, and we nursed them while we sat on the bed and talked.

Later we sat on the floor and looked through all my books, and talked and talked again.

As I grew older and my friends increased, we girls would spend weekend visits at each other's houses, talking until the small hours about life and love, of which we knew so little and expected so much. But even in my friendships I held an important part of myself back. My family and the Malthouse always made a good impression and I would not spoil that by talking of our inner tensions.

Nor did I ever speak of Clara, except to say that my real mother had died when I was very young, and I did not remember her. And I never showed her shawl to anyone.

I I

Some years are marked black on the family calendar, and 1934 was a bad one for the Schofields. They had been changing as a family since Uncle Eric graduated with distinction from Blackstone University and accepted a teaching post up in Edinburgh. And though he kept faith with tradition, and drove down each Christmas in his Morris Cowley to join the clan, we saw little of him.

In the March of this fateful year, less than three months after we had celebrated the annual family feast at Parbold House, and afterwards sat round the wireless to listen to the King giving his Christmas message, we were recalled for a more sombre occasion. Uncle Arthur had died in his sleep.

Of course we knew that he had been dying slowly, and yet the final leave-taking shocked us as much as if he had been in full health and strength. Dorothy took the loss particularly hard because Arthur knew and loved her in the same way as Michael did, enjoying her virtues and laughing at her faults. And Grannie took it worst of all.

Grandad kept hold of Grannie's arm from Parbold House to the graveyard, and squeezed it gently now and again. I could see that this comforted her, though she paid him no outward heed. Her lips moved as if in prayer throughout the service and burial. She was grieving the loss of a son whose dependence had made him dearer to her. As the clods hit the coffin, I stepped forward to clasp her hard little hand.

She nodded to show her thanks, and the other hand

automatically felt in her coat pocket for caramels, and remembered, and moved away.

I was sorriest for her and loved her most dearly then.

Of what was I dreaming, that June evening in my fourteenth year, floating swiftly to and fro in the beauty of the failing light, higher and higher, on the swing under the beech-tree branch. At regular intervals the toe of one sandal gave impetus to my flight. In a bower of transparent green and gold gleams I was losing myself gladly, shedding reality. My spirit leaped forth with the swing, to be restrained only by a jerk of the ropes when I reached maximum height.

I was dreaming of Clara. Though I had long since ceased to cry out for my mother in the night I still needed her as part of me, and as I changed I constantly renewed her.

Lilian Lacey and music were partly responsible for her latest image. In contrast to Dorothy's family mêlée Lilian ran a tranquil feminine household. While Dorothy rapidly lost interest in her appearance Lilian remained ageless and fashionable. And though Dorothy extolled the virtues of the married state, and told everybody what a happy and united family we were, I was not convinced. If that was marriage then I would have a career instead.

This idea had been grown over the years of hearing Aunt Kate's chagrin at the waste of her talents, by my father's belief in the importance of women's education, and most recently my teachers' passion for female learning and financial independence. So Clara, whose musical gifts had so far graced a domestic scene in my mind, now gave her recitals to a wider audience than my father and myself.

Her graceful Grecian knot bent over the keyboard of a concert grand piano. Her long pale fingers executed the most intricate runs. When she had played a final triumphant chord she lifted her head slowly, awakening from an inner to an outer world as the listeners rose to give her a standing ovation.

I dressed her in ivory for this debut: a long slim sheath of slipper satin. And as she bowed her head to those who paid her homage, she drew round her shoulders the shawl embroidered with birds. They fluttered in the folds, bright captured creatures of paradise. And then she turned to walk away into marriage and early death.

This vision of doomed beauty and talent had grown with me until I felt that I should take up the dream where she left off. To that end, some time previously, I had coaxed my father for extra music lessons.

He had looked at me objectively, a fragment of cold lamb poised on his fork, seeking the meaning beneath the words.

'For what purpose?'

I knew how to manipulate him.

'I want to take all the examination grades, as far as I can. Miss Lacey says I'm good. I always get A for music in my school report.'

'You mean you're thinking of becoming a music teacher?'

I knew better than to mention the prospect of becoming a concert pianist. That would be dismissed as fanciful and my father was stern with fancies. I compromised, telling the truth as far as possible.

'I hadn't thought of that exactly, but I do want to play the piano as well as I possibly can.'

'Can you do that on top of all your school work?'

He was warning me. Your education is the most serious business.

I had prepared my ground carefully.

'One of our prefects did, only last summer. She took three subjects in the Higher School Certificate exams. Music, French and English. She won a scholarship to Blackstone College of Music. And two years before that she won the Harriet Harcourt Music Cup.'

I added, using his favourite phrase of exhortation, 'And if she can do it I don't see why I can't!'

Dorothy, who had been chewing a pickled onion and listening, said, 'If I were in your shoes I wouldn't want to be a music teacher. What's the fun in that? Why don't you try for something more exciting like a concert pianist?'

So of course my father answered, 'Really, Dorothy! We were having a serious conversation!'

And Michael had to say, 'Mix a drop more soda with it, Mum!'

And I said nothing and silently hummed with fury.

'I'll think about it,' said my father. 'I shall need to consult Miss Lacey, and your music teacher at school.' But he had already made up his mind, for he added, 'And if I find that your schoolwork suffers as a result, then it's back to one lesson a week and no music exams.'

I returned to contemplate Clara, who was walking gracefully away from me, shawl trailing, the birds fluttering to the ground. But the vision was no longer sad, because she would come back in the end through her daugher.

Once more the audience took their seats and waited, and this time I was on the concert platform, hands poised above the keyboard of the Steinway grand. And even after, when I pictured us both in the context of music, Clara had always acknowledged the plaudits of the crowd and was walking off, whereas I was always about to play. And this was right. For Clara's music was over and mine just about to begin.

So, on a fine warm evening, homework done, I spent my leisure time swinging and thinking, swinging and dreaming, swinging and musing. Swinging and losing myself.

The rest of my family were pursuing their own dreams. My father was in his study. Michael was out exercising Flora. Julian was asleep. And Dorothy was sitting in her rocking-chair in the kitchen, with Tom Cat in her lap, reading *The Good Earth* by Pearl Buck.

At last I came to a halt, and laid one cheek against the rope in a half-trance, working out the fingering of a Chopin étude in my head. This exquisite problem had nothing to do with Lilian Lacey, who had said that my hand-span was not yet great enough, nor my technique good enough, to tackle Chopin.

'You're doing very nicely, my dear, and coming along even better and faster than I had hoped. But there's no point in pushing yourself beyond your present capabilities. That only leads to disappointment.'

As Jill said, it was useless to argue with an adult, but on a deeper level I reckoned that I knew my capabilities better than anyone else did. So I had learned to conform outwardly, while inwardly pursuing my own course, and this personal law applied even to the adored and revered Lilian.

Besides, there was something beautifully logical about fingering. Its resolution filled me with the same cool delight as an arithmetical problem. Tricky but fascinating. So for some weeks now I had worked on the étude by myself, and looked forward to the day when I should astonish the world with my prowess.

I wound my arms round the ropes and spread out my fingers. They felt more flexible. I wondered if they had stretched since yesterday.

The latch on the front gate lifted and fell, and I idled to and fro, listening, guessing. Should I disappear or join the company? As the visitors approached the gravel told me that these were deliberate feet, so they did not belong to children. Two pairs, one lighter and quicker than the other. A man and a woman? The footsteps went past the porch and round to the back door. Over the backyard wall I heard a small strained voice call through the open doorway. 'Anybody at home?' accompanied by a perfunctory knock.

'Grannie and Grandad!' I cried, deciding to return to earth.

And jumped up and left the swing to idle by itself.

The three of them were standing in the kitchen in a tableau which a Victorian painter would have entitled *Bad News*. Grandad had lost his smile and his portly stance. His shoulders and white head were bowed. Grannie's witch-like chin still tilted against misfortune but her face was dazed. Though it was a Friday they both wore their Sunday clothes. Dorothy, red-eyed from the sorrows of China, had stood up suddenly, clutching *The Good Earth* in one hand, while the other lifted momentarily to her lips in shock. Tom Cat was stalking sulkily away. As I ran in, they all turned and stared at me as if they could not comprehend who I was nor why I was there.

Grannie was the first to recover. She felt in the pocket of

her black cloth coat and brought out a packet of chocolate caramels.

'I didn't forget our Evleen, any road up,' she said to herself. I kissed her cheek, which was white and soft and cold, and his cheek which had lost its ripeness and colour. Dorothy set her book face down on the rocking-chair. I looked at her for guidance.

'I'll put the kettle on,' she said. 'Evie, ask your father if he can come down a minute. Tell him that Grannie and Grandad are here, and that they're in a bit of difficulty and would welcome his advice.'

Dorothy's voice was steady and her tone matter of fact. But as I closed the door I heard her revert to her honest self.

'Eh, God forgive me. Fancy letting you stand there! Sit yourselves down. Eh, I can't believe it. And our poor Arthur in his grave not three months since!'

My father glared over his reading glasses, displeased.

'What sort of difficulty?' he asked me abruptly. 'Illness? Death? Financial disaster?'

'Mother didn't say. They're in their best clothes and they look like they did at Uncle Arthur's funeral.'

'It'll be Eric!' said my father to himself. 'Crashed his damn fool car, I'll bet a pound to a penny. Tcha!'

To me he said, exasperated, 'We're holding the Oxford and Cambridge Exams at Grizedale's, you know. I've got enough to worry about without taking on your mother's family!'

Grannie's caramels sat mute and humble in my skirt pocket. I reminded him subtly of his kinder self.

'They're truly upset, Daddy.'

He took off his reading glasses and swung them gently, thinking. He answered the words I had not spoken.

'Yes. And they wouldn't ask to see me without good reason. Tell your mother I'll be down in a few minutes.'

I kissed his cheek in tribute.

And he was splendid, smiling as affably in the kitchen doorway as if no one had disturbed him, handsome and distinguished. Grannie and Grandad began to rise to their feet but he stopped them courteously.

He addressed his wife with gentle reproach.

'Why are your parents sitting on hard chairs in the kitchen when they would be more comfortable in the drawing room?'

They were more at ease in the kitchen but nobody dared say so, and they followed him obediently across the polished parquet of the hall. Dorothy stood in the middle of the kitchen, disorientated.

'*I'll* make the tea, Mother,' I said decisively. 'Shall I use the best tea service or the willow pattern? Do you want biscuits?'

'I don't know what they'll do,' said Dorothy, not answering me, staring through me at some bleak Schofield future. She said, 'As if they haven't had enough trouble already.'

I took her over, largely out of kindness and duty, but also relishing the novelty of being in charge. I bullied her benevolently.

'Mother! Go and sit down with them. I'll bring the tea in.'

At the door Dorothy picked up the household reins for a moment.

'Use the willow pattern!' she said. 'Your Grannie will only worry if we fetch out the best china. Oh, and I baked some shortbread this afternoon. Get it out of the cake tin and cut it up. With a sharp knife, mind, and straight along the markings, or it'll crumble.'

I nodded as if I didn't need to be told.

'But however will they manage?' said Dorothy as she went out.

As I balanced the heavy tray, preparatory to knocking at the drawing-room door, I heard my grandfather's voice, steadfast but curiously lifeless.

'. . . and would never have happened in his father's day, but young Mr Dewsbury never had any time for me, and he'd set out to trap me. So then he asked me to say, in front o' witnesses, whether or not I'd talked to the men about forming a trades union, and I couldn't and didn't deny it. And on the desk in front of him he had my records from forty years back. Every job. Every case. He'd gone to some trouble to get rid o' me, I can tell you. So I knew that though I'd done no wrong I hadn't a leg to stand on.'

Grannie's voice now rose in mournful pride.

'Tell Dr Fawley what you said to him, Sam!'

'Well, I could see there was nowt left but my bit o' dignity. So I said, "Well, Mr Dewsbury, it seems to me as you've got everythink on your side – barring the truth, that is. And all I've got is the knowledge that in all my life I never committed a dishonourable act, nor set out to harm any man. I think, between the two of us, as I'd sooner have my conscience than your own!"'

'He jumped up then, sharpish-like, and stood wi' his back to me, looking out o' the window. And he said to his sekertary, "See that this trouble-maker is paid a week's wages in lieu of notice, and get him off the premises as soon as possible!"'

'So I packed up my tool-bag and come home. And that week's wages is all Annie and me have got to live on until my national pension starts next year.'

His voice changed, sounding swollen and troubled.

'Nay, dunnot think as we've come a-begging, Dr Fawley. I wouldn't take a penny from nobody, and nor would Annie. But at sixty-four year of age, wi' three million unemployed in the country, what do I do to earn a crust, sir? That's what I'm asking of you. . . .'

Less than a month later, helped by a letter of recommendation from my father, Grandad was given a poorly-paid, foot-killing job as a door-to-door salesman of encyclopedias. He believed profoundly in the value of what he was selling, though he was inclined to spend far too much time discussing education with possible buyers, and this salved his dignity as man and provider. But it was hand-to-mouth money rather than a steady wage, and without financial help the Schofields would have starved slowly during the following year. Dorothy confided in me later how they had managed Grandad's pride between them. My father gave her an extra pound a week which she passed on to Grannie, who concocted heaven knows who many false stories to account for it.

So they were salvaged, but their way of life was not. That summer Grannie and Grandad left Parbold House, and moved into a terraced two-up two-down in Railway Street at the poor end of Hathersall. All the property in that part of town was due for slum clearance in a few years' time, but they could afford the rent.

Grannie had to wage constant war on cockroaches and mice, and there were rats in the allotments which ran down the back of the terrace. On these untidy strips a dozen unemployed men grew vegetables, and kept hens or pigeons in ramshackle huts covered with corrugated iron. Grandad joined them, but his attempts at self-support were dogged by industrial pollution. The main Blackstone-to-London railway line roared past the front of the houses, only an uneven pavement and an unmade road away, and the area was ringed by factory chimneys. Grannie's washing was sprinkled with smuts. All the white hens had grey feathers. And Grandad's cabbages came into the kitchen covered in a fine layer of soot.

The years of hospitality at Parbold House, with their air of bounty and their sense of family unity and family purpose, were over and done.

Dorothy was tiring of her role as the fulfilled married woman, and began to grumble about weekends, which she said were made for the convenience of everyone except herself, since our leisure meant more work for her.

On Saturdays, for instance, she rose as early as usual to cope with Julian and prepare breakfast while the rest of us did as we pleased. Michael, in his misery, had taken to lying late abed. I had my extra music lesson, and was allowed to practise instead of helping her. And my father retired to the drawing room as soon as she had lit the fire, reading the *Manchester Guardian*, and expecting cups of coffee at intervals.

Too much had been demanded of Dorothy that year, and on this particular Saturday my father precipitated a domestic crisis over breakfast, simply by making the following pronouncement from behind his newspaper.

'Your mother's house is too small to take all of us this Christmas. Besides, they can't afford to entertain as they did.'

Dorothy looked apprehensive. He shook the newspaper to emphasise his next point.

'I refuse to consider having the rest of that ragtag and bobtail she usually invites . . .' – he meant Grannie's sisters and their husbands – '. . . but your mother and father would be very welcome to spend Christmas Day with us here. And Eric too, of course, if he happens to make the journey.'

Relieved, Dorothy said, 'I've already dropped mother a hint along those lines, as a matter of fact.'

My father looked over his reading glasses, mildly surprised at this pre-emption of his plan.

'And is she agreeable to the idea?'

Her brother's death, her parents' plight, and the constant tug of divided loyalties between Michael and my father had taken its toll. For once Dorothy lost her temper with him in front of me.

'Agreeable? She hasn't much choice, has she? Apart from staying at home and frying up a bit of bacon, what else can she do? I can't see her eating humble pie with Aunt Beatrice. Agreeable? Sometimes I wonder if you live on a different planet from ordinary people!'

Astonished, he laid down his newspaper and paid attention to her.

'What *are* you talking about?' he asked reasonably. 'I've suggested nothing that disagrees with your own point of view, as far as I know. If you have other ideas then I'll endeavour to fit in with them. If you really want to invite all your mother's family then do so. I can always go to my study once we've eaten dinner.'

Dorothy's voice trembled as she gave Julian permission to get down from his chair in one voice, and in another addressed my father.

'Why make a point of going to your study because my

family comes over? You live in it anyway, whether they're here or not!'

'And what has *that* to do with the Christmas arrangements?'

'I'll tell you what it's got to do with!' cried Dorothy, ungrammatical in her trouble. 'It's got to do with the bloody life I lead, day in and day out!'

She had taken that phrase from Aunt Kate, standing over the ironing board one Tuesday evening, ironing a basketful of shirts for Uncle Harold, Alex and Leo.

'I tell you what I think, Dollie. I think – what a bloody life I lead, day in and day out!'

My father was electrified.

'The boy!' he said coldly. 'Think of the boy, if you please, before you use language like that in front of him.'

Dorothy only dressed up to go out these days, and had long since stopped trying to be pretty at breakfast. Her mass of ashen curly hair had been wound up rapidly and pinned into an untidy knot. She wore an old faded blue dressing-gown which needed dry-cleaning. Her face, though still comely, was not yet washed.

Immaculate as always, my father eyed her with slight distaste, and I did not blame him. She had come a long and sorry way from that stylish young woman in the pink velvet cloche, or the smiling bride in eau de Nil. I marvelled that she did not interpret his look and change her ways. I thought how I would have hated a man to draw his brows together like that, when once his eyes had courted me.

But Dorothy, at that moment, was not giving a damn how he looked.

She said furiously, 'Never mind sitting in judgement on me, Headmaster Fawley! I'm sick to death of trying to keep everybody happy and never having time for myself. All you ever do is to hand out orders. It's easy for you. And you've only got to do one job – *one job* – and even that's a job you like. I do a hundred different jobs a day, and I don't like any of them very much. I do jobs like a hen pecks up corn – a bit here, a bit there. But you can go to that precious study of yours every evening, like a priest to the shrine, and say to me over your shoulder, "I'm not to be interrupted!". Not interrupted? Well, you're very lucky. I'm interrupted all the time. And I'm left to sort everything and everybody out, and they all expect me to listen to them and look after them and speak up for them. And I've got nobody I really want to talk to, and nobody who'll listen to me, and I'm sick to death of it.'

She began to cry in earnest, wiping her eyes on the dressing-gown sleeve from time to time, sobbing out her rage and misery.

My presence was inappropriate, and would embarrass them both when they stopped quarrelling. Julian seemed to be absorbed, setting out lead soldiers in front of his fort. Tactfully, I took my breakfast things into the scullery.

I heard Dorothy start up again.

'I was better off when I lived at home with Mother and Father. I had a good job, and earned my own money and spent it as I liked, and people respected me. And my poor Michael was happy then. And I was comfortable. I was comfortable in my spirits. Oh, I was lonely. I'd rather – far far rather – that my poor Harry had lived. But I never felt hopeless like I do now. And there was a bit of fun in life. I've missed Arthur more than I can say. We used to have many a talk and a laugh together, and he was very wise, very brave. Poor Arthur. But now there seems nothing to look forward to – only everybody's worries and the same dull day over and over again.'

The silence that followed was punctuated by her sobs and sniffs and the sound of my father folding up his newspaper.

'Would it help,' he said at last, awkwardly, 'if we had a break and went off for the weekend together? We could go to London and see a show or two, like we used to do before Julian was born. Your mother and father could come here to look after the children. And it would be a nice change for them, after that place they live in.'

Evidently she shook her head. He reasoned with her.

'You need some new interest in life,' he said encouragingly. 'I appreciate that you find it dull being tied at home all day with a young child to consider. And the house is fairly isolated.'

He was doing his best, but she must have bruised him badly. His voice held a trace of reproach as he added, 'But you did say at one time that this was everything you wanted.'

I heard Julian, disturbed by his father's tone and his mother's tears, demanding to be taken on her lap. I came in again. He was scrambling up, putting his arms round Dorothy's neck, digging his face into her shoulder.

I said tactfully, 'Shall I take him for you?'

But she shook her head and wiped her eyes, stroked his silky hair and wiped her eyes again, held him to her and rocked him to and fro, patting his back, giving and taking comfort.

My father's skin had little colour at any time. Now it had none.

He continued to think her problem through.

'You read a lot. We entertain quite widely. You chat on the telephone.' His tone was kinder than usual on this point. Telephone bills usually brought arguments in their wake. 'But what you really need is an outside interest.'

They were both beginning to come round. He gazed ruefully at his only and beloved son.

'How old is Julian now?' For he never remembered ages or birthdays or anniversaries.

'He'll be four at the end of December.'

'So he won't be going to Moss Lane School yet?'

For Julian was to continue the educational experiment.

'Not until he's five. Over a year yet.'

Dorothy was looking guilty. Aware of her responsibilities as wife and mother she resumed both roles, though without her usual zest.

'Don't worry about me, Gil. I just got upset. You're very good to me, and you've been good to Mother and Father, and I've got a lovely home and a fur coat and a telephone and everything I want.'

The fur coat had been acquired when Julian was born, and the telephone installed after my crisis at school, but this was not everything she wanted. She had left a car out of her list of luxuries. I knew she was hoping for one. So did my father, yet his gaze remained as objective as his tone.

'But not everything you need. Obviously.'

'Who has?' she asked more cheerfully.

'None of us, but we can usually improve on a situation. Weren't you a member of Hathersall Dramatic Society before we married?'

'Oh, yes. But they're very keen. They rehearse twice a week, and put on three productions a year. I couldn't just go now and then.'

'I think a couple of evenings a week would fit the bill nicely. Julian goes to bed early. There's always at least one person in the house, and any one of us can look after him if he wakes up.'

'I hadn't thought of that!' she said, unexpectedly released.

She smiled at him, and her radiance was genuine.

What pictures were going through that extraordinary mind of hers, I wondered. Herself at the January audition, at least a stone slimmer, wearing a new dress, with her face discreetly painted, her hair possibly cut short and marcel-waved, being offered the sort of role she used to play in her twenties?

'Don't waste any time about it,' he advised, knowing her weakness for letting matters slide. 'Get in touch with some of your old friends from Hathersall Dramatic Society as soon as you can. Write to them, or ring them up, and make enquiries.' He got up and put one hand on Dorothy's shoulder, asking kindly, 'All right now?'

She came to life and nodded. She lifted her face for a kiss, which he gave kindly and without passion. It was not what I should have liked, in her place.

A weak November sun slipped through the misty trees and into the kitchen window. Relieved, Julian slithered from his mother's lap and set out a third line of lead soldiers. Released, I headed for the piano. Back to normal, Dorothy poured herself another cup of tea, and hummed a song which had been popular in recent years.

Somewhere the sun is shining. So, honey, don't you cry. We'll find a silver lining, the clouds will soon roll by . . .

*

My father stood, hands in pockets, smiling on me as I sat absorbed at the new Broadwood piano.

My fourteenth birthday had brought self-awareness with it. I had always been neat and tidy but now I became particular about my appearance. In imitation of Lilian Lacey's style, I was wearing a slim grey skirt and a scarlet jersey. I had washed my hair the previous evening with Amami, for Friday night was Amami night, and rinsed it with the contents of a twopenny packet of powder from Woolworth's, called 'Bronze Highlights'. Loosed from school plaits, it was brushed back and tied with a matching red ribbon, to mark that day as being different from the navy-blue of a school day. My body had lost the skimpiness of childhood and its future shape was plainly stated. I was intensely proud of my small new breasts.

My father cleared his throat gently to warn me of his presence, but he had come at exactly the right moment. I turned round laughing, clasping my hands overhead like a victorious boxer.

'I've got it, Daddy, I've got it! Come and look. Watch my left hand first. Then watch my right one. Then watch them both together.'

He gave me his full attention.

'Why do your little fingers hop out sideways like that?' he asked, interested.

'Because my handspan isn't wide enough. So actually my timing isn't precise. Most people wouldn't know, but I can hear it, and so can anybody who listens carefully.'

Then I paid tribute to his powers of observation with a little snort like his own, half-admiration, half-disgust.

'Daddy, you weren't supposed to notice *that*. You were supposed to watch the way I meshed my fingering together!'

He drew up a chair and sat down smiling.

'Play it again for me,' he said, 'and I'll watch carefully.'

I knew from his tone and expression how much he loved me, and as a child this would have been enough. But the growing woman in me spun his love into a web to capture many men. I imagined how they would worship me at the piano as I played, and how truly sorry I would be to send them away empty. For at this time love figured in my life only as something to be laid at my feet in homage, and lovers as admirers to be kept at a safe and beautiful distance.

12

Whereas 1934 had been a sad Pavane, the first half of 1935 was a brilliant Capricio Espagnole.

Dorothy's evening outings to Hathersall Dramatic Society had a tonic effect on her, and she would return full of news and good humour. Meanwhile my father and I had taken advantage of her absence to clean out the larder, which still tended to harbour remnants of grey apple pie, dried sauce bottles and furred gravy. We were all content with this new arrangement, but concessions in married life usually demand payment of some kind, and within a few months Dorothy's debt was called in.

Grizedale's had become an integral part of our daily lives, and my father acted as a barometer of its triumphs and failures. He began each term set firmly at Fair, hoped for Very Dry, feared Rain, and hovered mostly around Change. So the responsibility of any full-blown ceremonial occasion – so many risks to be taken, so much work involved – caused him inevitably to veer towards Stormy.

'Grizedale's isn't the only school in the country to be celebrating the King's Silver Jubilee, you know!' cried Dorothy, exasperated, as he sat in thunderous silence at the head of his dining table, in March of that year. 'All of them are doing something, and of course I'm doing more than everybody else put together! Blackstone High are having a festival, and Evelyn's in a school play, and wants me to sew her costume – a tunic and train, made all in leaves of silver lamé, thank you very much!'

She clapped down a pile of hot plates in front of him, and disappeared into the hall, still talking.

'Then there's the Jubilee Tea at Moss Lane School, and I've promised the headmaster that I'll supervise the catering. And they're giving a Bring and Buy sale beforehand to raise money for it, and asking people to provide things. So I'm baking two fruit cakes and two sandwich cakes and four dozen scones. . . .'

Her monologue came and went with her own progress, for my father had sensibly instituted a food trolley, which could be wheeled from the kitchen and parked just outside the dining-room door.

Dorothy returned with a steaming vegetable dish, still talking.

'. . . and quite apart from the Silver Jubilee, I'm supposed to be running a gift stall for the Townswomen's Guild's Summer Fair. Besides which, I'm stage-managing Hathersall Dramatic Society's Easter production!'

She went out again, saying, '. . . and as Julian starts at Moss Lane next January they've invited him to the Infants' Jubilee Tea, so he really ought to have a nice little navy blue blazer and grey shorts. And I haven't seen anything I like in Kersley, so that means an expedition to Barber's in Blackstone. . . .'

My father sighed. Michael and I winked at each other. Julian, spoon in mouth, watched the centre of his universe whisk to and fro.

Dorothy placed a large oval platter of chops, sausages, kidneys, tomatoes and mushrooms before her husband, who brightened noticeably.

'. . . so don't come grumbling to me about some little hitch in the arrangements for Grizedale's pageant.'

My father picked up the serving fork and spoon, saying in quite a different tone, 'This smells good, Dorothy!'

She had had her grumble, and as we began to eat with evident enjoyment her tone and expression softened.

'Has everyone got everything they want? Does it taste good?'

We chorused our appreciation, and she looked on us in

deep content. My father's face had relaxed, but he was plotting quietly to himself. I could tell by the secret smile he gave to his mushroom as he sliced it neatly into quarters. I was not surprised when he asked me to make coffee for them both afterwards.

'A small way of saying thank you, for yet another excellent meal,' he added, inclining his head towards Dorothy.

You would have thought he was making the coffee himself.

I speeded the process up and paused outside the drawing-room door. Eavesdroppers, Grannie Annie always said, never hear good of themselves, but they were not talking about me.

My father, at his most persuasive, was saying, 'All I am asking you to do is to come over to the school on Monday afternoon, watch the rehearsal, and give us the benefit of your experience.'

Dorothy's voice answered him hesitantly, flattered but afraid.

'But I've never produced a play in my life, Gil. I'm not sure I could. I'd rather you asked someone else.'

Her protest was feeble, halfway to acquiescence.

He answered truthfully, 'I haven't anyone else on the staff capable of taking over this late in the day. And poor Carswell won't be out of hospital for weeks.'

He had struck a false note. Annoyance edged her apprehension.

'Well, I've got too much to do already. Didn't you hear me say?'

A pause indicated that he was considering this remark seriously.

He said gently, pedantically, 'I not only heard, I listened.' He ran skilfully over the main heads of her meal-time conversation. I could picture him ticking them off on his fingertips.

'First. Evelyn needs a theatrical costume. I suggest that she makes her own, possibly with the help of your mother.

'Second. Why bake so much stuff for the Bring and Buy sale at Moss Lane? One good cake should be sufficient.

'Third. If you're helping us at Grizedale's then you can't supervise the sandwich-cutting at Moss Lane school, so that's out.

'Fourth. I can take Julian to Blackstone to buy his clothes.'

Dorothy was so silent that she must have been sitting there overwhelmed. The argument had reached the tip of his thumb.

'Fifth. The Easter production at Hathersall will be over well before the Silver Jubilee.'

He was on to the other thumb.

'Sixth. The Townswomen's Guild Summer Fair. When does that come off?' Dorothy murmured something half-heartedly and he repeated, 'Mid-July? Then you can forget it for the time being.'

His hands would be spread briefly in a triumphant gesture.

He said, 'You see how simple it is, Dorothy, once you sort out your priorities and begin to delegate? All you have to do for the Silver Jubilee is to produce Grizedale's pageant and bake a cake.'

I heard her burst out laughing. The laughter held rage as well as grudging admiration.

'You are the limit, Gil! What about everything else I have to do? The house doesn't run itself!'

He had the answer to that, too.

'Ask your mother to help out. She enjoys doing that. And get Mrs Inchmore to work on the afternoons you're taking rehearsals. She can pick Julian up from school and look after him until you get home. I'll pay for that.'

I knew that she was struggling, in the silence, to put forward her own point of view, but she was wasting her time and she was probably tempted by the idea.

'Well, I'm not promising anything,' she said, flustered, 'but I'll come in on Monday afternoon – just to give my opinion.'

'That's all I ask,' my father replied reasonably.

I could have told her that he was most dangerous when most reasonable, but Dorothy was not as finely attuned to him as I was.

Then unexpectedly I heard her come out strong and authentic.

'Just one more thing!' she said. 'If I do decide to take charge then I must *be* in charge. I'm not having advice, suggestions or orders from you or anybody else. Let that be understood from the beginning. Any interference and I shall walk out! I mean that!'

'I agree absolutely,' said my father in tones of respect. 'I should make the same condition myself.'

When I knocked and went in she was sitting upright, breathing hard and looking worried. He was sitting back, swinging his left foot.

Taking the tray from me absent-mindedly, she said to him, 'I'm not promising anything, mind!'

'Of course not!' said my father, reasonable to the last.

He was a fine judge of character and ability. He knew that Dorothy's love of drama and her desire to organise other people could be used on this occasion. He knew that she liked boys and would treat them with the right mixture of authority and camaraderie. What none of us knew was that Dorothy could organise and administrate quite as well as he, but had never been given the opportunity. And ironically, my father had released a genie from the bottle who would never go back. Dorothy was to savour power and freedom in the outside world. It could only be a question of time before she tried to savour it again.

In this the fates themselves would aid her, for darkness was spreading over Europe. The Babbages had come back from their Berlin holiday full of disturbing tales. Inhuman things were being done in the open streets and behind locked doors, and the number of distinguished Jews from Austria and Germany seeking salvation here and in America was growing. The question of German politics had been an intermittent subject for male debate over the past two Christmas dinner-tables. Now the debate was becoming general. I heard, but unlike my father I did not listen. Once I had believed myself to be immortal. Now I believed that my present world would last for ever.

Grizedale's, paying tribute to twenty-five years of paternal monarchy, epitomised that world for me. I remember middle-class England before the war as a fine warm afternoon in the May of 1935, through which privileged people saunter on shaven lawns.

The ladies were superbly hatted and gloved, clad in long slim floating gowns, carrying large smart handbags and silk parasols. Some gentlemen wore full morning dress, complete with grey topper and spats; others, less formal, were in double-breasted lounge suits and trilby hats. But none would have dared grace the occasion without his old school tie, grey or fawn gloves, and a cane. And only a rank outsider would have come bare-headed, in an open-necked shirt, sports jacket and flannel trousers.

I saw and heard in terms of music. Parents paraded and talked and smiled, performing the social minuet of meeting one couple and moving away, coming up to shake hands with the next couple and moving on again, while my father and his staff called the tune.

From the central tower of Grizedale's main building a Union Jack undulated languidly. Tubs of patriotic flowers, in red, white and blue, stood along the front terrace. The portico was decorated with silver greetings and enlarged photographs of Their Majesties King George V and Queen Mary. Pillars were swathed in red, white and blue bunting like giant barber's poles. Over the wrought-iron entrance gates an arch of silver cardboard trumpets and crossed flags proclaimed the Jubilee. And a vast white marquee had been erected on the main lawn, in which refreshments were served.

Dorothy had chosen a green clearing as the stage on which to present the pageant. Its shrubbery formed the wings, and a side lawn made an excellent auditorium, being on gently rising ground, where rows of folding chairs were set out in symmetrical half-circles.

Our family party was early in its seats, and Michael and I nudged each other as Dorothy herded her white-faced flock towards the shrubbery. They were gabbling lines beneath their breath or clenching their teeth so that they should not chatter in fright. We heard her clarion voice threaten them with her personal displeasure if any of them should forget a line or miss a cue.

'Poor devils!' said Michael, and was instantly taken to task by Grandad for profane language.

Our grandparents sat up very straight and stiff in their Sunday clothes, looking around them in silent exaltation. Then Grannie took a packet of peppermint creams from her pocket and offered us one apiece, with a whispered caution to behave ourselves.

We saw Dorothy's fingers prise two branches apart in order to peep though them, and heard her wrathful cry to the boys behind her.

'Silence! I will have silence!'

A little wave of amusement and expectation lifted the audience. I turned round and craned to see the time on the school clock, and saw instead a familiar stranger. The headmaster of Grizedale's was stalking splendidly towards us: a great black bird in his billowing gown, followed by a flight of lesser birds. The tassel of his mortar-board danced a little in the summer breeze. On his shoulders, beautifully draped, lay an azure hood trimmed with white fur.

My throat and eyes were full. Though my father could not see me in the crowd of spectators, and would certainly not have looked for me at that official moment, I smiled at him.

Punctual to the moment, he took his seat as the tower clock chimed two.

Where the shrubbery was thinnest I saw Dorothy's capable hand arresting the shoulder of the King's jester, waiting for us all to settle down. Only when the silence was at its deepest and most expectant did it loose its prey and give him a brisk tap.

I could imagine her saying, 'Right, my lad. You're on!'

Released, he leaped from the shrubbery and executed two perfect cartwheels into the centre of the stage.

We arrived home at seven o'clock, triumphant, with the heroine in our midst, to eat a supper of cold meat and pickles and bread and butter, tinned pears and cream. Then

Michael slipped out with Grannie and Grandad, saying he would escort them to the Hathersall tram.

We knew he would not return immediately. He was inclined, once out of the house, to disappear for a few hours and turn up around midnight. But on this flawless day my father would not say as usual, 'And where's that damned lad gone to now?' No, he smoothed out his frown and swallowed his temper, to keep Dorothy's happiness intact.

In the same mellow mood I offered to put Julian to bed and read *Little Black Sambo* to him, which he loved because of all the pancakes. And afterwards took a tray of coffee and biscuits into the drawing room, where my father and Dorothy were chatting. I had no desire to be with them. I wanted to be by myself and savour the day in my own fashion.

In the scullery, while my coffee cooled, I attended to Dorothy's bouquet, which had been left in a bucket of water on the floor, still wrapped in cellophane and a crimson ribbon. The heady scent of her favourite pink roses, released by warm air, delighted me. I made quite a ceremony of arranging them in a silver vase, and folded the ribbon for a keepsake.

Through the uncurtained window of the scullery I could see the chestnut tree beyond the backyard wall, lifting pale candles in the twilight. There was some May mood abroad of which I was a part, and this feeling persisted as I carried the vase of roses through the hall to show Dorothy, and heard my parents' murmured conversation as a concerto for two violins.

Their voices rose and fell in deep and private content. First one and then the other took up the main theme, reworked it and returned it. All was well and would be well.

Then in my head a 'cello began an adagio, sad and elegaic, and I remembered that trouble was never banished for good, had only lifted its bow for a while, waiting for the shining day to end, waiting for night to come.

13

The struggle to turn Michael into university material had continued, in a way, without him. Michael's own head-master had acknowledged defeat some time ago, but my father would persist, and fought a rearguard action over each inevitable step backwards. A lower grade of form, a year's delay, fewer subjects, all these concessions were won by his solitary persistence. Meanwhile, Michael gradually went to ground. He no longer protested or explained but became passive, as if awaiting a release of some kind.

Now seventeen, he was almost six feet tall and wonderfully handsome. His voice had deepened pleasantly and he affected a slight drawl. His fair hair glistened with Azora Viola cream, and he had developed the habit of smoothing the fine fair down on his jaws as if it needed constant attention rather than a thrice-weekly skim with a safety razor.

Our affection for each other remained constant even though our lives were different and we spent so little of them together. But one summer Sunday, when he had struggled all week over examination papers and been put through them again on the Saturday by my father, he did suggest that we played truant together. And so we got up early, made our sandwiches and pooled our pocket money, left a note for Dorothy, and set off with the dog for Tarn How.

The pattern of Tarn How days had been set long ago, so we did not need to talk, only to keep each other company and think our own thoughts, while Flora ran ahead of us and back again in delight.

As we ate our sandwiches underneath the curving rock, Michael said, 'I'm thinking of doing a moonlight flit.'

The day was warm. My face and hands felt cold. But both of us hated a fuss so I kept my tone and answer airy.

'Are you taking the family silver with you, and leaving a letter of apology on the mantelpiece?'

He looked at me sideways with a half grin, saying, 'I'd thought of borrowing your savings, actually, kiddo, and leaving an IOU inside the piggy-bank.'

'Cheeky devil!' I said, but could not swallow my sandwich.

I put it down and nursed my knees, staring ahead of me at the distant spires of Blackstone.

'When are you going, Micky?'

'When I'm driven to it, I suppose.'

'What will you live on?'

'I expect there *are* jobs for a prodigal stepson to do.'

But I attacked him in my distress, crying, 'What jobs, when so many men are out of work? And it would have to be unskilled labour. What fun is there in drudgery? You'd be completely wasted. You'd be worse off than you are now.'

That obstacle must have puzzled him too, for a long time, but he replied lightly, stoically.

'Apart from feeding swine, I could hop on a banana boat, depart for the colonies, or join the army and see the world.'

I would have laughed if I had not been so near crying.

'But I had to say it to you. I couldn't just hoof it without telling you. Okay?' I nodded hard. 'Then eat your blooming sandwich and stop wiping your eyes with your headscarf.'

I laughed and cried at once, then, and he patted my back until I felt better. Afterwards we finished the sandwiches and went down the other side to Dowson-under-Fell.

The atmosphere was cool when we returned home in time for Sunday tea. Dorothy and my father took us to task about our lack of consideration. Actually, they were jealous and would not admit it.

My father had rented a furnished house in Seascale for the month of August as usual. And, as usual, Grannie Annie joined us for a fortnight of that time, to help Dorothy while reaping the benefits of sea air and a change of duties. But this summer a cloud hovered over sun and sand and sea which had nothing to do with the weather. We were all waiting for Michael's results.

They arrived on a fine hot morning, and my father gave a short laugh when he read them.

'Congratulations, Michael, you've finally succeeded!'

His sarcasm suffused poor Dorothy with hope.

'What? Has he passed, then?' she asked joyfully.

My father gave another sarcastic laugh and did not answer her.

'No, Mother,' I said quickly. 'That wasn't what Daddy meant.'

Michael said nothing. Julian stopped fidgeting. Grannie Annie retreated tactfully to the kitchen.

Dorothy's expression changed from hope to utter wretchedness.

'All right, don't tell me,' she said, getting up hurriedly, also preparing to retreat to the sanctuary of the kitchen. 'I don't want to know. I've had enough trouble over this sort of thing.'

But she was not to be allowed to leave the scene.

'Well, your troubles are definitely over, Dorothy,' my father said, coldly genial, 'and so is my attempt to educate this son of yours. His headmaster can't accept him in the Sixth Form with these results. In fact, they're no use to him for anything as far as I can see. He has a credit in English Literature but has failed in English Language – which is, of course, a compulsory pass subject! He has a distinction in Geography and a pass in History, a credit in French and a fail in Maths.'

Then he lost his temper.

'It makes no sense. No sense at all. And I wash my hands of the whole damned futile expensive business.'

Dorothy fired up in defence of her elder son.

'Well, I think he'll do better when you leave him alone. He's not a fool, you know. He's clever at a lot of things. The trouble is that none of them happens to interest *you*.'

'Oh, I give him credit where it's due,' said my father, at his cruellest. 'He's worked hard for all his scout badges. And

155

had he been examined in the gymnasium or on the playing fields, or in photography and model-making and stamp-collecting, I have not the slightest doubt that he would have gained distinctions. Unfortunately, these are not qualifying subjects for even the humblest profession.'

Michael pushed back his chair and went out.

Dorothy said, trembling, 'You'll drive my boy away from home in the end. Do you know that? Is that what you're trying to do?'

I put my arm round Julian, who was sitting hunched and scared, staring from one furious parent to the other.

'Come on, old fellow,' I said. 'Let's go outside and say hello to the sea, shall we?'

He trotted out with me obediently, eyes worried, lips pursed.

Grannie was standing by the gas stove in the kitchen, drinking a cup of tea and keeping out of the way.

'Shut that door behind you, Evleen,' she whispered urgently. 'It's not our place to listen.'

As the door closed, we heard Dorothy cry, 'If Micky goes I shall go with him. I mean that. I shall go with my lad.'

I did not need to listen. I could supply my father's probable answer. He would prove every one of Dorothy's statements to be nonsensical, and remain cool and reasonable while his wife suffered and stumbled and made a fool of herself. I was truly sorry for her, and I could not forgive him. I would have liked to cry and shout and be hysterical, as she was being at the moment.

'Nay, dunnot upset yourself, love,' said Grannie, reading my expression. 'Our Dollie's only sounding off. She's got nowhere to go to, and nowt to live on, and she knows it. Think on!'

'It's not what she's saying,' I replied, sick at heart and stomach. 'It's what they're doing. They're trying to hurt each other inside. What's the sense of marriage if people live like that?'

'Eh, my lass,' said Grannie, stroking my hair, 'married life's not all roses. When folk get vexed they say more than they should, and more than they mean, often enough. I know

I have. But it's best to get it off your mind than let it fester. Your mam and dad'll be as right as ninepence by tea-time. You take our little lad out and play you on t'beach, sithee. I'll make thee a picnic later on.'

I kissed her, and said, 'Where's poor Micky?'

'He's gone back o' beyond. He give me a hug and a kiss, and whistled up Flora, and went off back o' beyond.'

Julian tugged at my hand. The phrase had opened up grand horizons for him. His face implored me.

'Let's us go back o' beyond, Evie,' he said.

'Not today, lamb. Not today,' I replied. 'It's too far to go.'

He picked up his bucket and spade, and I led him down the sandy steps and out to the glittering sea.

The quarrel continued long and went deep. Julian and I stayed out all day, sustained by Grannie Annie who fed us at intervals and reported progress.

By six o'clock the family, apart from Michael who had not yet returned, joined each other for a meal of boiled ham and salad. No one spoke much or ate much. My father was pale and silent, Dorothy red-eyed and subdued. Julian went to bed without a protest, too timid to ask for his usual story. Fortunately for him I remembered, and read *The Tale of Two Bad Mice*, which he loved because they messed up the dolls' house and stole its furniture.

I heard my voice bringing the story to life, and then explaining that the lady who wrote and illustrated the book had lived in the Lake District. And all that time, the tale of the prodigal son was running through my mind, but without its happy ending.

At sunset, as the sky donned its livery of mulberry and gold, a message arrived for Dorothy from the local post office, in the person of Mr Barraclough, our landlord. Michael had telephoned only ten minutes previously, to say that he'd be hiking for the rest of the summer holiday but would send a postcard from each place.

'And he said,' Mr Barraclough went on, 'to tell you not to worry, because he was all right, and that he'd be sure to keep in touch.' He could not forbear adding, 'Nothing wrong, I hope, Mrs Fawley?'

I felt the family close its ranks. We might cut each other to pieces in private but no one should gossip about us in public. Dorothy lifted her chin, though it quivered. Her words were prophetic, though she did not know this.

'Oh no. He's been planning this trip for some time.'

'Michael's a scout, you see, Mr Barraclough,' said my father, coming to his wife's aid, taking her arm and holding her close, 'and a very fine one. He's got nearly all his badges, and worked hard for them. This hike is by way of being an endurance test.'

'So very kind of you . . .' Dorothy began, in her best manner.

Then she could not go on, and it was my father who showed Mr Barraclough out and thanked him for his trouble.

Forgotten in the second turmoil that followed, Grannie Annie and I sat up talking late into the night.

'Eh, the lad'll be all right,' she said more than once. 'He were allus going off for t'day when he lived wi' us.'

'But not for two or three weeks, with a dog to look after,' I reminded her. 'And no food and no extra clothes, and above all no money, Grannie!'

For I had checked my savings box, hoping that Michael had found time to borrow its contents, and not a halfpenny was missing.

'Ah, but he's had his rucksack packed for the last two-three days,' said Grannie surprisingly. 'I noticed it in the shed, wi' his mackintosh strapped atop of it, but I thought it best to say nowt. And when I rec'llected it, and went to look, it'd gone '

I was relieved and glad, and I said so.

'The lad'll be all right, you see,' Grannie Annie repeated. She added, 'But I could wish that your grandad was here to give us his opinion. I set a store by your grandad's opinion. I do that.'

We sat awhile in silence, then I said, 'It would have been

easier for Mick if he hadn't taken Flora. She needs to be fed, too.'

'He'll look after her, and she'll be company for him. She's allus been his dog, you see. He wouldn't leave her behind to fret.'

'You don't think he's gone for ever, do you?' I cried.

'Nay, he'll turn up when it suits him. But unless him and your father have altered it'll start all over again, I reckon. I've been wondering – that's why I mentioned Grandad just now – as to whether it wouldn't be best if our Michael come and lived wi' us for a bit.'

She interpreted my look and said, 'Eh, your mam'd see we didn't go short. She'd give us summat towards his keep. But we could manage if we had to. He's still our lad. He were born at Parbold House.'

I said slowly, 'I suppose that's best. Oh, but I should miss him. And I daren't think what Mother would say and do!'

'Aye, she's the excitable sort is our Dollie, but she's got her head screwed on and her heart in the right place. She might well find it a comfort to know as he's content, and not to have to stand between him and Dr Fawley all the time.'

I had to ask her if she blamed my father, and she considered this question with some care.

'He spoke nasty-like this morning, but I wouldna say I *blamed* him,' she said at last. 'Dr Fawley is a just man. He's done his best for the lad, according to his lights, and our Michael hasn't worked at his books as he ought. I remember how our Eric worked – burning the midnight oil, he called it – night after night. But our Michael's been off wi' his dog, and off footballing, and off this, that and t'other. And Dr Fawley paid good money for his eddication, and he canna see owt for it. So he's bound to get vexed. Him and Michael don't see eye to eye, and I doubt they ever will. They're as different as chalk from cheese.'

'Perhaps it might be better if they didn't live under the same roof for a while,' I conceded.

I was glad that Grannie Annie did not condemn my father. She believed that most problems arose from misunderstandings, whereas Dorothy always took sides, labelling one right and the other wrong.

'You're a very wise person, aren't you, Grannie?' I said reflectively.

'Nay, I don't know about wise. I've just lived a long while,' she replied. 'I'd have to be daft not to have learned a thing or two by this time!'

'No. You are wise. I'm sure of that.'

'Well, I'm wise enough to know as you should be in bed, any road,' she replied, looking at the kitchen clock.

'I shan't sleep. I'm sure I shan't.'

'You're sure o' too much!' said Grannie Annie briskly, which made me laugh. 'Get you to bed, my lass. You'll drop off as soon as your head touches the pillow. See if I'm not right!'

'I expect you will be. So, good night, Grannie. And thank you.'

I was so much taller now than she that I must stoop to hug and kiss her. Then I looked directly into her eyes, so that no evasion or kindly lie was possible.

'Grannie, Michael will come back, won't he? Promise me?'

She answered with absolute faith.

'Aye, he'll walk in through t'back door o' Railway Street one o' these fine days, wi' Flora at his heels, as if he'd never been away. And I'll bet you a pound to a penny that his first words is, "Gran! I'm famished!" And then I'll put the frying pan on.'

I kept my arms round her neck, looking and looking into her face as if it held the secret to all truths.

'You're sure that he'll contact you first? Not Mother – or me?'

'Nay, he'll come to me first. He'll want to sound things out afore he tries Malt-housing, won't he?'

'Yes, I expect you're right.'

I kissed her again and said, 'I love you very much, Grannie.'

'I'm right fond o' you, and all,' she replied. 'I wish you got on half as well wi' our Dollie, but you're another chalk and cheese pair! If she studied you a bit more, and you critikised her a bit less, you'd be as right as ninepence together.'

'But I'm always very nice to her!' I said, amazed.

For I prided myself on being able to keep my temper and remain polite. But Grannie turned my thoughts inside out.

'Aye, soft words and hard looks. And often enough you say nowt and think the more, like your father. And that can be hurtful. I'm not saying as I blame either you or our Dollie for being like you are, but there's a place in the middle where everybody can meet if they try. So, think on!

'There, that's enough talk for one day. Night night, sleep tight, sweet dreams, God bless, and see you in the morning – all being well.'

14

Summer ended. Autumn came. On weekend walks our diminished family gathered wood for Bonfire Night, stacked it in a growing mound and covered it with a tarpaulin to keep dry. Dorothy brewed stone jars of ginger beer and baked a slab of parkin. I concocted a wonderful effigy from sticks and old clothes, and painted a mask, and frayed black darning wool into a beard and moustaches. And my father purchased the biggest and best box of fireworks from Addison's toy shop in Kersley.

Julian would be five at the end of this year: old enough to appreciate the meaning of an event but too young to wait in patience. Since October he had been crossing days off the kitchen calendar, and was now suffering the final hours.

'How long 'til we burn Guy Fawkes, Mummy? How long?'

'Oh, not until seven o'clock. Quite a while yet.'

'How long is quite a while?'

'For heaven's sakes, Julian,' Dorothy cried at last, 'get from under my feet and stop asking questions!'

He crawled beneath the kitchen table, silenced for a few minutes, and wound up his little black clockwork train.

'I wonder,' he murmured, just loud enough for his mother to hear, 'if Father Christmas will bring me a Hornby train set . . .' And whispered to himself, '. . . like Mick's!'

He had learned not to mention Michael to his parents. The subject made his mother cry and his father retreat to the study.

Dorothy kept Michael's weekly postcards and occasional letters in her handbag. They were addressed to her, ended by saying 'Love to all', and spoke only of general news. I sensed that this was a show put up for Dorothy's benefit while he worked something out for himself. She would read them aloud to us very cheerfully, making much, too much of his scraps of information.

'Fancy that! Michael says that the first time he tried to milk a cow it kicked its milk pail over, and then kicked *him*!'

'Michael cleaned out a monkey cage, and one of them tried to bite him. He pretended to bite it back, and it ran off. Isn't he a scream?'

'Well, I never, Flora caught a rabbit and Michael cooked it over a fire in the wood, and they ate it between them for supper.'

When she thought we were preoccupied and she un-observed, she would take the letters out and read them again. Sometimes she cried silently and said nothing, but mostly she perused the few lines as if they held uncoded secrets, and wiped her eyes as she returned them to their untidy stronghold.

Julian had grown tired of his clockwork train, which was a poor thing compared to the glory of a Hornby locomotive. He scrambled to his feet and stood on a chair to look through the kitchen window again, and make sure it was not raining.

'God bless that little lad!' groaned Mrs Inchmore, coming up from the wash-house. 'Let him enjoy hisself while he can, that's what I allus say. He'll sup sorrow soon enough, like the rest on us!'

She sat down heavily at the table, drying pink and wrinkled hands on her apron. Dorothy poured tea for us, and warm milk for Julian.

'How many times round the clock is it now, Mummy?'

'Oh dear me! Watch my finger. All round here. See? Not until Daddy comes home and we've had our evening meal.'

'Will it be dark?'

'Of course it'll be dark. If it wasn't we couldn't see the fireworks!' said Dorothy more sharply. 'Now stop asking silly questions, and sit down and drink your milk and be quiet!'

'Can I drink it under the table, please?'

'Yes, yes. Here, crawl in first and I'll hand it to you!' To Mrs Inchmore she said, 'I'll be glad when he goes to Moss Lane School next term. I really will. I can't keep him occupied for five minutes! He needs other children to play with.'

Julian embraced the cat, who walked away disgusted, and whispered into his milk, 'I wish Flora was here.'

Mrs Inchmore sighed deeply, heaped sugar into her tea, returned the wet spoon to the bowl, and leaned her elbows on the table. She addressed me first.

'Ill again, are you, Evleen?'

'Just a slight cold,' I replied curtly. 'I've been working at home instead of at school.'

'Ah! You want to watch them lungs,' said Mrs Inchmore. 'I lost our Nance wi' the consumption. Fifteen, she were, same age as you.'

I had long since ceased to marvel at the ability of her children, dead or alive, to point a moral or adorn a tale. She scrutinised my face, but I was not prepared to give her any satisfaction, so she looked for an easier prey.

'Have you heard from your Michael lately, Mrs Fawley?'

How often had I advised Dorothy not to lay herself open to this kind of prying? But she needed to talk about him, even to a traitor, and once she had started she could not stop. Round and round she went upon the wheel she forged for herself.

'I'm expecting to hear any day now. He never misses a week. I'd send money but he never gives me an address. He's hardly in one place before he moves to the next. I should like to send him something. I should like to write to him. It's terrible not to be able to answer. And then, the odd jobs he's been doing. Harvesting. Potato picking. Any odd job wherever he can find one . . . but what happens when winter comes?' Dorothy asked.

'Ah, poor lad,' said Mrs Inchmore, not caring.

'And yet he has so many talents,' Dorothy murmured to herself, 'and people love him. And in a funny sort of way he always lands on his feet. This may be leading to something important. . . .'

She dared not make such a statement in front of my father, who would reply, 'Such as what?'

'. . . but it's a come-down, whichever way you look at it. A fine young man like Michael, living like a tramp.'

'No better than a tramp,' Mrs Inchmore echoed mournfully.

'He sounds happy, though,' said Dorothy sadly. 'When I read his postcards or his letters I fancy I can hear him whistling to himself. Just so long as he's happy. That's all that matters.'

'Ah, being happy's one thing,' said Mrs Inchmore, enjoying herself, 'but staying happy's another!'

I nudged Dorothy to indicate that Mrs Inchmore had gone quite far enough, and she responded as if I had wakened her.

'I really must scrub a tray of potatoes for the bonfire party,' she said, and then resolutely, 'We're going to have such a good time.'

The evening crept up with the air of a conspirator, hidden in mist, hinting at change. Trees dripped quietly on their fallen leaves, reminders of a blustering afternoon.

'But it's not raining any more,' said Julian earnestly, and shook his head from side to side. 'It's not.'

He gazed anxiously at his father who had returned from a weather inspection. The hands of the clock pointed to seven.

'I don't have to go to bed,' Julian reminded his parents.

'We know!' cried Dorothy, amused, exasperated. She turned to her husband as to an oracle. 'What do you think?' she asked.

'Oh, the rain'll hold off long enough for us to enjoy ourselves! I've stood the gate open to welcome people anyhow. Are you ready?'

Dorothy swung into action, calling me up to help.

'Evelyn! Get Julian's outdoor things, will you?'

The child held out his arms obediently for his coat sleeves. In Dorothy's grief for Michael she had neglected her second son for a while, and I had taken her place out of pity for them both. He was an old-fashioned little mortal, as dutiful to me as to his mother. And since he feared to upset her with his confidences he confided in me, instead. As I buttoned up his gaiters he whispered a long litany about the Hornby railway, Michael and Flora and Guy Fawkes.

'You're tickling my ear!' I cried, laughing.

My father smiled down at his only begotten son. He took Julian by the hand. He rallied his family together.

'Come on, then! What are we waiting for? Let's light that fire while we can!'

He had engineered the evening's entertainment with particular care and skill that year. It was a way of telling Dorothy that he was sorry. He knew she liked chatting to people and feeding them, and he wanted to please her. This year he had suggested that we make a party of the occasion. And since relatives were inclined to bore him and he detested small talk so much that he had been known to fall asleep in his chair, he had invited more intellectual company: two of the masters from Grizedale's and their wives and children.

The demands of marriage never ceased to amaze me. By this time I should have thought all passion, if ever it existed, must be spent. And it seemed to me that both of them would be much happier on their own or with a more kindred spirit. Yet here he was, needing to reach and regain something in her which had gone with Michael. And here she was, concealing her grief, playing up to him like a trooper.

We stood around, waiting. Only Julian was honestly delighted. Then distant voices indicated that the Frasers and the Collinses were making their way up the lane.

'Here they are!' cried Dorothy gleefully, and stopped suddenly to listen. 'Is that the telephone?' she asked anxiously.

'I didn't hear anything,' said my father, uninterested, 'but if it's important they'll ring again.'

The gate clicked, and we turned as one to greet our visitors. My father's social smile was warm. He shook hands heartily. Dorothy was as joyful as if they were all close friends instead of amiable acquaintances. Julian ran forward to join the children, who were around the same age as himself. And

I prepared to play nursemaid for the evening while I thought of something else.

Meeting, guests and hosts said similar things in similar tones.

'Hello? Hello there? How are you? How lovely to see you! What an afternoon it's been. Yes, but it seems to have cleared up now. Yes. Not at all bad. We've been looking forward to this so much, haven't we? My word, doesn't everything look splendid? And don't you look well! How's life treating you these days . . . ?'

My father said, 'Give me a hand with this tarpaulin, will you, Frank? I wonder, Charles, could you help Evelyn with the Guy?' Together they unveiled the result of several weekends' foraging. Guy Fawkes was carried forth to exclamations of admiration and delight, and tied firmly to his stake.

'Stand well back!' my father said to his assembly. 'I have a surprise for you.'

He distributed the contents of a can of paraffin fairly over the pile. Took a box of matches from his pocket. Set the little flame to the end of a fuse. And rejoined us rather quickly.

We held our breath and watched the flame run into the heart of the wooden mountain. And all at once the night exploded into flames and stars. Fire ran up the sticks from a dozen points on the perimeter, lit a dozen Catherine wheels, licked up the breast of its sorry culprit, and roared through the clearing between the trees.

In momentary alarm, the men jumped, the women shrieked, the children shouted in terror and delight. Then everyone laughed and clapped, and the adults echoed each other's exclamations. 'That was a clever idea, wasn't it? Oh, wonderfully effective! Yes, wonderful. Oh, feel the heat. Oh, look how high it's going. Good thing those trees are no nearer – we might have a bigger conflagration than we expected! Lovely, though, isn't it?'

Now the fire crackled as it caught hold, and set free flakes of ash upon the shimmering air, and most beautifully lit the encircling trees, the watching faces.

The effigy was all ablaze. From his straw breast issued

spurts of flame. His mask blackened and curled. His ropes burned through. Released, he leaned forward to embrace his destroyer. And was gone.

Julian gave a long satisfied sigh and clasped his cheeks. But no sooner had we recovered from this ritual death than another glorious shock awaited us. My father and a chosen colleague stationed themselves at either end of the garden wall, struck matches in unison and sprinted back to join the group.

The wall became a thing of fear and splendour: a living mass of colour, noise and light. Rockets soared high above our heads and exploded with ear-splitting cracks and blasts into silent showers of silver and gold. Catherine wheels whirled. Fountains poured. Roman candles burned. Fluorescent lights blazed green and red. Rip-raps went off like a rattle of machine-guns, from a safe distance.

Julian jigged up and down, clapping his gloved hands. He was beside himself with excitement. His laughter came close to tears.

Round the group of children marched my father, with smiles and warnings, distributing his bounty of sparklers.

'Keep your gloves on. Hold them at arm's length. They spit.'

The bonfire was burning down. The men brought more wood from the out-house and stacked it round the sides, careful not to disturb its red-gold heart, into which Dorothy was popping her scrubbed potatoes, one by one.

I moved to and from the kitchen, hoisting and pouring the cold stone jars of ginger beer, jingling trays of glasses forth, answering questions and obeying requests automatically. Though present, I had absented myself. The flames ran in arpeggios. The rockets exploded in chords. The conflagration was an oratorio.

Now the party had welded together. The adults chatted and watched and sipped and smiled. The children shouted and danced round the bonfire, and wreathed a chain in and out of the rustling trees, shaking their sparklers against the night.

*

Afterwards Michael told me that he saw us, at that moment and for the first time, as his family, and knew how much he had missed us. His heart, though brave and steadfast, thundered in his breast. He had great hopes of acceptance, but with the experience of a wanderer had taken precautions against possible disappointment. The price of a night's lodging clinked in his pocket, should my father turn him out.

He said that we looked so splendid and sure of ourselves, so much an established unit, that it seemed as if we had always been like that and always would be. And he would very much have liked to arrive at the right moment, just for our sakes. But he could not gauge which that moment might be. So he walked forward into the firelight, with his rucksack on his back and Flora at his heels.

I saw him first and whispered his name under my breath, afraid he was an illusion of light and shadow. But Dorothy, seeing my face, and turning to look in the same direction, did not question this apparition. She forgot her dignity and status. She shrieked aloud, clapped her hand to her mouth, and then ran forward holding out her arms. She cried for joy. I followed, trying to hold my tears back. Julian came next, breaking away from the garland of children and fetching them after him.

There was a wild reunion, as all three of us embraced Michael and his rucksack, and Flora ran round and round our little group, barking and wagging her tail.

Last of all, excusing himself to his guests, my father walked forward, hand outstretched. Dorothy and I looked from one male opponent to the other, hopefully, fearfully. Neither man could speak at first. Michael swallowed. My father nodded. They shook hands.

'Pity you weren't here earlier, Mick,' said my father affably. 'I missed you. It really needs two of us to do this thing properly.'

'Mick! Mick! Mick! You should have seen the fireworks!' cried Julian, shaking his arm to attract his attention. 'They were the very best ever yet!'

'When did you last have something to eat, Micky?' Dorothy asked.

'Grannie cooked bacon and eggs when I walked in to her place at three o'clock. Then I had high tea with her and Grandad. But I could manage a jacket potato when they're cooked, Mum.'

So Grannie was right, I thought. He had gone to her first. And I knew that he had said, 'Gran, I'm famished!' And that she had put the frying pan on straight away.

'I tried to ring you earlier, from a call-box in Hathersall. But you didn't answer the telephone.'

'I said I heard it ring!' Dorothy accused her husband.

But the evening must not be marred. She changed her tone. She covered up his error.

'We were out here. We couldn't answer it in time,' she said.

'And how are you, Evie?' said Michael lightly, putting his arm round my waist. 'Come on. Give us a kiss, you sloppy old thing.'

He always knew how to dispel my awkwardness. I giggled and complied, then drew back surprised and looked at him closely.

'You rotten pig. You're all bristly!' I cried, and punched him, and hugged him, and drew him towards the crowd round the bonfire.

Still, the feeling of strangeness persisted, for he had changed. Something was there which had not previously existed, and something else had gone. I could not have named either of them, but realised that the boy in him had walked away for good.

Dorothy wiped her eyes. My father made introductions all round.

'You know Michael, of course?'

His guests were in a difficult position. They knew why Michael had been away so long and felt awkward in the midst of a family reunion. They attempted to leave early but were refused permission. We Fawleys spoke as one.

'No, certainly not. Won't hear of it. Michael's arrival

doesn't break the party up, simply makes it a better one! Besides, who's going to eat all this food if you go?'

The clutch of children had no such inhibitions. Having made sure that they were not to be cheated of a late night, they plagued my father to give them their table display, asked if the potatoes were ready yet, and demanded more ginger beer. The celebrations now moved into Dorothy's sphere, and she fed us even more lavishly than usual.

We had all learned something from Michael's absence. But whereas Dorothy and Julian and I were glad to have him back for his sake and ours, my father was only glad for Dorothy's sake. Even as we rejoiced, each of us must have wondered how things would work out now. For the men would only compromise so far, and then give no quarter.

Lighting a firework which oozed long grey snakes of ash, my father's face was grave and inward looking.

Was he thinking, 'Now it starts all over again'?

Julian restored me to the present, whispering into my ear.

'Evie, is it like when the progiddle son came home? Evie, has Mick been among swine? And, Evie, shall we roast a fat calf?'

15

Michael's welcome soon wore thin. Instead of coming to heel, as my father hoped, he had simply come home. He refused to go back to school, to be coached outside school, or to begin any formal apprenticeship or training of any sort.

'Do *you* know what the damned chap wants?' my father asked me.

I answered shyly, awkwardly, for Michael's ideas were easy to understand but difficult to express.

'He says he's finding out what he wants to do.'

'Piffle! He wants to do what he likes while I support him.'

I could not disprove this but I was on Michael's side. The way in which he had walked off in defence of personal liberty, in protest at adult injustice, appealed to my deepest instincts. Flight. The freedom to be oneself, to tell everyone else to go to hell.

'He wants to be free,' I said, and spoke for myself as well.

But my father had an answer for everything.

'There's no such thing as freedom. The best thing any of us can hope for is to serve under the tyranny of our choice.'

'Perhaps he wants a different sort of tyranny,' I said pointedly.

He ignored me. He coughed slightly, lifted his chin, looking into some dark future of his own devising.

'If it wasn't for your mother. . . .' he said.

Their quarrelling had started again. Though the bedroom wall was thick I could hear the rise and fall of their voices in discord.

Michael found one temporary job after another and

handed most of his slim wage packet over to Dorothy. She made a great point of saying that he paid for his keep, but I knew that she put it aside for him, and often gave some back when he was hard up.

The weekends were difficult because Michael lived a life apart from our own, and came home late on Saturday nights. Since my father would not allow him a front door key this problem again devolved on Dorothy, who lay awake listening for his return and then crept downstairs to let him in.

A new alliance now came into being, for she would knock softly on my door to indicate that Michael was back, and the three of us would secretly drink tea together and talk into the early hours. For Michael brought a breath of the outside world to Dorothy in particular, and she hung upon his words and watched his face in humble adoration, as though he were Harry Harland come to life again.

On the whole Michael and my father observed an uneasy truce for her sake. But I can still see my father sitting in state before the drawing-room fire on a Sunday morning, shaking open *The Sunday Times* and smacking the editorial page flat in deep displeasure. And he would redirect his anger with Michael, in tuts and snorts of rage, against the blindness of the British government, the dangerous ambitions of Germany and the growing power of the Nazi movement in Europe.

'We're on the brink of war, you know!' he would cry.

Truly reflecting the state within him.

Left to his own devices, Michael lived by instinct, from hand to mouth, from day to day. He worked hard, he kept himself employed, he paid his way and did not ask anyone for money. But the jobs were menial, and though Dorothy tried to spin a golden future from the straw of her son's present she admitted, in private, to being disappointed, while my father openly described him as a total failure.

'There's no purpose and no future in what he's doing. And even if there were he wouldn't stick to one thing and make a go of it. He's never stuck to anything. Hopping like a blasted bird from one twig to another, pecking up a crumb here and a crumb there. He's a regular Autolycus is that lad! A snapper-up of unconsidered trifles!'

And in another way Michael hurt his mother by renewing his relationship with the Harlands, for though they welcomed him back as Harry's son they did not include her, who was no longer Harry's wife.

So family life with Michael in the house was like sitting on the lid of some Pandora's box, trying to prevent it from springing open and discharging nameless horrors in the air. Certainly hope would always flutter forth at the end, but hope was a fragile thing and its wings were soon tattered, as I learned from experience.

My father arrived home, one January Monday in 1936, to find that Dorothy had been living on wireless bulletins and his meal was late.

'It's the King!' she cried. 'The King's dying! And to think that we only celebrated his Jubilee eight months ago!'

'I haven't got my coat off yet, nor seen the evening paper!' said my father tetchily, for he was hungry and wanted food and attention.

As she hurried to propitiate him he aired his views on the subject of the monarchy. He explained that people created royalty for the same reason that they created God, because they needed something to worship. He pointed out that the King was simply a figurehead with limited powers. One could be sorry for his present condition, but to prostrate oneself before the wireless all day on his behalf was nothing short of childish.

'But I feel I *know* him,' Dorothy protested. Returning to the wireless set, she said apologetically, 'I'll just switch it on for a minute. Round about this time there might be some further news.' Then, urgently, 'Hush! Hush!'

The grave and dignified voice of the BBC's chief announcer, Stuart Hibberd, repeated its message.

'The King's life is moving peacefully towards its close.'

How beautiful, I thought. And pictured King George upon a royal barge, wrapped all about in purple velvet and fine ermine, the sword and sceptre laid either side of him, the jewelled crown upon his breast, borne on dark waters to oblivion.

Dorothy wiped her eyes.

'A good ruler, and a friend to his people,' she said devoutly. 'We shall all be the poorer for his loss.'

'You know nothing about him!' said my father abruptly.

'I know what I've read about him!' Dorothy answered, equally annoyed, for he was spoiling her sorrowful enjoyment of the event.

'What? In women's magazines and the popular press? What value can you place on that sort of sentimental nonsense? It's written to keep the average citizen happy and the monarch on his throne!'

'It can't all be lies!'

'Why not?' said my father unkindly.

'Daddy, you're being unfair,' I said, reading his mood.

He had been warming himself on the dining-room hearth, backside presented to the fire, hands thrust into his trouser pockets. Now he swung the beam of his attention on me.

'I thought you were intelligent enough to distinguish between true emotion and self-indulgence, Evelyn.'

I paused. There was an answer to him somewhere, but at the moment I could not find it.

'The King is a symbol,' I offered.

He pounced on my reply.

'Exactly. One doesn't mop and mow over a symbol.'

'Well you're wrong, because I do!' said Dorothy, returning to battle. 'And *I'm* interested in the King even if you aren't. So after we've eaten you'd better go to your study while I listen to the wireless. I'll bring you a cup of tea at nine o'clock.'

And she retreated with some dignity to dish up the evening meal.

He gave his little snort of laughter, half-contemptuous and half-sorry. He knew he had gone too far, but truth was paramount so he would not apologise. Having estranged her, he now courted me.

'Are you giving me a concert tonight?' he asked amiably.

I knew he wanted to set up in cultured opposition to Dorothy, to sit by the drawing-room fire and listen to Schubert while the peasantry kept a royal death-watch in the kitchen. But I disliked this side of his nature and chose to thwart him.

'Thanks, but I've finished my practice, and I've still got heaps of homework to do.'

'Anything I can help you with?' he offered, slightly dashed.

'No, thanks. Just mugging up a lot of facts.'

He looked round for something to distract him and saw that the table was laid only for four of us.

'Where's Michael?' he demanded, in a different tone.

'He's dining with the Harlands, I believe.'

My father sniffed. He tossed his chin.

'What? Again? He was over there all yesterday. I don't believe it. He's probably cuddling some shop-girl in the back seats of the Princess Cinema in Kersley!'

He intended this as a double insult, since the Princess was the cheapest local cinema, known to its regulars as 'the flea-pit'.

Stung, as he intended me to be, I rounded on him.

'You don't know that, Daddy. And it's very unkind to say so.'

'That son of hers is no good, you know,' he said conversationally, relegating Michael and Dorothy to the lower depths.

He rattled the change in his pocket, grinning, speaking to me as if I cared no more for Michael than he did.

'He's a wastrel. A playboy. He'll come to nothing and I shall be expected to support him in idleness.'

I would not accept this Olympic statement, and for once I told the truth, which is usually unforgiveable.

'The real trouble is, Daddy, that you've never liked him. You don't care what he is. You'd rather blame him for what he isn't!'

Almost I cried, 'You're jealous of him!'

As it was, my temerity astonished me and my father, and I stopped short, the colour rising to my face.

'Where did you get that piece of homespun wisdom from?' he asked sarcastically, thinking I quoted Dorothy.

'From myself,' I said firmly, but felt afraid. 'It's what I've thought for a long time. You're not fair to Michael.'

He became remote and chill, as if I were no part of him.

'How old are you?' he asked.

'I shall be sixteen in September,' I said, chin up, making it sound as adult as I could.

'You're only fifteen, then,' he corrected me.

He paused before delivering the blow. He spoke deliberately.

'If I'd argued with my father like that when I was fifteen he would have boxed my ears.'

My own ears burned at the words. I lowered my head. I was back at school again, standing in the corner in disgrace.

He had never used so harsh a tone with me in my life. I stood there for a moment, trying to swallow tears, but the effort hurt my throat and I knew they must pour down my cheeks eventually. So I turned on my heel and went out, banging the door behind me, and bumped into Dorothy wheeling her trolley of hot food.

'Whatever's wrong with you?' she cried, mouth open.

'I hate Daddy!' I shouted, loudly enough for him to hear.

But what hurt me was that I loved him, and had betrayed him to her with the statement. So I pushed past her and ran upstairs sobbing, hearing her say behind me, 'What a family! What a way to live!'

I stayed in my room all evening, doing homework and growing hungrier. Fortunately, Dorothy encouraged my father to go to bed early, and while she lingered in her bath I crept downstairs to devour a cheese sandwich and Ursula's love affair with Skrebensky in *The Rainbow*. I was absorbed in opening the female flower of myself when Dorothy came padding down to continue her vigil.

'Got over your sulks, then?' she asked amiably, and switched the wireless on again. 'What are you up to now?'

I was drinking Skrebensky's kisses and cleaving my body to his. I answered briefly, so that she would leave us in peace, 'Just reading.'

A blown rose, Dorothy sat down at the end of the kitchen table in her old dressing-gown and yawned. She took no notice of the fact that I had returned to my lover but began to talk, absent-mindedly tracing a pattern on the oilcloth with her forefinger, looking at it with unseeing eyes.

'Your father gets irritable because Micky hasn't a proper job. I've been wondering whether it would be better for the lad to live with Grannie for a bit. I'll give her the money for his keep.'

Reluctantly, I drew away from Skrebensky again, and spoke as to a child who merely needs a sign of attention.

'Oh, Micky will find something, you'll see.'

Dorothy looked up at the kitchen clock.

'Twenty past eleven,' she said. 'What sort of time is that for old folks like the Harlands to be up? They're in their seventies.'

Another pause. She played unwitting gooseberry again.

'The Harlands always had a lovely home,' she said wistfully. 'Fresh flower arrangements in the rooms, winter and summer, and a parlourmaid to serve afternoon tea. Mind you, I never liked their tea. They drank Earl Grey and I always think it tastes pink. And they gave a garden party for the local bigwigs every year, in June. I asked Michael if it was just the same, and he said it was.'

'I'm sure it is,' I said impatiently, trying to concentrate.

'I just wish he'd reconsider taking the post that Grandfather Harland offered him at Harland's Mill. I know he'd have to start on the bottom rung of the ladder – well, that's only right and fair, isn't it? – but he'd be on the family board of directors by the time he was thirty. To think that he turned down an opportunity like that! I wished I hadn't told your father. I was so sure that Micky would take it, you see. And then when I had to say he'd refused. . . . Sometimes I don't understand that lad. I told him. I said, "Life isn't the Garden of Eden, you know. You'll have to face that sooner or later." But he doesn't listen.'

I frowned on her. I shut my book pettishly. She took no notice.

'I can't help wondering,' said Dorothy sadly, 'why the

Harlands don't invite me too. I mentioned it to Michael, and he said they always asked how I was and said they must ring me up sometime. But that's not a proper invitation.'

She knew the reason very well. My father had gradually but deliberately broken that connection. For her it could not be mended.

Alerted by distant sounds, I said, 'That'll be the London train coming in to Kersley Station.'

There was magic for both of us in the name of London. Dorothy's memories had roused my imagination. It was in a London concert hall that my musical daydreams took place.

The train thundered through the valley below. A triumphant whistle fluted through the frosty air.

'If he's not on that train then we'd better go to bed,' I advised her, 'because he'll be walking home.'

'He'll be on it,' said Dorothy, convinced.

She filled the kettle and brought the remains of a cold apple pie from the larder.

'Micky won't want anything to eat!' I said, laughing. 'He's probably had a six-course meal already!'

But it was Dorothy's way of welcoming him home. She padded across the hall to unbolt the front door and leave it slightly ajar. She turned the wireless off. In rapt silence, we waited and listened for his arrival, which was heralded by Flora leaping from her basket. As he opened the kitchen door we smiled at him and at each other.

He strode in like a young god, prepared to receive obeisance.

'Evening, girls! Has the old cock snuffed it yet?' he asked with cheerful irreverence, nodding towards the silent wireless set.

'Michael!' said Dorothy deeply, but could not keep up appearances. 'Micky!' she cried, excited, 'tell us what's happened!'

He timed his reply, smiling.

'I've got an absolutely ripping job!'

We cried out together and clapped our hands. Flora ran round the table barking with delight, and Tom Cat winked lazily on us all.

'What sort of a job? What will you be? Where? When . . . ?'

'I'm going to be a wine merchant – eventually!'

We shrieked again.

'It's all because of a chap I met . . .' he began, and we both laughed. 'No joke. Truly. I've known this chap on and off since I was at the Crown Corner garage last November. Name of Richard Blythe. Dickie, for short. He used to drop in for petrol when I was working the pumps, and we got talking. He's mad about engines. Pretty handy with them too. Runs a three-and-a-half-litre Bentley. Belongs to an aeroplane club. Loaded with money. We lost sight of each other and then, blow me down if his father wasn't a member of the country club at Fairlawn where I worked as a waiter over the Christmas period. His family gave a New Year party there. Tonight it turns out that the entire family are old friends of the Harlands. What about that for coincidence?'

'Michael, this was meant!' said Dorothy in her richest voice.

I giggled. Micky winked at me, and mouthed one of our favourite sayings, 'Madame Sosostris, the famous clair-voyant . . .'

'You can stop being cheeky, you two,' said Dorothy, on her dignity. Then, excited again, 'Come on, Micky. Tell us what happened.'

'Well, to cut a long story short, this evening was set up for my benefit by Grandfather Harland. A sort of "You must meet the Blythes!" occasion, and all very jolly and informal, except that I was really there to be summed up by Dickie's old man, with a view to being offered a job – or not offered it, according to how he felt! You can guess how bucked I was when they walked in! And how bucked Grandfather was that we knew and liked each other.'

'Did they mind about the sort of jobs you've been doing over the last few months?' Dorothy asked, discomforted.

'Good Lord, no! They aren't a bit snobbish. Dickie's old man said I was an enterprising young blighter. Anyway, it turned out to be a good thing for Dickie too, because he's been hanging around wondering what to do. And finally, Mr

Blythe said, "How about this for a proposition? I'll employ the pair of you for a trial period of six months, but I warn you that you'll be given no special privileges. You'll work your way up the ladder rung by rung, like everybody else, and work damned hard – or I'll chuck you both out on your ears!"'

He was radiant in remembrance, tilting back perilously on the chair legs, hands in pockets, smiling back at that magical evening.

'So Dickie and I said, "Done!" and "Thanks a lot!" And then Grandfather Harland got out a bottle of champagne he'd been keeping on ice, just in case we had something to celebrate, and they toasted us.'

'Champagne?' we cried out together.

'I haven't tasted champagne since my wedding – since I married your father, Micky,' said Dorothy. 'We only had sparkling wine when Gilbert and I were . . .'

She remembered my presence, and stopped. Delight for her son mingled with regret for herself. Once more she fell to tracing that elusive pattern with her forefinger.

'I've never tasted champagne in my entire life!' I said, marvelling. 'What's it like, Micky?'

'Andrews Liver Salts with flavour!'

'Oh, Micky!' we cried reproachfully, loving him.

'I'm only kidding. It's absolutely spiffing.'

'And what's this Dickie Blythe like? Why don't you bring him home for supper one night? Tell us about him, Micky.'

'Old Dickie?' said Michael proudly. 'He's a splendid chap. A year older than me. But he's the brainy sort. They thought he would have gone to Cambridge, but Dickie says he wants to live life, not study it. So he's been looking about him for a few months – rather like me – not knowing exactly what he wanted. . . .'

'Micky,' Dorothy pleaded. 'Do stick to this job, will you, love?'

'Now what's the use of promising anything?' he asked honestly. 'But I'll say this much, Mum. I like what I hear about it, and I get on well with Dickie and I respect his old man. I think I might very well make a go of it.' Then he shrugged and said, 'Anyway, it doesn't much matter what I do, because there's going to be a war and I'll be in it. So what's the point of worrying about the future?'

I felt as though the walls of the house had fallen away, leaving us exposed to the elements. Dorothy's colour and excitement vanished.

She spoke angrily, out of shock.

'War? What war? What are you talking about?'

'My dear Mum, you should turn from fiction to fact sometime! Read the old man's *Manchester Guardian* now and again. And if you find the editorials too heavy then take a gander at Low's cartoons. Only ostriches and optimists can talk about peace. For heaven's sake, Mum, Mussolini invaded Abyssinia three months ago! Did nobody tell you?'

'I know all about that,' said Dorothy, on her dignity. 'He's one of those Nazi dictators, and he's behaving very badly indeed. Dropping incendiary bombs on grass huts, and gassing a lot of helpless natives. But Haile Selassie will win in the end. He's not called the Lion of Judah for nothing!'

She loved both name and title. They had quite a ring to them.

'Mum!' said Michael, amused and annoyed. 'Your Lion of Judah has had his mane cropped and his teeth drawn already!'

'I know, I know!' she answered, anxious to impress him, 'but that was when Sir Samuel Hoare was the Foreign Secretary. Now it's Anthony Eden and everything will be all right. I'm not silly, you know!'

Despite the shadow of war, I had to smile. Michael and Dorothy at odds with each other were a comic spectacle.

'All right? Mum, you are a source of wonder to me!' Michael cried, enraged with her. 'Why do you suppose the Home Office has instituted air raid precautions?'

'Just to be on the safe side,' said Dorothy, sticking to her argument, but she was disturbed by his seriousness.

Michael flung up his arms and let them drop, disgusted.

'Besides, Abyssinia is a long way off,' said Dorothy briskly, 'and it's not our business to interfere in other people's affairs.'

'We'll bloody well have to interfere unless the Nazis are going to goose-step all over Europe.'

'And don't use bad language in front of Evelyn!'

'She's heard it all before. And you preach to me about living in a Garden of Eden? My God, Mum, you're the one who's living there, and I can tell you that there's something a lot nastier than an angel with a flaming sword outside!'

He had her worried momentarily. Then her face cleared.

'Oh, you mean Hitler and his lot?' She shrugged Hitler away. 'Shouting and raving, and sticking his arm up in that silly salute. And that funny little moustache. Just like Charlie Chaplin. He doesn't impress me, I can tell you!'

'Well, he impresses several million Germans,' said Michael, 'and anyone who puts guns before butter isn't planning a Peace Conference!'

She was silent, afraid for him. He was making ready for war.

'Well, he won't dare attack us,' she said stoutly. 'We've got the Royal Navy to defend us. Finest fleet in the world,' she added, to comfort herself and us. 'Britons never will be slaves. There was never a truer word spoken than that.'

War was too terrible to face. She poured out tea and spoke in quite a different tone.

'Tell us, Micky. When do you start work?' she asked.

Michael shrugged at me with wry philosophy. He turned to the more pleasurable topic. I rubbed my arms which had gone cold even beneath my cardigan sleeves, and warmed my hands round the teacup.

'I'm going in tomorrow to be shown the ropes. And I've got to get a passport. And I've got to do a crash course in Spanish. Because the firm will be sending us off to Spain sometime this year, under the wing of their chief rep, to learn a bit about sherry.'

'Will you be living at home?' Dorothy asked, in hope and fear.

'I shouldn't think so, Mum.' He looked directly at her, and said, 'It won't ever work, will it?'

Her chin quivered. She shook her head, and looked down

at the tablecloth, tracing the labyrinthine pattern of her thoughts.

'It's time I left home, anyway,' he said easily. 'I'm grown up now. Dickie and I thought we might share digs in Blackstone.'

I went cold again, but this time on someone else's behalf.

'What about poor Flora?' I asked, for she was sitting at her master's feet, watching him worshipfully.

Michael's brightness dimmed for a moment.

'I hadn't thought of that. I suppose there's no way I can look after Flora. Not in digs, and racketing about in Spain.'

Dorothy frowned on me, for his triumph must not be spoiled, and said, 'That's no problem. Leave her here. We'll look after her.'

The door opened suddenly, as if to catch us unawares, and the headmaster's voice said, 'What's all this noise about?'

We began to tell him everything at once, together. He lifted his hand for silence. And silence fell.

Michael said, polite but unsmiling, 'I've got a promising job with Blythe Brothers, the wine firm in Blackstone, and I shall be living away from home permanently.'

'Good!' my father replied curtly.

Then he realised that this was ungracious and unkind, and sought to make amends.

'Well done!' he cried, as heartily as he could.

Neither Dorothy nor Michael answered him, faces averted. He tried again, on a different tack.

'I suppose you've missed the news, in all this excitement?' he offered, conciliating us for once.

Dorothy's head jerked up. She looked questioningly at him.

'The King died peacefully at five minutes to midnight,' he said. 'I happened to switch on the wireless in our bedroom.'

'Well I never!' said Dorothy, disappointed. 'Fancy me missing that, after waiting all day with him!' She looked forward to a new allegiance. 'Oh well, the Prince of Wales will bring a breath of fresh air to the monarchy. He's a real charmer. We shall see some changes at Court, I expect. Not so much of that old-fashioned protocol.'

'He's a playboy,' said my father briefly, 'who is likely to cause a great deal of trouble, in my opinion.'

Again the remark was unfortunate. Again our silence shut him out. Then Dorothy diverted the conversation.

'Whatever were you doing, listening to the wireless?' she asked curiously. 'I thought you were fast asleep!'

'No. I was awake,' he replied quietly.

In those four words he conveyed unconsciously, for he neither gave nor asked for mercy, the many Saturday nights that he had lain awake, knowing that he was excluded from our company.

None of us could think of anything to say.

'It's pretty late,' my father offered. And as we did not move or answer, he said, 'I'll be off back to bed, then. I just thought you might want to hear the news.'

I looked steadfastly down at my teacup. Dorothy retraced her pattern on the tablecloth. Michael sat at his fair young ease, balanced on the back legs of the Windsor chair, hands in pockets. Flora looked expectantly from one face to another, awaiting a signal of some kind.

Then Dorothy said, as if the words were dragged from her, 'Micky says there's going to be another war, Gil. Is he right?'

Her husband looked on her very kindly then, because she was consulting his opinion, because she was afraid for her son. But he could not, even under these circumstances, soften the truth as he knew it. He cleared his throat.

'Oh yes, we shall go to war eventually,' he said. 'Probably, knowing us, at the last possible minute and totally unprepared. I've been saying for two years that those blasted Nazis meant trouble.' Unexpectedly, he added, 'I just wish they'd let me have a crack at 'em, but I'm too old now.'

Dorothy's eyes were wet for the husband she had lost and the husband she now possessed.

'At forty-seven? You're in your prime!' she cried indignantly.

Michael's interest, even his admiration, had been caught.

He said suddenly, 'What did you do in the last war, Dad?'

The name slipped out sweetly, surprising us all. My father answered in good fellowship, touched.

'I was a junior officer in the cavalry,' he said, and gave his self-deprecating snort of laughter. 'Cavalry! A typical British anachronism. Still, it had style.'

I looked up at him then. This was the young man in him, valiant and swift and dark, whom I knew better than any of the other guises. And my father saw me looking at him, and smiled an apology for our quarrel. He held out one arm, and I got up and moved into its circle, forgiving and forgiven.

'You're tired out, my lass,' he said gently. 'You've been working too hard. Go to bed.'

But I wanted to stay a little longer and hear more.

I said, half-joking, 'I didn't know you were a cavalier, Daddy. Did you charge into the enemy, waving a sabre?'

'Good God, no. We were equipped with rifles. They'd learned that much from the Boer War. We were supposed to go in after the tanks, but I never smelled so much as a whiff of battle. Blast them!'

'Weren't the cavalry used at all?' Michael asked, interested.

'As far as I know, they were kept behind the lines. But I was late joining up. I was teaching in South Africa for the greater part of the war. I came home in nineteen-seventeen, and volunteered for service.'

Michael interrupted him eagerly.

'Didn't you have to fight if you didn't want to?'

'No, I was safe where I was, and doing a useful job. But I felt I was shirking my responsibilities. England was my country, after all. I couldn't sit by and let everybody else fight for it.'

Dorothy shook her head and smiled to herself and traced her pattern, proud of him. My father snorted again in remembrance.

'Funny thing. I hadn't seen the family for four years. I thought there'd be something of a celebration when I turned up from South Africa, telling them stories of black boys diving for pennies in the waters of the bay, of old Boer farmers and black Kaffirs and herds of wildebeest. I'd even picked up a bit of Swahili, to show off! And do you know what happened? Harold had been awarded a medal for bravery and promoted, and he was home on leave, damn him! I became part of *his* celebration! Nobody wanted to know what *I'd* been doing. Ha!'

Again we did not reply but listened in sympathy.

'They shipped us over to France,' said my father, remembering. 'Horses, men, equipment, fodder, blacksmiths – a regular circus. Put us under canvas that first night, not far from the front. And I had a nightmare. Woke up shouting and sweating at two in the morning. I dreamed I'd been so badly wounded that they couldn't staunch the blood. It kept on flowing until I was wet through. And do you know what? It had been raining heavily and I was lying in a pool of water!'

He addressed himself to Michael, who had come to rest on all four legs of the chair and was watching him intently.

'War, Mick, is mainly a wet and muddy business. Damned uncomfortable at best. And, of course, damned dangerous at worst.'

He spoke to himself now, looking into the past we had not shared.

'Funny thing, war. The sound of thunder always brings it back. Like distant guns.'

16

Civil War broke out in Spain that summer while Michael and Dickie Blythe were accustoming their palates to sherry. It was an ominous time. Somewhere, under the wing of the wine representative, they were presumably trying to get home. Between rumours and silence we could only wait and hope, and the atmosphere at the Malt-house was as heavy and sultry as the days that followed.

The High School prize-giving ceremony on the last day of term happened to be particularly important to me, for I had been awarded the Harriet Harcourt Music Cup, given annually to the most promising student, and would play Ravel's *Jeux d'eau* to the assembled parents to show them how richly I deserved it. This triumph was shadowed from the beginning, since Grizedale's prize-giving coincided with that of Blackstone High School, so my father would not be able to come. Now, at the last minute, Dorothy refused to leave the house in case Michael telephoned.

My father permitted himself the vestige of a rebuke.

'If you stay at home, Dorrie, none of us will be there to see Evie collect her music prize.'

'Then I'll ask Kate if she can go instead of me. I'll just give her a ring. You'd like Aunt Kate to go, wouldn't you, Evie?'

I would have preferred it, but Aunt Kate had an unbreakable engagement somewhere else.

My father was becoming exasperated.

'But can't you find anyone who will sit by the telephone while you're away? You talk to enough people, God knows, surely one of them would help?'

But Dorothy could think of nothing but her son.

'If the prize-giving's as important to you as all that, why can't you get the deputy headmaster to take your place for once?' she cried.

She collected herself.

'It's not that I don't care about your prize, Evie,' she said to me, quickly. 'I'm just as proud of you as your father is. But I can't go. I can't. I couldn't rest in my seat for wondering whether Micky had tried to get in touch and I wasn't there.'

A family row on top of the other tensions would be too much. I decided to waive my rights.

'It's quite all right. I do understand.'

All the same I felt she had let me down badly. I knew that Clara would have come to see me on my day of glory, and put a smiling face on the event though she awaited news of half a dozen sons.

Dorothy sought some way to make amends, and found the wrong one.

'Anyway, you needn't worry about going to your music lesson afterwards,' she said. 'It would be too much for you as well as everything else. I'll cancel it.'

'No!' I cried, knowing that an hour with Lilian Lacey would compensate for what the day must inevitably lack.

She was so taken aback that I said more quietly, 'No, thank you. I shall manage it all perfectly well.'

My father backed this decision with deep approval.

'And while we're on the subject of Michael,' he added firmly, 'you should remember, Dorothy, that he holds a British passport and Britain is not at war with Spain. They've got enough trouble on their hands without upsetting neutral countries and causing diplomatic incidents. You must remember, too, that the telephone lines will be down and any form of transport will be difficult to find. But he's a resourceful chap, and used to looking after himself. He'll be in touch as soon as he can, and he wouldn't want you to be upsetting yourself.'

He looked at the clock.

'It's time Julian was off to school, so I'll take him on my way to Grizedale's. I don't want him to be kept at home, as he was yesterday. He can't do anything, and he can only be disturbed if he sees you crying. We must carry on as usual, Dorothy.'

'Besides,' I said confidently, 'Mick's luck is proverbial!'

Dorothy could only nod and try to smile. Her life had centred on wireless and telephone since the previous weekend. Her anxiety for Michael was genuine and deep but her way of dealing with any crisis was to dramatise it. She would have liked us all to suspend our daily lives until we knew he was safe.

So this day, which should have been my own and triumphant, hung on me like a winter overcoat: hot, heavy and cumbersome. Resentfully, I cleared my desk and locker of belongings and travelled home laden with books and sports equipment to find Dorothy still sitting by a silent telephone. Typically, she offered me a sandwich and forgot to ask about my prize. Whereupon, I refused all offers of sustenance, washed my hands and face, picked up my music-case, and the precious Harriet Harcourt music cup which no member of my family had seen me receive, and stalked out in a fury to catch the five-fifteen tram.

At Dowson-under-Fell the day was illumined by Lilian Lacey, who dispensed praise for my achievement, admiration for the cup, sympathy for my family's absence, and hope for Michael. She had a way of delighting and soothing which no one else could match. Temporarily mollified, I sat down to play, but all my energy had gone into the public performance of *Jeux d'eau*. My fingers either fumbled or fell like lead upon the piano keys. Lilian herself, though she had lit up beautifully at first, now seemed colourless and leaden. And whereas we were usually too absorbed to watch the clock, today we stopped promptly at a quarter past six.

She ordered iced lemonade for us both, and rested her head on the back of the armchair, exhausted. For me, on the other hand, the burden of the day began to slip from my shoulders. Obstacles surmounted, disappointments survived, tasks completed, I felt pleased with myself, inclined to chatter. Conversation with my music teacher was doubly sweet these days, for recently she had given me permission to address her as Lilian, a privilege which I vaunted on all occasions.

'I wish we had a refrigerator, Lilian,' I said, dunking ice cubes down with my straw. 'I'd have nothing but iced drinks all the time.'

She opened her eyes and smiled at the ceiling.

'I think you might find that the novelty wore off after a month or so!' she remarked mildly.

'When I grow up,' I continued, 'I'm going to live exactly as you do. I think you've got absolutely everything that anyone could want.'

She turned her head to one side and looked at me. Her expression was affectionate and ironic.

'Do you indeed?' she replied, amused. 'I lead an independent and comfortable existence, I agree, but most people would say that I was missing the best part of a woman's life.'

'Oh, you mean husbands and babies and things,' I said, and dunked another ice cube thoughtfully to the bottom of my glass.

D. H. Lawrence had persuaded me that lovers should not, even excitingly could not, be kept at a distance.

'But how can a woman have everything,' I asked myself and her, 'when men need such a lot of attention? I don't want to live like my stepmother, just running a family and a home. But women with a career and a family, such as Jill Babbage's mother, live like the Red Queen, running to stay in the same place. And what else is there?'

The smile lingered in Lilian's eyes and on her lips but she did not answer. I glanced up self-consciously, realising that I had been rattling on without a response, and rather too personally.

'Am I talking too much?' I asked. And, as she shook her head, 'Are you not feeling very well, Lilian?'

'I find this weather oppressive,' she replied listlessly.

Then she made an effort, and in her usual wry manner added, 'But I love to hear you philosophising about life, so do go on!'

'I've said something funny, haven't I? I just wish I knew what it was, because I'm being deadly serious. I'm a quiet person most of the time, then suddenly I burst out and can't stop. Daddy still calls me "Chatterbox"! When I was young he used to buy *Chatterbox Annual* for me every Christmas. And, do you know, I always thought they published it because of me!'

The doorbell rang. Lilian lifted her head and listened to the voices in the hall. Her demeanour changed instantly from apathy to a curious mixture of apprehension and expectation.

'I believe that's the father of one of my pupils,' she said, 'which means a minor crisis of some kind. Do you mind awfully, Evelyn, if I bundle you off instead of offering you another iced drink?'

'No, of course not! I've just finished, and I really ought to go!'

I jumped up to slip the music sheets inside my case.

'Dr Nash, madam,' said the maid. 'Wanting to know if you can spare a minute now, or shall he call back at a more convenient time?'

'Oh, I'll see him now, Mary. Evelyn is just going. Show him in.'

I stood with the music sheets in my hand, transfixed.

'I didn't know one of Dr Nash's daughters was your pupil. His eldest daughter, Marianne, was my best friend at Townley's. I haven't seen her since I left. . . .'

As a child I had been convinced that my father was right to send us to Moss Lane. As a young adult I was inclined to question this educational experiment. For Michael it had failed completely. For me it had cost four years of friendless exile, and by the time I regained social status Marianne Nash had gone to boarding school.

Lilian looked surprised, began to speak, checked herself, and said, 'I didn't realise that Townley's drew pupils from such a wide area. So you and Dr Nash will know each other?'

And Philip Nash, coming in with a smile, one hand outstretched to the teacher, was also surprised to recognise her pupil.

He stopped short and said, 'Is it Evelyn Fawley? Good heavens! I haven't seen you for donkey's years!'

Then he possibly remembered why, for he looked embarrassed.

He was a quietly charming and perceptive man, very proud of his fashionable wife and their four daughters. I had often wished he were our family doctor. He reminded me a little of Leslie Howard the film star, with his smiling eyes and high forehead, and fair hair that would wave in spite of being smoothed down with brilliantine.

'You were forgetting, Dr Nash,' said Lilian, into a difficult silence, 'that little girls grow up into young ladies!'

He smiled, picked up her cue, and said cheerfully, 'Yes, of course. You and Marianne used to hold dolls' tea parties, didn't you, Evelyn? Marianne is seventeen now. She'll be pleased to know that I've seen you. She must give you a ring sometime.'

Unimportant though this meeting had been, it depressed me. I had long since accepted the loss of Marianne Nash, had indeed replaced her with other friends and virtually forgotten her. Now I was troubled, standing at the tram stop in the early evening. Perhaps it was the phrase he used, so like the one with which the Harlands kept Dorothy at arm's length.

'She must give you a ring sometime.'

As Dorothy would say, 'That's not a proper invitation!'

With a flash of pride and perversity I resolved to telephone Marianne when I got home, and invite her to tea just to embarrass her. And then I walked into an atmosphere both light and joyful, and my Marianne-shaped cloud drifted away with it.

Dorothy was clicking the receiver into place, and turned round, crying, 'Oh, thank God! Micky's just telephoned, Evie. He's in London. He's safe! And you'll never guess what . . .'

'Oh, don't tell me!' I groaned in mock horror. 'He's missed the last train to Blackstone and he's living it up with Dickie and the wine representative – probably at the Savoy! Honestly! Oh, but I'm glad, I'm glad.'

We hugged each other spontaneously. We drew self-consciously apart.

'And he's coming over with Dickie tomorrow night,' Dorothy continued, 'so we shall hear all about it. My word, what an experience, eh? Fancy being on the spot when a war breaks out! Well, I'm blessed. I'm just going upstairs to tell your father. Oh, did your lesson go well? And was Miss Lacey pleased about your prize? Good! There's a plate of salad in the meat-safe for you, and some bread and butter, and I've set the coffee percolator ready, and there's a bowl of fresh fruit on the sideboard. Look after yourself, love.'

And she mounted the stairs, humming 'The Fleet's in Port Again'.

There was a gulf between her adoration of Michael and her good-natured indifference to me which I could only bridge with irony.

'And so the lady snaps her fingers,' I said aloud to the empty kitchen, 'at the Spanish Civil War – and, of course, the Harriet Harcourt Music Cup!'

17

December 1936

As a family we knew how to celebrate Christmas. From the first carol to the final thank-you letter we lived in a world immeasurably brighter and kinder than its usual self. And the older I grew the better Christmas became, because now I could help to create it.

Blackstone High School ended its autumn term soon after lunch, so I arrived home as the afternoon began to wane but before it grew dark. And in this primrose light I stood for a few moments, listening to the tram clatter off towards Dowson-under-Fell, watching the smoke of Kersley's mill chimneys send signals into the winter sky.

Presents for those I loved best had been bought from Barber's of Blackstone. They swung from my fingers in an elegant brown and gold carrier bag: the result of much saving and cogitation. My thoughts on their reception, and the pleasure on both sides when they were unwrapped, mingled with the sights and sounds of that late December day. I watching and listened for a while longer before marching briskly down the lane towards Dorothy's promise of afternoon tea, with fresh cream cakes from Clough's Bakery to celebrate the beginning of the Christmas holidays.

As I hurried along I rehearsed a speech for Dorothy's private ear. Its tone and content had changed a dozen times but its message remained the same: I could no longer help her with the evening washing-up, on top of School Certificate homework and music lessons. How to say this nicely and effectively had puzzled me for some time. I hoped, with the approach of Christmas, for a seasonal response.

But as soon as I put my head round the drawing-room door, I could tell that Dorothy was in a dangerous mood. Some crisis, personal or national, had occurred within the past hour or so. Her eyelids were pink, as if she had been crying, and yet there was an air of exultation about her.

The unknown lady visitor, sitting with her back to me, was wearing a smart little Tyrolean hat with a scarlet feather. She had slung her coat and silver fox furs carelessly over the arm of the leather sofa. The label on the thick soft coat read *Barber's French Collection.* Tea had been poured, but not drunk. On the round Indian brass table between the two women sat a plate of Clough's finest cream cakes, untouched.

And now Dorothy rose from her chair as she caught sight of me, and spoke in the high and thrilling tones which heralded a first-class domestic drama.

'Ah, here's *my* lovely grown-up daughter! Come in, Evie, dear. There's someone here you were very fond of, many years ago. And she's longing to meet you again.'

Oh God, I thought, either she's had an absolutely stinking row with Daddy, or Mick's decided to join the International Brigade instead of being a wine merchant, and gone to fight in Spain, or King Edward's changed his mind about abdicating and marrying Mrs Simpson and come back to reclaim the throne. And what on earth is this strange lady doing here?

In spite of these heretical thoughts I came forward, composed and charming as befitted the role of Dorothy's lovely grown-up daughter, and smiled upon the visitor, hand outstretched.

Far from being eager to meet me, this lady had now risen and was making nervous movements towards her expensive coat and silvery furs, anxious to depart. She had a high-nosed handsome face, heavily powdered around the eyes to hide tear-stains.

'Now, Evie, Evie. You don't need me to tell you who this

is!' Dorothy said roguishly. And rescued me by saying, 'Nice Mrs Nash!'

'Mrs Nash! Of course!' I said, as if I remembered perfectly.

The lady merely touched my fingers in passing, for she was picking up her handbag.

'Now isn't this a lovely surprise?' Dorothy cried. 'Would you ever have guessed?'

'Lovely!' I said, completely puzzled. And, 'No, I wouldn't!'

I knew Dorothy's weakness for engineering dramatic surprises, but did wonder as to the purpose of this one. I had never mentioned meeting Dr Nash in the summer and resenting Marianne's silence, so it could hardly have been an effort at reconciliation on Dorothy's part.

'I'm afraid I must be going,' said Mrs Nash, looking past me. 'You do understand, don't you, dear Mrs Fawley?'

Dear Mrs Fawley evidently did, and gave a tragic nod.

'Thank you so much. You have been so kind,' her visitor continued. 'So very kind. We really must . . .'

Whatever her intention, it tailed away into silence. Now she looked bleakly from Dorothy to me, who was taller than either of them.

'I should never have recognised you, Evelyn!' she said, and gave the light and artificial laugh which I remembered. 'You used to be such a quaint old-fashioned little creature! Still, no wonder you've changed so much, with a kind person like your stepmother. . . .'

She succeeded in making the fox bite on his woven black silk chain, though her fingers trembled. In the mirror on the wall she adjusted the angle of her Tyrolean hat, and tidied her hair. She tucked her handbag under her arm.

'Thank you so much!' she said again, holding out a gloved hand to Dorothy, who clasped it in both of hers.

'*I'll* show you to the door, my dear,' said Dorothy warmly, as if she simply could not bring herself to call the parlour-maid on such an auspicious occasion.

'Goodbye, Evelyn,' said Mrs Nash over one furred shoulder. 'So nice to have met you again.'

'Yes, indeed. Goodbye, Mrs Nash,' I answered automatically, but did not resist adding, 'Do remember me to Marianne. I really must give her a ring sometime!'

Dorothy returned in the role of Lady Bracknell: a part she had played with considerable success in Hathersall's autumn production of *The Importance of Being Earnest*. Her curious exultation had vanished. She was sombre and dignified.

She intoned the words, 'I have been deeply shocked!'

'Oh dear. I'll make some fresh tea, shall I?' I said callously, tired of the scene before it began.

Intending me to be her audience, she ignored the remark.

'It was all so sudden. I couldn't believe it. I still can't. To think of Mrs Nash sitting here, confiding in me as if we were sisters! We rarely meet, and yet we can talk as if we'd known each other all our lives. . . .'

Detecting a flaw in Dorothy's tale, I pounced unkindly on it.

'I didn't know you'd *ever* met!' I said, emptying cold tea vigorously into the china slop basin. 'Mrs Nash lives way out at Dowson-under-Fell, and our family parted company with her before you married my father. So why did you assume I was fond of her when you couldn't have known one way or the other? I happen to dislike her.'

Dorothy was studying an oval picture of a Greek lady gathering shells on the seashore, which hung on the far wall.

'The Ways of Providence are wondrous strange,' she murmured.

I had noticed on previous occasions that when my stepmother was acting out a scene she remained deaf to unsympathetic comments. For once I refused to play back to her or be silenced.

'Mrs Nash always patronised me, and even as a small child I resented it. But after she wrote that letter to Grandma Fawley I positively hated her. I heard Aunt Kate telling Aunt Maud about it. Marianne had told her I was going to Moss Lane School, and she penned one of her beastly pink notes – the sort that has a spray of briar roses in one corner and scalloped edges and smells sickly! – sorrowing because I was bound to lose all my nice friends, and could Grandma not use her influence with my dear clever father etc? Rotten snob. . . .'

'No, I never would have believed it!' said Dorothy dreamily, to the lady on the seashore.

'. . . and Grandma was silly enough, or aggravating enough, to tell Daddy – though Aunt Kate strongly advised her not to! – and they had an almighty row over that letter, I can tell you!'

I glared at Dorothy's back. She paused before a copy of Joseph Farquharson's *Glowed with Tints of Evening Hours* and conducted a little stage business. She straightened the heavy gilded frame. I picked up the tray, prepared to walk out on this performance.

'We were strangers, and yet she threw herself on my mercy,' Dorothy said, smiling in sad reminiscence. 'It was strangely moving.'

I stopped at the door and replied briefly and sensibly, as my father would have done.

'I shouldn't tell Daddy she's been here, if I were you. He'll be simply furious. He never forgives or forgets an enemy.'

Dorothy, brought down to earth, cried, 'Don't you adopt that tone with me, my lady, because I won't have it!'

'Look, I'm sorry if you're upset about Mrs Nash, but I really do need a cup of tea. I've been hauling my school kit all round Blackstone, buying Christmas presents, and I'm jolly tired.'

Surprisingly, for one could never be quite sure how Dorothy would respond, she dropped the role of Lady Bracknell.

'Then we'll have a cup of tea together. I rather wanted to have a little private talk, and we're not often by ourselves.'

Disconcerted, I said, 'Yes. No. Where's Julian?'

Dorothy put one hand on my arm, a gesture which I detested and suspected, and said, 'I took him down to Aunt Kate for the afternoon. The matter was of the utmost urgency.'

'In that case,' I replied, making the best of things, 'I must confess that I was hoping to have a private talk, too.'

The remarks we exchanged while replenishing the contents of the Indian brass tea-table were of little importance. I sat and sipped and waited, knowing that Dorothy could not contain whatever confidence was in store.

Surprisingly, she asked, 'How's Miss Lacey these days?'

She was jealous of Lilian, so I answered cautiously.

'Oh, much as usual. Apart from the weather.'

'The weather? What's wrong with the weather?' Dorothy demanded in her usual robust fashion. 'Or perhaps I should say,' she added with a light and artificial laugh which she had evidently learned from Mrs Nash that afternoon, 'what's right with it?'

I answered reluctantly, 'She's sensitive to changes in the weather. She was very tired in the summer. The heat oppressed her.'

'And now, I suppose,' said Dorothy, 'the cold numbs her?'

No longer acting, she looked hostile, spoke sarcastically.

'Has Miss Lacey ever mentioned leaving Dowson-under-Fell?'

'No,' I said, accepting a cream cake. 'No, I can't say she has!'

'I think you may very well find that she does.'

I set the cream cake down, feeling slightly sick.

'Of course, this mustn't go any further,' said Dorothy, 'but I feel you have a right to be warned.'

She bit generously into her own cake and watched my face as she munched. I did not answer. I recognised a personal attack, though why and about what I could not imagine. Her exultant air was unmistakable. She delivered herself of her news without finesse.

'Miss Lacey has been having an affair with Dr Nash for several months. And his wife has found out. She came to tell me.'

I folded my arms in a self-protective gesture as Dorothy cast the first stones, speaking with a familiarity bred of contempt.

'I'm not exonerating Philip Nash, but if a man's tempted

he's likely to fall. Lily Lacey should have been married years ago.'

She corrupted Lilian's name with delight, and smiled at my involuntary frown.

'This is what's likely to happen to an unsatisfied spinster of her age. Naturally she feels that life's passed her by. So she's set her cap at Philip Nash, and he's fallen for her. More fool him!'

My silence, composed of shock, distaste and growing anger, commanded Dorothy's attention.

She said, 'But I suppose you think that Miss Lacey – or *Lilian* as she asked you to call her, and I never thought much of that idea! – I suppose you think she's beyond criticism? Or don't you believe me?'

I set out to hurt her as she had hurt me.

'Oh, I believe that you're repeating what Mrs Nash told you, but she's nothing better than a social leech. I expect Dr Nash admires a woman like Lilian, who has style and quality and independence.'

Dorothy gave a laugh which was probably meant to be derisive but sounded uncertain. I attacked her from a different angle.

'Besides, it's only a couple of weeks since you were glued either to the wireless or the telephone, because of the King being in love with Mrs Simpson. That little contretemps cost a throne and a divorce, but what did you say when he abdicated? "Ah yes! The world well lost for love!" Or am I misquoting you?'

'Don't you talk down to me like that!' said Dorothy sharply.

'I won't talk to you at all. I'll take my tea elsewhere and drink it by myself in peace. I despise spiteful gossip.'

In one of her sudden bursts of temper, she cried, 'You'll stay here until I've finished speaking. Do you know that Mrs Nash is perfectly entitled to get a divorce and have her husband's name struck from the Medical Register? Do you know that she could ruin him? And instead of that, she's hushing the whole thing up. She's prepared to take him back. She's forgiving him.'

She deepened her voice when she pronounced the word *forgiving* and this annoyed me so much that I could have hit her.

I heard my father's biting commonsense in my reply.

'But if she ruined her husband she wouldn't have any money either, and then she'd have to cancel her account at Barber's of Blackstone, and the lady wouldn't like that, I can tell you! So it's to her advantage to take him back, as you call it. And what do you mean by saying *take him back*? He hasn't exactly left home, has he?'

'It's a manner of speaking. And I object to your tone!'

I did not care a fig for her objections.

'And how can you say that Mrs Nash is hushing it up? She came sneaking down here to tell *you* – and she doesn't even know you.'

'It was a kindness on her part,' said Dorothy loftily. 'She's found out the names of all Miss Lacey's pupils, and she's contacting their mothers to warn them. Oh yes, in the end Lily Lacy will have to leave Dowson-under-Fell. Mrs Nash will see to that!'

Now we were talking at the top of our voices. Standing up, with the tea-table between us like a brass referee.

'And why should Lilian be persecuted for the pair of them? That's downright immoral!'

'Immoral? Mrs Nash has given the best years of her life to that man. And what thanks does she get? He goes off with another woman.'

'But he *hasn't* gone off with her!' I cried. 'He's at home, being forgiven – God help him! Being *taken back*, as you put it. Oh, why can you never tell the plain honest truth, for heaven's sake?'

Dorothy stopped short as if I had winded her. There was a brief silence as we both gathered breath and strength.

'Are you saying that you approve of Lilian Lacey having an affair with a married man?' she asked, bridling.

'I'm saying that *if* they're having an affair, and we have only Mrs Nash's word for that, can you blame him? After all, what is Mrs Nash but a shallow-minded little snob who was once clever enough to make a good marriage?'

The allusion was not lost on her. She answered me with deadly deliberation.

'I thought I'd brought you up better than that!'

I told her something I had wanted to say for years.

'You haven't brought me up at all. You've fed me and ordered me about and never once considered how I felt. You don't talk to me, you talk at me. You're talking at me now. You're telling me what you think and what you want me to think, and you're wasting your time because I shall make up my own mind. Brought me up? You don't even know me!'

She sat quite still, registering the enormity of my words. Then she lost control.

'I might not have Lilian Lacey's style and quality,' she cried, 'but I'm not silly. Don't know you? I know you like the back of my hand. You're jealous and you're possessive. That's you. You never wanted your father to remarry. You'd rather he wasted his life mourning over that mother of yours. And you made your mind up a long time ago that I wasn't good enough for him or you.'

I had reaped the whirlwind. Fear sobered my anger, but I would not apologise. I stared back at her disdainfully.

'I'll tell you how well I know you, Evelyn Fawley. You think that music teacher looks like your mother, don't you? That's why you've made a little tin god out of her.'

She nodded her head, satisfied that she had scored a hit.

'Well, you're right. She's very like your mother. Clara Fawley was having an affair with another man before she died in that road accident. That's how much she thought of you and your father. Having an affair. And your father found out. And they had a terrible row.'

I put one hand out to the mantelpiece to steady myself.

'What would have happened eventually, I don't know. They patched things up for your sake. Yes, yours. Anyway, a few weeks later she walked smack into a car – daydreaming like you, I suppose, instead of looking where she was going. He'd have been all right by himself, but of course he was saddled with you. Somebody had to look after you. So he went back to his mother, and he was trapped there until he met me.'

Her voice changed. She spoke with sympathy and affection.

'We were both lonely, and we had a situation in common. We needed marriage and a home for ourselves and our children. He didn't attempt to hide anything from me. He told me things he could have spared himself. And then he said, "But I've finished with the past, and I've finished with Clara. Let's make a fresh start."'

Words and anger spent, there was a long silence.

At last Dorothy said, conscience-stricken, 'Mind you, your father would be very sorry to think you knew about that.'

I answered contemptuously as she hesitated over her next request.

'You needn't worry. I shan't tell him I know. Nor who told me.'

'Well, that would be best,' said Dorothy, crushed.

Our roles were reversed but my victory was a dark and bitter one. I felt the approach of tears, like a bubble swelling in my throat, and brought the words out brusquely.

'What happens about my music lessons? Are you going to cancel them now, or wait until Lilian says she's leaving, or what? I must know where I stand. I can't go there and pretend nothing's wrong.'

She was anxious to help me.

'Oh, don't you worry about that. I'll tell your father tonight, and let you know his decision. There won't be any unpleasantness. She'll just be made aware that everyone disapproves.'

I made my way slowly to the door.

'Where are you going?' Dorothy asked, alarmed.

'Only upstairs to my room. I want to be by myself for a while.'

'Should I fetch your supper on a tray?'

'No, thank you. If I'm hungry I can always come down and get an apple or make a sandwich. I don't feel like eating just now.'

'I've told you too much. I should never have said all that.'

'I'd rather have the truth.'

'Shall I give you a drop of brandy? You're very white-faced.'

'No, thank you. It would make me feel sick.'

'But what shall I tell your father when he comes home? You know what a state he gets in if he knows you've gone to bed upset.'

'Then don't tell him I'm upset,' I replied wearily. 'Just say that I've been doing my Christmas shopping and I'm tired.'

Dorothy followed me out helplessly. She even wrung her hands, though the gesture was sincere, not theatrical.

From the foot of the stairs she called up, 'Evie. I'm sorry. I do wish I hadn't told you. I do wish it hadn't happened!'

From the sanctuary of my bedroom doorway, I managed to say patiently, even reassuringly, 'I'd rather know the truth.'

'Evie? Evie? Just a minute. I want to say . . . I want . . . Evie, I know you've never liked calling me *mother*. And I understand. I do, really. And you're a young lady now. Sixteen. You can call me *Dorothy* if you like. I'll explain to your father that I feel we're friends more than mother and daughter. Is that a good idea?'

I held on to the door jamb as if it were a perfect gentle knight who alone could uphold me.

'Thank you,' I said. 'I should prefer that. Dorothy.'

She remembered something.

'What was it you wanted to have a talk about, Evie?'

I remembered the innocent request I had been nursing on the way home. It was a small point, but still valid.

'I just meant to ask you if I could skip the evening washing-up. I can't manage it as well as piano practice and swotting.'

She was so glad to be able to do something for me that her voice lifted, her face shone. She even invented a tale to fit the occasion.

'It's funny you should mention that. I was saying to your father, only the other evening, that you had too much work to do. Besides, you mustn't spoil your hands for piano playing. I'll stack the dishes and leave them for Mrs Inchmore in future.'

Wildly, I wondered what other requests she would grant, were I able to think of any.

Instead I said stiffly, 'Thank you very much!' And, interpreting her expression, 'Thanks a lot, Dorothy.'

Satisfied, Dorothy nodded and walked briskly towards the kitchen. Already recovering from a scene it would choose to forget, that amazing mind of hers was focused on the evening meal.

I closed and locked the door and sat on the edge of my bed for a long time. Then I lifted Clara's embroidered shawl from its wrappings and crept into bed with it, and lay there tearless and empty, holding it in my arms like a dead child, looking out beyond the bare beech trees to Tarn How.

18

The night was long, anguished and valuable. I drew no comfort from it, but I survived and learned from the experience. Now I was on my own. Michael, an earlier deserter, had gone for good. Lilian Lacey would be going. Clara, as I knew her, had never existed, and my father was her enemy. On the other hand, I had the measure of Dorothy. I slept shallowly for an hour or so, and woke in command of the situation. True, my position was nothing wonderful. It reminded me of a cartoon in a war-time *Boys' Own Annual* belonging to Uncle Eric, which depicted soldiers sheltering in a desolate shell-hole, and bore the caption, 'If you know of a better 'ole, go to it!'

Going downstairs the following morning, stubborn and pale-faced, I found Dorothy presiding in a subdued manner over the breakfast table and my father standing on his principles.

'I will not be influenced by common gossip. . . .' he was saying.

On seeing me he fell silent and returned to his newspaper, while Dorothy poured my tea and looked guilty.

'You're a bit pale!' she said to me.

'Oh, it's nothing much. I think I may be starting a cold.'

This mythical cold, which threatened me throughout the Christmas holiday, was my sword and buckler. It excused me from spending too much energy on outward events, and enabled me to come to terms with a new Lilian and a new Clara.

I should have had a lesson that afternoon, but a telephone

call from Lilian suggested that she was also in retreat from the outside world. Her voice sounded light, brisk and brittle.

'Evelyn dear, I've had an unexpected invitation from some old friends to spend Christmas and New Year with them, so I'm having to cancel today's lessons. I shall be away until the middle of January. I'll call you when I get back. Meanwhile, have a lovely time and enjoy yourself, won't you?'

Dorothy said later that Lilian had gone to a London hotel, and Philip Nash joined her there when he had done his Christmas duty at home. It may or may not have been true. I never found out.

Mrs Nash's campaign took less than two months to come to a successful conclusion, and was conducted in whispers. No one accused or confronted Lilian, they simply took their children away and sent them elsewhere. The parents of the few who remained, though under social pressure to conform, hung on. We went through the process of teaching and learning automatically, as a matter of principle. The atmosphere was tense as if we were waiting for something to happen. Lilian's maid gave in her notice, fearing that she might become unemployable if she did not leave the ship before it sank. And on the penultimate day of February we had a four-day blizzard which brought down telephone wires and snowed us up with thirteen-foot drifts. As winter was transformed into cold spring Lilian wrote a gently ironic letter to my father. For reasons of health, she said, she would be leaving northern England and going south in search of a milder climate. Before she went she would like to know that my future music lessons were in good hands, and wondered whether he would allow her to choose my next teacher? She was sad to terminate the close relationship with me and the very pleasant one with my family, and she thanked him for his kindness in the past.

Dorothy read the letter with a hint of chagrin.

'Why did she write it particularly to you?' she asked my father.

He did not answer her, for he realised as I did that Lilian was being true to the situation. She knew whose side Dorothy would be on, and which parent was genuinely interested in my future.

When he showed the letter to me he adopted Lilian's manner of admitting nothing and signifying much, and spoke a little louder than usual so that Dorothy should hear him as she bustled about.

'I shall write to Miss Lacey at once, saying that the north will be the poorer for her absence, and hoping that she finds a southern climate more equable, and I shall assure her that any advice she gives will be appreciated. I think that sums it up, don't you?'

I nodded and hugged him.

The veil of secrecy could neither be lifted nor rent, and so I did not thank him openly for his championship. I have often wondered why he adopted this attitude towards a woman accused of adultery, for he was a strict moralist. But he had not forgotten that Mrs Nash once tried to influence Grandma against him, and was instrumental in exiling me from my Townley friends. He may well have suspected her of acting out of jealousy, and so believed Lilian to be innocent of one sin simply because he had found Mrs Nash guilty of another.

On that April evening in 1937 I arrived early for my farewell to Lilian, and she was late in making a farewell of her own. I rang the front doorbell, peeped through the windows of the empty parlour and empty music-room, and finally walked round to the back of the house, which had never been the same since Mary left. The kitchen door stood partially open. Philip Nash must have been about to go and found yet one more lover's reason to delay.

They had been picnicking together in a curious mixture of the casual and the formal. The table was spread with an ordinary red gingham cloth, but daffodils had been arranged in a silver fluted vase at the table centre and the cutlery was monogrammed. Had she cooked for them? The humble remains of what Dorothy would refer to as 'a quick fry-up' littered two kitchen plates. A bottle of red wine presiding over the feast was still half-full.

They had heard the bell and misjudged the length of time

to answer it. They stood as close as they could, arms around each other's necks, looking not speaking. I had believed that he could be in love with her, worship her from a distance, but I had thought them both too old for passion. Now I felt their physical closeness as strongly as I had in reading of Ursula with Skrebensky. And though they were the same age group as my father and Dorothy I saw them as young again.

Then Philip Nash sighed and released her and stepped back.

He said, 'I must go. And you must open the door, my love.'

His last two words struck two chords: one in my throat and the other in the pit of my stomach. I would have given anything at that moment if some man called me his love like that. I knew for the first time that I was lonely, and this was a revelation. Enthralled, I continued to watch and listen, though honour told me to leave at once.

He put out one hand and touched her cheek, so reverently and with such exquisite care that it seemed he was afraid she might break. With equal care and reverence he leaned forward and kissed her on the lips, which my lips registered, and as she closed her eyes I closed my own.

In a moment the spell was broken.

'I must go!' he repeated, this time with more authority.

Mesmerised, I retreated to the back gate and crept down the back lane. I took three deep breaths to revive myself. At the front door I rang enquiringly, as if I had been waiting only a little while.

Lilian Lacey let me in with her usual smile of greeting, and though she sounded slightly breathless, she spoke as though this were a casual visit instead of a farewell.

'Sorry, my dear, I was packing crockery and pans in the kitchen and I'm still not used to answering the bell myself! Ridiculous, isn't it, to depend upon other people to do the simplest things? You've arrived at exactly the right moment. Come into the parlour. I've sorted out the last lot of books, the end is in sight, and I'm just about to take a break. That tea-chest is already nailed down. You should find it quite comfortable with a cushion on top.'

As I took off my best hat and coat, and put my gloves and handbag on the hallstand, she chattered on to fill up the silence of a house which is about to be left empty.

'Have you seen Gary Cooper in *Mr Deeds Goes to Town* at the Hippodrome? Or Charlie Chaplin in *Modern Times* at the Theatre Royal? They're both awfully good. I've been gadding about more than usual. I'm planning to catch up on the London shows when I reach Surrey. What a bother packing is! It's the small objects which make all the work. The large ones are just picked up and carted away!'

She chatted brightly at first, then the smile faded from her eyes and mouth. The only colour in her face came from the proximity of a little scarlet silk scarf tucked into the neck of her dress. She picked up a duster and put it down again. She sat on another tea-chest opposite. She spoke directly, acknowledging that I knew the real reason for her departure.

'I'm glad your father let you come and say goodbye. He's one of the few parents who has extended me that courtesy. He's been remarkably civilised about the whole wretched business, and I do appreciate that.'

I nodded, unable to speak.

'My dear girl, truly this isn't the end of the world.'

'It feels like the end of the world to me.'

'Yes, it will. This is probably your first sight of the social animal with its teeth bared. I can't say I've been hunted down before, but I've seen others at bay. Not a pretty spectacle!'

My colour and temper returned.

'I won't hear a word against you, or speak to anyone who does! It's no better than passing you the Black Spot, or giving you the White Feather!' I said with the utmost vehemence.

Lilian's smile shone spontaneously this time.

'You're still a funny little thing!' she said.

'I'm not little,' I said indignantly. 'I'm as tall as you!'

Then I laughed, slightly shamefaced, realising that I was taking a joke seriously. Lilian smiled back, but she could not sit still. She got up off the tea-chest and walked over to the window, arms folded. The curtains had not yet been drawn. In the street, the lamplighter was moving from post to iron post with his magic wand. As he passed, each gas-lamp shone forth in the dusk, bearing a misty halo, casting a pool of light on to the glistening pavement beneath.

'How long have I been teaching you, Evelyn? Six years? Six very important years in your musical life.'

I was young and passionate in my affections, anxious that she should understand my own suffering.

'All I can think of is how sorry I shall be when you've gone!'

She answered me with a kindness and wisdom which I was only to appreciate some wiser and kinder years later.

'I should be sorry if you weren't, for I shall miss you very much. You've been a source of comfort and delight to me, both as a pupil and as a person. But you know, my dear, personal considerations apart, I believe you will actually benefit from a change of teacher now. And your father has been kind enough, not only to ask my advice but to take it. . . .'

I nodded and swallowed.

'Good and bad fortune are usually mingled,' Lilian continued. 'In this case you're going to benefit by someone else's hardship. At the end of last year a distinguished Jewish professor of music, Aaron Feinberg, fled to England from Germany. We met at the Blackstone Music Society. He and his wife are living in rooms in the suburbs there. His natural sphere is immeasurably greater than his present position, and he is a far better teacher and musician than I could ever hope to be.'

She lifted one hand as my head came up.

'No loyalty, please. I'm being objective and should like you to be. Professor Feinberg is elderly, and he's lost everything, and must earn some sort of living. So he teaches part-time at the College of Music and takes in private pupils. I have asked him to consider you.'

I bent my head in silent response.

Lilian said persuasively, 'Perhaps you don't realise how extremely lucky you are? Your parents could never have afforded to send you over to Germany to be taught by him. In normal circumstances you would never have been offered such a splendid opportunity. I want you to make the most of it.'

A gleam of hope and ambition lit the dark wood in which I walked at that time, and this time I smiled at her.

'That's better,' she said, and smiled back. 'You see, I'm hoping that music will play quite an important part in your life, Evelyn.'

It was the opportunity for which I had waited.

I said, 'I should like music to be the whole of my life.'

She did not answer, trying to decipher my exact meaning, possibly hoping that I did not mean exactly what I said.

'I want to be a concert pianist, Lilian.'

As soon as I had spoken the words I knew that they had altered the mood of the evening. She hesitated by the window and then came and sat down again on the tea-chest opposite.

She said uneasily, 'Of course, you've worked tremendously hard and well, and you're very talented, but I had no idea . . . you keep your deepest thoughts and feelings very much to yourself, you know.'

Embarrassed and appalled I could think of nothing to say. She forgot her own trouble momentarily, in contemplation of mine.

'Oh, my dear child!' she said helplessly. 'Is this a shock?'

She began to explain rapidly, concerned for me.

'You're intensely and delightfully musical, and the music is very necessary to you and will be a source of joy to many others besides yourself. But, my dear, there is an enormous gap between the highly specialised life of an artiste and that of a very talented musician. And I'm not elevating the one or demoting the other for a moment. But you should – and would – have started much younger if you had possessed that necessary spark of genius. . . .'

I had forgotten my present sorrows and answered her indignantly, 'But that was because of Miss Hibbert. . . .'

The movement of one hand silenced me.

'A thousand Miss Hibberts would have made no difference. Even a Miss Hibbert would have recognised she was dealing with someone far out of the ordinary. And though it's not necessary to be born into a musical family, it does help.

Every star, in any sphere, needs an enormous amount of understanding, support and encouragement. Theatre people joke about the mothers of baby ballerinas, forever trotting round after them, fighting and scheming and working for them – most often failing to achieve their hopes. But that sort of dedication can make all the difference. . . .'

I could not accept her judgement.

'Then I've got nothing,' I cried, accusing her. 'I might just as well be dead.'

And in an instant I was all tears.

I look back and marvel at her, a provincial music teacher in her middle years, suffering the trauma of a late love affair, driven from her home by public opinion, preparing to start life again in a strange place. While I in the egotism of youth, with all my life before me, mourned the loss of an adolescent dream and demanded her last crumbs of emotional energy.

'Evelyn, my dear girl, don't take it so much to heart. I blame myself. I should have realised. To think we should be so close and I so blind! But you have such a range of abilities that I assumed you and your father were aiming for university. Of course, you might consider music college – I feel that he would be happier if you took some specified training, with a diploma attached to it. Think about it, anyway. And believe me, my dear, I wouldn't dare suggest you as a pupil to Aaron Feinberg if you weren't rather special. He taught Lucia Barowska. Evelyn, Evelyn, the sun will shine again, believe me. There'll be another spring, you know. . . .'

'I know it,' I said, mopping away with a borrowed handkerchief, 'but I can't feel it, and spring never lasts!'

'I think we both need a cup of coffee,' said Lilian, and led me into the kitchen. There she picked up the half-empty bottle and said, 'On second thoughts, a glass of wine might be better. Would your parents mind? You're not teetotal, by any chance, are you?'

I paused in my wretchedness to shake my head, and so tasted burgundy for the first time.

The sharpness of my disappointment had cleared the air. I shared the last of the wine with her, feeling bruised but better.

'It would help if you learned another instrument as well, of course,' Lilian went on. 'That would give you more options in the future. A violin, perhaps? A clarinet? If you became proficient enough you could join an orchestra. Otherwise, it would mean teaching. . . .'

I thought of the difficulties in persuading my father to allow more time and money for music, quite apart from suggesting I join an orchestra. Besides, if I took a diploma in music he would expect me to teach. So I discounted her advice. Also, I had committed myself to the piano. I loved it, and was faithful in my love.

Lilian said, musing, 'Heavens, how I wish I were your age again, with life stretching away in front of me like a road full of adventures. I didn't think so at the time, of course. My father died when I was about your age, leaving my mother and I in reduced circumstances. We had to give up our home and find something more modest. Instead of pursuing music for its own sake I had to learn to make a living by it. Towards the end of the war I became engaged, but my fiancé was killed before we could be married. My mother pulled me through that, as I had pulled her through father's death. Then life smiled on us again. An aunt left us some money. We bought this house and I established myself as a music teacher. But within two years my mother died. So I've had my share of sorrows. I find that the first year after any loss is the hardest. Then you put down a tender root or two, and gradually build a new life.'

I pondered this, sipping my wine, and dared to ask personal questions.

'But surely the most important thing in the world is whether two people love each other? And if they do then why must they stay with other people who make them unhappy, instead of living together?'

Years would pass before I realised how much it must have cost Lilian Lacey to reply so frankly and charitably.

'I don't think we could build a good life on the foundation of other people's misery. Our personal happiness would have cost everyone, including ourselves, far too much.'

I did not equate passion with such drab considerations.

Could one imagine Romeo and Juliet deciding not to upset their families?

'But surely – just to be together – isn't it worth any price?'

'The world well lost for love?'

'Well, yes, I suppose so.'

Lilian said gently, 'I think that's a young person's point of view. The young are all for glory and the moment. Loving someone is wonderful, but love can be an intensely selfish emotion. You forget everybody and everything else. Then suddenly you come down to earth with a bump and have to face the situation squarely. I know that people are saying I tried to break up Philip's marriage, but I would never ask that sacrifice of him – or his family.'

'Well Mrs Nash wasn't quite so thoughtful,' I said, in the freedom of my cups. 'Gossiping all over the place. I hate Mrs Nash.'

'Certainly, Mrs Nash and her allies are responsible for my leaving here rather more quickly and with less dignity than I could have wished, but I had already decided we must part.'

'So you wouldn't have – wouldn't ever have – run away together?'

Lilian shook her head.

After a suitable pause and another sip, I said, 'Might I ask where you're going, Lilian?'

'I'm staying with an old friend in Kent while I look around.'

'Will you give me your address, please? May I write to you? Can I come to see you when you've settled down?'

'That will depend upon your father. We must trust his judgement and abide by his decision. . . .'

I nodded, in a pleasing stupor of weariness and wine. Her voice came in waves from far away, washing upon the shores of my understanding, to be remembered and treasured in later years for different reasons.

'. . . and we've shared friendship and music and learned a great deal from each other. Perhaps it's time for us to part. And we shan't forget each other, even at a distance. Distance is not important. Remember, Evelyn, that we never lose anyone by letting them go, only by trying to hold them back.'

So Lilian Lacey went, and took the scandal with her as if it had been an illegitimate child. Mrs Nash, having used Dorothy, took no further notice of her: a point which my father raised when Dorothy would have liked it to be overlooked. His attitude towards the whole affair had surprised and slightly shamed her. She made no protest when I was allowed to write to Lilian, and always asked how she was when I received a reply.

And I, clinging to the advantage I had gained at such a cost, kept my stepmother at a distance for some months afterwards, and read Lawrence with renewed fervour. For now I knew that this miracle could happen, and regarded young bachelors in quite a different light, mentally trying my prince's suit of love on each of them and finding it did not fit.

19

Grandad Schofield had a heart attack that summer, while I was in the middle of my School Certificate examinations. He had walked up a steep hill on a hot day to deliver a set of encyclopedias, and being out of breath and thirsty he sat down and asked his customer if he might trouble him for a drink of water. When Mr Fosdyke returned with the glass Grandad had died, sitting in the chair.

Grannie wanted to stay in Hathersall but, apart from twenty pounds in the Post Office Savings Bank and her Co-op dividends, she had only ten shillings a week pension on which to exist. Chivalrously, my father helped out by paying the rent, and she managed well enough for a few months. In the end it was not lack of money which drove her from her own territory but lack of purpose.

She had looked after other people all her life and did not know how to look after herself. First she stopped baking bread, cakes and pies. Then she could not be bothered to cook at all. She kept a small brown teapot stewing at the side of the hob, and drank cups of this brew frequently. If she felt hungry she would add a slice of bread and margarine, spread it with jam, and make a meal of that. One autumn afternoon I called in on my way back from school, and found her sitting in a cold kitchen by an empty grate, hands folded in her lap, doing nothing.

On being questioned, Grannie said that she had plenty of coal and would light the fire presently. She did not remember when she had eaten last, nor did she seem particularly concerned about it, but seeing that I was worried she offered an explanation.

'Eh, I canna be mithered wi' myself, Evleen. The sooner I'm underground wi' my Sam the better it'll be.'

I lit the fire and brewed her a pot of tea and went straight out to telephone home. For whatever faults Dorothy had as a stepmother she was a responsible and affectionate daughter. Her reaction was prompt.

'Stop with her until I can get over. I shall have to sort things out here, but I'll be with you as soon as I can. Have you got enough money to buy yourselves some fish and chips? Good. Do that and I'll pay you back. And you were right to tell me, Evie. You've done well.'

I felt warmer towards her then. By the time I had hung up the receiver I knew that the uneasy truce of the past ten months was over. Michael and my father had solved their difficulties by living apart. Dorothy and I must soldier on together until I left home.

'So now it starts all over again!' I said to myself ironically. And went out to find a fish and chip shop.

Grannie looked rather frightened when her large and capable daughter surged in, and offered no resistance to the ultimatum.

'Right, Mother! Gilbert says I'm to fetch you home with us!'

So Grannie came to live at the Malt-house. She stayed in bed for the first week, puzzled how to adapt to her new way of life, but there is always plenty to do in a large household, and gradually she joined the mêlée and made herself useful.

While Mrs Inchmore did the cleaning Grannie went out shopping for Dorothy. When Mrs Inchmore had gone she washed up while Dorothy cooked. She was always ready to look after Julian while we others went out. She liked ironing, and made a special effort with my father's shirts out of gratitude, for he had taken her under his protection. But this genuine respect for her son-in-law did not make her feel any easier in his presence, and their conversations with one another were limited to the weather and their state of health.

There were difficulties, of course. For instance, Grannie would have preferred to eat by herself in the kitchen, but my father insisted that she join us in the dining room, and he always served her first as a mark of respect. Still, after the evening meal Grannie made a point of refusing their coffee and company, and retreated to the kitchen and contentment. There she sat for hours by the fire: darning socks, drinking stewed tea and reading the *Hathersall Weekly Advertiser*, which Dorothy ordered for her. In a material sense she was better off than she had ever been. Her food, clothes and housing were free. Her pension was now her pocket money. Alternately, she hoarded and squandered it in sombre enjoyment.

Life at the Malt-house flourished anew. The knowledge that Grannie was always there to look after Julian gave Dorothy a degree of freedom she had not known before. The world outside beckoned, as it were, and she entered it with delight.

At thirty-nine, she was still an attractive and ebullient woman, popular with both sexes and having many blessings to count. But I suppose that no female can view her fortieth birthday with complete nonchalance. Dorothy's flesh, though fair, had become over-abundant in a decade of good-living, and each year saw last year's clothes hanging in the wardrobe, too tight for comfort.

'It's no use! It's no use!' she cried, as I struggled to close an obstinate zip-fastener at the back of her best dress. 'I shall have to do something about it. I've got nothing nice to wear. I'll ask Kate for one of her diets. Just look at me!'

Dismayed, she was comparing my reflection with hers in the wardrobe mirror. Fair, fat and forty stood beside dark, slim and seventeen. Time had cheated her.

'I'll get a diet from Kate and start next Monday,' said Dorothy, nearly in tears, as she fastened the waistband of an old skirt with two safety-pins and covered it with a cardigan.

On the following Sunday she ate as much as she could of everything she liked best, and found it easy to starve the next day. But she lapsed on Tuesday, struggled back on Wednesday, fell by the wayside on Thursday, gave up on Friday, made a fresh resolve over the weekend, and started again with a Sunday orgy. This became a regular practice, and she had three standard excuses to explain why she failed to lose a single pound.

We realised that she needed encouragement and support but did not know how to provide it. My father's embarrassed little jokes provoked tears or quarrels. Grannie made only one remark about her daughter's increasing bulk, spent the day regretting it, and never mentioned the subject again. And anything I said was construed as boasting about my figure or criticising hers. It was Michael, coming home on Christmas Eve, bringing a dozen bottles of Blythe's finest sherry sack with him, who took Dorothy cheerfully to task.

He had always talked to her as though they were equals. And since I called her Dorothy, he referred to her as Dot.

'You're a very big girl, Dot,' he remarked frankly, 'and if you don't tackle yourself soon you're going to be a very fat one!'

'It's my bones,' said Dorothy, looking wistfully on this gallant reincarnation of Harry Harland. 'I've got such big bones.'

'And how the blazes do you know that?' Michael asked, grinning in spite of himself. 'When there isn't a bone in sight, Dot!'

Dorothy put forward her second excuse humbly.

'Kate hasn't found me a diet that works yet, Micky.'

'I'll bet you don't stick to any of them, that's why!'

She offered the final excuse.

'Slimming makes me ill, you see. I get dizzy from lack of food.'

'Then try giving up sugar. Just while I'm here.'

To please him she did try, making great play of refusing it over Christmas in coffee or tea. But on Boxing Day he caught her spooning sugar into the breakfast pot, and none of her protestations could convince him or us that this was a single lapse. She needed some over-riding reason to be slim, and it was provided early in 1938 when Hathersall Dramatic Society held their annual social, and asked Dorothy if she would take charge of the refreshment buffet.

She clapped the receiver back into place and sat holding the telephone to her bosom, looking pink and huffed.

'So that's the way the wind blows!' she remarked. 'They're going to push the catering on to me. A woman of *my* experience. I've done everything but produce for them, and they don't have women producers. To think I should stoop to providing refreshments!'

My father said reasonably, 'But you're an expert caterer.'

Dorothy's voice trembled. Her chin shook.

'But I don't go there to do catering. I go for the theatre work.'

She was riven, nursing the telephone.

'I know who's behind this,' she said. 'It's Mavis. She's the same age as me and she's had the same amount of experience. She wanted to play Lady Bracknell, but I got the part. Anyway, she hadn't the *presence* for it. She's – she's slimmer than I am. She was always jealous of me when I was Leslie Ormerod's leading lady nearly twenty years ago. And that's another thing. I should have thought that Leslie Ormerod had more sense than to see an actress of my calibre stuck behind a refreshment table!'

Grannie surfaced from the Deaths column of the *Advertiser*.

'Les Ormerod?' she cried. 'I thought he left years ago?'

She had grown a little deaf and Dorothy raised her voice to answer, 'Yes he did, Mother, but he's coming back. They've invited him to produce our autumn play. *Lady Windermere's Fan.*'

'Eh, fancy that. I remember Les Ormerod. He used to see you home every night, regular as clockwork, after the performance. He were a right bobby-dazzler in them days. I daresay he's older now.'

'We're all older,' said Dorothy, and her untidy head drooped.

We were silent for a moment or two in homage to past youth, and then my father returned her to the point.

'You can please yourself whether you do the refreshments or not, but go to the social anyway and find out how things stand. It seems to me that you're jumping to conclusions without having any proof.'

'What?' said Dorothy. 'And find out I'm right, and have them all whispering about me? And come home feeling an inch high?'

Out of pity for her I said, 'If you want some moral support you can take me with you. I know I'm not a member but it's a social evening. You can say I had to help you to carry the refreshments.'

She looked at me doubtfully.

'We're short of young people. They'll probably ask you to join,' she said, obviously wondering whether this was my hidden motive.

Grannie picked up the wrong end of the conversation.

'Aye, take our Evleen with you, Dollie. She's nearly as old as you were when you first started. They'll be glad of a bit of new blood, and she's a bonnie young lass.'

'Well they needn't bother asking,' I said outright. 'I've neither the time, the talent nor the inclination.'

My father gave his little chuff of laughter.

'Take her along with you, Dorrie!' he said proudly. 'Evie can snipe at them if they don't behave themselves!'

I giggled, Grannie smiled, and Dorothy recovered sufficiently to draw up a generous buffet menu. And so I took on the role, for the first time in my life, as her protector.

I had admired the Hathersall productions on stage but I found the members disappointing at close quarters. Except for the wardrobe mistress they were all playing the parts they hoped to get that year. And as Dorothy humbly pointed out the leading lights I wondered why she was so concerned to impress them.

'That's Mavis!' she said bitterly, of a middle-aged woman with a disappointed expression and dyed black hair. 'She's always after the men. She's caused some heartache in her time, I can tell you!'

I could not understand why any man wanted her, until I saw the men, who were either young and pimply or middle-aged and seedy.

'And there's Les Ormerod!' said Dorothy wistfully. 'Don't you think he looks rather like Ronald Coleman?'

'I suppose he does, rather,' I said doubtfully.

Evidently Mr Ormerod also thought he looked rather like Ronald Coleman, and had encouraged the likeness. In middle-age his figure was thick and his glossy dark hair thin, but he cultivated the famous slim moustache and exercised a long lingering look on the ladies, as if his dark brown eyes were about to melt with admiration. He was spruce and debonair, wearing his fifty-five shilling suit from Montague Burton's as if it had been tailored in Savile Row. And he had toned down his Lancashire vowels, though they tended to return when he was off guard.

Personally, I thought he was absolutely awful.

'And he's such a laugh!' Dorothy said. 'He used to have us in stitches. And he's no fool. He's worth quite a bit of money, you know. He owns three tobacconist's shops. But he should never have married. He was unhappy with her when I first knew him, and she's very jealous of him. She made him leave at one time. He hasn't been back here for years. But Mavis told me recently that he and his wife were going their own ways. Staying together, of course, for the sake of appearances and the children. . . .'

'What better solution could you have?' I murmured drily.

But she was not listening.

'Hathersall's lucky to get him back, and they know it. He's a marvellous producer!'

Her voice deepened as she said, 'The theatre's in his blood!'

Then in her natural, homely fashion she added, 'And besides, I don't expect there's anywhere much to go in the evenings. He'll be glad of the company and a bit of limelight.'

Cowed by encroaching fat, she had busied herself in the background with the tea and coffee pots, and put me out front on the serving table, where I had already attracted a great deal of attention and three requests to join the society. So I was not surprised when Leslie Ormerod sauntered up, one hand in the pocket of his tweed jacket and a silk Paisley scarf tucked into the neck of his shirt.

His twisted smile and cocked eyebrow were pure Coleman, but they were not intended for me. His melting eyes stared past the florentines and cheese straws to the stout lady behind me.

'Don't I remember you?' he cried. 'Dollie Harland, isn't it?'

I could tell that Dorothy was delightfully surprised and touched, but she adopted her most dignified manner. She even cleared her throat first, in order to deliver the speech with perfect tone and diction, and hid a chicken vol-au-vent she had been eating.

'Dorothy Fawley nowadays, actually,' she said, with Mrs Nash's social little laugh. 'I remarried many years ago.'

'You were a damned good little actress,' said Leslie, ignoring the marriage. 'Pretty girl. *The Second Mrs Tanqueray* in 'twenty-three, as I recall. *Passing of the Third Floor Back* in 'twenty-five?'

Dorothy inclined her head graciously, and pushed the chicken vol-au-vent further behind the teapot.

'Leslie, this is my lovely daughter, Evelyn!' she said, offering me up as a social sacrifice.

'Oh yes? Hello, Evelyn? Nice to see you, dear.'

He was not in the least interested in me. I was not his sort. He focused on Dorothy and talked past me.

'I say, Doll, I hope you're going to audition for a part in my production. Do you fancy any of 'em?'

Her expression was so poignant that she must have been thinking of the days, long gone, when she could have played Lady Windermere. She filled his cup thoughtfully, and handed it to him in what she would have termed 'a speaking silence'.

'Would you like a cocktail sausage, Mr Ormerod?' I asked briskly.

He did not answer me, and took a finger of shortbread. He came round the table and joined Dorothy at the back.

'There comes a time,' she said deeply, intimately, 'when one should retire into the wings. That time has come for me, Leslie.'

'What? A good-looking lass like you, and in her prime?'

Dorothy's eyes were full. She attempted to shrug the compliment away with another of Mrs Nash's little laughs.

Someone came up and asked for tea. She poured coffee and did not hear the protest.

'You'd be damned good as Mrs Erlynne,' said Leslie unexpectedly.

'Mrs Erlynne?' she cried, astonished into honesty. 'Never!'

'I'm not promising and I'm not canvassing,' said Leslie. 'And if an absolute natural for Mrs Erlynne turns up I'll have to take her, but *you* could do it.'

His liquid brown eyes were full of admiration and some sadness. Perhaps he was thinking of a time when they were both young and could command leading roles as of right.

Dorothy was trying to regain her matronly dignity.

'Actually, I've been specialising in the older character parts.'

His eyes were not convinced. She bent her head before them.

'I'm – I'm not – they don't – I was Lady Bracknell in the last Wilde play,' Dorothy confessed.

He tackled her directly, as Michael had done.

'That's because you're too fat,' he said frankly. 'If you lost a couple of stones you could give any girl here a run for her money. Your face is young enough, but you've got a middle-aged body. The slim girls win every time, Dollie.'

I could see that Dorothy was both deeply pleased and deeply hurt, and had entirely forgotten about refreshments. I took over her job and mine, and tried to hear their conversation while taking orders.

'I happen to be on a very strict diet,' said Dorothy loftily.

He stared hard at the half-eaten chicken vol-au-vent.

'Then stay on it,' Leslie advised. 'You could be your li'l ol' self by the autumn. I shan't be holding the auditions until April. You could lose quite a few pounds by then. Come in to read Mrs Erlynne, anyway. And tell us all outright at the beginning that you know you're overweight but you're dieting for the part. If you don't feel you can say that then let me bring it up as a question. I'll handle it in a friendly and tactful manner. There might be a few smiles but there won't be any sneers, I promise you. You're a popular lass. God help me, Dollie, isn't it worth a joke or two and a bit of effort to corner the best female part in the play?'

I was now bobbing to and fro like Figaro.

'Surely Lady Windermere has the . . . ?' Dorothy began, dazed.

He brushed the remark aside before she finished speaking.

'Lady Windermere's got the title role, not the best part. When all's said and done, she's only a pretty girl. But Mrs Erlynne's a damned handsome woman with a colourful past. I know who I'd rather take to the pictures! Think on, Dollie!'

He winked at her, nodded, and strode off.

My stepmother remembered her duties and elbowed me aside.

'That's my job!' she said ungratefully.

She no longer needed my moral support. In fact I was in her way.

'Here, love,' she said, mollifying me. 'Have a nice cup of coffee yourself, and go over and talk to some of the younger members.'

From a distance I watched her trembling hands and heard her flurried laugh. She was busy absorbing the full import of Leslie Ormerod's words, from 'You've got a middle-aged body' to 'You'd be damned good as Mrs Erlynne!'

In the arrogance of my youth, I wondered how he could equate the worldly-wise, the infinitely seductive, the coolly brilliant, the unexpectedly heroic Mrs Erlynne with the stout, middle-aged wife of a Lancashire headmaster. He must have been deluding himself. Well, he had a partner in delusion. Dorothy's face was wearing that rapt look which betrayed inner drama. No doubt she was imagining herself sweeping across the stage, elegant in a feathered hat, making play with her parasol. And the inner drama was influencing her outward actions. There she was, handing out slices of veal-and-ham pie and offering chocolate éclairs fearlessly, even with an air of disdain.

Was she thinking, 'They cannot tempt me now!'

20

The blast of war was blowing in our ears that year, but far from imitating the action of the tiger we slunk uncertainly. In March, Hitler annexed Austria. In May, Hitler and Mussolini met in Rome.

'Deciding what to take over next!' cried my father indignantly. 'We're letting them get away with murder! What's the matter with the damned government? We shall be fighting with pitchforks on the Dover beach if we're not careful!'

Michael was evidently of the same opinion, for he dropped in one summer evening to tell us that he and Dickie were both joining the RAF, and brought a bottle of champagne to celebrate the decision.

'But why are you joining up before you have to?' Dorothy cried. 'Don't you realise that you might get killed?'

This remark made everyone but herself laugh.

Eyes bright, head erect, my father raised his glass, saying, 'The toast is to you, Michael, to Dickie, and to all our brave young men! We shall have need of you.' Adding, 'By God, I wish I was young enough to join up. I'd go as a rear-gunner and pop at them myself!'

We laughed again.

Then the conversation turned to Dorothy, who had stuck to her diet with a tenacity we did not know she possessed, and was already a stone lighter. We were amazed that the prospect of playing Mrs Erlynne could triumph over her relish for good food.

As my father said humorously to me in private, 'I'd have

bet a pound to a penny that Thornton's chocolates would win!'

They did not, though she was often and cruelly tempted. And I, who was no admirer of Leslie Ormerod, had to admire his tactics. He had given Dorothy the part on condition that she lost weight steadily. As a safeguard, or a threat, he also appointed Mavis Cartwright to be her understudy. Not for nothing had he played Professor Higgins to Dorothy's Eliza Doolittle in '26. Within a month, apparently, Mavis was word-perfect and waiting for a chance to take Mrs Erlynne over, which kept Dorothy at her fighting best. I am sure that whenever her appetite threatened to bolt she thought of that predatory female and reined it in.

'You're beginning to look like you did when I was little!' said Michael. 'How's my best girl, then?'

He gave her a great hug, looked over his shoulder, and asked, 'Where's the rest of her gone to?'

And we laughed again, excited and pleased with him.

My father, entering into the spirit of the conversation, replied, 'I don't know, but she must have taken her wardrobe with her. I've had to pay for a dickens of a lot of new clothes!'

'That's because we're having a few days' holiday in London!' said Dorothy coquettishly. 'I can't go looking like a scarecrow. They're all very smart there.'

'Dorrie wants to see Emlyn William's new play *The Corn is Green* – and probably one or two others, if I know her!'

'Do you think I look nice, Micky? Do you?' Dorothy asked.

'You look wonderful!' he said honestly.

He kept one arm round Dorothy and held out the other for me.

'And who is this dark-eyed gazelle? I say, isn't Evie becoming a beauty? Any boyfriends yet?'

My hasty disclaimer was echoed by that of my parents.

'Not until she's left school,' said Dorothy.

'Time enough for that sort of thing!' said my father.

Michael answered them with understanding, grinning.

'Lock up your daughter, eh? I should lock your wife up too, if I were you, Dad, or you're liable to lose her as well!'

My father smiled then, delighted by this obscure compliment.

'And what about you, Micky?' Dorothy asked curiously. 'Have you got a girlfriend?'

'Several, Dot, several. There's safety in numbers.'

'No one you'd like to bring home?' she asked wistfully.

'Certainly not. The sight of you would make them jealous, Dot!'

'Oh, Micky!' she said, smiling, reproachful, knowing he had evaded the question.

We laughed a lot that evening. Everything we said seemed to be witty or funny. And yet, looking back, I find it immeasurably sad. The seeds of destruction were growing in us and in the world outside. By the end of September we were on the brink of war.

'At what stage,' cried my father, from his favourite rostrum of the drawing-room hearth, 'shall we stop placating a German war-lord?'

'Oh, Gil,' said Dorothy, despairing, because she was already late for rehearsal, 'I can't listen now, love. I'm trying to find my gloves. Czechoslovakia is thousands of miles away from us. And all that Hitler wants is the part with the Germans in it.'

'He said that before he reoccupied the Rhineland and marched into Austria!'

'Well, I'm sure the Prime Minister will patch things up.'

'That's exactly what I'm afraid of! Trotting to and fro like a dog at his master's bidding. With his winged collar and his damned umbrella. Like some blasted undertaker. Tcha! Can't stand the man. Couldn't stand his father, either!'

Grannie had retreated to the kitchen from this hail of politics, or she would have helped her daughter to find the gloves.

'Oh, what a terrible week it's been!' cried Dorothy, nearly in tears. 'Nothing but worry and talk of war. And the British Fleet mobilised. Whatever will come of it all?'

'That Chamberlain fellow will worm his way out of it!' said my father wrathfully, chin tilted, colour high. 'Peace without honour! That's what it'll be. Mark my words.'

'Oh, here they are!' cried Dorothy, finding her gloves tucked down one side of the leather sofa. 'However did they get there?'

'I expect you left them there! What time will you be back tonight? And when does this damned play begin?'

'If I've told you once I've told you a hundred times. Three evenings at the end of next week, and a Saturday matinée. But who's going to bother to come if we're at war?'

The first night of *Lady Windermere's Fan* was perhaps the most stupendous success that Hathersall Dramatic Society had ever achieved, and part of that triumph was due to the public release of tension. After the terrors of the previous week, we all needed to celebrate what the Prime Minister described as 'peace in our time', even though we did not at bottom believe it. As the audience clapped and stamped its feet, and the cast took curtain calls to the point of delirium, everyone understood that this was only peace for the moment: a respite, a breathing space, while the country prepared for war.

Still, on this October evening in 1938 we celebrated in style. Each member of the cast could expect a cigar or a spray of flowers, and real bouquets, crackling in cellophane and tied with satin ribbon, were handed up to the leading ladies. Dorothy had two, and took a personal curtain call which was frantically applauded. And still we asked for more.

Sweating through their Leichner make-up, the company linked hands as the curtain rose for the fifth time. They swept forward. They lifted their chins and smiled up at the lights. They bowed low before their applauders and drew back. Then Lord Darlington stepped forward to ask for silence.

'Ladies and gentlemen. On behalf of the cast I should like to thank you very much indeed for being such a wonderful audience. We've all enjoyed ourselves. But none of this would have been possible without the inspiration and hard work of our producer, Leslie Ormerod. Let's give him a big hand, shall we?'

He turned towards the wings, and cried, 'Come on, Les! We know where you're hiding!'

And the audience called, 'Producer! Producer! Come on, Les! Let's see you, lad!'

Excited, delighted, Leslie Ormerod walked onstage, smoothing his hair, adjusting his silk neck-scarf, one eyebrow cocked quizzically at all the fuss.

My father and I had been standing at the stage door for almost half an hour, watching other members of the cast come out in their usual role of ordinary citizens. Impatiently, he lifted the gold fob-watch from his waistcoat pocket and checked the time.

'Still talking to people, I expect!' he said to himself. 'Never knows when to stop! Evie, pop in and ask your mother to hurry up, will you? The car takes a while to start in this weather. It'll be past eleven o'clock by the time we're home, and Grannie's waiting up.'

The contrast between the brilliant crimson and gold auditorium and this poorly lit corridor, with its dirty green walls and dank odours, struck me unfavourably. In the theatre world everything up front was magical and splendid, but backstage – what a shabby affair.

There were only two large rooms in which the cast could change and keep costumes: one for each sex. I peeped round the open door of the ladies' dressing room and found only the wardrobe mistress: a small elderly lady with a mouth full of pins, who kept her eyes on the hem she was repairing.

'Awfully sorry to bother you, Mrs Perritt,' I said, seeing that the pins must be removed before speech was possible. 'I'm looking for my mother. Can you tell me where she is, please?'

Mrs Perritt transferred the pins skilfully to their cushion.

'Is it Evelyn? You do look grown up! Your mother went about ten minutes àgo, love. They've all gone, bar Mr Ormerod. He's allus the last to leave because he likes to lock up. Have a look on't stage, love. He's there somewhere abouts.'

'Thank you. Awfully sorry to interrupt. The pins, I mean!'

I hated empty theatres. Like rooms, the morning after a party, they were lost places, bereft of purpose. Silently cursing Dorothy for putting me to all this trouble, I walked down the dim corridor towards the stage and past the men's dressing room.

That door was closed but light slid from underneath it. I heard a man's muffled laugh and a woman's half-hearted protest, and knocked and called his name before I realised that this was an intimate conversation. Immediately, the light went out. The silence that followed was alarmed. The occupants of the room had stopped talking by common consent. The atmosphere became clandestine.

So he was fooling around with some female member of the cast? Probably Mavis! Well, I was not surprised. I had marked him down as a lady-killer when Dorothy introduced us. Now what to do? I decided that it would be more tactful to pretend that nothing was amiss. Nervous but determined, I knocked again.

'Is that you, Mr Ormerod? It's Evelyn Fawley.'

This time the silence was one of hesitation, followed by small quiet sounds which did not want to be heard. Then Leslie's voice answered. He was trying to be laconic but sounded deeply uneasy.

'Half a mo', Evelyn! I'm in here coping with the electric light. The bulb's on the blink. Be with you in a minute.'

I did not believe him. So he was a liar as well as a cad? Well, that was his business. I waited, idly translating faint noises. Two sets of whispers. Stockinged feet padding carefully. A piece of furniture, bulky rather than heavy, being lifted and moved stealthily. The stage had been set for the scene which would follow. Now came the performance. Leslie's muttered commentary was entirely for my benefit.

'Where's that chair gone to? It's as dark as pitch in here.' A match scraped. 'Ah! now I can see what I'm doing.'

Much fumbling with a celluloid lampshade. Suddenly the light went on. He got down from the table and swung the door open, whistling.

'Sorry about that!' he said heartily. 'I tell you, the wiring in this place has to be seen to be believed. Now what can I do for you?'

I could tell that he disliked me as much as I disliked him.

'I'm looking for Dorothy,' I said clearly. 'We've been waiting outside the stage door for over half an hour, and I can't find her.'

Leslie put his arms akimbo, grinning. His reply was too clever.

'Well *I* haven't hidden her!' he said.

I knew then, with a sense of shock, that this was exactly what he had done. And he was a fool as well as a rogue, for I never would have suspected that the woman was Dorothy.

I glanced over his shoulder and saw a screen standing near the window at the end of the room. They had moved it in the dark, so that it would be as far as possible from the door. And Dorothy must be standing behind it, court shoes in hand, holding her breath and listening. Mrs Erlynne offstage as well as on.

'I didn't suppose you had!' I replied coldly.

Leslie knew he had made a bad mistake.

'Only my joke, dear!' he said.

He assumed a worried and responsible air.

'Now where can she have got to?' he said. 'There's nobody here except Mrs Perritt and me. Did you say you were at the stage door? Ah! That might explain it. She was talking to somebody in the foyer, earlier on. I'll bet a pound to a penny that she's been standing in front of the theatre while you waited at the back.'

'I wonder why none of us thought of that?' I said sarcastically, disgusted with the pair of them.

He knew I had guessed the truth. His frown was heavy, sullen, dangerous. I was glad that he would not dare slap me. He wanted to, I could see. Slap me and probably knock me down as well.

'Good night, Mr Ormerod,' I said.

I would not hurry down the dim corridor. I was too proud to seem afraid of him, and I needed to calm down before I told my father a thumping good lie. He was standing there, watch in hand, tutting.

'And where the blazes have *you* been?' he cried, past all patience with women.

'It's the old story!' I said, laughing. 'Apparently, she's

234

been chatting to somebody in the foyer, and they think she might be at the front of the theatre. Wouldn't you know it? Come on, Daddy!'

Dorothy was standing there, holding her bouquets as if they were wreaths. She was badly frightened, but waved in a light and joyful manner and hurried towards us. She could act better than Leslie Ormerod. She managed to be unreasonable in her usual style.

'And where have you two been, might I ask?' said Dorothy. 'Do you realise I could have caught my death of cold standing around?'

But there was no spirit in her tone, no spirit at all.

On the last night of *Lady Windermere's Fan* I spent the evening with my father in the drawing room, playing his favourite pieces, while he sat by the fire and rested his head against the back of his chair and closed his eyes in quiet delight.

At nine o'clock I made tea, left Grannie to drink hers in peace over the evening paper, and carried in a tray for us.

'This is a rare pleasure, my lass!' he said, smiling at me.

'Yes. We're both so busy usually. We're all so busy. It's lovely just to stroll through an evening instead of hurrying. Sugar?'

'I suppose so! I ought to give it up and take saccharine, like your mother. I think I'm beginning to put weight on.'

'Not so's anyone would notice,' I said loyally.

I had already seen that slight bulge of the waistcoat, but did not like admitting it any more than he did. I preferred to think of him as perennially lithe and handsome.

'Your mother did well the other night!' he remarked. 'Excellent performance. She stole the show, I thought. Looked splendid, too. She's a different woman these days. As Mick said last weekend, I shall be losing her if I don't watch out!'

He chuckled. An attractive wife was a compliment to his taste, but I did not think of this at the time. I had spent two nights mulling over Dorothy's secret life, and I was bent on justice.

'The only thing you're likely to lose her to is Hathersall

Dramatic Society,' I said lightly. 'I wonder what part the great Mr Ormerod will find for her in the next production? Perhaps they should do *Pygmalion* again. She played Trilby to his Svengali, so she told me, sometime in the nineteen-twenties.'

'Which one is Mr Ormerod?' my father asked, mildly interested.

'Daddy! You don't remember people from one minute to the next unless they're something to do with Grizedale's! Dorothy introduced him to you on the opening night. He's the producer. He's the man who's been playing Svengali in real life – promising her the part of Mrs Erlynne if she was slim enough. He must have some faith in her, I must say. I never thought she'd starve herself for eight months! Daddy, you must remember Mr Ormerod. He looks like a faded film star. Glistening hair oil and a thin moustache. Dresses as if he's a country gentleman, and isn't – either countrified or a gentleman, I mean!'

I was chattering on in an excellent imitation of my usual style, and watching what impression it made.

My father lifted his head. He considered the opening night as if it were imprinted on the wall opposite.

'Was he that unctuous chap in the hired dress suit?' he asked, in quite a different tone.

'Oh, Daddy! Who said that men were never catty? Yes, that's the famous Mr Ormerod. I don't like him, personally, but he's been a good friend to Dorothy, so each to her own taste.'

I allowed the information and my previous remarks to sink in. My father stirred his tea thoughtfully.

'Reminds me of a manager at a seedy cinema,' he said, and sipped.

'I think he's paying court to the outrageous Mavis,' I continued.

'Did I meet her, too?'

'I don't think so. Dorothy and she are great rivals. Mavis was dying to play Mrs Erlynne. Anyway, she may not have got the part but I think she's got the man. When I was wandering round looking for Dorothy on the first night, he was in the men's dressing room with the door shut, having a very intimate conversation with a lady, judging by the whispers. He switched the light out when he heard me knock. And, lo and behold, when the door opened again after a string of excuses, no lady could be seen!'

My father was now wholly concentrated.

'Are you sure a woman was with him?'

I touched my ears, and nodded.

He frowned. 'That's a bit off!' he remarked. 'I don't like that sort of behaviour. Can't say I liked him, either!'

'Well, don't mention it to Dorothy, because they're old friends. It might not be Mavis, of course, but she has a reputation of being a man-hunter and he's certainly a lady-killer. I shouldn't be gossiping about him. Except, as Dorothy always says, nothing beats a bit of hot gossip! More tea, Daddy?'

The mahogany clock on the mantelpiece chimed in contemplation.

'Half past nine,' said my father to himself. And to me, 'What time does the performance finish?'

'Ten o'clock-ish.'

'I'll go and meet her,' said my father. 'She'll need some help, carrying her costumes and make-up. It'll save her getting a taxi home.'

'Do you want me to come with you?' I asked casually.

'No, no. No need. Stay with Grannie. She'll think we're always clearing off and leaving her. Mustn't take advantage of her kindness.'

He was speaking of Grannie and thinking of Dorothy. His face was chilled and colourless, his eyes troubled. Old doubts and fears were attacking him. I had opened the lid of his Pandora's box, and heaven knew what would fly out before it was safely shut again.

Slightly chastened, I joined Grannie in the kitchen. She lived mostly in the past nowadays, and would pick up a conversation as if you had been living it with her. It took mental agility and a good memory to reply at once. Tonight, however, she was pursuing a similar line of thought.

'Your grandad had occasion to speak to that Les

Ormerod, at one time,' she said, with a grim little jerk of the chin. 'He used to walk our Dollie home from rehearsals at ten o'clock. We allus thanked him, but we never asked him in. Anyway, that night the clock came round to a quarter of eleven, and still our Dollie wasn't home. So Grandad walked up the road, being worried-like. And when he got to the Rose and Crown she came out, arm in arm with Les Ormerod. Grandad were never one for mincing his words. He said, "You're a married man, Mr Ormerod, and I value my daughter's good name. I was never over-fond of you seeing her home, but I most certainly won't have her kept out late at night, drinking at a public house. In future I'll come and fetch her from rehearsal meself!"

'Our Dollie were that vexed and upset. Well, she were in her twenties and married – widowed, I should say – and she tried to argue with Grandad. But he said to her. "As long as you're under my roof, and you've got no husband to protect your reputation, I shall make myself responsible." And so he did, though Dollie cried and carried on. And then your father come along and everything turned out right.

'Mind you, I'd got nothing against Les Ormerod. He were a pleasant, good-looking chap, clever and hard-working in his own way, and nobody's fool. But when a man's got a cold wife and a cold hearth he starts to look round for summat else. Only it were no use looking at our Dollie, and that's why Grandad nipped it in the bud.'

We went to bed soon afterwards, and I lay awake in the dark long enough to doubt the wisdom of my domestic plot. The first surge of astonishment and self-congratulation had been succeeded by fear of the consequences. In my desire to bring Dorothy to justice I had quite forgotten that my father's comfort of mind and body and all our daily lives depended on her. Second thoughts brought disturbing questions in their train.

Supposing that my father turned her out of doors, who would take her place as organiser of the Fawley household? I doubted that Grannie was capable of it, or that we could afford a full-time housekeeper.

It would be me, I thought in panic. I'd have to give up my

life to look after Daddy and Julian. Yet I had to acknowledge that I had brought it on myself, that such an expiation would be majestically right. Then, having thought of myself, I turned to the others. What effect would this trauma have on poor little Julian, so secure in his present world? How could Grannie live on my father's charity with her daughter cast out in disgrace? What would Michael think of me when he found out that I had betrayed her? And how could I make up to my father what I had taken from him? I remembered Dorothy saying of his life at Grandma's house, 'He was trapped.'

I no longer saw myself as an avenging angel but a dangerous and destructive meddler, no better than Mrs Nash whom I had despised.

The Lord, I realised, had good reason for saying that vengeance was His. Only He could dispense it justly and remain untouched by it. Human beings were too small and too involved to execute one another. My vengeance shamed, branded and diminished me.

Oh God, please don't let him find them, I prayed sincerely.

They unlocked the door and came in without speaking. I heard my father shut himself in the spare room, that sanctuary in which one or the other partner healed themselves of marital wounds. I heard her walk across the hall and into the kitchen.

When I had made sure that my father was safely shut away I crept soft-footed down the stairs and paused at the kitchen door. In a rush of honesty I had decided to confess and apologise, to bring the full storm of Dorothy's wrath upon my head and thus be absolved. But as I hesitated I heard sounds which froze me. A muffled sobbing, punctuated by gulps and gasps. China chinked. Cupboard doors opened and shut. A chair scraped across the floor.

I stood, head bowed, knowing what was happening.

She was raiding the larder and meat-safe, bringing out everything she had relished and denied herself for months, piling it on to plates, cramming the food into her mouth as if she were starving, and crying for the man who had recreated her.

I realised then that confession would only help me and hurt her more deeply. I must bear the consequences of my action. So I crept away and left her to pile on the flesh which would prevent her from ever straying again.

She never suspected me, but I have had to make reparation in many ways since then, often surprising her by my forbearance.

'Sorry, love!' she says, apologising for a flash of temper. 'I know I'm sharp-tongued. And you're always nice. You never snap back.'

And so I go on repaying that old debt, and will do so until I am granted some other absolution.

21

July 1939

It was just over two years since I had seen Lilian Lacey and Philip Nash making their farewell in Lilian's kitchen. Two years since she dealt my musical ambitions a near-mortal blow. And the dream of being a concert pianist had been replaced by a dream of love. Not the dear familiar love of putting my arms round my father's neck, courting his smile, coaxing what I wanted from him. Not the mystical love I still felt for Clara. Not the sibling love I had for Michael nor the old child-like affection for Grannie, but a love that set me aflame. I wanted a man to turn and look at me as Philip Nash had looked at Lilian Lacey, and to touch my cheek and kiss my lips as if they were precious things. I wanted a love I could die for. I wanted, oh I wanted the inconstant moon. And I lived in purdah.

School regulations were strict, and applied to our appearance as well as our morals. Cosmetics and coloured nail polish were forbidden. Full school uniform must be worn in school hours, and kept immaculate. Hatted, gloved, stockinged and impeccable we averted our eyes from the Grammar School boys. To be seen chatting to them meant a detention. Flirtation meant grave warnings and a possible letter to our parents. Continual bad behaviour led to expulsion. Even at weekends we behaved decorously in public lest we were recognised by some sour all-seeing eye, and reported.

At home the same rules prevailed, though in domestic guise. Dorothy's hospitality was generous and she had a maternal weakness for young men, so I met a number of Michael's friends and the junior members of my father's staff. From my eighteenth birthday, Dorothy began to cast a calculating eye over her bachelor guests, to put me on show and to keep me out of reach. They were allowed to admire me socially, but would not have dared ask me to go out. I was being saved up for eventual marriage and must not be allowed to make myself cheap.

That last year at school chafed me. Girls I had known at Moss Lane were wheeling prams while I was still in uniform, and I could see they pitied me. I pitied myself.

And now I must confess that Michael's boon companion, the famous Dickie Blythe, had been a tremendous disappointment to me at first. Michael had spoken so highly of him that I expected a Greek god, but the sight of Dickie destroyed all thoughts of romance, for what is love if the lover is not handsome? To me it was a piano out of tune, food without savour, a moonless night.

Dickie Blythe gangled. He was even taller than Michael, almost as thin as poor Uncle Arthur, and his ears stuck out. He had a plain big-nosed face, expressive when he talked and faintly sad in repose. His eyes were an indeterminate colour, blue or grey according to mood, and his straw-coloured hair was plastered to his skull with Viola hair cream. He spoke with a drawl which sounded affected, and he dressed with an elegance that was almost foppish.

Dorothy, with her instinctive worship of the upper class, took to him at once. My father and I reserved judgement. But before the end of the evening he had captivated us all. No one could help liking Dickie. The first impression over, his honest goodwill shone forth, and he was incredibly funny, with a humour that was lighter and more fanciful than Michael's dry wit.

So when my beloved brother asked us in private what we thought of old Dickie, we chorused our approval.

'A very nice fellow!' said my father. 'A very intelligent

fellow! Too bright, I should have thought, for the wine trade.'

Dorothy said quickly, to cover up this gaffe, 'I think he'll do very well as a husband for Evie in another few years!'

This kind of remark tended to be made more frequently as I grew older, but I was always careful to convey that he was not for me. Still, I became very fond of Dickie. In fact he was the only young man I knew, apart from Michael, whom I could regard as a genuine friend.

'Forty years on . . .' sang the ranks of schoolgirls gaily, disbelieving that such a thing could happen to them.

'. . . when afar and asunder,' sang the rows of single lady teachers who had suffered time and separation alike.

Sun poured through the stained-glass windows of the main hall, frivolously colouring the sepia portraits of the school's suffragette founders. Strong faces and cottage-loaf coiffeurs, high-necked blouses and swelling bosoms, were jewelled in ruby, emerald, sapphire and amber. They had sacrificed personal happiness and invited social hostility by pioneering for women's emancipation. They had maintained that to educate a boy was to educate only one person, whereas to educate a girl was to educate a family. They had won those rights for us, and I am afraid we took such privileges for granted.

'. . . parted are those who are singing today.'

Simultaneously, I felt my eyes smart with tears and was amused to see that our headmistress's petticoat was hanging below her dress.

Miss Boswell had hitched on her gown absent-mindedly, and it hung longer on one side than the other. Her mortar-board sat at an angle which would have looked rakish on anybody else. But her dignity remained intact. She sang lustily and her expression was in no way nostalgic. She had, as she often told us, chosen to teach rather than to marry, and she abided by her decision without regret.

'I have the greatest respect for Miss Boswell,' my father had said from the beginning. 'I value her judgement and her common sense.'

The previous day, with my sixth-form colleagues, I had heard Miss Boswell's speech to school-leavers delivered clearly with perfect diction. A charming Scots lilt, which sometimes surfaced in a relaxed moment, had been sacrificed for clipped King's English. I was inclined to think it a pity, for there was a music in the lilt that her King's English lacked, but our speech-training mistress always held up Miss Boswell's accent as an example to us all.

'"Man's love is of man's life a thing apart. 'Tis woman's whole existence,"' she had begun.

The quotation was delivered sarcastically, followed by a pause and a toss of her fighting chin, as she pitched into both sentiment and poet.

'It was, of course, Lord Byron who believed this nonsense, girls! And of course it suited him, and many other men, to believe it. But if you are leaving us tomorrow, feeling that marriage is your only goal, then you and we have failed!'

She searched our polite young faces. She clarified her argument.

'I expect every girl here to become self-supporting and self-sufficient before she even thinks of marriage. Remember that the best of husbands can be mortal, and the worst can leave you flat!'

She permitted herself and us a chuckle at this uncharacteristic piece of slang. She liked to amuse while she instructed.

'In fact, I should strongly advise you to play the field and enjoy yourselves for the next five or six years!'

We laughed appreciatively.

'Marriage can be a blessed state, but the yoke is not easy and the burdens are not light. Nevertheless, if you do marry, as most of you will, you should continue to take an intelligent interest in the world outside. Learn, and keep on learning. Pursue your education throughout life, provide your children with an intelligent background, and when the time comes – send your daughters to us!'

She smiled with sincere goodwill, saying, 'I hope you won't forget us. Do join our Old Girls' Society and send us your news, and do come and visit us from time to time. We are always pleased to see our old girls. Jolly good luck to you all!'

Answering smiles and a chorus of thanks poured forth. For freedom was in sight, and coffee and biscuits would shortly be served in the headmistress's study.

Of course, only a miserly percentage would follow her advice: some because it suited them, others by chance, and a few because they could never find a man to dissuade them from it. The majority would head like lemmings for the cliffs of wedlock as soon as possible.

Still Miss Boswell must have remained optimistic, for the brief sermon she preached had apparently not changed in over thirty years.

Now the school orchestra struck up *L'Arlésienne* overture and the first row of juniors began to march out. The violinists put their heads on one side and plied their bows industriously. Miss Fawcett, the music teacher, conducted with flashing eyes and flailing arms, glaring in the direction of false notes and squeaks and squeals, endeavouring to keep them all in time. Usually I fought down my giggles. Today I accepted the effort and the mistakes with loving kindness, for I would never hear them battling against Bizet again. Today I listened not to the sound but to how they meant to sound.

It was the prefects' turn to leave. Jill nudged me. Margaret and Pamela pushed me.

Sibilantly, gleefully, they whispered, 'Wake up, Dollie Daydream, Pride of Idaho!'

And we wheeled and marched from the platform for the last time, heads high, conscious of our supreme importance, waiting until we were released into the mill of parents and pupils outside the Queen's Hall before we exchanged con-gratulatory smiles. For this, our first afternoon of adult freedom, we four friends had planned a private celebration.

So we took leave of our respective families, handing over our gift bibles and form prizes, and promising to be home for the evening meal. Each member of our group had brought a carrier bag containing her weekend clothes. A little high with excitement, we caught a bus to Barber's, made for the Ladies

Powder Room, and there paid a penny each to go into the lavatory as a schoolgirl and emerged as a young lady, dazzling even ourselves with the results.

'Let's stay here for tea!' I suggested, powdering my nose.

'I think we'd be safer to go down to the Kardomah in Priestgate,' said Jill, 'and sit in a dark corner where we can't be spotted.'

'But who's going to see us? And anyway they can't give us a detention now we've left school,' I protested.

For I loved Barber's balcony restaurant. The gipsy ensemble was quite good. I could listen and muse.

'Suppose any of our parents decide to do some shopping, and then come and have tea here before they go home?' said Margaret.

'Yes, we don't want to be caught smoking,' said Jill, who had been stealing her father's cigarettes for the past year.

'I must say, I can't see my mother going home without looking round Barber's,' said Pamela.

'But it's not three o'clock yet. They won't be likely to have tea until four,' I pleaded. 'Let's stay for half an hour. Just tea and cakes. No smoking. And then go on to the Kardomah.'

'All right, then. Half an hour!' said Jill good-naturedly.

We trooped into the restaurant, which was almost empty and sat at a table near the edge of the balcony. I struck an attitude, cheek on hand, eyes uplifted. Affectionate derision followed.

'Don't bother to order tea for Juliet. She'll only sit there letting it get cold while she wonders where Romeo is!'

'What will happen when she goes to the College of Music, I wonder? Will food ever pass those painted lips again?'

'Shush, girls! Shush!' I cried, sitting up. 'Here they come!'

The gipsy players had been enjoying a short break, but this influx of customers must have caused them to drain their teacups, stub out their cigarettes, and return immediately. Barber's ensemble was famous in Blackstone, composed of romantic black-haired young men dressed in bright satin costumes and playing fiddles. There were usually a dozen or so, but the number varied and the turnover was fairly high. Though unrelated to gipsies they shared the compulsion to move on, and music college students had been known to fill gaps in the ranks during the summer vacation.

Automatically the players looked up at the balcony, preparatory to giving the little bow which said they were honoured to be recalled. Then, seeing the four of us smiling and clapping in anticipation, they bowed very low in true homage.

Fluttered and excited, we budding Juliets smiled back and inclined our gracious heads. Adult life had begun.

'You see?' I could not resist saying. 'Isn't this nicer than smoking in the Kardomah?'

Still, we ended up at the Kardomah after all, and ate a variety of things on toast, and drank a great deal of excellent coffee, and parted after a final cigarette. Our promises to keep in touch, to meet in twelve months' time and compare notes, were sincere. We had been friends for nearly six years, and nothing, we thought, could change that.

But Jill would be taking a medical course in Edinburgh, Pamela would read English at Oxford, Margaret study for a Physics degree at Imperial College, London, and I had won a scholarship to Blackstone College of Music. Other people and other places would lay claim to us. We were bound to change. But we were too young to realise that, and so promised eternal allegiance.

My first cigarette had made my head ache. An appalling assortment of snacks churned in my stomach. I threaded my way listlessly through the crowds who were flocking towards home and high tea, and joined the Kersley bus queue. It might cost twopence more than the tram but in this condition I could not bear to be rattled and banged about.

The conductor's arm barred me from the first bus, and I leaned against the post and sighed as I waited for the next. A hand touched my sleeve, delicately, courteously, to attract my attention.

'Excuse me. Pardon me,' said a man's voice. 'Miss Craig?'

He was fine-boned, slim and black as a Spaniard, not much taller than me. He had worn his handsome face for thirty years or more, but his present pleasure lent it an air of youth.

'It *is* Felicity Craig, isn't it? I thought I recognised you!' he cried, as if he had been granted a most precious wish.

His voice was most pleasing, light and mellifluous. My head ceased to throb, my stomach began to settle. He was so easy and friendly and good-looking that I could not reply with the cool courtesy due to a total stranger. I smiled radiantly back.

'I'm afraid you haven't recognised me at all,' I answered.

'*Not* Felicity Craig?' he insisted, searching my face.

'Not a bit of it. My name is Evelyn Fawley.'

He raised his dark velour hat. I noticed that his leather gloves were also a little worn, that all of his clothes had been of good quality but were now old.

'Ah! My name's Hyde. Christopher Hyde. I apologise for troubling you, Miss Fawley.'

I felt that 'Not at all!' was the proper reply.

'You see, Felicity is the kid sister of an old friend of mine. We've been out of touch for years. You have a certain resemblance.'

He hesitated, and I tried to think of something which would hold his attention. The carrier bag full of school clothes prompted me.

'I left school today, Mr Hyde.'

'Ah! Then it must have been a wonderful day. What happens next, Miss Fawley?'

We were smiling at each other as if we could not stop.

'I shall be studying music at the Blackstone College. I begin this autumn.'

'Talking to strangers!' said a stout woman who was standing next to me in the queue. 'There's such a thing as the white slave traffic!'

She spoke loudly, so that we could both hear, and her companion answered her in the same challenging tone.

'Aye, I've read about that in the *News of the World*!'

They both looked meaningfully at us.

Christopher Hyde gave me a reassuring wink and raised his hat for the second time.

'Best of luck, Miss Fawley. My apologies once again in mistaking one lovely face for another.'

And he was gone, he was gone, hurrying along the hot and dusty summer pavement, brief case in hand.

The Kersley bus bore down on our queue but I was not aware of it. My loud-voiced neighbour pushed me. The conductor told me to hurry up.

'You want to be more careful, you do,' said the stout woman, elbowing me forward. 'That chap was trying to pick you up. Pretending to know you. I've seen that trick done before.'

The pressure of the crowd deposited me on the bus platform in a rush. Scarlet with shame and pleasure, I found a corner seat, but the two women came and sat on either side of me protectively.

'Just in case he's followed you!' one of them said, nodding.

Nervous, desirous, joyful, petrified, I waited: wondering whether he had indeed slipped undetected on to the bus, ready to accost me when I was alone. My two guardians bought tickets to Hathersall and regaled me with stories of white slave trafficking. After a while they realised that I was not listening, and spoke across me to each other until it was time for them to get off.

'It's a good thing you didn't tell him where you lived!' they said. 'Now if he comes downstairs after we've got off you tell the conductor that he's making a nuisance of hisself!'

But he did not appear. In relief and disappointment, I knew now that he would not come. I relaxed. I sat raptly in my seat and told his words to myself over and over again. I felt an inner radiance which must have been outwardly visible, for I caught the attention of several male passengers as they boarded or left the bus at different stages. But I paid attention to no one but a fine-boned handsome man in his thirties, with Spanish-black hair. I heard nothing but that simple heart-stopping declaration: 'My apologies once again in mistaking one lovely face for another.'

I could not wait to get home and consult my mirror. Mirror, mirror on the wall, who is the fairest of them all?

I dodged Dorothy's questions and exclamations at my

appearance, made a grimace at the smell of frying sausages, and ran upstairs to lock the door of my room.

In privacy, I brushed out my hair and swept it up once more into its Grecian knot. I lifted the embroidered shawl from its leaves of tissue paper and drew it round my shoulders. Turning, I consulted the oracle. And Clara's daughter, newly-minted by a stranger's compliment, gleamed palely, darkly at me from the glass.

I stared at her as if I had met her for the first time, and she stared back, as shy and startled as Eurydice surprised by Orpheus. I saw her as Orpheus, or Christopher Hyde, might have done: a deep-eyed nymph with a high silk knot of hair, and a long neck rising above the aviary of glittering birds.

And Christopher Hyde had been quite right about her face.

It was lovely.

22

My father had been preparing for war all that year. He bought a very large, expensive and handsome map of the world, and a packet of small, coloured paper flags through which he drove long pins. On the Ides of March, when German troops invaded the rest of Czechoslovakia, he mounted this map on the kitchen wall and marked all Fascist and Fascist-occupied territory in Europe with black flags. It was a forbidding prospect.

'Now we're for it!' he remarked, with sombre pleasure. 'And the only one who's surprised is that idiot Neville Chamberlain!'

He tutted, eyes bright, colour high. He mimicked the Prime Minister's bewilderment.

'"Is this an attempt to dominate the world by force?"'

And answered the question roundly, 'Of course it is! Winston Churchill and I have been saying as much for years! No good throwing a bone to a jackal like Hitler. He wants the whole carcase. We've now lost the Czech army, a defensive strip comparable to the Maginot Line, and one of the most valuable arsenals in Europe!'

Dorothy, practical rather than political, was curious to know why he should choose her kitchen rather than his study in which to follow the complexities of war.

'What's the use of putting that map up here?' she asked.

He replied tetchily, 'Because this country is an island which relies heavily on imported goods, and we shall go short of food and fuel. We certainly shan't have enough coal to heat this damned great barn of a place – I told you before we

251

moved in that the house was too big! – so we shall all be living in the kitchen during the autumn and winter months, and I want to keep my eye on things.'

The thought of my father presiding over her domestic evenings was too much for Grannie to contemplate.

'Eh, surely we can find enough coal for your studying room?' she said. 'You canna do your thinking in the kitchen.'

Otherwise, she could see herself going to bed by nine o'clock.

'Perhaps they'll allow us a bit extra!' said Dorothy hopefully.

'I doubt it!' said my father with gloomy grandeur.

I could see we were due for another political lecture, and turned his thoughts in another direction.

'Daddy,' I said, 'would you like me to draw a swastika on those black flags, in white ink?'

'That would be a good idea, if you can spare the time,' he said, brightening up.

'And what colour flags are you giving to our country?'

'I hadn't thought. What about green?'

'England's green and pleasant land? It's a lovely idea, but if you used the white ones I could colour Union Jacks on them.'

'Are you sure it's not too much trouble, my lass?' he asked, softening at the prospect of my co-operation.

'Not a bit. I simply love doing that sort of thing. I'll get my coloured inks out after supper. We can't have Germany, Italy and Spain dominating our map!'

'Aye. Rule Britannia!' Grannie cried, with unexpected patriotism.

Dorothy headed for the telephone, chin set.

'I'll just have a quick word with the coal merchant,' she said.

The word 'shortages' had alerted her. She was determined not to have her war years blighted by want. As she passed her husband she took the opportunity of giving him a piece of her mind.

'And then I'm going to ring up Kate,' she said resolutely.

'I don't care two hoots whether you and your brothers like each other or not. If we have to be registered with a food shop it may as well be with Fawley's. Blood's thicker than water when all's said and done, and I've been one of their best customers for years – in spite of your nonsense about buying our groceries elsewhere. Elsewhere, indeed! They're the finest grocer's for miles round. Besides, none of the other shops give such long credit!'

Her voice was disappearing into the hall. We caught the last of her diatribe before she unhooked the receiver.

'It's always the men who make the trouble in this world, and the women who patch it up. I've never had a wrong word with any of your family, and I get on with Walter and Harold a treat! And what does the Bible say? A house divided against itself cannot stand. . . .'

My father cleared his throat and smiled sheepishly. Grannie came to his rescue, bypassing her daughter's criticism.

'Eh, none of us'll go short of owt while our Dollie's in charge!'

That evening I transformed quite a supply of little flags, which was just as well, for three weeks later Italy invaded Albania.

War was approaching, like the tread of marching feet. A month later I walked in from my music lesson to find Aunt Kate sitting very upright in a kitchen chair, resplendent in her best parma-violet costume and matching hat. The fact that she was taking milk and sugar in her tea, and eating a Kunzel cake, indicated a major crisis. But she turned from the waist just as gracefully, and her smile was as wide and warm as ever.

'You'll never guess what! All Kate's men have joined up!' said Dorothy, full of sympathy. 'The lads volunteered for the army, and your Uncle Harold went with them and wangled himself a desk job in his old regiment. We've been sitting here all afternoon, drinking tea and talking and having a good cry – haven't we, Mother?'

Grannie, sitting apart from them in her low chair by the

kitchen fire, replied, 'Aye, and they won't be the last tears as we shed, neither, if I know owt about it!'

I dropped my music-case, put both arms round Kate's neck, and hugged her tightly.

'You smell of Devon violets, Aunt Kate! Is it to match the suit? Don't you worry about Alex and Leo. They're lucky ducks, like Michael. And Uncle Harold will be far safer in a desk job than roaming round as an air-raid warden.'

'I'm not so sure – silly old fool!' said Kate, furious and fond at once. 'He nipped out with our boys while my back was turned. He's itching to grab hold of a rifle and go into battle again. And he's such a cunning old fox that I wouldn't be surprised if he managed it!'

'So you'll be left with Aunt Maud and Uncle Walter? How very dreary!' I said frankly. 'You must come and visit us more often!'

'My words exactly!' cried Dorothy. 'But tell Evie the rest of your news, Kate!'

'You'll never guess! Your Aunt Maud's getting married.'

I lifted my eyebrows, in what I hoped was the manner of Merle Oberon, and said 'To whom?'

'Eh, don't she sound like her father?' cried Grannie.

And Kate and Dorothy laughed.

'Aha! Not the knock-kneed idiot you might think, my superior young lady!' said Kate. 'He's a retired sea captain called Patrick Ridley, with a loud laugh and plenty of yarns to tell. A bit of a rake, in the nicest possible way. Bright blue eyes and reddish-grey side-whiskers. They're going to live in Southport.'

She gave her famous giggle, and said, 'I rather fancy him myself! I can't think how she landed him. But they're very fond of each other. Always squeezing hands or pressing feet under the table. Of course, she's the old-fashioned sort, all sweetness and light – not like Dollie and me! – and he's used to being in command . . .'

'I've invited them all for supper on Saturday night!' Dorothy interposed. 'Harold and Kate and the boys, and Walter, and Maud and the Captain. A sort of hail and farewell. . . .'

'. . . and Maud's had her hair cut short and marcel-waved and gone all girlish,' Kate continued. 'And the other day I caught her writing *Mrs Patrick Ridley* over and over again on a piece of paper! And she's taken her savings out of the Post Office and spent them all on new clothes and bed linen! I tell you. Wonders will never cease.'

'And that isn't all!' said Dorothy, busy orchestrating the conversation. 'Tell Evie about Walter, Kate!'

'Well, Walter and Harold had *such* a row when Harold joined up!'

'You *do* surprise me!' I said ironically.

'Have a Kunzel cake, love!' said Dorothy, and pushed a cup of tea towards me.

'Walter said he wasn't going to do Harold's share of work in the shop while he fooled round in the army. And Harold said that in that case Walter couldn't go on living with us rent-free. The house is ours, you see. That miserable old bat left it to Harold in her will. But of course we'd never dreamed of asking Walter for rent! Anyway, Walter is buying Harold out and moving into the old living quarters over the shop. He should feel at home! His mother and father started married life in those rooms, and he was born there. Anyway, when the hullabulloo had died down I had a quiet word with Walter . . .'

Dorothy looked at me significantly, as if to say, 'See what we women have to contend with?'

'. . . and he's agreed to pay the money into my bank account. Because if I didn't take care of it Harold would buy a fur coat for me and a Daimler for himself, take us both to London for a fortnight, and then find he was penniless except for his army pay!'

'Then there's no need to stay at The Laurels any more,' I said. 'So why don't you buy one of those nice convenient new bungalows they're building outside Kersley?'

'That's exactly what I said!' cried Dorothy. She included Grannie again. 'Didn't I, mother?'

But Grannie was brooding over the red coals, seeing a war which had gone, and robbed her in its going.

'Oh, I'll give the old mausoleum a try for a year or two,'

said Kate. 'I've never liked it, but Harold and the boys were born there, and it's always been home for them. Besides, Harold will be stationed in Blackstone for a while, so he'll be trotting to and fro. Anything can happen, can't it? With a big house like that, and Blackstone Barracks overflowing, I might have to provide billets for soldiers.'

She gave a tremendous giggle.

'My word, that would make Harold jealous!' she said gleefully. 'I'd give him cause, too, if I got a nice middle-aged officer. And serve the old fool right for deserting me!'

'And Katie's paved the way to my having a private word with Uncle Walter when he comes over on Saturday night,' said Dorothy, giving me a significant look. 'He'll look after us if there's rationing.'

I giggled and choked over the last of my cake, saying, 'I think you're both absolutely ruthless!'

'Is Walter still fond of macaroni cheese, Kate?' Dorothy asked.

'Yes, but he doesn't get it very often. My boys don't like it.'

'Oh, that's all right. I'll make him a macaroni cheese all to himself. In a big dish,' she added.

As soon as Grannie came to live with us Dorothy had ordered the Schofield's daily paper as well as the *Hathersall Weekly Advertiser*, on the pretext of making her mother feel at home. In fact Grannie only read the *Advertiser*, so Dorothy had the *News Chronicle* to herself and was henceforth spared the intellectual effort required by the *Manchester Guardian*. She also took a new magazine called *Picture Post*, which combined fine photographs with pithy journalism. She was now well-informed and anxious to impart her knowledge.

'What are we doing about an air-raid shelter, Gil?' she asked from behind the pages of the *Chronicle* at breakfast. 'They were giving out those Anderson shelters in London at the end of February, and we ought to have some protection. The Ministry of Health reckon they'll need between one and three million hospital beds for those killed and injured in the first air raids. Are you listening, Gil?'

My father withdrew his attention from the *Guardian* leader and considered this speech.

'Londoners will have priority, of course,' he said, 'being a prime target. But those air-raid figures sound excessive to me. And shelters aren't given out like sweets, Dorothy, they have to be paid for. Still, I must think about that.'

'And the sooner the better! Now let me tell you where I'm going this morning. Down to the Town Hall to join the Women's Voluntary Service. People always need feeding. I can organise the catering somewhere. The women will be in the front line, this time. Young ones in the forces, older ones in munitions and war work. No idlers.'

Sensing that part of this speech was directed at me, I left the aubade in my head to play by itself. Dorothy's war was becoming unpleasantly personal.

'I shan't have to join up, shall I?' I cried, alarmed.

My father spoke calmly and deliberately to reassure me and to reprove his wife.

'No, Evie. Your mother's overstating the case. As usual. Students will be exempt from call-up while they pursue their studies.' He had to add a moral rider. 'So be grateful for the privilege and make the most of your opportunities.'

'Well, I think a year or two in one of the women's forces would do Evelyn a world of good!' said Dorothy robustly. 'Look what a difference the air force has made to Michael! And what will *you* be doing in the way of war work, Gil?'

He sighed and put down his newspaper.

'Apart from being responsible for the safety of six hundred boys and an historic building,' he replied sarcastically, 'I'm already organising fire-watching rotas, fire-fighting lectures and air-raid drills at Grizedale's. And as soon as war is declared members of staff will take it in turns to sleep there. As headmaster I shall head the list of volunteers. So you can expect me to be away from home at least one night a week.' He added, 'For which I shall require a thermos flask of Ovaltine and a packet of sandwiches!'

Grannie said humbly into the silence, 'What can I do, Dollie?'

We all answered at once, for her humility made everyone her champion.

'Knit socks and balaclava helmets for the troops, Grannie! You're the best knitter in the family!'

'You'll be able to take my place when I'm at the WVS, Mother!'

My father said, 'Just keep the home fires burning, Grannie. That's the most valuable job of the lot!'

He feared that his tone had been too warm, his statement too sentimental. He corrected it with irony.

'I have noticed, in times of national crisis, that Dorothy invariably forgets to light the fires!'

'Nonsense!' said Dorothy vigorously.

There was a short pause until she found something else in the paper and returned to the fray in quieter mood.

'It looks very serious all the way round, Gil! Do you think we ought to book the house at Seascale this summer?'

'Yes, I do!' said my father, folding his *Guardian* emphatically and slapping it down on the table. 'I'm not letting those damned Huns spoil our annual holiday! Book it for August, as usual.'

Then he paused, looking down at the toast crumbs on his plate.

He said, 'Better ask Mick if he can put in for some leave and join us there. It might be the last holiday we have together as a family for quite a while.'

Public buildings were padded with sandbags, windows plastered with criss-cross strips of brown paper, trenches scored deep in recreation parks. Parlourmaids, weary of domestic service, gave short notice and marched off to serve their country instead.

At the Malt-house my father decided that the safest place for an air-raid shelter was the long cloakroom under the staircase. He had the partition taken down, and used the narrow end for stores of tinned food and candles. Dorothy raided Michael's camping equipment and set up spartan sleeping and eating quarters. Water was already laid on. A little window opened out on to the backyard. Even in the event of a direct hit he reckoned we could survive until someone dug us out.

Then he bought a stirrup pump, and made everyone except Grannie learn how to use it.

We queued at a local community centre to be fitted for our gas masks. Behind the mask, cool and flabby and smelling of rubber, I felt completely isolated. Drawing the first breath was a terrifying experience. I sucked in air frantically, heart beating. The thought of living this way for hours in a gas-filled world was a nightmare.

Grannie followed the air-raid warden's instructions. obediently, and came out flushed and tearful from the gas mask, murmuring, 'Eh, my poor Arthur!'

Inside its sleeping-bag mask a baby kicked and yelled silently.

Our family crises usually brought some material benefit in their wake to anoint the bruises. The row over Leslie Ormerod had resulted in a Morris saloon, to Dorothy's great delight. So when summer arrived, warm and beautiful, we locked up the Malt-house as usual and gave a key to Mrs Inchmore, and my father drove us up to the Lake District. But the holiday was curtailed, for on the twenty-third of August, as half the country experienced a trial black-out, Russia signed a non-aggression pact with Germany, and Michael's leave was cancelled.

We dropped all pretence of relaxation and listened to every news bulletin on the wireless. My father drove several miles to buy a copy of the *Guardian*, and walked in waving it, crying, 'They're pushing an Emergency Powers Bill through Parliament!'

Then he said fretfully, 'I should have brought my map!'

It was Dorothy who made the decision. Dorothy, in charge of Kersley's catering plans for London evacuees, walked up to the Post Office to telephone the head of Kersley WVS for advice, and arrived back grim and gleeful at once.

'Right! Let's start packing,' she said. 'We're going home.'

On Sunday morning, the third of September, my father put his head round the kitchen door to deliver a highly important announcement.

'The Prime Minister will be speaking in five minutes!'

I set the coffee percolator to bubble on the gas stove. Julian put away his homework. Flora came out from under the table. Dorothy ceased to beat Yorkshire pudding batter and called to Grannie who was peeling potatoes in the scullery.

'Mother! It's nearly eleven o'clock. Time to listen to the Prime Minister.'

Grannie dried her hands on her apron, anxious to oblige, and we followed my father across the hall. In the drawing room we stood in a solemn half-circle round the wireless set, with Flora at our feet, ears cocked. The room was bright and peaceful in the September sun. I can visualise it now, in those last moments of peace. The front of the wireless set was decorated with a carved wooden tree, spreading its branches like a blessing. A large copper bowl of roses bloomed in the empty grate. The furniture glowed, the cushions were plump, the carpet was well-groomed. Ebony and gilt-framed pictures hanging from chains on the walls showed life as it should be: rural idylls, mystical events, romantic meetings.

Dorothy said, 'Julian, you must remember this day. This is a day which will go down in history.'

Grannie said, 'I wonder where our Michael is now?'

My father looked at us kindly, and placed a finger on his lips.

The clock struck.

The words were spoken.

Between one moment and the next we were at war with Germany.

Part Three

1940–1944

23

Our first attempts at a black-out were makeshift and did not reach the standard required by local air-raid wardens. So Grannie and Dorothy spent hours treddling away at their Singer sewing machines, making a set of lining curtains for each window in the house from regulation black cloth. Since even these let chinks of light escape from the top, my father paid a carpenter to put up wooden pelmets and stain them a dark-oak colour. And at last we were warden-proof.

Light. I had never realised how much I took it for granted. The nightly ritual of lighting street lamps had been a beloved part of my childhood. Now those lamps were out for the duration of the war, and lamplighters became obsolete. Everyone carried a pocket torch, and even this must be shone carefully on the ground, not waved about, for enemies could be watching from the air.

Lights in buses, trams and trains were dim and heavily shaded. There were no longer any signposts or names of towns and cities displayed. At night we found our way cautiously under a pall of darkness in a strange land.

Autumn was warm and mild, heavy with blackberries. But winter came, in this first year of the war, not only bitterly cold but black. Travelling to and from the city became a formidable venture, but there were compensations. The music college formed a fire-watching rota of teachers and students, and once a week I took my turn as part of a team, sleeping in a camp bed when I was off duty. Protests from parents, fearful for their daughters' virtue, made no difference. 'There's a war on!' was the standard reply. Mind you, the strictest proprieties were observed. Females occupied one room and males another, and two members of staff supervised us. But that was not good enough for Dorothy, who bought me a pair of very ugly flannelette pyjamas and a pair of slacks to put over them. Still, it was a novel experience, and the thrill of meeting a strange man with a coat over his pyjamas, on the way to the lavatory, was quite indescribable.

I would have enjoyed it still more had my imagination not leaped ahead of me, painting lurid pictures, of which the worst was being caught in a Blackstone air raid. I saw myself falling like a flannel-clad doll, arms and legs whirling, machine-gunned from the parapet. I pictured myself entombed in the cellars of the music college, dying slowly beneath the rubble. I felt and heard fire raging above and about me. Pipes burst, inundating me with water, poisoning me with gas. I died many deaths a day, and at night they disturbed my dreams. For I was dreaming vividly, feverishly, in the heightened atmosphere of war.

I saw Clara, older now and forsaken, staring out of a window, companionless in a cold house. Lilian Lacey, remembered only once a year in a Christmas card letter, held out bandaged hands in mute appeal. Michael dived from the sky in a comet of flame. And the elusive Christopher Hyde hurried forever away from me down a hot and dusty pavement.

The New Year, and a new decade, began with the coldest January in a century. Water, land and people froze. At the end of the month a great blizzard blanketed the Pennines. I stayed home that week and practised the piano in a chilly drawing room, wrapped in layers of woollies. The music sounded flat, the keys were cold, my fingers turned white and stiff. Vitality was low and spirits ebbed. No one could help me. They had their own problems.

All Dorothy's good work had gone for nothing. Only four months ago she had organised the reception, bedding and feeding of nine hundred and forty-four London evacuees. Before Christmas, all but a few of them had trailed back home. She went down daily to the Town Hall to take her part in the WVS activities, but these had dwindled to knitting squares for patchwork quilts and running whist drives, and she needed greater challenges.

At Grizedale's ancient pipes burst, enraging my father who had been urging their replacement for years. His two fire-watching nights were purgatory for us as well as himself. By the time he had driven off, loaded with blankets and pillows, a hot water bottle, a thermos flask and a packet of sandwiches, his gas mask and his tin hat, we felt as if we had set up and personally supplied an Arctic expedition.

In this month, also, Dorothy reckoned the war really began.

Her weekly grocery order was delivered by Fawley's High-Class Grocer's van promptly at half past four on a Friday afternoon, in two large cardboard boxes. And while she unpacked she liked to chat to Fred the delivery man, who came in time for tea and biscuits. This was always a delightful domestic ceremony, particularly enjoyed by Michael and me when we were children. For she allowed us to put away the hand-weighed, hand-packed, brown, white and blue bags of dry goods, the painted tins and gleaming jars and shiny packs, the yellow slabs of cheese and butter, and the thickly-sliced best back bacon. And there was always a complimentary paper cornet of chocolate peppermint creams for Dorothy, to thank her for her custom.

This savage January day she had three unpleasant surprises, the first being the delivery man, who did not arrive until half past five and proved to be a total stranger.

'Why, where's Fred?' Dorothy asked.

For this old fellow with his cap and muffler and frayed gloves, puffing and grumbling at the weight of his load, was hardly the sort of person Fawley's employed. They liked them good-mannered, smart, bright and reasonably young. Fred had been with the firm for the past twelve years, was immensely popular with all the ladies and reckoned that the customers' tips paid for his Blackpool holiday every year.

'He's joined up, missis,' said the man briefly.

'Oh!' said Dorothy, betrayed. Then, censoriously, 'You're very late. I'm in the middle of cooking our evening meal.'

'Tha'rt lucky to get it at all,' said the man. 'Van's been off t'road sin' Tuesday. Garage were short o' spare parts.'

'Indeed? And what might your name be?'

She was on her dignity, but he refused to truckle to her.

'Mr Leadbetter,' he replied, with a slight emphasis on the *Mr*.

'Well, let me tell you something, Mr Leadbetter,' emphasising the *Mr* sarcastically. 'Shortages are one thing, but good service and good manners are another. I'm not used to this sort of treatment.'

'Happen tha'll have to get used to it,' he said ironically. 'And when t'petrol ration runs out tha'lt have to fetch thi own order!'

Grannie had not heard this revolutionary exchange and though Dorothy was mouthing 'No!' and shaking her head, she poured him a cup of tea and offered a plate of biscuits.

'Mother, would you like to put the groceries away while I check everything?' Dorothy asked. And to Mr Leadbetter she said curtly, 'You'd better sit down.'

A short note was attached to her long shopping list, written in Uncle Walter's clerkly hand.

'Dear Dorothy, I am very sorry to say that owing to the present situation Fawley's can no longer supply the customary gift of sweets, and we are unable to fulfil all of your requirements. I am sure you will understand that this is through no fault or wish of our own, but due to wartime shortages. Yours sincerely, Walter.'

Mr Leadbetter watched her face as she read this, and though Dorothy tried not to look disappointed, she failed. He gave a sour little smile, and dunked a second biscuit in his tea.

There was only one cardboard box, and three small packages had slipped down the side of it. She fished them out, puzzled. She unwrapped them and stared in disbelief.

'Never!' she cried, aroused. 'Is this all we get?'

Mr Leadbetter tightened his muffler and pulled his cap further over one eye. He stood up.

'Aye, them's your rations, missis,' he said with evident satisfaction. 'Butter, sugar and bacon. I've never tasted butter in me life, sithee, but I daresay you use that much for breakfast. Well, now it's got to last the week. We're all being treated alike, missis. Rich and poor. I've taken orders round all day to t'big houses, and watched folk's faces drop – like yours did just now. And I'll tell thee, summat – it's been the best bloody day o' my life!'

He turned at the threshold of the back door, adding, 'I shouldna waste thi time complaining to Fawley's about me, neither. They're having enough trouble finding staff as it is. So, as long as t'petrol lasts, missis, thee and me'll have to put up wi' one another! And then it'll be Shanks's Pony all the way to Kersley and back for thee! That'll take a bit o' weight off thee, any road!'

In the awful silence that followed his departure Grannie said timidly, 'That van driver seemed to be very opinionated.'

'Opinionated?' Dorothy burst out. 'He's downright impertinent! I know his sort. They're either at your feet or your throat. He'd have been as nice as pie if there wasn't a war on!'

In her fury and fluster she invented a new expression. 'He's a fair-weathercock, that's what he is! A fair-weathercock!'

Mrs Inchmore proved to be the next fair-weathercock. Her legs, acting as a barometer to the climate of her soul, played up something terrible that winter. The Malt-house in war-time was a large cold place, and the flagstones outside the wash-house proved to be an ice-rink, as her legs discovered when they slithered the length of them one bitter Monday morning. Fortunately she landed on her behind and no bones were broken, but her legs were badly shocked. They went home early and took the rest of the week off.

On the following Monday, slyly, sulkily, they made their way to the labour exchange and found her a better-paid job in a factory, where they could sit down all day. Then they took the tram to Tarn Brow and broke the news to Dorothy.

'I can't believe it!' Dorothy said to anyone who was prepared to listen. 'She's been with me since nineteen twenty-eight, and never a wrong word. She's been part of the family. And to walk out like that, with not so much as a by-your-leave, or even a week's notice.'

'Times are changing,' said Aunt Kate, who was at present playing the role of confidante. 'I can't find a charwoman for love or money. Lord, what wouldn't I give to have dear old Ada alive? That sort of family servant has gone for good, Dorothy, believe you me. And we're all in the same boat. Not one of the local doctors' wives has a parlourmaid to her name.'

'Never fret, our Dollie,' said Grannie gallantly, though the prospect of tackling a ten-roomed house must have daunted her. 'I've been cleaning for sixty year. I can do it a while longer.'

But dust settled, silver tarnished, parquet floors grew dull and furniture wore a blue bloom. There were spots of iron-mould on the table linen. The weekly laundry, once washed on Monday, ironed on Tuesday and aired on Wednesday, took up permanent residence with us and hung about all the time. The Malt-house was becoming a hotel which had seen better days.

So far the war had been in cold storage along with the weather, but in the spring of 1940 they both warmed up. My father, who had been grumbling about the lack of movement on his map, began to worry about the Nazi advance instead. For suddenly, within five weeks, German troops had occupied Denmark, Norway, Belgium and Holland, taken Amiens and reached the French seaside town of Abbeville in Normandy.

Late and unprepared, as he prophesied we would be, the British prepared to fight. But first we exchanged the leader who had craved peace for one who loved to battle, and our family gathered round the wireless set to hear Winston Churchill speak as Prime Minister. He had one ardent follower among the Fawleys before he began.

From his rostrum of the drawing-room hearth, my father said, 'Now we shall get somewhere. At last!'

The voice was that of a warrior and orator. He offered us

nothing but blood, toil, tears and sweat. He told us that we must wage war by sea, land and air, with all our might and with all the strength that God could give us. He promised victory at all costs. Victory in spite of all terror. Victory, however long and hard the road might be.

None of us spoke when he had finished. He had said everything that was necessary.

Aunt Kate was worrying about Alex and Leo, who were in France with the British Expeditionary Force. She had not heard from them for some time, but even when they wrote they did not know how to sustain her. They loved her, no doubt of that, but their letters were brief, infrequent and unsatisfactory. Nor did Uncle Harold help, for he was a natural soldier, and accepted discipline and deprivation as part of the adventure of war.

'Kate's fretting again,' he would say jovially. 'She's worried in case the lads haven't enough clean socks!'

And when she flared up in anger, or broke down in terror, he did not know what to do, but strode up and down the room, twisting his greying moustache, saying that physical danger and hardship turned boys into men.

In those lovely late-May days Aunt Kate often walked the mile up to the Malt-house, fashionably dressed and hatted, to cry to Dorothy and Grannie and me, who were afraid for Michael and could sympathise.

My father's little line of black flags moved inexorably on. The enemy were only a few days' march from Paris. The Dutch capitulated. The Belgians were about to follow. The French were in total disarray. Abandoned by their allies, the British troops retreated to the beach of a Flemish town called Dunkirk. And having got as far as they could, had no choice but to stay there.

'Hard and heavy tidings?' said my father, repeating Churchill's sombre warning to the nation. 'That means we've lost the expeditionary force and all its equipment.'

'Oh, don't say that to Kate!' said Dorothy fearfully.

'My dear Dorrie, we're not much better off than Alex and Leo. There's only the Channel between us and the damned Germans, and our defence lies in the hands of an untrained, part-time civilian army without guns or uniforms!'

He thought for a moment.

'I suppose I ought to go down and sign on with them,' he said. 'I've still got my rifle. I could shoot it out, if the worst came to the worst.'

I had never really liked Alex and Leo, and when Alex came home alone I felt as guilty as if I had killed Leo personally. Uncle Harold was away in the Midlands, and we took upon ourselves the responsibility of listening to and comforting poor Aunt Kate. Sometimes Alex came over, for he was on extended leave, still suffering from shock and exposure. What comfort he got from us nobody knew, for he sat there silently throughout each visit, either with his hands clenched between his knees or smoking cigarette after cigarette, looking at nothing.

'Best to take no notice,' Dorothy advised. 'Just act naturally.'

My father had always disapproved of Harold's boys and their supposed influence on Michael. But it was he who tackled the problem when the three of us were in the drawing room one Sunday afternoon. I had been playing Schumann, because Dorothy thought that music might be therapeutic for my cousin, and my father had been listening and swinging his reading glasses.

In the tranquillity that followed the last notes he said easily and pleasantly, 'Tell me what it was like at Dunkirk, Alex.'

And so opened the floodgates.

'We'd been sitting on the beach for days, waiting. We didn't know for what. I suppose we hoped somebody would do something. It was all pretty desperate. And then we saw that hotch-potch fleet of boats coming in. Everything from posh sailing yachts to motor launches. The RAF was with them, to fight off the Gerries, and there was stuff coming at us from all over the place.

'There were thousands of us on the beach, but they began to organise us into lines. Wounded first. Orderly retreat.

'We were wading out to the boats, Leo and me. We kept talking. Nothing that mattered but it helped to keep our spirits up. Leo still had his rifle, which he held up over his head. I still had my boots. I knotted the laces and slung them round my neck. We hadn't shaved or eaten or slept properly for days, and – short of dying – we'd been through the bloody lot.

'"Keep moving, lads!" the sergeant yelled. "This isn't a bloody Sunday School picnic!"

'Leo shouted to me, over the din, "He never saw *our* Sunday School picnics. Do you remember when we started that fight in the back of the charabanc? And when we lit those squibs?"

'It made us laugh. Funny sort of laughing, nearer to crying.

'I said to Leo, "You've got a dirty face and you stink!"

'And he said, "Same to you, mate!"

'My legs were unsteady.

'Leo said, "If I cop it and you have to identify me, you'll find the imprint of Mum's slipper on my bum!"

'I didn't tell her that. I thought it would make things worse. We never minded her hitting us. But I must tell her that sometime. We only made a fuss for the hell of it. She didn't really hurt us.

'The boats were coming in as close as they could, shipping water as they went, with the weight of men on board. Neither of us is – was – what you'd call tall. Not like Mick. And Leo was a couple of inches shorter than me. Our uniforms were sodden with sea water. He must have been more tired than I was. Falling behind. He spoke in jerks.

'The Gerries were coming down to machine-gun us. There were bullets spurting in the sea all round us, and the water was up to our chests. The boats seemed to get further off, instead of closer. We were all thrashing about like fools to reach them.

'The skipper of one pleasure boat leaned over the side and held out his hand.

'"Come on, mates!" he said. "We've got to get out of here."

'I had one hand on the boat when something made me turn round, and I saw that Leo had stopped a few yards off and was staring at me. I keep going over and over this in my mind. I dream about it. He was trying to tell me something, just looking at me. And I looked back at him. Then he lost his footing. I saw it happen like a slow-motion picture. He kept looking hard at me, frowning a bit, with his mouth open. Then he simply went under. The last thing I saw was his rifle. He was still holding it over his head.

'I started to push my way back, calling him.

'Someone shouted, "He's copped it, mate!"

'I didn't believe him. I was punching and fighting my way back. Then the sergeant grabbed me and gave me a sock on the jaw. I was groggy, but I could feel them hauling me aboard. Two of them propped me up. There was no room to lie down, or even to sit. I stood jammed between them and cried like a baby.

'The sergeant said, "He'd had it, lad. The bastards machine-gunned him. He was dead before he dropped."

'But do you know what I was thinking? I was wondering how I could tell Mum. Because I remember Leo being born. He was lying in one of those cots with frilly curtains round it, and Mum was sitting up in bed with a frilly jacket on.

'And she said, "This is your baby brother, Alex, and you're to look after him."

'He'd have been twenty-one this month.

'So I kept on crying and saying, "It wasn't my fault, Mum! It wasn't my fault!"''

24

In Hitler's view the war was over and he offered peace. It must have seemed logical to him and inevitable to everyone else, but we British were an obstinate people. In pugnacious mood, Winston Churchill told the world that we would never give in.

'Look at it this way,' said my father, as we listened to a roll-call of allied anthems being played before the nine o'clock news, 'we've got all these foreign servicemen here prepared to fight, and we rescued most of our army from Europe, and we've enrolled over a million in the Home Guard. It's not as though we were defenceless.'

Invasion. Children evacuated from coastal towns. Children sent to America for safety. Concrete tank traps on beaches. Old men and teenage boys in civilian clothes, drilling with kitchen brooms.

In my dreams, the skies were black with winged invaders. Church bells jangled warning. Parachutists drifted down like dandelion clocks. Spies disguised themselves as nuns. Friends turned traitor. Posters came to life, flapping and shrieking, 'Be careful what you say. Careless talk costs lives.'

How long now, we thought? The world seemed to hold its breath for a while, and then the Luftwaffe swooped down for the kill.

Through the splendour of those long hot summer days, young men became legends, donning their flying helmets, taking to the air in legendary 'planes. On the south-east coast people came out to watch the air battles. The victors performed a victory roll. The vanquished fell out of the sky, incinerated in a pyre of flame or landing crazily but safely in a field of hay. The headlines of evening newspapers notched up the day's total of Nazi 'planes destroyed like sports scores. And we held on until autumn approached, the threat of invasion receded and the enemy changed tactics.

Early in September 1940 the indiscriminate and persistent bombing of London began.

For three months, while the capital city was battered night after night and fired with incendiaries, the local sirens around Blackstone wailed at half past ten each evening and celebrated the all-clear at half past six each morning. Sometimes the warning signalled the approach of German bombers, but these were merely passing over Kersley on their way to an industrial target, and there were never very many of them. Often we would hear nothing all night.

'I expect it's a way of keeping people safe indoors,' said Dorothy. 'A sort of curfew.'

'And we're waiting again,' I said.

For I was as finely attuned to silences as to sounds.

'We're waiting to see if London holds up to this lot,' said my father grimly.

'Poor old London,' said Dorothy sadly. 'I've always loved it. I can't bear to think of those beautiful buildings being destroyed. Why, you've never even seen it, Evelyn. The lights in Piccadilly Circus and the pigeons in Trafalgar Square, and Kew Gardens in the spring.'

'We've got a few beautiful old buildings up here, too, in case the Nazis run out of cultural targets!' said my father sarcastically.

He was thinking, of course, of Grizedale's, but I, who had been wondering how to introduce a different subject now found the way.

'The Royal Victoria Concert Hall in Blackstone is beautiful,' I said. 'They built that before Victorian architecture got so fussy. And do you know what I'd like to do for a family Christmas present? I'd like to take you all to hear Handel's *Messiah* there. Is that a nice idea? I mean, everybody. Grannie and Julian as well. He's not too young to hear it for the first time, and Grannie used to love listening to Grandad sing in the Hathersall Church Choir.'

The short silence could have boded well or ill. The adults smiled uncertainly. Julian spoke first, with ten-year-old frankness.

'Is it instead of a proper Christmas present? Because I'd rather you bought me something for my Hornby train set.'

And Grannie said, 'It's very good of you, love, but Blackstone's too far off for me. I canna manage the buses and trams like I did. And then to sit for two-three hours in a public hall. And my hearing's none so sharp these days. Don't waste your money on me, love.'

I appealed to my father and to Dorothy.

'But I thought it would be such a lovely idea. A family outing on a Saturday afternoon. We'll be back here by six o'clock. And Malcolm Sargent's conducting the Huddersfield Choir – you simply can't hear anything better than that. And Isobel Baillie is the soprano!'

My father, hating to disappoint me, spoke apologetically.

'The days are short and the transport's difficult, Evie. Besides, the Germans have been blitzing industrial cities recently. We don't want to be caught in an air raid, miles from home. I wouldn't mind if we could go by car, but I haven't enough petrol coupons.'

"And is your journey really necessary?" Julian quoted under his breath.

An unexpected ally arose in the shape of Dorothy.

'I know where I can *buy* some petrol coupons.'

My father was shocked.

'Good heavens!' he said. And then again, 'Good heavens!' And then, wavering, 'Suppose we get found out?'

'Surely you're clever enough to think up a good excuse?' said Dorothy sarcastically. 'I'll get the coupons anyway. You never know when they'll come in useful.'

'I'm not at all sure that I approve . . .' he began.

'Leave it to me,' said Dorothy firmly. 'You needn't know anything about them. I'll take the blame. Just use them and say nothing.'

While he hesitated, she said, 'That's settled, then!'

She turned to rally the others. 'Now, Mother, we're going in the car, so you've got nothing to do but sit there in comfort. And it's time you went further than Kersley market. You're growing into a regular hermit these days, and that'll never do. Why not come with us for a Christmas treat? My father thought the world of the *Messiah*.'

Browbeaten, Grannie acquiesced.

'And as for you, Julian,' said Dorothy, 'you can either come to the *Messiah* with us, and your father will treat us to tea at Barber's or Peeble's afterwards, or you can manage without a Christmas present from Evelyn altogether. Which is it to be?'

'Oh, well. Thanks, Evie, I'll come.'

Dorothy swept past his reply.

'When did you say it was, Evelyn? The Saturday before Christmas? Then that should put us in the right mood. And by the way, everybody, I've managed to order a turkey from a local farm, and Uncle Walter's letting me have a few extras, and I saved a pudding from last year, so Christmas will be as good as ever.'

She received our congratulations with a satisfied nod, but remembered one absence.

'I just wish Michael could be with us,' she said.

I thanked her afterwards, wondering what random impulse had caused this alliance.

'Oh, that's all right,' said Dorothy. 'They only needed sorting out. If we don't make an effort we shall just sit at home in the black-out, brooding about the war. Besides, it's important we do things together as a family. Fambly comes fust! Remember Ma Joad in *The Grapes of Wrath?*'

So that was how Dorothy saw herself these days? It was a far cry from Mrs Erlynne. I felt a little sad.

My father drove in some trepidation to Blackstone. He was now worrying in case the petrol coupons had been forged.

'Forget it,' Dorothy said, 'and leave the talking to me!'

But no one arrested us. Breathing more freely, my father parked in a side street and shepherded his flock into the concert hall.

I produced my sheaf of tickets proudly. I had booked five seats in the front row of the balcony: a choice which had demanded personal sacrifices in the way of transport, lunches and trips to the Kardomah for the whole of the autumn term. The family, shown to their places, were touched and impressed. My father wanted to buy a programme, but I could not allow that.

'My treat!' I said firmly, and bought them one each as a memento. 'Now, Julian, come and sit by me, and I'll tell you how Handel came to write the *Messiah*. And when the orchestra starts to tune up, I'll point out the different instruments.'

I settled down and looked round the Royal Victoria Hall with delight. It reminded me somehow of Lilian Lacey. Elegant and restrained. And then it hinted at Clara, who had also been musical. I resolved to write a long letter to Lilian tomorrow and tell her all about it.

'The acoustics are marvellous, wherever you sit,' I explained, flushed with success, 'but you get the best view from here.'

My father put his arm round my shoulders and squeezed me affectionately.

'You're a generous lass,' he said. He made a little joke. 'In fact, everything's going according to plan – provided we can keep your mother out of prison for fiddling the petrol coupons!'

'It's not worth their while to put me in prison,' said Dorothy promptly. 'I'm too useful. But if they do then I can take life easy for a change – which is more than I've been able to do since I married you twelve years ago!'

She nodded emphatically to underline this point. My father winked at me, and laughed.

I smiled back, and continued to pay delicate attentions to all my guests, but inwardly I was already withdrawing from them, preparing to immerse myself in musical waters and be baptised anew.

We came out into a rosy winter afternoon, and like the people who walked in darkness we had all been changed. My father and Dorothy strolled arm-in-arm affectionately. Grannie was communing with old memories. Julian looked pleased with himself, as if he had cleared a cultural hurdle. And I felt downright exalted.

Dorothy was deciding what the family should do next.

'What time is it? Half past four? Shall we stay in Victoria Square and have tea at Peeble's, or take the car up to Barber's? Still, we might not be able to park so easily at the centre of town. I suppose we could leave the car here and walk up Victoria Street. On the other hand, Mother might not be able to manage that far. Oh, Mother says she can, and she'd like to look in the shop windows.'

We strode briskly in the cold, our conversation forming a family oratorio.

'Do you know, our Dollie, I've been counting up on my fingers, and I haven't been in Blackstone for above three year!'

'That's what I said, Mother. It's done you a power of good to have an afternoon out.'

'I've always admired the skyline of this street,' said my father, musing aloud. 'The Victorians weren't afraid of civic grandeur. They didn't mind spending money. And they built for posterity. None of the gim-crack arty stuff we put up nowadays.'

Obediently we lifted our faces to admire the skyline with him.

Julian said, pointing to the silhouetted chimneys, 'It looks just like the drawings in *Film Fun*.'

Barrage balloons floated in the evening sky, their silver and grey flushed to pink as the light failed.

'Clear and frosty,' said Dorothy. 'Poor old London'll be for it again tonight. And did I tell you that Lord Haw-Haw mentioned us on the wireless the other day in *Germany Calling*? He said, "The Luftwaffe hasn't forgotten the small towns!" and he read out a list, and Kersley and Hathersall were on it.'

'He's a fool and a traitor,' said my father curtly. '*Germany Calling*, indeed. I'd shoot him, for two pins! You shouldn't listen.'

'Why not?' said Dorothy. 'He makes me laugh most of the time.'

I said nothing, borne on the crest of the 'Hallelujah Chorus.'

An aftermath of a great occasion, the evening passed in a desultory fashion. It was too late to warm my father's study. Heavy with a stew which was composed largely of potatoes and carrots, we sat in the kitchen pursuing our own thoughts, sometimes in silence, sometimes aloud.

'I wonder why onions are so scarce?' said Dorothy. 'They were raffling one down at the WRVS last week. I bought five tickets, but I didn't win it. And this time last year I had a proper joint sitting in the meat-safe ready for the Sunday dinner, and now I've got a miserable bit of stuff there that you couldn't put a name to if you tried. I said to the butcher, I said, "What part of what animal does that come from, Mr Breerton?" And do you know what he said? He said, "Let's be thankful it isn't horse-meat, Mrs Fawley, though we might come to it yet!" What do you think of that?'

'Eh, Dollie, take a look at this piece in the *Advertiser*. There's a man in Hathersall been had up before the magistrates for selling petrol coupons, and they're sending him to prison!'

My father glanced up from the *Blackstone Evening News* and said briefly, 'Julian. Nine o'clock!'

Reluctantly, my young brother put away his tools. He was making a De Havilland Tiger Moth out of balsa wood.

'Did you know that Mick was trained in one of these?' he said, trying to start a conversation.

'Yes, love, we did,' said Dorothy briskly. 'Now night night,' lifting up her face for his kiss, 'and thank Evie for giving you such a lovely treat, and thank Daddy for the tea. No offence, Gil, but the balcony restaurant isn't what it was. Slow service, and that gipsy ensemble's on its last legs! And what sort of tea would it have been if I hadn't brought some butter along with me?'

We were deeply embarrassed by this recollection.

'However do people manage on their ordinary rations?' she wondered, ignoring our discomfiture.

'We shan't know that, apparently,' my father replied with fine humour, 'since you seem to have solved the problem for us.'

'They've had somebody up before the magistrates for buying butter from this here Black Market, our Dollie. Wherever's Black Market? I've never heard of it.'

My father said crisply, 'Bed, Julian, if you please! Don't let me have to tell you again.'

Grannie left her gossip column and hurried into the scullery to fill the kettle. I set aside my score of the *Messiah* and laid the tray for our evening cup of tea. Dorothy bustled into the larder and brought out one small tin, half-filled with digestive biscuits.

'Black market or not, I can't perform miracles!' she said.

In that instant Flora whined and the cat dived under the table. The earth shuddered and the house shook as if it were being thumped by some cosmic bully. Teacups jingled, teaspoons tinkled, saucers chattered. The clock stopped on the wall.

We stood open-mouthed, frozen in the movement we had been making at the time of impact.

Then my father said, 'Listen!'

An armada was droning steadily, purposefully, overhead. We heard another stick of bombs fall further away. And another. Then the sound of bombs and bombers mingled like some fearful double concerto, above which a frantic and familiar wail now rose and fell.

'Incompetent idiots!' my father cried wrathfully. 'The only time the damn siren is needed – and it's late! Into the shelter everyone!'

An excited voice from the top of the stairs cried, 'Daddy! Daddy! Is it our turn to be blitzed?'

Dorothy grabbed the tea-tray, saying, 'Evelyn, bring Flora and the cat with you.'

She saw Grannie scurrying in the wrong direction and hailed her.

'Wherever are you going, Mother?'

Confused, Grannie replied, 'I'm just getting my hat and coat from the back of the door, Dollie. Have you seen my handbag?'

'Leave them, Mother. You won't need them, and we haven't time.'

The noise of the bombers was loud enough to thrill the nerves.

I heard my voice, high and strained, crying, 'Julian! Help me. I've got Flora's lead on, but she won't move. You take her!'

Then I crouched down, trembling, lifting the chenille fringe of the table-cover, and called, 'Tommy, Tommy, Tom Cat!'

'Put the lights out and use your torches!' my father ordered.

I shouted, 'Daddy, this blooming old cat won't come out!'

'Let him take his chances. He should be all right there. Evelyn! Did you hear what I said? Leave him! At once!'

We had been sitting in the shelter for several minutes, blankets round our shoulders, warming our hands on the teacups rather than drinking, when the telephone rang imperatively in the hall.

'That'll be for me!' said Dorothy, convinced.

'Then bring it inside the shelter!' said my father. 'The lead's long enough. No use standing in the hall. Think of flying glass.'

She grabbed the telephone and brought it in at a run. Her voice sounded unusually loud in that enclosed area.

'Yes? Yes! Where? Ah! We thought it was near. Right. Can you send anyone for me? I'll be ready as soon as you are, then. Will you ring Mrs Sawyer and Mrs Betts and pick them up, too? Right!'

She hooked up the receiver and spoke to my father.

'I've got to go in a few minutes. They dropped that first stick of bombs right across the middle of Kersley. The one nearest to us demolished a row of houses in Moss Lane. All the windows have been blown out of the school and church. They don't know how many casualties there are. They're setting up a relief centre in the Town Hall. I'm off to do the catering.'

The telephone rang again, making us all jump.

'This must be for me,' said my father prophetically. 'Yes, Dawson? I was afraid so! Who's with you on fire-watching duty? Just Freeman? Where did it drop? The playing fields could be worse. Oh, next to the new gymnasium? And there were incendiaries too? Have you sent for the fire brigade? They don't know how long they'll be? I'm not surprised. I think we shall have to deal with this ourselves. I'll be there as soon as I can. Ring every member of staff and ask for volunteers.'

To us, he said briefly, 'I'm off. Expect me when you see me.'

'But what about your thermos and sandwiches?' Dorothy cried, automatically mindful of his comforts.

'Oh, damn all that nonsense, Dorrie. Grizedale's is burning down. Where the hell's my tin hat?'

Then we all realised that at best we must manage without each other until the air raid was over, and at worst might not survive it.

Julian was sitting in his dressing-gown with his arm round Flora, who whined and shifted restlessly. Grannie and I sat hand in hand. It was difficult to know who was comforting whom.

'Now you'll be perfectly safe,' said my father firmly, 'just as long as you follow the rules we've laid down. And on no account must you come out until you hear the signal for the all-clear.'

Julian said, 'I'll look after us all, Daddy.'

For that is what Michael would have said, in his place.

'Good chap. We'll be back as soon as we can.'

Dorothy kissed and hugged us passionately. We guessed what was going through her mind, and it was not reassuring.

'Good thing you got those extra petrol coupons, Dorrie,' said my father, giving praise where it was due. 'I'd have had to walk to Grizedale's without them. The place might have been gutted by the time I got there!'

She kissed him. They held each other briefly. The

front-door bell signalled that Dorothy's car had arrived. Then they were gone, and only a majestic staircase and a cloakroom door stood between the three of us and destruction.

The shock had been too much for Grannie. She sat patiently in a canvas garden chair, saying at regular intervals, 'Is it over yet, Evleen?' And she fretted about her hat, her coat and her handbag until I broke the first rule by going out of the shelter to get them.

Curious, in spite of my fear, I drew back one curtain from the scullery window and peered out, remaining there fascinated, until I remembered that the others would be worried by my absence. But as nothing dreadful had happened and I was growing used to the idea of an air raid, I also stopped and knelt by the kitchen table to coax out Tom Cat. He gave a grateful meow, but refused to join me.

Julian was still sitting with one arm round Flora when I got back. He looked pale and strained. Grannie was muttering to herself and shaking her head.

'You shouldn't have done that, Evie,' he said reproachfully, as I slipped in.

'I know, but . . .' and I nodded significantly at Grannie. 'Here you are, Grannie!' I said loudly.

I helped her to put on her hat and coat. Suitably attired, she clutched her handbag and sat upright, ready for anything.

'What's it like out there?' Julian asked curiously.

'As bright as day. Everything's lit up. I looked out. . . .'

'Evie, you shouldn't have done. . . .'

'I know, but I'm glad I did. The bombers are coming over like a swarm of locusts. And there are searchlights crisscrossing everywhere. Though why they bother I don't know. It's bright as day outside. The sky looks just as it does on bonfire night, only more so. There's a red glow radiating up from the horizon, and when the bombs fall the red turns gold. Actually, if it wasn't so horrible it would be beautiful.'

He accepted this with a nod.

'Shall I make us all some cocoa?' I asked, glancing at

Grannie. 'And I think we deserve an extra spoonful of sugar in each cup, because we've all had a bit of a shock.'

Julian followed my eyes and nodded. He understood me perfectly.

'I'll light the primus,' he said. 'Flora's settled down.'

His presence was soothing. He had grown up all at once. His words to my father had not been mere sentiment. He was taking care of us.

I said the nicest thing I could think of.

'You remind me of Micky when he was your age.'

Julian flushed up and smiled.

'I wish he was here,' he said. 'Mick's a good chap to have in a tight corner.'

We drank our cocoa and checked the time. One o'clock in the morning. The noise outside had not abated.

'They only seem to have bombed us once,' I said.

'Yes. We were the flare path,' said Julian, displaying unusual knowledge. 'It's Blackstone they're after. The Path-finders lit us up so that our fires could show the others the way.'

Grannie would not remove her hat and coat nor relinquish her handbag. We persuaded her to lie down fully dressed. Then we lay down, too, with Flora at our feet, and dozed.

In that half-world between sleeping and waking, I connected the armada of destruction with a composer.

And murmured, 'Wagner. Of course. *Götterdämmerung*.'

Grannie muttered and snored and walked through my dreams. Outside, the holocaust continued to rage.

At seven o'clock by torchlight I sat up on my mattress, moving stealthily so as not to wake the others, and crept soft-footed to the door. My father, mindful of all things, had oiled the latch. I blessed him for that, and eased it gently open, but Julian's whisper stopped me on the threshold.

'Hang on, Evie. I'm coming with you.'

Flora lifted her head, yawned, stretched, and padded softly after us both. Leaving Grannie fast asleep we stole out into the sane and lovely world of the Malt-house.

It was not quite dark. Furniture shapes were emerging as

day broke. Colours took on life-tones. The parquet floor felt cold and slippery beneath our stockinged feet. Brass and silver gleamed dully. In the empty fireplace a bowl of bronze chrysanthemums stood sentinel. Their shaggy heads rustled in the wind which came down the chimney. Otherwise all was quiet. Julian and I spoke in whispers.

'Has the all-clear gone?' he asked.

'I didn't hear it, and I'm sure I would have done. But they've gone away. It's over. I'll make us some tea.'

A conspiratorial joy possessed us, as if it were a far-off Christmas Day and we had come downstairs early to unwrap our presents. The house was exactly as we had left it the previous evening. The kitchen seemed particularly welcome, and Tom Cat wound round and round my legs, congratulating, complaining.

'Don't put the light on just yet,' I said, and threaded my way quickly across the darkened room and drew back the curtains.

'Come and look!' I said, beckoning.

A dull red dawn seemed to be breaking, but its light flickered and changed from pink to gold to dirty crimson, and was over-hung by a pall of smoke. Above it the sky was still the deep rich blue of night.

'That's Blackstone, burning,' I said, and rubbed my arms.

We stood side by side in silence until the all-clear sounded its single note of comfort and triumph. We had survived the night.

'The fire's still in,' said Julian. 'I'll make it up.'

I started to speak, but decided to hold my tongue. He had never dealt with the kitchen range in his life, so far as I knew, but he rattled out the ash confidently until the coals glowed, and coaxed flames from the coals with the aid of a newspaper.

I watched him, arms folded, smiling and enlightened.

'Of course, I forget that you're a scout. Just as Micky was.'

He placed the coals strategically and coaxed the flames again, while I marvelled. I was his elder by ten years and had played the part of a second mother to him. He could never mean as much to me as Michael did, but overnight he had become a companion.

'Better be quick with the tea,' said Julian, 'or Grannie might wake up and have another fit of the collywobbles.'

The tea brewed, I peeped in on her, but she was fast asleep, her cheeks patched with red like those of a clown. I left the cloakroom door open so that she would know when she awoke that all was well.

By common consent, Julian and I wrapped ourselves up warmly, took our mugs of tea with us, and walked in the garden with Flora, who squatted beneath favourite trees in relief and ritual homage.

A fine hard frost made the ground ring. I turned my back on the smouldering city and saw, with new eyes, the frozen wave of Tarn How forever about to break over its grey ridge. The grass crumbled under my feet. In the cold sunlight a spider's web glittered. I had not known what it was before just to be alive, and glad of life.

We heard the back gate open and close, and shouted with delight as my father came into view.

His voice was hoarse. He held out blackened hands.

'Don't touch me!' he commanded from a distance. 'I'm filthy!'

But we ran forward and hugged him just the same.

'Have some of my tea!' I said, holding it to his lips.

He drank it right up, and handed the mug back.

'Glad of that. Your mother and her pals didn't turn up until the fire brigade arrived at four o'clock this morning. Then the firemen took over and the WRVS served us with tea and sandwiches. Your mother seemed to be enjoying herself!' He gave his little snort of laughter. 'Bossing everybody about!'

He searched our faces for the truth.

'All right, then?' he asked.

We nodded vehemently, linked his arms and led him to the house. He was very tired, too tired to stop talking.

'What a business! The fire brigade had to finish it off for us. Those stirrup pumps don't work on a big scale. And the blighters up there kept dropping incendiary bombs into the

286

fires they'd already lit. I know they couldn't all have fallen on Grizedale's but it felt as if they had. We've been dashing from one place to another for hours, trying to keep everything under control, like – like that musical fellow with all the pots boiling over at once. . . .'

'The Sorcerer's Apprentice!' I answered promptly.

'Yes. That chap. Well, we haven't lost the school, but it's in one hell of a mess. Probably looks a lot worse than it actually is. But the new gymnasium's been completely gutted, and the fire from there spread to the adjoining buildings. The library and dining hall are damaged, and the kitchen roof doesn't look too good. I shall have to go back and assess the damage when I've had a sleep. I know one thing – we've got a hell of a lot of cleaning up to do before we can start the new term. . . .'

Dorothy arrived at nine o'clock. She had eaten breakfast at the Town Hall with her volunteers, and handed over to her assistant on the day shift. She was just as weary and talkative as my father, but not as dirty, and had brought home various spoils left over from the sandwich-making, the best of which was a blue bag half-full of sugar.

I could tell that the area of her interests had spread. She no longer saw herself as Ma Joad, with the fambly coming fust, but Grannie's eccentric air and appearance did capture her attention.

'Are you all right, Mother? What are you up to?' she asked.

For Grannie, now dressed in her Sunday best with a clean apron over all, had folded her coat and hat and put them on her kitchen chair, with the handbag on top, and was inspecting her best gloves.

'Just making ready,' said Grannie. 'I don't want to be caught on t'hop next time.'

Dorothy opened her mouth to explain, to talk down, but I put one hand firmly on top of hers.

'Just let her do what she wants to,' I said meaningfully.

'We can take care of her,' Julian added importantly. 'Just leave Grannie to us, Mum.'

Dorothy realised then that if she left a gap behind her it

would be filled somehow, and the thought seemed to dash her for a couple of seconds, but the night's adventures were too wonderful and terrible to relinquish. Like my father, she had to talk herself out.

'Kersley Civil Defence were caught napping. They were drinking tea and playing cards when the first bombers arrived. Still, credit where credit's due, once it'd started they never stopped. Shifting rubble with their bare hands, fetching out the living and the dead. Folk are wonderful when they're in trouble. Wonderful. . . .'

Propping up tired heads, sipping gloriously sweet tea, we rode with her on the canteen van into the thick of the fray. Burning beams crashed on every side. The fire was so hot that it singed our hair. The water from the hosepipes turned to steam. And at each stage along the route firemen with blackened faces crowded round, to hold a thick white mug of tea in hands that shook with exhaustion, to eat a thick sandwich, and to walk back again into the furnace. Dorothy wiped her eyes several times as she told the tale.

'Brave lads, every one of them,' she said. 'Brave lads.'

She sat looking at her empty cup, tracing a pattern on the table, thinking. Then she roused herself for a final effort.

'As soon as I've sorted out the Sunday dinner I'm going to bed, because they're calling for me at five o'clock to run the evening shift. We shall be ready for them tonight!'

My father, now bathed, shaved and dignified in his Jaeger dressing-gown, said gravely, 'Let's hope it will not be necessary.'

'Well we all hope that, but we don't know,' said Dorothy briskly. 'Better to be safe than sorry.'

But, truthfully, I believe she did not want it to end. The catharsis had washed her clean, made her exalted as music made me. I could tell from her rapt silence that she would have liked to go on and on, in a war in which no one was hurt but the same drama and need of her prevailed.

25

Methodically, and with terrifying precision, German Path-finders returned at exactly the same time the following evening, and dropped another stick of bombs across Kersley only a hundred yards away from the first, to light their way to Blackstone again. On those two nights the courses of all our lives were changed.

Grannie had lost her bearings. My father's health was to suffer from the struggle to cope with conditions at Grizedale's throughout the war. Dorothy, launched upon public service, had outgrown her domestic role for good. Julian's education, both at Moss Lane and later at grammar school, would be conducted between makeshift classrooms and air-raid shelters. And I was musically homeless, since Blackstone Music College had been hit by a landmine. Yet these burdens were comparatively light. For we were alive and healthy and we still had a roof over our heads. We could be counted among the lucky ones.

'Very lucky indeed!' said Dorothy aggressively, coming home late on the Monday morning, red-eyed with pity. 'And let no one forget it.'

She took half a pound of bacon from her bag, slapped it on the breakfast table, and sat down heavily. I poured her a cup of tea. In this mood she had to be humoured.

'It's Christmas Eve tomorrow, Dorothy,' I said conversationally.

I waited for comment and received a sniff.

I asked, 'What do you want me to do about Christmas?'

'Oh, don't come whining to me about Christmas,' said

Dorothy curtly, unfairly. 'There are two hundred and fifty people in Kersley without a rag to their backs. I'll be out all day tomorrow – if I'm not called out again tonight, that is. And on Christmas Day we shall be cooking a dinner for the homeless.'

I decided to tackle her head on, and replied equally curtly.

'Look, this is your household and you'd be the first to complain if I did something without asking you. I was offering to help – if only you'd listen.'

Dorothy quietened down and said, 'Oh, all right, then.'

'You said something about a turkey. Well, where is it?'

She chewed her toast reflectively and added another scrape of butter. She looked as though she were trying to take an interest in someone else's past life.

Finally she said, 'I put a five shilling deposit on it. It ought to be collected from Foxhole's Farm tomorrow afternoon.' Then she lost patience and said, 'Oh, I don't know. I can't be bothered. I'm tired out. I'm going to bed for a few hours. If they come back again tonight we can cross Christmas off altogether!'

My father was in bed already after another night's fire-fighting. Julian had gone off to Moss Lane School to view the damage and swap horror stories with his classmates. Grannie sat by the fire in her coat and hat, handbag over one arm, and shielded her face with one hand against the blaze.

I'm alone, I thought. Bloody well alone.

I felt better for swearing, even in thought. I sugared my stepmother's tea generously and prepared to be firm.

'Dorothy, if you're going to be out then I'll have to make a Christmas for us,' I said, woman to woman. 'Just tell me what I have to do, and as far as I'm concerned you can sleep for a week. You see, we haven't even collected the tree yet, let alone decorated it. And you said something about a pudding, but I can't find it. And have you made the mincemeat or can we buy it?'

Dorothy paused, toast in air, and said, 'What does it matter?'

I could have hit her. Metaphorically, I aimed at a soft spot.

'It matters for Julian's sake, doesn't it? He's only a child.'
Then I stopped, out of honesty.

'No,' I said. 'It's not just Julian. It matters on principle.
We've always had lovely Christmases. I'm not giving up
because we've been blitzed. I mean, *you* were the one who
was talking about the family sticking together. Remember?
Ma Joad in *The Grapes of Wrath*?'

Dorothy's eyes narrowed. She weighed up the situation.
She would have liked to slap me down, but I was too old to be
called impertinent and told to mind my own business.
Moreover, it was me or nobody.

'Find me a pencil and paper and I'll write it all down,' she
said sensibly. 'And here,' she took out a large black leather
purse with dividing pockets, and removed a number of
pound notes. 'Here's my week's housekeeping money. Try to
make it stretch. But if you can't manage then ask your father
for some more.'

I accepted this small fortune with awe, and thanked her.
Then, lawyer-like, as one had to be with Dorothy, I stated
my case.

'You're letting me make all the preparations for Christmas. Is that right? It's my responsibility and no questions
asked. Right? And if it isn't exactly what you want then no
post-mortems. Right?'

Dorothy nodded in answer to each question. She finished
her breakfast and rose. She stared round as if unsure what to
do next.

'Don't worry about anything,' I said. 'I'll take care of it.
Would you like me to wake you with a cup of tea at five
o'clock?'

Dorothy relinquished her authority.

'Yes, I would,' she said. 'That'll be nice. I won't disturb
your father. I'll sleep in the spare room. And, thanks,
Evie.'

'You're more than welcome,' I replied, most graciously.

When the door had closed I poured myself and Grannie
another cup of tea, and read the list.

'Now, Grannie,' I said briskly, to the monument by the
fire. 'We've got a lot to do this morning. I'll ring up Uncle

Walter and have a word with him. And as soon as Julian is back he can collect the order for us, and do the running about while we organise everything. Quite apart from the Christmas preparations, this house is a downright disgrace! You'd better let me help you off with that coat and we'll find a couple of clean aprons. . . .'

So I took charge of the Malt-house, and Grannie came to me like a child, thankful for orders in a world of chaos.

That night we slept in our beds, in peace. The Blackstone blitz was over in time for Christmas.

I could not effect a miracle in twenty-four hours, but I could give the impression of one. The Malt-house was dusted and tidied from top to bottom, and Grannie polished the silver and brass. I changed all the bed linen and sent it to the laundry. The turkey was resting in the larder. Uncle Walter had sent a handsome grocery order, and packed a number of seasonal kindnesses by way of food. A large green fir tree leaned against the balustrade in the hall, waiting to be planted in its tub. And the table was properly laid for breakfast.

My father entered the kitchen frowning, carrying his shoes. 'Where's your mother?' he asked. 'These haven't been cleaned.'

I was sitting in her chair at the end of the table, wielding the china teapot as if I had queened the household for years, and I answered him in a tone which was both firm and friendly.

'Dorothy's gone to have breakfast at the Town Hall. They're setting up a Christmas canteen for the homeless. I'm afraid, Daddy, that if you want those shoes cleaned you'll have to do them yourself.'

He dropped the shoes as if they had bitten him, and accepted a cup of tea while he considered this proposition. In the typical Victorian household of his youth there must always have been a humble pair of female hands shining his shoes in loving duty, proffering them in homage. Even in the First World War they would be cleaned by his batman. He cleared his throat, and spoke pacifically.

'I've never had to do them myself, you see, Evie,' he said.

He hesitated, but I did not offer to clean them. He looked hopefully at Grannie, and dismissed the idea. Then his face cleared.

'Where's Julian?' he asked.

'He's had his breakfast and gone to collect the green-grocery order. He's got a hundred things to do for us, Daddy. We're all three of us working like mad all day.' A delightful demon possessed me that morning. I had tasted domestic power. 'Oh, and I've got a little list of things which only you can do.'

He did not even ask for his newspaper. He drank his tea and ate his toast almost surreptitiously, watching me.

'Where can I have put it?' I said. 'Ah, here it is!'

I handed over a piece of paper. I translated his expression.

'Daddy, I'm sorry, but it's every man for himself this morning. I'll show you where everything is. You've got one problem sorted out, anyway – I've tidied the shoe-cleaning box.'

He had never bothered about this piece of domestic equipment before, but being tidy-minded like me he could picture the state it must have been in. He answered as heartily as he could.

'Oh, have you? Well done, Evie! Right we are, then.'

I urged him to finish the marmalade, since Uncle Walter had sent another jar. I stood guard against any female weakness which might have rescued him. I knew I could not indulge him as Dorothy had done. But later, hurrying through the scullery, I saw him sitting on Julian's old washing-up stool, wearing one of Dorothy's ample aprons, polishing his shoes. He was bringing all his thought and energy to this ordinary task, forehead furrowed in concentration.

'Goodness!' I cried. 'I can see my face in them!'

He glanced up, pleased beyond measure.

'If a job's worth doing, it's worth doing well, eh?' he said.

'Always, Daddy!' I replied. Brisk and matter of fact.

But outside in the garden shed, hunting for the Christmas tree tub, my conscience did smite me.

*

We stood round the hall fire that evening, shivering a little in our finery, waiting for Dorothy. Since she would spend Christmas Day in the service of others, I had decided to hold the family celebration on Christmas Eve. And, as a precaution, I had sent Julian down to the Town Hall earlier in the day, with a message whose velvet invitation concealed an iron command. I said that we had organised a lovely surprise for her, and please would she get home as near to six o'clock as possible, and ring the front doorbell rather than use her key?

I had broken another tradition by using the hall instead of the drawing room as the centre of festivities. In my opinion it had always seemed to be the perfect place. The tree, glittering with pre-war baubles, towered over its heaps of gifts. A tray of sherry glasses winked in the firelight, surrounding our last bottle of Blythe's Finest Oloroso. A very few luxuries were heaped up in three very small bowls: nuts and raisins, a handful of green olives and another of silverskin onions, all from Uncle Walter. I was setting my face against fear and misery, creating a pre-war Christmas.

And I was quietly delighted with myself as a symbol of the occasion: draped fashionably against the mantelshelf in a long green silk gown which once belonged to Aunt Kate, my hair twisted into a Grecian knot at the back of my head. I kept glancing into the oval looking-glass on the far wall, and every glance returned a compliment. Even Julian said, 'You do look nice, Evie!' Even my father turned a complaint into a question.

'Evie! Are you sure we afford the coal for all these fires, my love? Kitchen, hall, drawing room, dining room. . . .'

Julian answered him, in his new adult manner.

'Only the kitchen one is coal, Dad. The rest are an old sleeper which I nicked from a pile in the railway yard and chopped up.'

'Good God!' said my father, appalled at yet another instance of depravity in his family. 'You could have been arrested and charged!'

Grannie, in the best black satin which graced all

occasions, said, 'Nay, we shan't want for owt while our Evie cares for us.'

She had transferred her allegiance from Dorothy to me.

My father was yearning for sherry. He must have needed a drink after the upheavals of the past three days. The hall clock chimed the quarter hour and he tutted pettishly.

'Late already. She's been looking after other people all day. You'd think they would have the decency to let her come home in time.'

'Daddy, she's always late,' I said, with good reason. And added, 'She always has been and she always will be.'

The doorbell rang tremendously. And as if that were not enough, the door knocker rapped three times. Flora began barking.

'All right! All right! We're coming!' we called.

And still, as Julian ran through the vestibule with Flora yelping excitedly at his heels, and my father and I following, the doorbell shrilled and the knocker demanded our immediate attention.

'Hang on! Hang on!' my father cried, amused, annoyed.

We flung open the door, laughing. Flora leaped, like an arc of welcome, straight into the arms of an RAF officer. And we stood, silent and motionless, staring in joyful disbelief at Michael.

We were all talking at once.

'Here!' said my father, handing his stepson the first glass of sherry. 'Knock that back – instead of knocking my front door down! What the blazes are you doing here . . . ?'

Michael was saying, 'But are you all okay, then? Is everything okay? We didn't hear until yesterday about the Blackstone blitz. I tried to ring you but they were having to bypass Blackstone telephone exchange and I couldn't get through. I moved heaven and earth to get here. They've given me twenty-four hours' compassionate leave. . . .'

'Eh, fancy seeing our Michael. Nobody told me he were coming. You never know what's going on from one minute to the next. . . .'

'Mick. I looked after Grannie and Evelyn and Flora. And, Mick, the bomb's mucked up Moss Lane School no end. . . .'

'Micky, they've wiped out the lovely Royal Victoria Concert Hall and we heard *The Messiah* there on its very last day. . . .'

Michael said, 'Where's Mum?'

The doorbell rang again, not quite so dramatically, but with shrilling resolution.

'Half an hour late, as usual!' said my father, making one of his dry little jokes.

The old magic was working. Michael and I had the same thought at the same time. We nodded at each other. He placed one finger on his lips, and walked softly to the front door. He allowed it to ring once more, opened it and hid behind it, so that Dorothy looked down the length of her festive hall to the smiling group by the fire.

'Well I never!' she cried, moved and delighted. 'Well, I never!'

She came forward a few paces and stopped. She stood quite still, as we had done a quarter of an hour earlier. Her expression changed from pleasure to fearful hope. She turned, trembling.

'Happy Christmas, Dot!' said Michael, holding out his arms.

'Well I never expected this!' said Dorothy, arm-in-arm with husband and son. 'Did you know Michael was coming? Why, this is the best Christmas I could have wished for!' In quite a different tone she said, 'I can smell that turkey from here, Evelyn! Is it all right?'

'Yes, Dorothy. Everything's under control,' I answered, pleasant but firm. 'It's resting in the bottom oven. As soon as you go upstairs to change, Grannie and I will dish everything up.'

Grannie came to life as her name was mentioned.

Child-like, she said, 'I'm ready for me orders, Evleen.'

And I answered her soothingly, as if she were indeed a child.

'There's no hurry, Grannie. You sit down for a while and enjoy yourself. You've worked like a Trojan all day.'

'Aye, and you've worked and all, my lass,' said Grannie.

But she was still troubled by one unorthodox piece of behaviour.

'She's sent the bed-linen and towels to the laundry, our Dollie. I'm feared they'll wear them out. I told her. I said, "Your mother and me have never sent a sheet to the laundry in all our lives!" I said.'

My father swept aside this domestic heresy.

'More sherry, everybody? Grannie, another glass of ginger beer?'

'Did you manage to wangle some eggs from Foxhole's Farm, Evie?' Dorothy asked. 'Good. Well, I've brought a pound of sausages home. You can have bacon and egg and sausage for your breakfast, Michael.'

'Sounds like the morning after a bombing raid!' he remarked, grinning. 'They always feed us up when we get back.'

We realised, with a sense of shock, that he was inflicting the same horrors on Germany that had been inflicted on us.

Dorothy said unwillingly, 'I know that war's war and we've got to fight back, but it doesn't help me to think that some poor Germans are being dug from under the wreckage.'

'It helps me!' said my father contentiously. 'Blast them all!'

This time Michael steered the conversation back on course.

'Sorry, chaps. Not a tactful topic,' he said cheerfully. 'Dad! You'll be pleased to hear that I haven't come empty-handed. Dickie gave me a bottle of wine, and I got hold of a bottle of whisky. We reckoned that, if the worst came to the worst, I could always sit in the smoking ruins of the Malt-house and drown my sorrows! And if all was well – as it is – we could celebrate. . . .'

His tone was airy, his smile never faded. He turned aside every attempt to find out how he really felt. Michael's war was a gallant and stylish affair, rich in comradeship, spiced with adventure.

There were, it appeared, seven warriors in his fighting troop. Six air crew and the Whitley, to whom he referred as 'the old girl'. The bomber, apparently, had moods and a mind of her own. A mother rather than a mistress to them, she lumbered over to occupied Europe and dodged back again. She was, for those tense, cold hours of flying time, their home. They loved her, laughed at her, relied upon her.

He parried all our questions beautifully.

'What's it like up there, Mick?'

'Like being Guy Fawkes on bonfire night!'

In that green and eerie world of searchlights, they hoped the old girl possessed magical qualities which would shield them from harm.

Julian sat on the hearth rug, hugging his knees, looking up into his elder brother's face. He had shed the responsibilities of the last few days and become a boy again now that Michael was home.

'Mick. Mick. Has the old girl ever been hit?'

'We've had one or two shaky dos. Once I nursed her across the Channel on a single engine.'

'Gosh! What was it like, Mick?'

'Okay. We flew in carrying part of a hedge between the wheels.'

'Gosh! How long did she take to mend?'

'The chaps had her ready for the next night.'

'Well done,' said my father, mellow with whisky. 'Well done.'

'I wish you could meet our bods,' said Michael. 'They're good types. You know Dickie, of course. He's our navigator. Jimmie, the rear-gunner, was a plumber from Glasgow. Andy, my co-pilot . . .'

We were all with him in the Whitley. Our breath smoked on the air. The drone of the engine held dominion. It was a cold, noisy, metal world, but this time we were on top of things, not hiding underneath and waiting for the bombs to fall. We crossed the French coast. Dickie said, "You should see a river now, Skipper. . . ."'

I listened and watched and rubbed my arms. This dream could turn to nightmare in a moment. The old girl was mortal. That roll-call of young names had a sonorous ring to it. The last story might not be told. I loved him, and was afraid for him.

Unconsciously picking up my thoughts, Julian said soberly, 'But Mick, what happens if the old girl loses *both* engines sometime?'

'We bail out, laddie. The brollies open up, and down we go, over land or over sea.'

'Do you bail out last like the captain of a ship? Suppose you fall into the sea?'

'We've got our Mae Wests to keep us afloat, and a rubber dinghy to stooge around in while we're waiting for the air-sea rescue bods.'

'Suppose you land in occupied territory?'

'We'll be prisoners of war. Still, life could be worse than playing a long game of dominoes, and waiting for Dot to wangle illicit food parcels through the Red Cross.'

'But, Mick, what if the old girl doesn't have time to let you bail out? What if she just blows up?'

Michael said, smiling, 'Then we've bought it, old chap. Gone for a Burton. Scrubbed. Jolly bad show.'

The spell had been broken, the listeners sobered. But the storyteller was ready for this, too.

'Did I hear you mention mince pies, Dot?' Michael asked.

Midnight struck. We had wished each other a Merry Christmas, exchanged gifts and thanks and kisses, and now hovered on the upstairs landing, unwilling to end the party.

'All praise to Evie,' said Dorothy, being fair-minded. 'We'd have had no Christmas without her. She's given us all a lovely surprise.'

I said, 'The best surprise was the one I didn't plan.'

Dorothy, warm with food and sentiment, said, 'We'll have a proper Boxing Day breakfast together, tomorrow, Micky. Just like old times.'

But it was not like old times, at all. War had made itself manifest. This was merely an interlude. The luxuries had all been eaten. Christmas was over. Michael was going away again, and would not cease from mental fight nor let the sword sleep in his hand. As for we civilians, we had simply endured a few turns of the martial thumbscrew. A long racking lay ahead.

26

January 1941

Dorothy's knuckles performed a brisk tattoo on the bedroom door.

'Evelyn! Evelyn! Time to wake up.'

Until recently it had been Grannie who rose early, sweetening her morning call with a cup of tea, but since the blitz she had risen later and later. At first she apologised frankly, annoyed with herself. Then she laid the blame on her alarm clock, without attempting to remedy the matter. Finally she did not refer to it at all, but stayed in bed longer and retired earlier, stopped reading her newspaper, and generally lived in a world apart.

Dorothy mentioned this change of behaviour to Dr Gould, who dropped by on a pretext and drank hot Oxo in the kitchen, observing Grannie as he talked.

'I don't think there's anything wrong with the old lady that a dose of sunshine won't cure,' he said to Dorothy, as he left. 'Old folks find the winter hard-going. She's hibernating. Keeping herself warm. Conserving energy.'

But the trouble went deeper than that. Grannie was retreating. She would begin a task, work up to a certain point, and then something in her came to a halt. Then she repeated the business of the alarm clock: apologies, excuses and finally silence. So Dorothy and I took over more and more of Grannie's domestic tasks, while she sat by the kitchen fire in dozing communion with the red coals.

Christmas had been a brief dream, created in one supreme effort, when I restored the Malt-house to its former self. For a few days I believed I could continue to organise it, but it was too big and too demanding, and I had neither the time nor the temperament to devote myself fully. Dorothy found me, on New Year's Eve, half-crying with frustration as I cleaned the brass and silver.

'It's only a week since I polished this lot,' I said, voice higher than usual, 'and I've been sitting here for two hours doing it all over again! Two whole hours. I ask you.'

'Don't tell me you're upsetting yourself over a bit of routine housework!' said Dorothy, setting down her shopping bags with a thump.

I wiped my eyes with the back of my hand and shook my head.

'No! I'm upsetting myself because the house won't co-operate with me! I want it to be comfortable and shining and beautiful, like it was before the war. I hate living in a place that looks like a run-down boarding-house!'

'Well, there's no point in getting worked up about that,' said Dorothy prosaically. 'There's a war on. Where's Grannie?'

'Gone to lie down for half an hour, with a hot-water bottle.'

Dorothy took off her hat and coat and slung them casually on a kitchen chair. As I had sorted out all the hats and coats, and hung them neatly up on the hall-stand, this was the last straw.

'All afternoon,' I said wildly, 'all afternoon the Walrus and the Carpenter have been talking in my head. And do you know what they were saying, Dorothy? "If seven maids with seven mops swept it for half a year, then do you think," the Walrus said, "that they could keep it clear?" "I doubt it!" said the Carpenter, and shed a bitter tear. Well, that's just what I'm on the point of doing. Shedding a bitter tear. I'm damned well sick and tired of making no impression on it!'

'I will not have you swearing!' said Dorothy emphatically. 'However old you are. It's unbecoming in a woman.'

Yet she was briskly sympathetic.

'When you get to be my age you'll know that three days' dust is no worse than one. That's why I'd rather cook. I don't mind how much trouble a meal takes because I feel I've created something at the end of it. But the endless, mindless treadmill of housework always did get me down.'

'Oh, thanks very much! So *you've* given up and *Grannie's* given up and we can't get a charwoman for love or money? Well, that leaves just me to try keep the Malt-house going, and I'm under enough pressure as it is. Just you try practising the piano in an unheated drawing room! And when I go back to the music college I shall have an extra bus journey and a long walk to our new place in Ducie Grove!'

Dorothy clattered the kettle on, saying over her shoulder, 'It's no good getting on your high horse with me, my lady. *I* haven't asked you to clean it. As far as I'm concerned we can wrap that silver up and put it away in the sideboard cupboard until the war's over. And while we're on the subject of housework, let me tell you something. Your beautiful Malt-house used to cost seven days a week of my time and five mornings of Mrs Inchmore's. So you may as well forget it.'

She added a short homily, to improve my character.

'You did a grand job at Christmas, and I appreciate what you're trying to do now, but you must face up to reality, Evelyn. You want everything to be lovely all the time, but life's not like that. And now that Grannie isn't as bright as she used to be, you and I must pull together!'

So I no longer lay abed, warm and languid, musing over the coming day with a cup of tea, but jumped awake to the sound of Dorothy's knuckles, which rapped on my bedroom door like so many hard facts, appealing to me to face reality.

Reality, that first term after the blitz, was grim and bitterly cold. Life at college had become a makeshift affair, and Blackstone a makeshift city. The Royal Victoria Hall was a crater, the Victoria Street skyline a mouth full of smashed teeth. There were gaps in every block and square, whole streets reduced to rubble, railway lines and stations damaged, dusty little recreation parks ploughed up, sooty trees burned down. Clearance and repair had become part of the daily round. Yet from behind boarded windows and under tarpaulins, in temporary quarters, life went on.

We might be down but we're not out! declared a placard outside one small shop which looked nothing more than planks and sandbags.

We were all alert, too. We knew now that this could happen to us. We checked our bearings constantly, noting the nearest air-raid shelter so that we could run in the right direction if need be. We all carried our gas masks, the cardboard container smartly covered in a cloth or rexine holder. We liked to get home before it was dark, if possible, and to stay there.

My love life, if so it could be called, was at a low ebb. My code of sexual behaviour had evolved from a private consultation with Aunt Kate, for I would never allow Dorothy to come too close. Between us we reckoned that if I had been going out regularly with a young man, say for half a dozen dates, an arm about the waist and a good-night kiss was permissible, but no more.

'No spooning sessions!' Kate warned.

'We call it *necking*!' I corrected her, demurely.

'No necking sessions, then. You can go further than you mean to. Keep it on a light and easy level. And when you fall madly in love, my girl, for heaven's sake come back to me for another round of advice, because that's a different situation altogether!'

Leo had taken his mother's high spirits away with him. Kate's rich giggle had not been heard since he died, her hair was turning grey, but she brightened up during our conversation. I had left her sitting in the front parlour with her hands folded in her lap, her thoughts years away, and a little smile on her mouth.

But that was fifteen months ago. The first excitement of making a date had worn off. The first kiss had been a tepid affair. And the first fumbling hand round my waist had met with a sharp slap. I longed for love, I made myself ready for it, and it did not come. Rather liking a young man was my strongest emotion so far, and over the past year at college I had gained the reputation of being unattainable.

Purely out of chagrin that cold January day, I refused a cinema date with a third-year music student whom I had encouraged the previous term, and joined the Kersley bus queue in the early evening.

Music was still my first love, and the day's music trailed through my head as I waited. The light had faded most beautifully over Blackstone, softening the broken skyline of Victoria Street, filling the gaps with promises, turning the mounds of rubble to gold, reviving the waste land. Now the city became a kingdom of night in which music was paramount. Joyful, ordered, transcendent.

The wailing protest of the siren tumbled me down to earth, threatened chaos. The bus queue turned as one body and began to run. Drawn along with them, I did not know where I was going, whether I would get there, or what would happen if I did. My throat closed in protest. Suffocating in the crush of people, I gasped for air, afraid of fainting, of falling and being trampled.

'Let me out!' I cried, unheeded and unheard. 'Let me out!'

The movement of the crowd was forward. Instinctively, I pushed and pummelled my way sideways, and found myself cast up against a policeman who was trying to organise the retreat.

'Not this way, miss. That way!' he shouted to me.

But I drifted past him and sat down on the low stone wall which bordered the bus station gardens.

'You can't stop there, miss!' he shouted over his shoulder. 'The siren's gone. You must get under cover.'

I ignored him. I knew that he was too occupied to leave them and deal with me. I sat breathing hard, elbows propped on my knees, my face buried in my hands. The throng was diminishing: a host of leaves on the wind. Footsteps still pattered past me: stray leaves on the outskirts of the storm. Time slowed almost to a halt. The siren wailed down to its close. In the moments of waiting, I was aware of voices, speaking above me. Two men hoisted me to my feet, not roughly but urgently.

'Come on now, miss,' said the policeman. 'You can't stop here.'

'I can if I want to,' I said childishly, stubbornly. 'It's my life. It's my life.'

The warden shouted, 'Drop!'

The three of us dropped together, and I felt the bomb take the ground beneath me by the scruff of its neck and shake it, harder and harder until my teeth chattered in my head. Flashes pierced my closed eyelids. I sobbed in anticipation of the next assault.

Nothing more happened. No armada cruised in to feed the fires. We scrambled up, shaken.

In the uncanny silence the warden said, 'I towd thee!'

'Are you all right, miss?' the policeman asked.

I nodded. Apprehension remained, but the bomb had blown my panic away.

Ashamed, I said, 'I'm very sorry. I do apologise.'

'Nay, that's all right, love. Best get underground now, afore the rest on 'em come,' the warden replied.

'Are you all right, sir?' the policeman shouted to a man getting up from behind the bus shelter, dusting his knees.

The man answered airily, with a hint of humour.

'Never felt better. Jolly close shave, though, wasn't it?'

The tone reminded me of Michael when he talked about war. The voice immobilised me. I remembered it perfectly. I remembered the way he had placed one hand gently and enquiringly on my sleeve. The memory of our meeting had been laid away as if it were a wedding dress waiting to be worn. He was a mystery I longed to unfold, a stranger I felt I knew, a key to the love I needed to give and receive. I had actually dreamed of him two or three times.

The worn and handsome face of Christopher Hyde loomed up, smiling, holding out my music-case which had skidded away.

'Does this belong to the young lady?' he asked.

I formed his name with my lips and could not say it. His smile changed from courtesy to delight. He swept off his hat with a flourish.

He said, 'This time I know you're not Felicity Craig. How very nice to meet you again.'

'Eh, hurry up and get under cover!' said the warden, tired of niceties. 'There's a bloody air raid on!'

Christopher Hyde held out his arm grandly. Graciously, I accepted it. Together we went down into the shelter as if to a great hotel which was holding a reception especially for us.

The atmosphere was convivial, the company mixed. We were greeted like old friends, and responded as such. But after a while, feeling that we had done what was required of us socially, we withdrew into ourselves and were left alone.

'Evelyn Fawley was the name, if I remember rightly. And you'd just left school that afternoon, and were looking forward to studying at the music college – but wasn't it badly bombed?'

I found my tongue and kept my tone as light and friendly as his.

'You have a very good memory, Mr Hyde.'

'You're not easy to forget, Miss Fawley, I assure you.'

The compliment was deliberate, but he did not labour it, moving easily from one point to the next.

'How have you been managing since the college was bombed?'

'Not badly. We're housed, for the time being, in two disused buildings at opposite ends of Ducie Grove. It's inconvenient in bad weather, walking to and fro, and of course I have a long bus journey and a tram ride on top of that. But we all manage remarkably well. Surprising what you can get used to! Do you live or work in the city? Have your premises been bombed?'

I listened to myself. I sounded wonderful. I hoped he had not seen my exhibition of panic.

'I'm the junior partner in a small firm of architects. Berryman, Yates and Hyde, at the back of Marygate. No, we've been fortunate. I think ours is the only complete block of offices left in that district.' He picked up one of my remarks. 'Do I gather that you live a fair way out of the city?'

'We live at the upper end of Kersley. Near the Cheshire border. Where do you live?'

307

'In Cheshire itself. A little village near Wilmslow. The only trouble with Cheshire is that it's too flat. I used to be a great hill-walker. I know your town quite well. I've stood on the top of Tarn How many a time and looked across Kersley. Wonderful views.'

I was instantly and recklessly transported by the name.

'Oh, Tarn How is my favourite place in all the world. You can see the roof of our house from the ridge. We used to come up from the Kersley side, eat our sandwiches at the top, and walk down to the tea-shop with the Hovis sign at Dowson-under-Fell.'

'Good Lord,' he said, and threw back his head and smiled. 'I'd forgotten that tea-shop. Run by a highly genteel lady called Miss Waterman. Everything homemade and plenty of it. Full for a shilling, and blown-out properly for one and sixpence!'

I giggled. I had forgotten the air raid, the shelter and the war.

'And who was *we*?' he asked, smiling on me.

'First of all, my father. Then he married again and we never went for walks by ourselves afterwards.' I paused in recollection. 'Then my brother Michael and I – he's my stepbrother really, but I never think of him as that. He's a bomber-pilot in the RAF. . . .'

And so we exchanged our histories until the all-clear sounded in the middle of Christopher Hyde's twenty-first birthday. The air-raid warden tapped him on the shoulder.

'I'm sorry to break up t'party,' he said sarcastically, 'but don't you want to go home, sir?'

We became aware that everyone was filing quietly but jubilantly past us, up into the ordinary world outside. Apart from a flickering glow against the night sky, a few streets away, Blackstone seemed much as we had left it.

'Nobbut a spit in the eye,' said the warden cheerfully. 'There were only the one Junkers. He must've got lost, else got left behind, and he unloaded on us afore he turned tail for home.'

'Anybody hurt? Much damage?' Christopher asked, looking at the glow in the distance.

'It might've been worse. A warehouse on t'canal. Fire brigade's sorting it out.'

Shining my torch on the face of my wristwatch, for this could be any hour, I said, 'Better than I thought. Only half past seven. Oh, but I must telephone them at home. They'll have had the air-raid warning, too, and they'll be frantic about me.'

Before he spoke, I knew what he was going to say. I waited, accepting the offer silently.

'Look, telephone by all means, but why don't we try to find somewhere to eat? Brooks's Chop House should be open. I've had nothing since lunch. I don't suppose you have, either. Please allow me to invite you to dinner. Oh, and do assure your parents that I am a most respectable person, who will look after you properly and see you safely on to a bus home. I'll speak to them myself, if you like.'

I was not a child. I corrected him politely but coolly.

'Thank you, but I always speak for myself!'

He inclined his head in apology as well as acquiescence, but I saw the ghost of a smile on his mouth, rather like Lilian's when she said I was a funny little thing.

My father answered the telephone. His relief and his long influence persuaded me to be honest, and yet I felt too shy about Christopher Hyde to share him. Disliking to tell an outright lie, I formulated a half-truth.

I said in a rush, 'Daddy, it's me, Evie, and I'm all right. I've been safe in an air-raid shelter with a very nice crowd of people, and I'm awfully hungry, and some of us are going down to Brooks's Chop House for a meal. And they'll see me on to the bus afterwards. Is that all right?'

He accepted my story without question.

'Yes, of course, my lass. Order yourself the best meal they've got. I'll pay for it. And try not to come home too late, Evie. We'll be glad to see you. It's been a very long two hours, wondering how and where you were.'

'Daddy, you're not to worry. I'm absolutely fine. But thank you for worrying, Daddy. And, Daddy – I love you very much.'

I hooked the receiver tenderly back.

Oh, you beastly little Judas! I thought, disgusted with myself.

Then the incredible sight of Christopher Hyde waiting to escort me to Brooks's turned me at once from Judas to Juliet.

He said, 'May I call you Evelyn? My first name is Christopher.'

I answered, 'I did remember.'

We walked arm in arm, shining our torches carefully on the ground before our feet, oblivious of time and place.

27

Since the war began, the first two months of each year had been bitter enough to break weather records, and a bitter January was followed by a February blizzard. In such a climate as this it demanded an effort of will to get up or to go to bed, for the place was arctic and the wind whiffled down chimneys into empty grates. Most of the rooms in the house stood in chilly silence, collecting dust.

Left alone all day, Grannie sat by the kitchen range and kept the fire stoked. Apart from washing up in the icy scullery, she did little else, and she wore a hat all the time to keep her head warm. The first week in March she caught a cold. It was nothing much, but as it seemed inclined to linger Dorothy made her stay in bed, warmed her room with an electric fire, and called the doctor.

Neville Gould strode in, slapping his leather gloves against his thigh. His step was almost as brisk, his voice almost as hearty as ever. He carried his troubles gallantly. One son lay buried in Normandy, the others were serving overseas, and his wife suffered from various nervous afflictions. Whether age and grief had changed him I did not know, but he no longer frightened or embarrassed me.

Perhaps, I thought, it's I who have changed.

He examined Grannie carefully and with delicacy.

'I wish my heart was as strong as yours, Grannie!' he said aloud.

Then he turned away from her, to ask in a lower tone, 'How old is your mother, Dorothy?'

'She'll be, let me see,' counting on her fingers, 'seventy-four next week!'

He nodded. He glanced round the room. I had tidied it up only an hour ago, and picked the brave snowdrops which were drooping their heads in a blue cup by the bed. The grate had been boarded up to exclude draughts. The electric fire burned hot and bright.

'Well, you look very comfortable to me, Grannie!' he said. 'I think you should stay there until the end of the week, and then I'll drop in and see you again. And if that handsome young grandson of yours calls at my surgery this afternoon, I'll have some medicine to soothe your cough.'

I followed them downstairs, hearing echoes of my childhood.

'Is she all right?' Dorothy was asking.

'I can't find anything worse than a cough and cold, apart from *anno domini*. Keep her in bed and keep her warm. Plenty of fluids.'

'I'm out all day, you see,' said Dorothy apologetically. 'And so's Evelyn until the end of term. It's difficult to nurse her.'

He snorted. He reminded her that he had predicted this sort of thing when Marie Stopes started her damned nonsense.

'So make sure that she's got everything to hand before you go. Keep that electric fire on the tiled hearth, and put a guard in front of it. Leave her a thermos flask full of tea, a jug of orange squash and some sort of snack. Try to go out a bit later and come back a bit earlier. Do your best for her. Winter and war are hard on old folks.'

Grannie was pretty good at first, but when he advised her to stay in bed for a second week she began to fret. A lifetime of hard work is not easily shrugged off. She was used to keeping busy, and at last habit overcame commonsense.

Arriving home sooner than expected one chilly afternoon, I found her in the backyard, filling the coal scuttle. She was wearing her winter coat and hat, but an east wind riffled the folds of her flannel nightgown, her legs were bare, and an ancient pair of carpet slippers slopped on her feet. When she saw me she put the coal scuttle down quickly, and stood, head bent, twisting one button of her coat.

'Don't tell our Dollie!' she pleaded, like a child in disgrace.

I was more worried than angry, but concern sharpened my tongue.

'For heaven's sake, Grannie, whatever are you doing out of the house? You shouldn't even be out of bed!'

'I wanted to set the kitchen fire to rights.'

'But you don't need to, Grannie. We made it up before we went this morning, and damped it down with slack. It stays in beautifully. You're to come back inside this minute.'

And I swept up the coal scuttle and hurried her into the kitchen. There I touched her cheeks and hands.

'Lord above, Grannie, you're freezing. I'll make two hot-water bottles for you. Grannie, you really have been very naughty!'

She spoke querulously, trying to distract my attention from her misdemeanours.

'I nearly fell downstairs in these owd slippers. I need some new'uns.'

'I'll buy a pair for you tomorrow, if you tell me what you want.'

'I don't need you to buy them. I can pay my way,' said Grannie boastfully. 'I've got a ten shilling note in me handbag this minute, and two weeks' pension to come!'

Her bravado faded.

'Don't tell our Dollie about me, Evleen. She'll be that vexed!'

Grannie had been my ancient child for the last three months, and I loved her. I would not have worried or frightened her for the world. Still, I spiced my reassurance with a little threat.

'I won't say a word this time, I promise. But if I catch you again I shall not only tell Dorothy – I'll tell my father, too! Now, upstairs, and let's make your bed again and sort you out!'

Thoroughly chastened, Grannie scrambled between the sheets. Her little heels were yellow, worn and shiny. Her scalp showed pink through the white hair. Anxious to make up for her faults, she gave me a wide false smile as I tucked her in.

On the following morning, she apparently said nothing to Dorothy about her condition, though she must have known she was ill. And Dorothy told me afterwards that her own mind was on her job rather than her mother. But Grannie did ask for help in another way.

'Stop wi' me, our Dollie,' she said, as her daughter glanced anxiously at the clock ticking on the mantelpiece.

'Why? Don't you feel so well, Mother?'

'Nay, I'm all right.'

At a superficial glance she seemed better, with her high colour and bright eyes. Still, she tried to persuade her daughter.

'I just wish as you'd stop at home wi' me, today, our Dollie.'

The request came at a difficult moment in a difficult period of Dorothy's working life. Since Blackstone could not be blitzed every week she was widening the sphere of her activities, and had come up against the stone wall of internal politics. Always there was someone manouevring for the position she held, and someone else machinating for the position she was trying to gain.

'Mother, I can't. I've got an appointment to go before a special committee at eleven o'clock, and an interview in Blackstone at two this afternoon. I'll be lucky if I can snatch a sandwich in between. But it's Evelyn's early day. She promised to be back by four o'clock, and she says she's buying you some carpet slippers. And we'll all be home this weekend, and perhaps Dr Gould will let you get up for an hour or two. That'll be nice, won't it?'

Grannie did not answer.

Dorothy said, 'Well, if you've got everything you need I'll leave the rest. I'm late as it is. Now are you all right?'

Grannie rolled over on one side, turning her back on her daughter.

'Aye, I'm all right, our Dollie.'

Dorothy's conscience assailed her, but time and circumstances were not on her side. She scribbled an explanatory note to me, kissed her mother goodbye. And left her.

Popping my head round the door at four o'clock, I saw Grannie lying with her face to the wall, and was momentarily chilled.

'Grannie!' I said apprehensively. 'It's me. Are you all right?'

Her head moved fretfully on the pillow.

'Aye, what should be wrong wi' me?' she replied hoarsely.

'Merciful God! What a mess!' I said, seeing the state of the bedroom. 'Didn't Dorothy tidy you up this morning?'

'She did what were needful,' said Grannie, loyal even in adversity, 'but she hadna time to do more than wash me and make the bed. She's left a note.'

I read the note, which had been written at slapdash speed on a torn sheet of paper.

'Too busy?' I said bitterly. 'We're all too busy. Typical!'

I did not possess Dorothy's robust constitution nor her tremendous stamina, but I was quicker and more efficient and could achieve a better effect. Within half an hour Grannie was propped up on the pillows, hair brushed and face washed, holding a cup of fresh tea, while I set the room in order and replaced the snowdrops with a bunch of crocuses I had picked from the garden.

'Now you're looking more like yourself,' I said, though the improvement lay in the room rather than in Grannie. 'Would you like some bread and butter?'

'Nay, I want nowt to eat. I just wanted me tea.'

I was busy unwrapping a brown and gold cardboard shoebox.

'You'll never guess what I've got, Grannie. Pre-war carpet slippers at a pre-war price, from Barber's, no less! They only had them because you take a size two-and-a-half! Look, a lovely soft blue. Leather soles, real wool, and pretty white fur linings. What about that for a bargain?'

She inspected the new carpet slippers listlessly, gave me her empty cup and lay back.

'Don't you want to try them on?' I asked, disappointed.

315

Grannie said, trying to please me, 'Nay, there's no need. They'll fit lovely. You know best, Evleen. They're grand.'

She seemed to drop off into a doze then, but as soon as I made a move towards the door her eyes opened.

She said pitifully, 'Nay, don't leave me, love. I've been laying here by myself all day. Stop wi' me a bit.'

But there was the fire to be coaxed, a meal to be prepared, washing up to be done, and Julian not there to help because he played football on Friday afternoons.

'Grannie dear, I will as soon as I can. I promise. But I must sort things out before everyone comes home. Look, I'll put Daddy's walking stick by your bed. Knock on the floor when you want anything.'

'Nay, I'll not mither you, love,' she said, accepting solitary confinement.

In the following two hours the telephone rang twice. First of all my father, battling with a contractor over repairs to Grizedale's, said he would be late. Then Dorothy, hatching a political plot with a sympathetic committee member, said she would be late. 'Just for once,' she added guiltily.

Mentally I consigned the pair of them to hell, served up Julian's meal and saw him off to the scouts. By this time I was too tired to eat with him, and put the rest of the potato pie in the bottom oven to keep warm. Then I made more tea and some toast, and out of kindness rather than inclination went upstairs to share it with Grannie.

My company was welcomed tearfully.

'Eh, you have been a long while,' said Grannie. 'Stop and talk to me, love. Tell me . . .' I could see her casting about for some subject which would interest me. 'Tell me about your music master,' she said. 'That foreign gentleman. He makes me smile.'

Eating, sipping, talking, scorching my legs pleasurably in front of the electric fire, I began to entertain her with tales of Aaron Feinberg. But once I was underway, Grannie dozed off uncomfortably with snorts and starts and mutterings, just as she had done on the nights of the blitz. And I, released, returned to the on-going mystery of Christopher Hyde.

*

316

We had met only three times since the air raid, though that was due to the weather, and none of them had been as dramatic or satisfying as that unexpected evening at Brooks's Chop House. The time of day, the places and the atmosphere were all wrong. My idea of romance was not a Saturday lunch at the Kardomah, followed by a cinema matinée, a cup of tea and a handshake at the Kersley bus stop. And though his admiration was open, his manner teasing and tender, he did not commit himself further than the next meeting nor did he suggest that we telephone each other. He seemed to want, and not to want, to see me. His attitude was puzzling. I lacked the experience to interpret it, but was shy of consulting Aunt Kate because he was so much older than I and she might say he was unsuitable.

The sentinels that were my ears alerted me to a change in Grannie's breathing. She was mumbling and restless, panting for breath and in great distress. As I bent over her she sat upright, grasped the covers, threw them aside and tried to get out of bed. I prevented this unexpected move with some difficulty. The strength in her wiry little body was astonishing.

'No, Grannie, dear! No! Tell me what you want and I'll fetch it.'

As suddenly as she had arisen Grannie fell back, and I saw that the bed was wet.

'All right, Grannie. Stay where you are. I'll sort things out.'

I tucked her in as tightly as possible. Leaving the door ajar so that I could hear what was happening, I went to the airing-cupboard for clean sheets. There were none. Cursing Dorothy under my breath, for she was supposed to send them to the laundry, I ran into the bathroom and inspected the contents of the dirty linen basket. It was crammed down and beginning to overflow. A faint but distinct odour warned me that these could not be used again, even in an emergency.

Capacious as it was, the basket could not possibly hold Dorothy's entire store of bed linen, so where was the rest? Instinctively, I looked in the most unlikely place: the cistern cupboard. And there was another slovenly hoard, warm and dusty and over-ripe. I suspected that if I went down to the wash-house I would find other, and older horrors than this. I should have known she could not be trusted.

A crash and a cry brought me scurrying back to Grannie's room, to find that she had fallen to the floor and was crawling towards the fire. I managed to lift her to her feet, coaxing and scolding alternately, but as I steered her towards the bed she began to struggle again with unsuspected strength and purpose. She was muttering something about a chop for Sam's tea, and saying, 'Nay, I must get to back o' beyond afore dark.'

I realised by this time that she was light-headed, and I was not sure how to handle the situation.

Helpless and frightened, I shouted, 'Oh, get into bed, Grannie, and don't make such a fuss!'

She started, as if I had wakened her from a nightmare, and obediently allowed herself to be brought back. She looked so old and frail and ill that I was instantly ashamed.

'I'm sorry I shouted, Grannie, but I'm trying to find clean sheets,' I explained, 'and I'm all by myself. I can't be everywhere at once. Please promise me that you'll stay in bed, will you?'

Grannie nodded and lay back, squeezing her eyelids shut. Two tears found their way beneath the lids and trickled down her cheeks.

Near to tears, myself, I ran to Julian's room. It was now the private retreat of a ten-year-old boy but had once been his nursery. Knowing that Dorothy was a natural hoarder, I opened all the drawers and cupboards, banging them shut as they disappointed me. And then I found what I was looking for: a pile of old clean cot sheets and a rubber underlay.

Wiping my eyes on my jersey sleeve, I carried this treasure hoard back, and found Grannie out of bed again, sitting on the floor, trying unsuccessfully to put on her new carpet slippers.

'All right, Grannie,' I said, resigned. 'Stay there, then.'

I can't perform miracles, I thought.

I found a clean nightdress in her chest of drawers, and

hung it over the fireguard to warm. The hall clock chimed eight. Julian would be back in an hour, but I did not know when the others were coming. I began to make up the bed, talking all the while to reassure Grannie.

'What do you think of those slippers, then? Wasn't I lucky to find them? Aren't they a delicate blue . . . ?'

Grannie gave a wheeze and a gasp, keeled over like an old rag doll, and lay still. For a few horrific moments I thought she was dead. Then she began to fight for breath. I eased her into a sitting position, reached forward, and pulled the eiderdown from the bed. Wrapping it round her, I held her upright while she struggled for air.

'Can you move, Grannie? Can you help me to move you?'

Grannie's eyes were fixed on some goal which demanded unwavering attention. Without looking at me, she gave one sorry shake of her head and continued to keep watch and to strive for breath. So we sat together on the floor until Julian came home, and I called out to him.

He telephoned the doctor, who was not at home, and left an urgent message with Mrs Gould. He telephoned Aunt Kate, but no one answered. He helped me to carry Grannie back to bed, and we propped her up with pillows. He made tea for us both, and watched Grannie while I drank mine. Then I took over again, because he was too young to witness Grannie's plight, and I felt that his presence might distress her.

'Gran's very bad, isn't she?' he whispered at the door. 'If you need me for anything, knock on the floor and I'll come up.'

So I sat by Grannie's bed and spoke to her and stroked her restless hands, and did what little I could to make her comfortable.

At ten o'clock I heard Dorothy coming up the stairs as fast as she could. She had not even taken off her best hat and coat, but hurried into the bedroom and stood there, smart and stout, taking in the scene, grasping the situation.

'Evelyn, I'm sorry. I really am sorry,' she said sincerely.

319

I nodded and swallowed. I would not speak just yet, lest the fury and apprehension of the past six hours flood forth. Grannie needed our undivided attention, and in spite of my desire to make Dorothy suffer, my anger was tempered by relief. For she was a good nurse, and I hoped that her experience could turn the tide of Grannie's illness.

She spoke quietly to me, feeling her mother's hands and cheeks, 'I've told Julian that if Neville Gould hasn't turned up by half past ten he's to ring Dr Lewis. We must have a doctor.'

She listened to Grannie's laboured breathing, looked into her eyes and spoke to her kindly, reassuringly.

'The doctor's coming, Mother. He'll have you right in no time.'

'Cold,' said Grannie from a long way off. 'Cold.'

'Julian's made relays of hot-water bottles for her, but her legs are like ice,' I said. 'I've put an extra eiderdown on the bed, and a shawl over her cardigan, and rubbed her hands and feet, and still I can't warm her.'

My voice shook. Dorothy sat down heavily on the bed.

'I blame myself,' she said simply. 'She begged me to stop with her, this morning. I should have guessed there was something amiss. I should have known. She's looked after everybody else all her life, and never asked a favour of anybody. I should have stayed. I'll never forgive myself. Never.'

With that sudden and astonishing strength Grannie thrust the covers aside and tried to scramble out.

'No, don't bother, Grannie. It doesn't matter. It doesn't matter!' I cried. 'We've got plenty of sheets.'

I turned on Dorothy, crying, 'She's wet, you see. I could change the sheets but I couldn't change her nightie and I couldn't ask Julian to help me. Where the hell were *you* when you were needed?'

Her mouth quivered. She looked as if she were about to cry, but before either of us could give way to anger or remorse the front doorbell rang, and in a moment or two we heard Neville Gould's voice in the hall.

'Thank God!' said Dorothy.

His expression did not change as he examined Grannie. He remained cheerful and non-committal.

'Now what's all this about, Grannie?' he asked heartily.

His voice carried across the gulf that separated her from the living world, and she paused in her work to gasp and nod at him.

He held her hands reassuringly in his while he asked me what had happened. He nodded his head as if this was an everyday occurrence. His attitude calmed and comforted me. I was amazed that Grannie did not instantly respond to this confident manner, but laboured on to her mysterious goal though the ground was rough and the going hard.

He patted the old woman's hands before he relinquished them, booming, 'You're doing well, Grannie.'

But to Dorothy he said quietly, 'Your mother's dying, my dear. There's nothing I can do for her, and I don't think she'll be long about her business. I'll stay here with you to the end, but I think Evelyn should go downstairs.'

'I'm not leaving her after all we've been through,' I said obstinately. And added, in final proof, 'I'm not a child, you know. I'm twenty years old!'

Neville Gould did not argue.

He said, 'Then sit by your grandmother, Evelyn, and put your arm round her. Now, Dorothy, can that young son of yours bring me some boiling water? I want to sterilise this syringe. I'll just give her a mild sedative to relieve the discomfort.'

He cried heartily across the gulf, 'Better soon, Grannie!'

The effect of his injection was miraculous. Her breathing became quieter. She ceased to struggle. She looked round at us all, recognising us. She even tried to voice her thanks and apologies.

'Sit at the end of the bed where your mother can see you, Dorothy,' said Neville Gould. 'She's over the worst now.'

He withdrew to the back of the room and waited.

I could feel Grannie's body relaxing against my arm, and kissed the top of her head compassionately. Then the extraordinary happened.

Grannie said quite clearly, in wonder, 'Eh, look. Look.'

I could not see her face but I read Dorothy's expression, moved and reverent. I felt a small cold wind blow over my shoulder.

Grannie drew three breaths, each finer and softer than the last, and stopped on the threshold of the next. Herself enlightened, she became a part of the mystery.

Still I kept my arm round her, and kissed the top of her head, for I could not believe that she had left us. And still Dorothy, with the tears running down her face, held her mother's small cold hands.

But Neville Gould said quietly, 'It's over. She's going to her long home now, my dears.'

And came forward to close her eyes.

28

April 1941

That my first encounter with death and my first love affair should come together was somehow fitting. The charged atmosphere of wartime enhanced them both.

'You're very pale. You're very quiet. Your father says you're withdrawn. Are you having nightmares? I should never have let you stay to see Grannie die! You're too sensitive. I'm full of remorse. . . .'

So Dorothy discharged her own emotions by heaping praise and sympathy on me, and blame upon herself.

'Evelyn was wonderful when mother died, but of course it's left her deeply shocked. . . .'

I was not shocked, I was punch-drunk with genuine experience. My childhood had been sheltered, my adolescence monitored. In such a cloistered existence only thought and imagination could roam freely. Mentally, I was the most accomplished girl in the world. I had commanded armies and lovers, worn the crowns of queens and saints, and travelled far. In fact, I had been asleep and dreaming until I met Christopher Hyde again. Awakened, I waited for my first real kiss: not the callow and embarrassed offering of some young music student but an event of the first magnitude.

We should have met on the day after Grannie's death, but as I did not know his telephone number at home I rang his office to make my excuses. He sounded regretful and sympathetic but slightly remote. He said he would be away the following weekend, but perhaps we could meet in a fortnight? Same time, same place?

Grannie's death had sharpened my appetite for life. I was riven at the thought of a further two weeks without him. Besides, the time and place were both wrong. I was tired of eating Welsh rarebits in a dim corner of the Kardomah, and I did not need his company to cry over such films as *How Green Was My Valley*. Still, I must not seem too eager. Aunt Kate had told me. Hold back. Keep them guessing. Let them do the running.

Clutching the telephone to my thundering heart, I spoke lightly, airily, as if the idea had just occurred to me.

'That will be well into April, and the weather is bound to be better by then. Wouldn't it be nice to go for a long walk instead? I could bring sandwiches and tea for both of us. We could make for Tarn How, if you liked, from the Cheshire side of the fell.'

He laughed, and answered just as lightly.

'My dear girl, we'll do whatever you say. But don't bother about sandwiches. I'll give you lunch. There's rather a jolly little pub in Stansfield called The Fox and Grapes. Suppose we meet there?'

We took the long steep slope of Dowson Fell in measured strides. The sleeves of my best russet cardigan embraced my neck. I had taken it off in the warmth of the climb and the mildness of the spring afternoon, and pushed up the sleeves of its twin sweater. I stood aside from us both, seeing us as if we were a drama about to be played. I was striding easily and well, hands on hips, but Christopher had fallen slightly behind me, an old raincoat slung over his shoulder, hat thrust to the back of his head. For the past hour we had not spoken to each other, but the silence was one of understanding. Smiling to myself, I turned to look at him and saw an answering smile on his mouth. We moved steadily, rhythmically up the hill, in unison. The woman in me was exultant. The girl in me broke the spell.

'Race you to the top, Christopher!'

He made a gallant effort, but I was quicker and younger than he, and after all it had been my idea. Triumphantly, I flung myself down on my stomach in the coarse grass, and waited until he lay panting and laughing beside me. I plucked a stalk of grass. I would have liked to tickle his nose with it, but did not dare. I chewed it instead, and we lay there looking down into Kersley, and along the ranks of mill chimneys to the faint outline of Blackstone on the horizon.

He seemed content to lie by my side wordless, eyes half-closed, but I was intent on the second part of my plan. I needed to talk.

'Weren't we lucky? This must be the first mild Saturday in the year. Aren't you glad that we're not sitting in some stuffy cinema in Blackstone? I thought it was high time we breathed fresh air, and this is my favourite place. Look! That's our house among the trees!'

He made a polite noise which could have meant anything. I sat up and delivered my invitation as casually as possible.

'Why don't you drop in and take pot luck with us this evening, instead of going back home? You needn't worry about rations. Dorothy manages very well for us. She's very hospitable. And she'd enjoy a surprise visitor.'

Adroitly, he evaded the issue.

'A surprise visitor? So I'm not expected? Don't they know that you're out with me this afternoon?'

I considered his questions, embarrassed. I did not know how far I was supposed to take our friendship for granted. I knew that he liked me, that he was attracted to me, but nothing had been said.

Never trap a man into any admission, Aunt Kate had told me. They like to take their own time. You could ruin everything by pushing.

So I said, 'They know I'm walking with a friend, but I didn't mention you. I haven't mentioned you at all. What with the winter. And Grannie dying. I wanted to be sure we were friends before I introduced you. I thought it might be a good opportunity today.' Then I could bear it no longer, and asked, 'We are friends, aren't we?'

He smiled round at me without answering, and the smile was lovely but not enough.

He sat up, and felt in the pockets of his tweed jacket, saying 'Let's have an apple!'

'You haven't told me whether you're coming to tea, or not.'

His hand paused over the apple.

'Best not, Eva,' he said, very nicely.

'But why not?' I asked stubbornly.

He tried to make a joke of the matter.

'Eve – have an apple?'

I shook my head and sat up, hugging my knees.

'Eva, let's be sensible about this. How old are you?'

'I shall be twenty-one in September.'

'I'm thirty-five now. Suppose they thought I was unsuitable company for a young and lovely lass like yourself?'

'That wouldn't make any difference to me.'

'Oh yes, it would, Eva. The good opinion of your family is very important to you.'

He was quite serious, and quite right.

I thought this over, humiliated. My heart seemed to be beating in my throat, making me breathless. Slowly I got up and walked away from him, pretending to look at the view from the other side of the fell. Tears came to my eyes but I whisked them away angrily. My pride, as well as my feelings, had been wounded.

When he spoke I could tell by the direction of his voice that he was looking at me, and was sorry.

'My dear girl, if you're going to take this so much to heart then our very pleasant friendship is bound to change.'

'I was only inviting you to take pot luck with us, for heaven's sake. It was only a thought. You'd think I was asking for the moon!'

He was ruffling the grass with his hand, thinking.

He said simply, 'I'm married, Eva.'

My world turned over, and as it tilted I caught a glimpse of Clara smiling round the corner of her pink cloche hat, of Lilian in Philip Nash's arms.

I'm doomed, I thought. Like them.

And sat down on the grass suddenly.

He turned towards me, speaking urgently.

'I had no right to begin any kind of friendship in the first place. I was old enough and experienced enough to know better, and you were not. But I was so damned lonely. I tried to fool myself, tried to take it lightly. I put off – I put off this moment. But I did, and do, love your youth and beauty, and your sublime belief in life, so much.'

My world came the right way up, and radiant.

'You love me? You really love me?'

'Of course I love you!' he said, as if that were obvious.

'But you've – you've never even kissed me goodbye.'

According to Aunt Kate, the kiss came before the declaration.

'Where would kissing end?' he asked gently.

I sat and twisted my hands in my lap, and stared at his face to engrave it on my mind for ever. I had not thought this question through. The kiss had been of such immense importance. Nor had Aunt Kate given me any rules which coped with married men, for they were not supposed to figure in my life. So I spoke the truth.

'Oh, but I love you, too, Christopher. I love you more than anything in life. I have done ever since the first time we met. The day I left school.'

I reckoned that if he loved me he must logically want to marry me. Naturally, my parents would not be too pleased about a divorced son-in-law but they must put up with that.

'Christopher, if you love me, I'm prepared to wait. I don't mind how long it is. I don't expect it to be easy.'

'Listen to me, Eva. . . .'

I interrupted him. I wanted to think of everything and sort it out to the complete satisfaction of all parties.

'I daresay you have children, too. I understand how you must feel about them. But so long as you love me, I can wait. . . .'

'Eva! There is nothing to wait for!'

His tone was a slap, and I stopped and quivered as if I had indeed beeen slapped.

'Eva,' he said, softly now, 'There are no children – which is a blessing, under the circumstances! – and I have no intention of divorcing my wife. Janet suffers from a nervous illness and lives in a nursing home for months at a time. We've been married for ten years. I can hardly walk out on a sick woman.'

He had composed himself with that declaration, but I sat in chaos.

'Janet's in the nursing home now,' he went on quietly, 'or I shouldn't be with you at all, my dear love. I married this sickness when I married her. It's part of us, and we try to accept it. And I do try to keep faith. It was wrong of me to involve you. A situation like this isn't fair on any of us, and there's no honourable way out.'

I looked up, keeping my voice as steady as I could.

'I'm not asking – for a – way out. I'm not – asking for anything except – that we should meet when we can.'

For that, I felt, was the only solution: to give what I could, to accept what was offered, to demand nothing.

'Christopher, we can go on just as we are. Not telling anyone. Meeting when we can. And then no one will be hurt.'

He said, 'There's no future in it for you, and you can't tie yourself up for life.'

I swallowed, and shook my head vigorously. I answered with increasing difficulty but with great determination.

'You're all I want, Christopher, truly. And you said you were lonely. We'll keep each other company while we can.'

'But, my dear love, when Janet comes home I'm on duty and must take care of her. I'm all she's got. Even a whisper of scandal would upset her equilibrium. That's why I may have sounded rather distant when you rang me at the office. And I was sorry. Believe me, I was and am sorry, because you deserve nothing but the best, my love. . . .'

My love, he had said. *My love*.

'. . . to go on seeing each other would mean secrecy, and you won't like that, and I don't like it for you. And when Janet comes home then we can't see each other at all.'

I swallowed. But if that was the cost of love then that was what love cost. My tone was fairly steady.

'When is that – likely to be?'

'I have no idea. It could be weeks or months. She's a voluntary patient. She decides, with their help, whether she goes or stays.'

'And how – how long – will that last?'

He shrugged his shoulders.

He said, 'It's a life sentence, Evie. For better or worse. But it's my life sentence. Not yours. And the kindest thing I can do for you is to walk away and not see you again.'

My mind was made up. In terms of experience I could not even swim but I waded out fearlessly, ignorantly, into the raging sea.

'I accept the situation as it stands. I don't want to lose you. I won't lose you. I'll ask nothing of you, except that we stay together. I accept.'

He got slowly to his feet, held out both hands, and pulled me up to stand face to face with him. That moment, which should have been sheer happiness, was poignant.

He said, 'Have you ever been kissed, Eva?'

I ducked my chin in acknowledgement, but added, 'Not properly. Not by anyone I ever really wanted to kiss me.'

'You break my heart,' said Christopher Hyde.

He held me very carefully, as if I might indeed break, and kissed me on the lips. We stayed like that for a very long time, on the edge of Tarn How. I would not have been surprised or horrified if we had fallen slowly, slowly off the rim of the world.

It was everything I had dreamed of, and real into the bargain. I could have fainted with joy.

29

Neither by nature nor upbringing was I fitted to conduct a clandestine love affair. I began bravely and meant well, but my lack of experience caused me to make one false assumption after another.

Fragments of Aunt Kate's advice floated, unasked and unwanted in my giddy head, as we pressed up against each other in dark alleys and shop doorways.

'. . . when you fall madly in love . . . that's a different situation altogether . . . you can go further than you mean to . . .'

As Christopher had said, that afternoon on Tarn How, 'Where would kissing end?'

My body as well as my emotions had been aroused. So far my upbringing held me sternly in check, but very soon the kisses of which I had dreamed, for which I had yearned, left me as dissatisfied as the lack of them had done. Already, we were infringing Aunt Kate's rules about spooning.

The hunger of love stifled all other considerations, including my music. Unlike music, it provided neither harmony nor haven but kept up a continuous clamour. Our meetings were of necessity infrequent, and I fitted the rest of my life around them. In order to stay out late at night, to spend a Saturday or Sunday with him, I was forced to tell lies, which meant living in a state of continual apprehension with an outraged conscience.

One May evening we missed the last bus to Kersley. Neither of us looked at the other as we watched it disappear into the dusk. My desire for him vanished. I became a child in disgrace, terrified of facing my father.

'Oh, what can I do?' I whispered to myself, hands over my mouth. 'Whatever shall I do now?'

For once I would have given a great deal to be well away from him. Silent, he took my arm and walked me to the recreation park behind the bus station. We sat down on a bench, and I moved slightly apart from him, trying not to cry. Sensing this, he laid aside the role of a lover and became a thoughtful friend.

'Eva, I know exactly how you must feel, but you're not to worry. We'll sort something out. I can find you a hotel room if necessary. At a pinch, I can put up you for the night myself.'

An incipient sob died in my throat.

'What?' I said, astonished. 'Out in Cheshire?'

'No, no. Not there. I've got a room in town. Nothing grand. Sometimes I have to work late, and then I stay overnight.'

I was out of my depth.

'What about my parents? I must 'phone them. What shall I say?'

He took command of the situation and tried to lighten it.

'With whom are you supposed to be out, tonight?'

The lie tasted sour on my tongue.

'I'm supposed to be attending a meeting of the Music Society.'

I was ashamed of myself. I had behaved badly, shoddily.

He put one hand under my chin and lifted it so that I should look directly at him.

'Eva, I hate this even more than you do, because I'm responsible for it. Don't turn away from me. Please.'

I gave the merest grimace of a smile. He smiled back and tried to make a joke of the next question.

'That's better! Now am I always the Music Society or do I play other parts?'

'Sometimes you're the group. There are six of us. All music students. We started off in the first year together on fire-watching duty. Ann and Bob are engaged, but the rest of us are just friends. . . .'

He was waiting patiently for me to come to the point. I gave a sigh which came from a long way back. Life was like that. There was always a catch in it somewhere.

'. . . Dorothy and my father have vetted them, and they've been passed as suitable companions!'

The resentment came from a long way back, too. He ignored it. 'Good. Then I suggest that you tell your parents that you're staying with one of the girls in the group. Would one of them be prepared to back you up on that?'

I answered slowly, 'I think Ann would. I think she might.'

'Then telephone her first, to make sure that's all right.'

I had never asked anyone to lie for me before, and evidently Ann did not like the situation any better than I did. Reluctantly, she agreed, and I knew that she thought the less of me. Then I had to lie to Dorothy, and ask her to pass the lie on to my father.

My stepmother was perturbed, I could tell. She told me exactly how upset my father would be, and asked if she could speak to Ann's mother. Horrified, I put my hand over the receiver and whispered this to Christopher. But in an instant he had taken over, and was speaking to Dorothy with assurance. He introduced himself as Ann's father, said his wife was in the kitchen making cocoa, that I would be quite safe with them and Dorothy was not to worry in the least.

She swallowed it whole. She thanked him graciously.

I was sinking to the lowest depths of shame. Deeper and deeper.

'I'm sorry I had to do that,' said Christopher, reading my face, 'but I couldn't think of anything else on the spur of the moment, and if you have to lie then tell a good one. Now would you prefer me to find you a room in a hotel?'

Numb and dumb with misery, I stood there thinking. Then I shook my head. It was stupid of me, and perhaps unconsciously I wanted to push us to a conclusion, but it was mainly innocent. I loved him and therefore what he did was right. He had asked me to trust him. I did.

*

His room was in an apartment building in a poorer quarter of the city. Nothing grand, as he had said, but clean and tidy. One person's complete living quarters had been tucked into this twelve-foot square. The kitchen was composed of a wall cupboard and a gas-ring. The bedroom was a single divan and a clothes' rail. There were two hard chairs and an armchair, and a thin carpet of nondescript pattern. He had done his best to make it less impersonal. On the small card table, covered with a red gingham cloth, stood a candle in an old wine bottle. There were a few paperback books on the mantleshelf, and a Toulouse-Lautrec poster on one wall.

Christopher said, 'Wait for the pop!' And lit the gas fire.

He came over and warmed my hands in his own.

'I'll make you a night-cap. What do you want, my love? Tea? Coffee? Ovaltine?'

My spirits were picking up. Mentally, I refurnished the room, supplying what it lacked.

'Oh – tea, please!'

He was anxious to put me at my ease.

'First things first,' he said cheerfully. 'You sleep on the divan, and I'll sleep on the floor. I've done it more than once, when some old school friend has spent a night in town. And I know how to make myself comfortable. There's an extra eiderdown on the bed, rolled up behind the cushions.'

And so there was. I sat in the easy chair, relaxed, warming my hands on the cup. He sat on the carpet at my feet. Apart from involving Ann in my lies, I was enjoying the adventure.

He began to talk about his past and his future, skirting neatly round his marriage.

Before Tarn How we had talked socially. After Tarn How we had been too bemused by love to talk of anything but us. Now he was thinking aloud, personally, intimately, as to a close friend.

'. . . I'm not only older than you, my dear, I'm a great deal less fit, that's why I puff behind you up the steep slopes, and why I shan't be called up. I did volunteer, but I'm Grade Three. Not up to snuff, as my father would have said! In one way I'm sorry about that. In another I'm not. I want to keep my job warm. I wish there was more money in it. These old men live for ever.

'I should like to be rich. I could build my own house, then. I have designed it – I'll show you the plans some time. Very fine, very expensive! Still, I have my little house in Cheshire, and I'm not only an architect I'm an amateur builder. I've done a lot to that place, spent a lot on it, too. It was derelict when I bought it. I restored it to its former self, but with modern amenities. The garden was a wilderness. I landscaped that, in keeping with the house. . . .'

In the silence he was saying, 'I wish you could see it!' And I was answering, 'Yes, I'd love to!' But we knew this was not possible, and so the silence communed with itself.

'My family had plenty of money at one time,' Christopher was saying. 'Lashings of it. I was the only son and the youngest child in a family of girls, so you can guess how I was spoiled. But my father died when I was at school, and all that changed.

Childhood. Best part of my life. I seem to have been looking for it ever since! So much hope. Such great expectations. And then the nothingness, the clothes that grow shabby, the body that ages, and the love that grows cold. *In sleep a king, but, waking, no such matter!*

He came to, and found me watching and listening, nursing my cup of cold tea. He smiled.

'That's one of the things I love about you, Eva. The hope and the expectation, and above all the belief that life is about to be wonderful. I've warmed my heart on you, many a time. Many a time.'

In the silence that followed I set my cup down and came over and put my arms round his neck and kissed him. He stroked my hair and ran one finger along my lips. We spoke more softly than usual.

'If you continue to look like that, Eva, all my good and honourable resolutions will fly out of the window.'

'I don't care. The only thing I care about is your nothingness. I want to make it somethingness.'

'You want to prove that youth and beauty and hope

and expectation will prevail? That the miracle will always happen?'

I laughed then, because he had said what I could not put into words. I nodded emphatically.

He kissed my lips and drew back a little, smiling.

He said, 'I think you are about to have an affair with me.'

I wanted to say that this was not an affair but a matter of fate, that we were meant to love each other. But talking time had run out.

Looking back I give him credit for being a considerate lover. At the time I was only aware that the experience seemed more clinical than ecstatic.

Afterwards he said, 'Tell me truthfully. Did you like that?'

'Not madly,' I admitted. 'It wasn't exactly what I expected.'

I had hoped that the earth would move for me, as for Maria in *For Whom the Bell Tolls*.

'But you didn't find it too dreadful?'

I was most beautifully tired, now that the decision had been made. I shook my head slowly from side to side, and yawned. He laughed, and bent forward and kissed my forehead.

'You'll come to like it a lot, later on.'

Yawning and yawning, I murmured, 'Transports of delight?'

He put his arms round me and rocked me to and fro gently, murmuring back, pressing his face against mine.

'Yes, transports of delight. Now let's get you to bed before you fall asleep on the carpet.'

Slipping into oblivion my mind officiously supplied the first half of Christopher's quotation. 'Thus have I had thee, as a dream doth flatter . . .'

I was received coldly at home the following evening. As well as this strange new state of body I had to endure my father's silence and Dorothy's recriminations. Between them, they made sure that I would never miss the last bus again. And our love affair, once started, had no mercy on me either. We had to be twice as careful and secretive as before. Meetings were difficult to arrange and even more difficult to alter. He left notes for me at the college. I left messages at the apartment house. We had each other's home telephone numbers, but these were to be used only in dire emergency, accompanied by a false identity.

'In case my cleaning woman answers, you'd better say you're a client, cancelling or making an appointment. Call yourself – what? Something that's not likely to be mistaken. Mrs Maxwell Forbes.'

'It doesn't sound like me,' I said sadly. 'I'd never be a Mrs Maxwell Forbes. I think the safest person for you to be is someone who wants to join the Music Society. That could be anyone. . . .'

Lies, and more lies.

I was obsessed by fear of pregnancy, even though he was reassuring about the precautions he took. But I was shocked when he said I mustn't worry, because he would always pay for an abortion. We quarrelled violently over that, unable to reconcile his practical approach with my emotional one, and then healed the quarrel with love-making, which was wonderful and brief and did not solve anything.

Our relationship made us outsiders, turned us in upon ourselves. We avoided places where we were likely to be recognised. We avoided friends and acquaintances. On summer Saturdays we avoided his part of Cheshire and my part of Lancashire, and walked in unfamiliar places and talked in unfamiliar tea-shops.

When I dared to think at all, I wondered how it would all end. Most of the time I kept the worry and occasional panic to myself. Sometimes I tried to talk them out with Christopher, but he would grow impatient with me, reminding me of my promise to accept the situation as it was. And so our summer drew towards its close. More than once I caught him looking at me speculatively, instead of lovingly, and our quarrels were important issues in trivial disguise.

'Why are you looking at me like that?' I asked. 'What are you thinking?'

He answered coolly, 'You're trying to make this room into

a home. Leaving a magazine lying around. Buying a bunch of flowers.'

'What's wrong with that?' I asked, embarrassed and annoyed.

'It's not a home. It's a temporary place. It simply serves a purpose. That's all.'

I whisked the flowers out of their jam jar, picked up my magazine and walked out. This time he did not run after me down the stairs. I sat in the Kardomah by myself, drinking coffee and wiping my eyes, and then I crushed my pride into a manageable ball and went back and knocked at the door, and crept into the circle of his arms, which was not as tight and warm as it used to be.

Once, he said, 'You're getting tired of this. I can read the signs. You need more than I can give you. I knew it would happen.'

'It's not true. We've been cooped up in here all afternoon because of the rain, and it's put you in one of your nothingness moods! Let's go out and walk round, even if it is wet.'

And what will happen, I thought, when winter comes and there is nowhere else to go and nothing else to do?

My question was never answered, because Janet Hyde returned home unexpectedly.

We should have met in a tea-shop at Romiley that Saturday afternoon, but he did not come. The shop was busy and I ordered tea for one, to justify my presence. I had lingered over it for half an hour when the waitress brought a message for me. A Mr Hyde had just telephoned to say he was unable to meet me as arranged, and please to excuse him. He would ring me that evening at six o'clock.

'But didn't he ask to speak to me?' I asked, chilled.

'He did say he couldn't wait, miss, and please to excuse him.'

I finished my tea without pleasure. A telephone conversation meant surreptitious use of the call-box at Tarn Brow.

I reached home, hot and tired, to find the Malt-house in its usual state of Saturday turmoil. Dorothy had gone out shopping at two o'clock and never been seen since. Julian was playing cricket and not expected back before eight. And my father had been driven to make himself a pot of tea.

'But I couldn't find any cake or biscuits,' he said, injured, 'and I don't know what she's planning by way of a meal. She may have it with her, for all I know.'

Myself in need of comfort and soothing, I soothed and comforted him. I searched the larder and meat-safe in despair and disgust, finding only the week's rations, two rusting tins of haricot beans and a packet of Chivers raspberry jelly. Wearily, I made coffee for us both, and tidied up. At ten minutes to six, desperate, I seized on the excuse of Dorothy's lateness to slip out of the house.

'I'll just see if she's coming up Tarn Brow,' I said, and disappeared before my father could offer to join me.

In the musty booth, smelling of stale cigarette smoke, I kept my back to the road so I should not be recognised, and pretended to be thumbing through the directory for a number while I waited for the telephone to ring.

Christopher was evidently under stress. His voice sounded curt. He explained and apologised unemotionally, factually. Janet's return had caught him by surprise. It had been necessary to take a taxi and pick her up that afternoon. He had contacted me as soon as he could.

'Oh, Kit! When shall I hear from you again?'

'I don't know. I can't tell.' With a touch of hostility, he said, 'It's a question of Janet's health and well-being. I'll contact you as soon as I decently can, but that could be some months.'

'But surely we can write, or telephone, or see each other before then? Even if it's only for a cup of coffee and a talk. Just something to keep us going.'

'Eva, my dear . . .' My dear, not my love. 'Best not. It's far too risky, for you as well as for me.'

Confused, discarded, I could think of nothing to say.

'Look, my dear, I must go. I've had to make an excuse in order to come out, and this is the second time today. Janet will be wondering where I am. And she seems so much better and happier that I mustn't risk disturbing her peace of mind.'

At the end of my tether I cried savagely, 'And what about *my* peace of mind? Why can't you say that you love me and understand how I feel, and that you'll miss me – instead of just leaving me flat!'

He answered just as angrily. 'We've been over this subject again and again. You obviously don't understand my situation at all!'

'Oh, I do understand. You're in a tough spot. And so am I. But the situation doesn't upset me half as much as your attitude. You sound as though you don't care twopence about me. And you can talk of several months as if they were nothing, when I've counted minutes and hours and days, waiting to see you. . . .'

He interrupted me wearily, 'Oh dear! I did want to avoid a scene. Can't we part with a little dignity and restraint?'

My mind cleared. Why, I thought, this is what the conversation is all about. It's about us parting. Janet has nothing to do with it. Today, this minute, is the end of us.

I was cold and calm now.

'You don't expect us to meet again, do you?'

He said nothing.

'Then we'd better say goodbye, Kit. And for good.'

I did not wait for his reply. I saw my hand slot the receiver into its hook. I walked out on to the warm evening street.

The knowledge of what had happened overwhelmed me. Love had taken far more than I could afford to give, and short-changed me into the bargain. I had lost my pride and self-esteem as well as my virginity, and I sensed that the full cost was still to be counted. The hurt he had dealt me manifested itself as a pain in my stomach. I folded my arms protectively over it and began to walk away. I could not go home.

Behind me a car horn blew and a man's voice shouted, but I took no notice, walking aimlessly on.

In another moment a taxi drew alongside the kerb and kept pace with me. I glanced sideways, confused and alarmed. The driver was smiling to himself as if at some private joke. Behind me the door swung open and the man jumped out. The nightmare was complete. I gave a little shriek, which sounded like a small animal caught in a trap, and began to run. And the man was running after me, catching my arm, calling my name. I opened my mouth to scream and he swung me round to face him and shook me hard.

'Evie!' he shouted. 'What the hell's up with you?'

The nightmare shivered to a stop.

'Micky?' I said. 'Oh, Micky. Micky.'

Head on his shoulder, I began to cry as if I would never stop.

Dorothy's voice said, 'Whatever's the matter?'

'The kid's upset about something. Here, Dot, take this and pay for the taxi. Let him help you with those baskets.'

I held on to my brother and could not stop crying.

'We'd better get her home,' said Michael.

'Well, what a thing!' said Dorothy, deflated.

We walked slowly up the lane together, laden with shopping baskets. I accompanied Dorothy's soliloquy with hiccuping sobs.

'She's always been the same, no matter what. Up one minute and down the next. And when we were going to have such a lovely evening together, with Micky on three days' leave. I couldn't believe it when I saw him step off the bus – though why he can't tell us when he's coming home I'll never know! And a taxi up, instead of struggling on and off the tram. And then to find Evelyn in this state! I know what's wrong with her. It's a man. I can read the signs. She's been neither use nor ornament the last few months. Moping round the house or going off on long walks. Staying out late. Missing buses. I can't tell you when I last heard her practise the piano. And never a word or a sign of him, whoever he is. There's something very wrong somewhere, and it's high time we got to the bottom of it. . . .'

Michael said with dry good humour, 'For Christ's sake, Dot, why don't you belt up!'

He was wonderful. Negotiating the Scylla and Charybdis of my alarmed and curious family, he took me up to my room, helped me into a sitting position on my bed, and gave me his handkerchief to cry in.

340

'I'll be back in ten minutes!' he said. 'Don't cut your throat. It makes such a mess on the carpet!'

Gradually I ran out of tears, and lay against the pillows, emptied of everything but grief.

Michael returned bearing a cup of tea, well-laced with whisky. Behind him came Flora, more sedately than of old, but full of quiet delight in his presence. She inspected me first, and then settled down at his feet.

'Here you are, kid. Get this down you. I've got them all sorted out. Julian's eating my chocolate ration. Dot's cooking black market delicacies. And the old man's cleaning his rifle.'

This last point was not lost on me. I managed a giggle, and he sat on the side of my bed, grinning.

'It is a man, isn't it? Do you want to tell me about it? No need, if you don't want to, but I can act as go-between with the family, and you can trust me. Cross my throat and hope to die!'

His face did not change as I poured out my saga. When I had finished he sat with his hands between his knees, thinking.

Then he said, 'Okay. Now, Evie, I want you to do as I say! You must leave all the talking to me. . . .'

We were back in our childhood together. I heard a boy's voice saying, 'You're likely to tell them anything they ask you. I know how much to say to keep them quiet, and when to keep my mouth shut.'

Michael said, 'We're going to concoct a final lie to end this affair for good and all, Evie, because they must never know how far it went. Suppose I tell them that he was in the services? We can work out the details. Name, age and so on. Let's say he was a soldier, based at Blackstone Barracks. Not long since he was drafted overseas, and today you heard from a friend of his that the poor chap had been killed.'

I answered shakily, 'What about the evening I missed the bus?'

'You stayed with Ann. Okay, you'd been out late with him. But after all, kid, he could hardly invite you back to the barracks! I'll make it water-tight. I'll say that you don't want to talk about it, and I'll give the impression that he was very young, and it was merely a high-minded, shy and secret romance. They'll believe that of you.'

I was still very frightened of being found out, the more so since I would be alone and in the open.

'Suppose Dorothy meets Ann's parents sometime, and thanks them? I've been terrified of that happening.'

'Is it very likely?'

'No. No, not really. But anything's possible.'

'Then you stayed in a hotel, lied to them because you knew they'd be worried, and your chivalrous young soldier tried to cover up for you. It's not good, but it's the best I can muster. You see, kid, you shouldn't take a risk until you've reckoned the cost, and you must always be prepared to pay for it.'

I nodded. I had learned a great deal in the last few months. I was learning more now. I had much to learn later.

He patted my knee.

'If I bring up a light supper tonight, and toast and tea in the morning, do you think you could make it downstairs for Sunday lunch? Dot seems to have cornered an old hen, and she's talking about stewing it. I'll have the family primed and tamed, and I'll back you up.'

I nodded again, and thanked him.

'Okay, kid. Don't worry about a thing.' He paused at the door, looking speculative. 'Christopher Hyde, you said the name was? Works for a firm of architects in Blackstone and lives in Cheshire? Right.'

'You're not going to see him?' I asked, panic-stricken.

'Yes, if I can track the bastard down. I'm going to put a spoke in his wheel sometime while I'm on leave. Either at work or at home. Wherever I find him first.'

'But – his reputation in the firm – he's a junior partner . . .'

'Hard luck.'

'At home – his wife – Janet – she might go mad . . .'

'I doubt if Janet exists,' said Michael. 'Her breakdowns and recoveries sound too convenient. I reckon he rents a room in town for fun, and keeps his house private. He doesn't have to bother about marriage because he's supposed to be married already, and he spares himself nasty scenes on home

342

ground because no decent girl will risk upsetting poor Janet. I'll bet that all his girlfriends are young and inexperienced, that he meets them in much the same way he met you, hands out the sob story and admits he loves them. Then plays the protesting gentleman every inch of the way, until one night he helps them to miss the last bus home. Let's face it, kid, he's a fake.'

'But he did love me. I swear he did.'

'Why shouldn't he? You're quality goods and he got them cheap.'

I found more tears, saying, 'But we had that meal at Brooks's Chop House, and it was very beautiful and expensive.'

'Did you ever go there again?'

I shook my head.

'You could hardly call the Kardomah and the Odeon high living? And a crummy room at the wrong end of Blackstone isn't the Ritz!'

My mind, unclouded by love, began to think. My eyes dried. I picked at the coverlet.

Finally, I said, 'I can forgive myself for loving someone, but not for being stupid.'

'That's the price of experience,' said Michael kindly. 'We all pay it, one way or the other.'

'I wonder if Felicity Craig ever existed?' I asked myself.

Still, I had known love through Christopher Hyde, and in his fashion he had loved me too. I had a tenderness for him.

'Micky, you won't – won't – hit him or anything? He's – not strong. He's – Grade C. . . .'

Michael said, 'By the time I've finished with that bastard, he'll feel like Grade Z!'

It was my love affair, and my lover. I made up my own mind.

'No, Micky. Please. I don't want that. It's over. Let it go.'

I came down to lunch the following day, white-faced and red-eyed, to find my own drama had been upstaged by the news that Germany had invaded Russia. But everyone was hushed and tactful with me. No one remarked upon my lack of appetite for the stewed chicken, and they covered my silence with chat of the sort that does not matter but is somehow comforting. And that evening, when the Prime Minister had declared the Russians to be friends in a common cause, and the 'Internationale' was added to our symphony of allied anthems, my father was busy with his map.

'Hitler's gone too far this time!' he said jubilantly, hunting through the flag box. 'He's overstretched himself. The damned fool!'

'Well, you're the only one who thinks so,' said Dorothy, in argumentative mood. 'He mopped up Europe and now he's going to mop up Russia. And we can't help them, we can't even help ourselves. Just count the swastikas all over that map if you don't believe me!'

'Never you mind my map. You look at your history books!' my father retorted. 'Even Napoleon came a cropper over Russia. Wait until the winter comes. Yes, we must bury our differences with the Bolsheviks. For the time being, anyway. And I'll tell you something else, too. They won't be bogged down with chivalry and fair play, like us. They'll know where to stick their bayonets! They'll give those blighters hell – and serve them damned well right! Ah, here we are. Red flags for this lot!'

He turned to me automatically, and then hesitated.

I translated and obeyed the look. Sighing within myself, for ordinary life was about to begin again, I brought out a bottle of white ink and a pen.

'Hammers and sickles, Daddy?' I asked.

Later I closed my door on the world and sat cross-legged on the narrow bed, hands clasped loosely in my lap, looking out at Tarn How in the evening light. Love had cast me forth again, and my heart was sore. I knew that months of loss lay ahead of me, time to be paid painfully out, time to endure. And yet my mind and conscience were at peace. On the piano in my head Satie was picking out the first contemplative notes of the *Gymnopédies*.

30

Michael's luck was still holding, at a time when the RAF was losing a bomber for every ten tons of bombs dropped, and the death toll of British pilots was higher than that of German civilians. His old girls were less fortunate: riddled by cannon-shell and flack, coaxed home on a single engine, patched up and sent out again until they accomplished one mission too many. The doughtiest of them all, a Vickers Wellington given up for lost, flew on for some time after her crew had parachuted to safety and finally crashed in the Fens.

In the autumn of 1941 he and Dickie Blythe came home on leave.

'We should have had six months off!' said Michael jauntily, 'but the RAF can't manage without us, so they're giving us a fortnight's holiday and a new bomber instead. Oh, and you won't hear from us for six weeks at least, but you're not to worry because we're going to a secret destination and it's all to be kept hush-hush.'

'And how much of that nonsense is true?' Dorothy asked, utterly content to have him back.

My father forestalled the answer.

'All of it, I should imagine! Mick should have been rested for six months after his first tour of duty, but there aren't enough experienced pilots to allow for that. A new bomber sounds as though he'll need a conversion course. And the secret destination is probably somewhere in Scotland. Am I right, Mick?'

'Perfectly deduced, Sherlock!'

My father gave his snorting laugh.

'Are you allowed to tell us about the bomber?' he asked.

'Only if you keep it under your hat. It's one of the first four-engined heavy jobs. They're calling it the Lancaster.'

He was in time for my twenty-first birthday, and we made it a private family celebration, dining, by courtesy of his old connection there, at the Fairlawn Country Club. And then dined there again as guests of the Blythes, who gave Michael and Dickie a farewell party on the last night of their leave.

At the end of that year, while U-boats sank our shipping and the Russians retreated to Moscow, Japan attacked Pearl Harbor, bringing America into the fray. And now the whole world was at war.

When Michael came on leave again, early in the New Year of 1942, it was in his usual style, unheralded and full of surprises. This time he tracked me down to a dusty practice room in one of the music college buildings in Ducie Grove.

He must have opened the door very quietly, to avoid disturbing us, for I was playing a Debussy *Image*, making reflections in the water of the music, and I finished the piece before I realised he was there. Aaron Feinberg sensed his presence first.

Turning round, registering the uniform and Michael's expression, he said almost coyly, 'Someone important is come to see you, Evelyn.'

My absorption vanished. Returned to a world with Michael in it, I jumped up to hug and be hugged, uncertain whether to laugh or cry.

To my teacher I said, 'This is my brother Michael, professor.'

'Then no more music today,' he replied, bending his head gravely and benevolently. 'Go home now. Music has all time to be played. Brother has not so much time as music.'

We stood shivering, smiling, in the wintry street. It was almost four o'clock.

'I'm taking you to the *thé dansant* at the Victoria Hotel,' said Michael. 'There's someone I want you to meet.'

I guessed by his tone that this was also someone of importance. Not Dickie Blythe, or he would have said, 'Let's go and have a noggin with old Dickie!' Nor a man, for that was, 'You'll fall for this bod!'

'Who is it, Micky?'

He did not answer at first, summoning up a taxi from nowhere. His uniform gave him this, as well as other, priorities.

In the taxi, he said, with only the slightest tremor, 'She's called Judith Mitchell, and I'm going to marry her.'

For a few moments I stopped breathing. Our long comradeship was over. She would be closer to him, more necessary to him than I had ever been. And I had no one who could take the place of him. But I had come of age in more ways than one. I drew breath again, and put my smile and congratulations out in front, to cover my initial reaction.

'Micky! How utterly marvellous. Am I the first to know?'

He said ruefully, half-amused and half-afraid, 'Of course you're the first to know. Who else is capable of handling Dot in this situation? She's not going to be pleased about Judith.'

I watched his face, though I could hardly bear to see it so bright and open for someone else. And if this news affected me so deeply, how much more deeply it would affect Dorothy?

'A son's a son 'til he gets a wife!' I could hear her saying.

My social self answered, 'Oh, thanks a million. Put me in the firing line, of course! Tell me, why shouldn't Dorothy be pleased? And do you always call your lady *Judith*, never *Judy*?'

'Judith always. You'll see why, when you meet her. And I'll give you two reasons why Dot won't be pleased. First of all she's not going to like any girl I marry. Ever. Secondly, she won't be able to boss Judith about. Ah, here we are!'

Like every other building in that area which had survived the blitz, the Victoria Hotel had exchanged its blackened grandeur for plain shabbiness.

Keeping my smile steady, trembling slightly with the effort of seeming casual, I stepped out of the taxi. I held my coat collar up to my face to shield it from the north wind which swept into Victoria Square. I followed Michael past the shivering doorman, who saluted him, and through the revolving doors, and came into light and warmth and a world before the war.

Between marble columns, at spindly tables, conversation was still conducted in a subdued monotone. There was still a hard core of middle-aged ladies wearing hats, carrying gloves, and talking of difficulties with servants. But there were no longer any young waiters, the waitresses were elderly, the number of cakes was rationed, and a notice at the end of the afternoon tea menu regretted that the cream was artificial.

The centre of the floor was crowded with young couples, one or both of them in uniform, dancing to the music provided by a decimated ensemble. And not a very good one either, in my opinioin.

'There's Judith, bless her!' Michael cried. 'She's been keeping places for us in the scrum.'

A fair young woman rose halfway from her seat, wearing the same rapt bright look as Michael. No one else existed for either of them though they tried to disguise the fact. Michael looked at her lips but kissed her cheek.

'Judith, this is my sister Evelyn.'

Ten years ago Judith was probably just a pretty girl. Experience and possibly sorrow had honed her into the sort of woman at whom men look twice. Her country tweeds were old but well-cut and had been expensive. A camel-hair coat was slung over the back of her chair. Beneath a jaunty feathered hat her hair waved naturally to her shoulders. She wore hardly any make-up. Smiling, self-possessed, she held out her hand.

Oh yes, I thought, you couldn't Judy this woman. And Dorothy won't dominate her. She must have been born adult and able to cope.

Then I read anxiety in Judith's grey eyes, a tenseness about her mouth, a 'Will she like me? Shall I like her?' look, and I relaxed, shook hands firmly and smiled warmly, determined to give this new relationship a flying start.

'Such a wonderful surprise!' I cried.

'Lovely of you to come so promptly. I'm afraid we must have interrupted your work. Mike's told me all about your music, and how dedicated you are. . . .'

So she called him Mike, as Dickie Blythe did.

'Not so dedicated that I could miss seeing you both.'

'Was our news a frightful shock?' Judith asked. 'I begged Mike to introduce me by degrees.'

'Micky never does anything by degrees,' I said truthfully. 'It would probably shock us if he did!'

'I've got a week's special leave, by the way,' said Michael, 'but don't tell Dot just yet. I shall only be at home for the weekend. We're getting married on Monday.'

'Good God!' I said involuntarily.

Their laughs were nervous.

'How splendid!' I added quickly.

A commentary from Dorothy began to run through my mind.

'Getting married on Monday? Why, what's the hurry? You don't suppose she's . . . you know. Do you? And look at her. She's years older than he is. Mind you, I can see she's out of the top drawer. Not that I'd expect anything less. Michael being a Harland.'

For Judith's refinement would bring out Dorothy's snobbishness.

Michael was ordering tea, turning the double charm of himself and his uniform on the waitress. Judith left him to it, and addressed herself to me.

'I'm afraid everything is going to be a frightful rush, including today. I have to get back to Knutsford before six o'clock. My mother's looking after the children, but I like to be home in time to read them a story and put them to bed.'

'Children?' said Dorothy's voice in my head, appalled.

'Children?' I asked tentatively.

'My husband, Alec, was a pilot in the same squadron as Mike. Alec was killed a year ago, and Mike wrote to ask if he could help in any way. He made a point of visiting us whenever he was on leave. He's been so good to us. Tim and Liz adore him. At first it was simply friendship, and then . . .'

She was looking at him, and Michael left the waitress for a moment, as if he felt the look, picked up Judith's hand and kissed it.

Dorothy was saying, 'Friendship, my foot! She was out to trap anybody who'd take on a war widow and two children. Burdening a lad of twenty-three who's got enough on his plate already.'

Known her for a year? I thought. The sly old boots! And he never told us. Never so much as mentioned her.

'How lovely. How old are they?' I asked, as if my brother took on other men's children every day of the week.

'Tim is five. Liz is three. I have photographs. . . .'

She was hunting through a large leather handbag, face alight, handing over proofs of their identity.

'This is the best one, although they've grown up quite a bit since then. Daddy took it when we were at Rhyl last summer. We've been living at home since Alec was killed. . . .'

'No money and no home of her own,' Dorothy continued. 'How does she suppose he's going to keep them all?'

But I, studying the snapshot, imagined that Judith would be a good mother, endeavouring to make up for her children's loss while bearing her own. She stood there, hatless, one hand in her mackintosh pocket, the other trying to prevent her hair from blowing in her face, smiling gravely into the camera. But Tim and Liz were irrepressible. They made helmets of their buckets, presented arms with their spades, and laughed.

'Oh, they're very sweet!' I said sincerely.

I found something favourable to say about each snapshot before handing them back.

The waitress was going away, prepared to bend the rules.

'It's an RAF officer,' she would say in the kitchen. 'Lovely young chap. What's an extra cake when the lad might never come back?'

And Michael was joining the conversation, relieved and pleased to see that we were getting on well together.

'Tim and Liz are grand kids,' he said. 'We enjoy each other. I made friends with them first, actually. Judith took a while to come round, didn't you, my love?' He shook her

350

hand to shake away the shadow, and added lightly, 'She's the only grown-up in the family!'

Judith smiled, then. It was a private joke which had grown out of the differences between them.

'She should be ashamed of herself,' said Dorothy's voice. 'One husband hardly buried and already looking for another.'

No, it hasn't been easy for either of you, I thought. Micky's had to wait and learn, instead of getting all his own way at once. And Judith's had to make up her mind to risk herself for a second time, and risk her children with a man who isn't their father. I like her. I could make a friend of her. I know why Michael loves her. She's a good choice, a fine and adult choice on his part.

On the bus journey home I told him so, and he squeezed my hand.

'How do you think Dot will react to the news?' he asked, as if this were a joke.

And as if I shared the joke, I replied, 'I tell you naught for your comfort, and the sky grows darker yet. Getting married on Monday doesn't give Dorothy a lot of time to adjust, does it? When are you going to let her know?'

Tacitly it was understood that my father would be no problem.

'I'll play it by ear,' said Michael. 'Would it be better to wait and tell her when it's all over.'

I said drily, 'And expect her to swallow the fact that she didn't come to the wedding, on top of everything else? And what about the wedding breakfast? I know Judith said it was only drinks and snacks with the family afterwards, but surely they'd be rather surprised if we didn't turn up? Honestly, Micky!'

'I know you're right,' Michael answered ruefully. 'Evie, do you think there's any chance they'll like each other?'

I answered honestly, 'Not really. But neither of them will quarrel. I imagine Judith doesn't quarrel anyway, and Dorothy likes to keep up appearances. She'll probably go out of her way to be nice to Judith, and tell us what she really feels afterwards. You can always rely on Dorothy to keep the family flag flying. But after springing a surprise like this on her I don't think you can expect more.'

Michael said philosophically, 'Fair enough!'

I thought of them together, and thought of myself alone. After a few minutes' silence Michael spoke apologetically.

'Evie,' he said hesitantly, 'I'm not asking you to make a friend of Judith, because friends aren't made that way, but will you keep in touch with her when I've gone back? She'll have to go on living at home until I can find a place for her and the kids. It isn't easy.'

He had been more than good to me when I was in trouble. I was content to pay my debt and pay it gladly.

I answered truthfully, 'Oh yes. You needn't worry. She's part of you. Part of our family. She's my sister, now.'

He looked as if he were about to say how much that meant to him, how much I and our long alliance meant to him, but it was not his way to make set speeches about deep emotions.

He said lightly, 'You're a good little egg, Evie! And Evie, how do you suggest I handle this? Judith and I have only got a few days together. I don't want a Dot-sized cloud hanging over them.'

I answered in the same tone.

'I suggest that you open that bottle of wine you've brought, as soon as we get in. And tell the family what we're about to celebrate. It's quite the best thing you can do under the circumstances.'

Knowing Dorothy, I could not help adding, 'We might even have a party instead of a wake!'

This third successive winter of the war was also bitter, and there was a coal shortage which strained even Dorothy's connections and resources. In the coldest February for nearly half a century, Judith rang to say that Michael's aircraft had been reported missing.

My father answered the telephone, courteous and kindly with this new daughter-in-law, of whom he approved. Then he walked slowly and thoughtfully into the ice-palace of a drawing room, to confide in me.

The one-bar electric fire had made little impression on the temperature. The area around the piano was merely a few degrees warmer than the rest of the room. I was a bundle of old woollies, pink-nosed and cross with cold.

'Oh, what is it now?' I cried, over my shoulder.

'We're in real trouble,' said my father simply.

He poured a glass of sherry for Dorothy and made her sit down. He cleared his throat. He reminded her that Michael's luck was legendary and that he had survived other accidents.

'He was flying a very strong and well-made aircraft, of which he spoke highly. He stands a better chance than he did in the Whitley or the Wellington. A Lancaster will take some punishment, and afford considerable protection, before it goes down.'

He was talking her through the first shock, trying to keep her steady while she digested the news.

'And Mick isn't the skipper of an air crew for nothing, you know. He has particular qualities which fit him for leadership. He's young and in tip-top condition, highly trained and resourceful.'

Though she nodded and seemed pleased to hear him praise her son, Dorothy's eyes told another story.

'I'm not holding out false hope when I say that he and his crew have all probably parachuted safely down somewhere,' my father went on. 'And you can rest assured that wherever they've landed people will be looking for them. It's too early in the day to despair. So keep up your spirits, Dorrie. We must all keep up our spirits.'

She had not fully comprehended him. When she spoke, her questions were random and she did not listen to the answers. Beneath her terror lay an emotional resentment which had begun with Harry Harland's death and been compounded by Michael's marriage.

'Missing? Is that all she said? Is she keeping something back from us? Why did they tell her first? Why didn't we hear first?'

'Judith is his wife, Dorrie. She's the official next-of-kin.'

Dorothy was recovering her prejudices.

'I knew no good would come of that marriage. She's the possessive sort. I could tell when I met her. Missing? Where is he missing?'

'They don't know, Dorrie. He simply didn't come back.'

She looked up at him fiercely, accusingly.

She said, 'You can pull strings, Gil. You know who to contact. Ring up the Air Ministry.'

'My dear Dorrie,' he said patiently, 'they can tell us nothing more than Judith has told us.'

Now Dorothy had a target at which to aim, however wildly.

'How did she find out? Was it a letter or a telegram, or what?'

'She didn't say. And I didn't think to ask.'

'Exactly,' said Dorothy, with supreme conviction. 'She's holding something back. Ring her up and ask her.'

My father was frowning, disturbed.

'Why should she? You're talking nonsense, Dorrie. Besides, Judith is a woman of great integrity.'

Dorothy was attempting to blunt her fear by charging into a fray of her own making.

'What integrity? Trapping a boy of twenty-three into marriage? Do you call that integrity? No, you just can't be bothered.'

She unleashed the old grievance.

'You don't care twopence about poor Micky. You never did.'

My father would not walk out, because she was in such trouble, but he turned away from her and stood with his back to us, staring out of the kitchen window into the frozen garden. I did battle for him.

'Dorothy, you're being unreasonable, do you know that? Totally unreasonable! Think how poor Judith must feel. She and Micky have only been married a few weeks, and she's facing this sort of crisis for the second time. She's lost one husband in the war already.'

'So have I!' Dorothy cried from her wilderness. 'So have I! But she can find another husband. I can't replace my son.'

354

My father and I exchanged looks of anger and sorrow. I attempted to pacify her.

'All right, I'll ring Judith up to condole with her, and ask exactly what the telegram, or letter, or whatever, said.'

Dorothy's mood changed from pathos to aggression.

At her most maddening, she said peremptorily, 'Don't bother. You'd be wasting your time. She'll only tell you what she wants you to know. We'll find out soon enough.'

My father gave a despairing shrug. We stood in silence, waiting for inspiration, while Dorthy glared at the kitchen fire, and nodded as if it were Judith, caught out in expected treachery.

Scarlet with cold and exercise, Julian burst in, rejoicing. Under one arm he carried Michael's old football. He was about to speak, but our stricken faces stopped him. Grasping the situation without being told, he set the football down, went straight over to his mother and put his arms round her.

Dorothy's chin came down several degrees, and wobbled. She pulled Julian to her and began to sob: ugly sounds that hurt her and us.

Over her head, Julian mouthed to me, 'Missing or killed?'

'Missing.'

He bent over his mother, hugging her ample shoulders, stroking her untidy hair. 'There's no need to take on like that, Mum,' he whispered to her softly. 'You should know by this time that old Mick always lands on his feet. Don't cry, Mum. Please don't cry.'

We waited all that winter day for news, and through a winter night and into a winter morning, and the cold was part of our bones. My father appointed himself keeper of the telephone, and relayed its messages through me. When Judith's call came he turned to me for the comfort and support he could not expect from Michael's mother.

He spoke stiffly, head averted, unable to varnish the truth.

'A trawler picked up two airmen in a dinghy. Michael and

Dickie Blythe. Dickie's in poor shape but still alive. Michael died of wounds and exposure.' Then he looked up at me. His chin quivered. 'Evelyn, I don't know the right words. I don't know what to say to Dorothy.'

I told her, and held her, and listened to her. I fed those who could eat. I played the go-between, because she would have nothing to do with my father. And he, heroically understanding, shouldered the funeral arrangements to help Judith, and dealt with all the official business of a death. He nerved himself just once to speak to Dorothy, clearing his throat, looking to me for support.

'I'm going down to Dover tomorrow, Dorrie, to bring the – to bring Michael home. And Judith thinks that he should be buried here. In Kersley. Not in Cheshire, as we might have expected. She felt that it was only right. I thought it was good of her. I'll fix everything up. And whatever you want Michael to have, whatever you want me to do, Dorrie, I'll do it. You only have to say the word.'

She kept her back to him and did not answer.

'Do you understand what Daddy's saying, Dorothy?' I asked.

She gave a jerky nod. She swallowed and spoke gruffly.

'I'm grateful – for that. Harry was – buried in France. I've never – seen his grave. And you do – need a grave. Somewhere to – put flowers. Somewhere – to go – on a Sunday. And remember . . .'

I got up at dawn to see my father off, and cooked our bacon ration for his breakfast, and made him a thermos of coffee and sandwiches, because God knew when and where he would eat on that long journey to the south. I kissed him goodbye with more than usual tenderness, and watched him go with some misgivings, for he seemed to have grown old overnight. And it was a hard thing for a man to face such an ordeal, and then the funeral on top of his trouble and grief, and to receive no word of thanks or praise from his wife.

*

The funeral was over, the mourners had gone. Michael's room was cold, but I was so much colder that I hardly noticed. I had spent the last dreadful days giving of myself, and receiving nothing.

'Naught for my comfort,' I told myself stoically.

I sat on Michael's bed and looked around me at the sum total of his life, from his ancient teddy bear to his final sports cup.

Dust could accumulate, domestic battles with the Malthouse be daily lost, and the general housekeeping totter along from one crisis to the next, but Dorothy kept her son's room always ready for his return.

In other places which had known him, a similar welcome would prevail briefly. Sheet turned down, counterpane smoothed, bookmarker keeping the place at which he had stopped reading, leather slippers side by side beneath the bed, dressing-gown hanging on its hook.

At the other end of the corridor Dorothy was lying blotched and swollen with grief, snoring slightly in a drugged sleep. My father had banished himself to his study, taking the electric fire with him. Julian had whistled up Flora and said he was going back o' beyond. He had kept his face turned away from me, trying not to cry, because he was now eleven years old and a boy never cried: except, perhaps, on the lonely slope of Tarn Fell, with Michael's dog for company.

The telephone in the hall rang yet again, but this time I let it ring. I could not bear the burden of sympathy.

Michael's room was very peaceful and very empty. I had thought I might find him here, where he had retreated from my father in those wretched early years, where he had been glad to rest in the time of his freedom and fulfilment, but he did not come.

I slipped off the bed and walked over to the window, arms folded, to look out on Tarn How.

Michael, in death as in life, had gone ahead of me, walked on without looking back, as he did when we were children. He had never been a sentimentalist, and the prospect of a new adventure would find him ready to leave the old adventure behind him. He could not be expected to wait while I grieved.

So I went out, and closed the door behind me, and left the room to keep a vigil for him.

31

April 1942

The first smile in weeks hovered round Dorothy's mouth, though her hand automatically reached for the handkerchief in her apron pocket. My father, alert these days for any sign of improvement, looked hopefully at the letter and cleared his throat.

'Something nice for you, Dorrie?' he asked.

'Yes. Very nice indeed. A letter from Dickie Blythe. I've always been fond of Dickie.' She handed it to him, and blew her nose. 'Let Evelyn have it when you've finished. There's a message for her, too.'

'Dear Dorothy

'Sorry to have been so long putting pen to paper, but I was in pretty poor shape when they fished me out of the drink, though practically fighting fit again now.

'There's no way of saying how sorry and angry I feel about Mike's death, and how much I miss him. He was the best friend I ever had or ever hope to have, because we went through the worst as well as the best together, though I realise that my loss can't be as heavy as yours. I know that my Mama has been in touch with you, but I swore a great oath that as soon as I could put pen to paper I would write. You must be wondering what it was like for Mike, bobbing round in a rubber dinghy in freezing weather, waiting to be rescued, with only an idiot like me for company. Actually, he kept up amazingly well, and talked about you a lot. His family meant a great deal to him, and he had so much to live for, but loss of blood and exposure got him before the trawler picked us up.

'I'm convalescing fairly near to you for the next few weeks, in a rather jolly little cottage hospital at Dowson-under-Fell. I thought of you all, and the ever-hospitable Malt-house, as the ambulance drove through Kersley. If you can possibly forgive me for being a survivor, and bring your generous and kindly self to visit me, it would cheer me up no end, and I think I can set your mind at rest about Mike.

'No need to peer round for a bandaged warrior. I'm sitting up, all clean and recognisable – ugly as ever, as old Mike would say – and eating as many square meals a day as I can scrounge. Actually, there's nothing wrong with me, but the nurses have to earn a living somehow. My best regards to you all, and my sympathy – but you know that.

Sincerely
Dickie

'P.S. I just hope you can read this dismal scrawl. Please don't bother to bring me fruit or flowers or anything. My locker is bursting at the seams already. I'd just like to see your friendly face.

'P.P.S. If Myra Hess can tear herself away from the keyboard it would be nice to see her, too, but don't let me interrupt the concert!'

My father said, 'When are you going to see him, Dorrie?'

She reached for a piece of toast, considering.

'I don't see why I shouldn't go this afternoon. It's a Saturday and I'm not working. I'll ring up the hospital and ask them about visiting times. You'll come with me, won't you, Evie?'

'Yes, of course I will,' I replied, making a grimace at the postscript.

We saw that Dorothy was preoccupied in a different way, not brooding over Michael but thinking about Dickie Blythe. She buttered her toast quite briskly, and when Julian offered her the marmalade she accepted it. This was promising. She had lost weight since Michael's death and it did not suit her. Her skin looked sallow. Her clothes hung from her in unbecoming folds.

The past two months had been horrendous, particularly for my father, who took the onslaught of her rage and grief. She had to have some target and he was the obvious one. Sometimes, unable to bear her trouble, she would flare up at him in front of Julian and me. Mostly she restricted herself to the privacy of the marital bedroom.

Night after night I had lain awake, hearing muffled sobs and accusations as she dredged up my father's misdemeanours. Often, one of them would leave the other, to go downstairs and make tea and sit in the kitchen until the small hours of the morning. Frequently, my father would seek refuge in the guest room.

Taking him tea, one evening after the funeral, I had found him sitting in his study, head propped on one hand, staring through the window at the budding garden. Careful not to disturb him, I put the cup down and walked softly away, but at the door his voice stayed me.

He said, 'I was no good for Michael. No good at all.'

I came back, saying as stoutly and confidently as I could, 'Daddy, you did what you thought was right, and you did your best. Grannie Annie always said so. She said you were a just man.'

His voice was so thick that I was afraid he might cry.

He said, 'But not a merciful one.' And added painfully, 'Your mother told me I'd been a rotten stepfather.'

I imagined that Dorothy had gone even further than that, and said he had been a rotten husband, too. I put one arm round his shoulders and kissed his cheek.

'Well, you've always been a wonderful father to me,' I said. 'The best in the world.'

We stayed silent for a minute or two. Then he patted my hand as a sign to release him, and said, 'Thanks for the tea, lovie.'

Still I persevered, not liking to leave him in this wilderness.

'Daddy, you and Micky became friends once he'd grown up. You were good friends in the end, and that's what counts.'

My father shook his head.

'No,' he said stoically. 'A young man can take care of himself. A boy can't. She won't forgive me for that.'

He fell silent once more. I thought he had finished, and was about to steal away when he spoke again.

'I don't know that I can forgive myself.'

Then he cleared his throat and changed the subject.

'It looks as though we might have a nice spring to make up for the winter,' he said, lifting his cup.

Picking up the thread of his thoughts, I added mentally, 'But Mick won't be here to see it.'

Dorothy and I saw Dickie Blythe the moment we entered the ward. He was sitting up hopefully, ears at attention, watching the door.

The hospital sister said, 'He was so pleased when he heard you were coming. Mrs Fawley, I wonder if I might ask a favour of you? If you see him looking a bit tired, would you be kind enough to make an excuse and leave – and give me a nod as you pass the window? He's lucky to be alive, and he's not nearly as well as he makes out!'

'Yes, of course, sister,' said Dorothy, delighted to be on confidential terms with the staff.

'Brave lad!' she said to herself.

And hurrying forward she cried, 'Hello, Dickie! Here we are. And we've brought you some chocolates. You didn't mention *them*!'

'Don't talk so loud,' Dickie said, grinning. 'Someone might hear you, and I shall have to hand them round. I say, this is awfully good of you. I do appreciate it. Hello there, Evie! How are you doing with the old pi-yanner?'

Dorothy sniggered. She liked to have my music taken down a peg.

'I see you're as exasperating as ever,' I replied airily. 'I'm sorry I gave up my sweet coupons for those chocolates.'

'You shouldn't say things like that to him,' said Dorothy,

scandalised at this treatment of a hero. 'I'll give you some of my coupons next month if you need sweets that badly!'

Dickie winked at me and said, 'Pull up a couple of chairs, girls, and give me the gossip.'

We managed to be amusing for a few minutes. Then Dorothy's tone and expression changed.

She said humbly, 'I'd be obliged, Dickie, if you could tell me about Michael. I was wondering, like you said. I'd be obliged.'

I sat back, observing them both, and saw Dickie put on a different mask. I listened to his light and pleasing drawl as it related the death of a hero. The story was new, but told in the same old debonair fashion.

Yes, of course it was a serious business. It was hard and dangerous. You did suffer. You were afraid. But underneath you knew that you were on the right side, and would eventually prevail. And even if you didn't come through, you'd done a good job, and the knowledge of that upheld you. Thoughts of home and family kept you going, cheered you on. You loved and were beloved. Often there were good times, probably the best times in your life if only you knew it. And on the whole you were a jolly lucky chap, and everything would come right in the end somehow.

'He'd lost a lot of blood, you see,' Dickie was saying, 'so he was pretty weak. He didn't grumble half as much as I did, and I think he was too numb to feel pain. He talked a lot about you, and the happy times when he was a little chap.'

Dorothy cried, from a full throat, 'They weren't all happy times, and I can neither forget nor forgive that.'

I saw Dickie change direction. He spoke affectionately. He almost echoed the words with which I tried to comfort my father.

'But all he remembered in the end was the happiness, and that's what really matters.'

Dorothy's fierce wet gaze softened. She nodded, bent her head, twisted her gloves. He waited to hear what else she wanted of him.

She spoke with difficulty, keeping herself under control.

'It was a long time, though. You were in the sea a long

363

time, Dickie. Towards – the end – it mustn't have been easy.'

'He slipped into a coma,' Dickie said, 'and never came out of it. I thought he was asleep. I was pretty drowsy myself, by that time. In extreme cold you feel sleepy.'

Dorothy kept her head down and nodded.

Then one hand went up to her eyes and she said, 'You'll have to forgive me, but I can't help it. I shall have to go. But I'll come again. And we'll talk about other things. God bless you, Dickie.'

She got up, fumbling for her handkerchief, and blundered down the ward. I was about to follow her when I saw a nurse come forward and take her arm, and so sat down again.

Bereft of animation Dickie's face became sad and plain: the face of a clown whose act is over. He lay back on his pillow, and stared at me in tired surprise.

'Bit used up, I'm afraid,' he mumbled in excuse.

'Yes, I'm sure you are, Dickie.'

I felt very kindly towards him then. He had done his best for Dorothy. I just wanted to make sure that he did not confuse her needs with mine.

'Dickie, I'm going now, because you must rest. But sometime you might tell me exactly what it was like – because, quite honestly, I don't believe a word you said!'

He smiled then.

'Oh, I will, sometime,' he promised. 'Mike once said, "If you get back and I don't, cushion the tragic news for Dot, but Evie can roll with the punches – and she likes to go all ten rounds!"'

I had listened almost unmoved while he comforted Dorothy, but the authentic voice of Michael shook me badly.

I rose as hurriedly as Dorothy had done, saying, 'Bless you, Dickie. Take care of yourself. We'll come to see you lots of times if you can bear it.'

And followed my stepmother down the ward, full of tears and loss.

My father, in sombre mood, did not shave on the Sunday morning, and when Dorothy remarked upon this he said that his wrist was painful from sawing logs. He asked me if I would cut up his toast for him.

Dorothy gave him a shrewd and wifely look, so like her old self that his face lightened for a moment or so. Then he was thoughtful again. This depression persisted throughout the day, despite the fact that Dorothy had conjured a leg of mutton from somewhere, which we celebrated in our former Sunday style: the meat roasted for lunch and sliced up cold with pickles and bread and butter for supper.

Watching him sit and eat without true appreciation, his right hand lying on the table as if it were no part of him, Dorothy was alerted. She waited until Julian was out of the way, and then tackled him in a comradely fashion.

'Come on, Gil. Tell us what's wrong.'

He drew a breath so deep as to be a sigh.

'It's my hand,' he said, glad to confide. 'I woke up with it like this. I can't move it. It's – paralysed.'

He was adrift without a compass. Dorothy and I looked at one another, momentarily paralysed ourselves. Then she dropped domestic anchor. She became her old brisk self.

'I'll get the doctor right away,' she said. 'I know exactly what it is. You've been working too hard and worrying about Grizedale's.'

She did not mention the trauma of Michael's death. She preferred to lay the blame on the war.

'Trying to run a great place like that under those conditions. No proper gymnasium. A kitchen that can't produce more than snacks. Roofs leaking. Borrowing other folks' playing fields. Workmen in the classrooms – whenever they choose to turn up! Shoddy repairs having to be done over again. All the young men on your staff called up, and the old ones brought out of retirement. And that fire-watching twice a week – I'm sure nobody else does it twice! What can you expect?'

She was comforting him with this tirade, as she would comfort a child who had fallen and hurt itself.

'Yes, it's all been too much!' she cried. 'You need a rest, and so do I. I'll stop at home and look after you. We live like gipsies in a field. If Evelyn hadn't dusted this room, and run the Ewbank over the carpet just before supper, we couldn't have sat here. And I'm not bothered about giving up work. There are plenty of jobs going for anyone willing enough to do them. We'll get you better first. And I'll find a char-woman, too. I'll bet there's some poor body in the back streets of Kersley who'd be glad of part-time cleaning and a bit of extra money. I'm just going to 'phone the doctor. I'll be right back. Don't worry, Gil. . . .'

At the door she stopped and said what was really troubling her. She said it in front of me, which showed how much she cared.

'And Gil, I know I've been unkind in the past few weeks, but I didn't mean it. I didn't mean what I said about poor Micky.'

He was facing disablement and oblivion. For I guessed that he had found no reason to trust in this life, and knew he did not believe in a life to come. So he must hold to the truth, though he put it as considerately as he could.

'My dear Dorrie, you meant every word. And in many ways you were right. But I accept that you wish you hadn't said it.'

Ostensibly Dorothy returned to the bosom of the family to nurse her husband, for my father had suffered a mild stroke. He was ordered to rest for the whole of the summer term, and advised to take life more easily thereafter. But she was also healing herself, since the distraction of his illness took the bitterness from her grief. She concentrated on bringing him back to full health and putting her house in order. And she began this new régime by inviting Aunt Kate to a sociable cup of coffee instead of crying on her shoulder or over the telephone.

'Charwoman?' cried Aunt Kate, giving a little shriek and throwing up her hands. 'You'd better learn the new domestic vocabulary before you start asking round! They're called *cleaning ladies* now – and they don't work so much as oblige. And the old rate of half-a-crown a day and a hot dinner is over – they charge a shilling an hour. What's more, they're about as easy to find as a pair of silk stockings.'

366

But Dorothy could nose out staff when she set her mind to it, and within a week she tracked down a young woman called Nellie Crayshaw.

Nellie had worked for eight years as a chambermaid at the Victoria Hotel in Blackstone, which was sufficient recommendation in itself. But unfortunately, at the treacherous age of thirty, she had fallen for the passing charms of a commercial traveller. Sacked without a character reference, she and her new baby were at present living with her widowed mother in genteel poverty.

Dorothy took me with her to call on Nellie, whom she addressed then and afterwards as *Mrs* Crayshaw. Dignified and gracious, she admired the baby, who was a strangely wizened little creature but very clean. She listened to the widowed mother's recital of Nellie's wrongs and her own shame, and assured her that she was right to stand by her daughter. She then offered one shilling and twopence an hour wages, referred to the post as 'housekeeper', and persuaded old Mrs Crayshaw to look after the baby while Nellie worked.

My father, hearing that I had accompanied Dorothy to this den of vice, said in mild reproof, 'But, my dear Dorrie, what of the moral influence on Evelyn? I hope you made it clear that though you are trying to help this person you do not condone her behaviour!'

'Oh, stuff,' said Dorothy robustly. 'We need a cleaner. Nellie needs the money. And Evelyn's old enough to know better. Besides, times are changing. We must change with them.'

He did not stand in judgement on her attitude, as once he would have done, but humphed quietly to himself, and he was always exceptionally polite to Nellie.

Before summer came, the Malt-house had recaptured some of its pre-war splendour. And despite the threat that hung over him, my father was enjoying his convalescence.

He breakfasted in bed and rose late. He shaved and dressed and sat in the drawing room in state, reading old favourites: the essays of Ruskin and Benson, the plays of

George Bernard Shaw, nature books such as *Eyes and No Eyes*. In lighter mood he chuckled over the outback ballads of Banjo Patterson, or puzzled his way pleasurably through the criminal mazes of Margery Allingham, Agatha Christie and Edgar Wallace. When the afternoon was warm and fine he sat in the garden and dozed, with the *Manchester Guardian* lying open on his knees to show everyone that he took a serious interest in politics.

He had time to enjoy programmes on the wireless. He listened to *ITMA* with the rest of his family, and picked up nationally-famous phrases which had so far eluded him.

'Can I do you now, sir?' he would say under his breath, when Nellie knocked respectfully on the drawing-room door.

And once, in a deep voice, to delight Julian, 'This is Funf speaking!'

But to *The Brains Trust* he responded as if C. E. M. Joad, Commander Campbell and Julian Huxley were colleagues, and he participating in their discussion.

'Pure sophistry!' he would say. Or, 'Ah, that's more like it!'

In the evening he listened to the agreeably modulated tones of Alvar Liddell or Stuart Hibberd reading the nine o'clock news, brought his map up to date, and went early and contentedly to bed.

'Slow death!' said Aunt Kate, grinning. 'You're killing him with kindness, Dollie.'

She had brought half a dozen new-laid eggs for the invalid, and was departing with a basketful of scraps for her hens.

'Rubbish!' said Dorothy automatically. Then, interested, 'Father used to have hens on his allotment. Tell me, Kate, do you think we could keep hens somewhere?'

She was thinking, as always, of food and barter.

'I doubt it. Julian's growing vegetables for victory in your back garden. So you'd either have to fell the trees or dig up your front lawn and flower-beds. And fourteen hens in a coop aren't a pretty sight from the drawing-room window.'

'Why should we have fourteen?' Dorothy asked curiously.

'Because you have to declare your egg production to the Ministry if you have more than that. So you might as well keep fourteen and have the eggs for your family and friends!'

Dorothy's hospitality was in full flood once again, though minus the banquets of former days. Dickie Blythe, now out of hospital, brought his parents with him for Sunday tea. It was the first time the two families had met since Michael died, and Dorothy and Connie Blythe went into the kitchen and apparently shared comfort and tears over the cress sandwiches, because they emerged damp-eyed but smiling.

Dorothy told us afterwards that Dickie had suffered mental stress as well as wounds and exposure, and was on leave for an unspecified length of time while the top brass made up their minds about him. They were not sure whether he was fit for night-flying.

'But Connie says he's as keen as mustard to go back. Brave lad!'

On another Sunday Judith came over for the day with Tim and Liz, bearing as gifts a bunch of Dorothy's favourite pink roses, *Trent's Last Case* for my father, a record of Schnabel playing Beethoven sonatas for me, and Michael's fountain pen for Julian.

Repenting her errant tongue, Dorothy confided in me as we laid trays for tea on the lawn.

'It's very good of Judith. She's put a lot of thought and expense into those presents, and she hasn't much money. I know from my own experience that life can't be easy for her. A young widow living with her parents, trying to bring the children up on her own. There's not a lot we can do for her, either. We haven't really had time to get to know one another, and she lives too far away to drop in. The best thing that could happen is for her to marry again, but that'll take some doing. Life's smacked her down twice already. Poor thing. Poor thing. And, Evie, I'm sorry for what I said about her when poor Micky was reported missing. I didn't mean it. I always lash out when I'm upset. And I'm always sorry for it after. . . .'

Judith sat on the lawn and talked to my father. Her

children ran and shouted and explored the garden, as once Micky and I had done.

Much later, Dorothy sponged the front of Liz's dress, saying, 'Don't be vexed with her, Judith. It's not the child's fault. The trees are dirty, even this far out of Kersley.'

'Should I light a bonfire for them?' Julian asked, enjoying his superior status. 'We've got plenty of old rubbish to burn.'

'And we could put some potatoes to roast in it!' I offered.

Tim and Liz jumped up and down, shouting, 'Yes! Yes! Yes!'

'Our garden's always been a children's paradise,' said Dorothy, flattered by their evident delight. 'Did you know that Evie and Mick found it before we did? Yes, fourteen years ago. The little monkeys were trespassing. Climbed over a wall, and got in through a side window – that'd be *his* idea, of course! – and ate their picnic sitting on the drawing-room floor in the dust. They didn't tell us for a long time.'

She stopped, afraid she had been tactless.

But Judith said, 'No, don't stop. Even if it makes me a bit weepy at times, I love hearing you talk about Mike. People don't mention him, you see, in case it upsets me. But you keep his memory alive, and that comforts me. And you know more about him than anyone else does. You've known him all his life, not just a little piece of it. I feel as if he's here with us, this afternoon.'

She stayed as late as she could, prolonging the visit. As she shook hands with my father and kissed Dorothy's cheek, she said, 'I'm going home happier than I came. You've all been so kind to us, so good to us. I feel I can face tomorrow now.'

'You must come again,' said Dorothy sincerely. 'Don't stand on ceremony. Come as often as you like.'

Even my father was reinstated as she accepted Judith.

'You married our son and we look on you as our daughter. That's right, isn't it, Gil? This is your home. We're your other family.'

So death had accomplished what life could never have done. If Michael had indeed been with us, the irony would have appealed to him.

*

When Judith had gone, Dorothy said wistfully, 'I did enjoy having Tim and Liz this afternoon. They're lovely children and she's a good mother. I wish – I do wish she'd had Michael's baby. I'd have loved that. Something to remember him by.'

My father, opening his detective novel, answered with a sadness that had grown in him since his illness.

'My dear Dorrie, that girl's got enough responsibility without another child to complicate her life. There are too many widows and fatherless children already. Who's to look after them? How can anyone make it up to them?'

He tapped his lips thoughtfully with his reading glasses. He was thinking, as the rest of us were, of Michael.

'A man dies and it's like a ship going down. Nothing left but floating wreckage. Flotsam! That's what we are. Flotsam!'

Then he put his glasses on and began to read *Trent's Last Case*.

32

Outside our temporary college building in Ducie Grove, Dickie Blythe was propped up against a lamp-post, hands in pockets, wearing civilian clothes of pre-war cut and quality. His fair hair was plastered neatly to his skull. He seemed thinner and longer than ever, and his face in repose was young and grave. But as soon as he saw me he brightened up, winked, and began to sing a George Formby song which had been popular in the late thirties.

'. . . leaning on a lamp-post at the corner of the street, till a certain little lady comes by . . .'

With the wry affection I reserved for him, I said, 'Dickie! You're a clot!' And gave him my music-case to carry.

'Thank God you're not a 'cellist!' he replied. 'I say, I've got a bit of good news. Thought I'd like to share it with a musical friend. Are you coming for a noggin?'

'At this time in the afternoon?' I asked, smiling.

He held out his arm in exaggerated chivalry.

'Why not? We can drop in on the old firm and do a spot of wine-tasting. You've never toured our cellars, have you?'

'No. I wasn't considered old enough for such places when you and Micky were budding wine-tasters.'

'Well you're old enough for anything now. Let's grab a taxi!'

And he hailed one, as Michael had done only a few months earlier. My heart ached as I stepped in.

'Funny thing about loss,' said Dickie, watching my face. 'Pops up when you least expect it. One minute you're jogging along nicely. Next minute – Zap, Wow, Ouch and Garooh!'

I had to smile.

'Like losing a leg,' Dickie continued. 'The phantom limb hurts. Hardly fair, that. Going through it over and over again.'

'What's your news, Dickie?'

'Well, you know we had a new AOC-in-C, just before Mike and I were ditched? Apparently he's been hotting things up for Jerry ever since. Bomber Harris, they call him. A gentleman of great discernment. He took a gander round and said, "Where's old Dickie Blythe these days? Night raids haven't been the same without him!" So they've asked me back.'

'How do you feel about that?' I asked cautiously, remembering what Dorothy had told me about his nerves.

Dickie's guard was well up. He answered breezily.

'Absolutely wizard. Nothing beats chumming up in a Lancaster! I was afraid they were going to make me chair-borne. No joy. Sitting at a desk, coping with lots of bumph. Took a dim view of that.'

'Dickie,' I said, raising my eyebrows, 'just for once, would you mind telling me how you feel, and in King's English.'

He laughed.

'Oh, I'm not pretending I shall enjoy the flack, and I've developed a slight aversion to being shot down, but other-wise tophole. I did a spot of amateur motor-racing before the war for the same reason. Like wearing a tight corset — wonderful when it's on, and such a relief when it's off. Not that I've ever worn one.'

I said frankly, 'I think you're quite amazing. I should probably be sick on the spot, or so frightened that I lay down and refused to move. If they wanted me on board a Lancaster they'd have to carry me!'

He looked as if he were about to answer this seriously, but stopped himself and changed the subject.

'It is this summer that you take your finals, isn't it? What happens next?'

'I don't know. I imagine that the Labour Exchange will have a part to play in that decision. They might direct me into munitions. Or perhaps I'll join up. . . .'

'What do your parents think about that?'

'They want me to live at home and teach music. But music might not qualify as helping the war effort!'

'What do you want to do?'

I sighed and said, 'I'd like to get a job and live in a place of my own, but since Micky died I feel that they need me more. I've never been anywhere or seen anything, apart from the Lake District, and there's a whole world outside – even if it is at war.'

Again he was about to speak seriously, but this time he was interrupted by the taxi-driver telling us we had arrived.

'So we have!' said Dickie cheerfully. 'For *Blythe Bros* read *Sots Unlimited*. I told the old man we might be dropping in. We'll have a preliminary glass of sherry with him before running the gauntlet of the entire staff. I'm afraid it's going to take ages to get to the cellars. We shall be treated with hushed respect. How's your royal wave and handshake?'

And it really was in the nature of a royal visit. Everyone knew Dickie and wanted to meet him and shake his hand. He greeted everyone by name, stopping to speak to senior members and to introduce me as Michael's sister. His smile never faltered. His seeming confidence never wavered. As we left the office he turned to smile on them all, and gave a confident salute. Victory was in the bag, that gesture seemed to say, and they loved that. Perhaps it cheered them rather than convinced them, for we were losing the war on every front.

'Goodness, what a reception!' I said, as we descended.

'Some chaps were born with a silver spoon in their mouths,' said Dickie lightly. 'I was born with a cork. Dad will be thinking of retirement in ten years. He'd like me to take his place eventually. That's a decision I'll face when I get back.'

He did not say 'If I get back', but he must have been thinking it, as I was.

The vaults were cool and quiet and dimly lit. While our guide explained the mysteries and beauties of wine we were silent. This was his kingdom. These were his charges. There was something both magnificent and soothing about the vast barrels maturing their contents, the regiments of dusty bottles waiting to come to perfection. War and the dangers of war receded. I should have felt quite safe here in an air raid.

Later, as we sampled a bottle of Pouilly Fumé with Mr Warburton, I said, 'I've never thought about wine before, but it's by way of being an art as well as a craft, isn't it?'

Mr Warburton approved of this remark, but as wine was a man's business he relayed his appreciation to Dickie.

'The young lady puts it very nicely, Mr Richard. I shouldn't be surprised if she developed quite a palate, given the opportunity of course. Now I'll just introduce our oldest inhabitants. . . .'

Dickie whispered in my ear, 'The young lady was drunk for breakfast and dead drunk for lunch, but she developed quite a palate!'

And I, picturing myself looking slightly squiffy and holding a glass of champagne aloft, giggled.

'Tell you what, Evie,' said Dickie, 'I know a jolly little place where we could have a spot of dinner. Dyson's Cellar. Not been open long. Run by a couple of ex-RAF bods. One's lost a leg and the other's lost an arm. You'd never notice.' He raised his voice, saying, 'The food's good but you have to take your own wine.'

Whereupon Mr Warburton, with a small dry smile, produced the very bottle needed for the occasion, and another for good luck.

'I must ring Dorothy to say I shan't be home for supper,' I said, as we returned to the upper world.

Warm, relaxed, I accepted the offer of Dickie's arm, realising that the unaccustomed drinking had gone to my head. There was nothing wrong, however, with my ears. On the telephone, speaking carefully to make sure no words were slurred, I detected an exultant undertone to Dorothy's voice which sobered me instantly. Evidently, she was doing a little matchmaking in her head. Dickie was so eminently suitable. I did hate having my life run for me.

'Anything wrong?' he asked, as my lips tightened.

'No. Nothing.'

What else could I say? It was not his fault, after all.

My contrary frame of mind was instantly dispelled in the ambience of Dyson's Cellar, where we arrived half an hour early and knocked at the kitchen entrance. Here Dickie was hailed with a delight which they also extended to me as Michael's sister. I had seen maimed servicemen from a distance, but never known any until now. I prepared to act as if nothing was amiss. They insisted that I noticed the difference, and shared in the joke. We drank one bottle of wine with them and took the other into the little restaurant.

'Good bods!' said Dickie. 'Good cooks, too.'

I raised my third glass of wine to him. I had forgiven him for Dorothy's misdemeanour.

'And good company!'

For Dickie was always good company, and time for once was unimportant. I stood on the threshold of my own world, and tasted freedom in every sip of claret.

Over coffee, Dickie said, 'I've got a few days spare. Reporting for duty on Monday. Any chance that you can spend them with me? We can go out and about. I know lots of places. Lots of people, too. We could have picnics and things.'

Through the haze of wine I began to wonder whether Dorothy was alone in her hopes. Dickie was looking vulnerable.

Objectively, for I was fond of him, I considered the situation. If he intended to court me there was no way in which I could avoid hurting him. I tried to warn him off.

'I think I know you well enough, Dickie, to tell you something that only Michael knew. Can I confide in you?'

He nodded, and his face brightened. I cursed his hopefulness.

'A year ago I was in love with a married man. It's over for good. But I'm still . . . I still . . .'

I was hunting for the right words, trying to strike the right note. Not sentimental, I thought, but not offhand either.

Dickie suggested brightly, 'Still suffering from a hangover?'

It was less elegant than I could have wished, but I nodded.

'Fair exchange is no robbery,' said Dickie, unmoved.

'Allow me to tell you that I was cruelly repulsed by a Queen Bee a year ago. . . .'

'What on earth is a Queen Bee?' I asked, coming off my dignity.

'The senior WAAF officer on our station. A dazzling popsie. But already married, and some years older than my humble self. Not that age matters.'

He poured out the last of the wine. He raised his glass.

'Oh, queen of bees, I salute thee!'

Piqued, I raised my glass too, saying somewhat coldly, 'She must have been a remarkable person.'

'She was indeed. And underline the *was*,' Dickie said. 'Life is short.' Then he added seriously, 'Recent experience has proved to me that life, above all else, is short.'

The wine was taking its toll of me. I sipped, and swirled the claret in my glass, and nodded dolefully.

Dickie said, 'But with all due respect to our past loves – and may they rest in peace – why should you and I not spend the last few days of my leave, convalescence, call-it-what-you-will, together? No names, no pack drill. Just friendship and fun, and I promise not to make a pass at you even if I'm yearning to. What do you say?'

I was unable to think clearly, let alone say anything. So I touched his wine glass with my own. It slopped slightly.

'Good-ho!' said Dickie.

He had an excellent head for drink, and was in good practice. He smiled on my flushed face with benevolence.

'I'll bet you thought I was going to propose?' he remarked, in his most beguiling tone.

Released by alcohol, relieved by this artless approach, I said, 'It's just that Dorothy's rather keen on the idea, I'm afraid.'

'So are my parents,' said Dickie, grinning.

'Really?' I said, amazed.

'Oh yes. The old man thinks you're a lovely lass – and I wouldn't dispute that! – and your Mama and mine are always putting their heads together and saying how nice it would be. Even old Mike was guilty of dropping a heavy hint from time to time.'

377

He was evidently amused, taking their matchmaking in his stride.

'I do propose something,' he went on. 'I propose that we be good friends. Real friends. Or is that not possible between members of the opposite sex?'

'It's perfectly possible!' I said very emphatically. 'And let me tell you something – I've regarded you as a friend for a long time.'

This evidently amused him as well. He closed one eye and drew down one corner of his mouth.

'We can fox them, can't we?'

I laughed aloud.

'Dickie, you turn my mountains into molehills. You do indeed.'

He peered at his wristwatch in the candle-lit gloom.

'But night hath fallen,' he remarked, 'and I must take thee home, Kathleen. And as I should hate us to stumble over the threshold of thy father's house, giggling in an unseemly fashion, I feel that more black coffee is called for.'

'We shall have to watch our feet anyway,' I said, giggling already. 'The floors are full of holes. Honestly! They open up like magic, overnight. Daddy's written a letter to the house agent about it. The other day Grannie's chiffonier tilted sideways. No warning. Just tilted slowly and with enormous dignity, like a tipsy duchess! And would you believe it? The legs had gone through a rotten board. Actually, Grannie never called it a *chiffonier*. She called it a *sheffaneer*. It was years before I connected the two. . . .'

'You're getting garrulous,' said Dickie with great enjoyment. 'You'll be tilting over sideways in a minute, like the chiffonier!'

I excused myself, making sure that I walked straight because he was watching, and went into the Ladies Room which was rather damp and smelled of mushrooms. I peered anxiously into the mirror and saw an exceedingly pink and bright and wispy young woman. I tidied her hair and powdered her nose. I put more lipstick on her mouth, careful not to blur the edges. Satisfied, I walked carefully back.

The sight of his face in grave repose reminded me of the serious question I wanted to ask.

'First,' I said, sitting down rather quickly, 'do I look sober?'

'Apart from the red leather lips, absolutely spiffing.'

I dabbed my mouth surreptitiously with my dinner napkin.

'Second?' Dickie asked, smiling.

Then I tackled him.

'You're leading two totally different lives, aren't you? What people expect, and what you really feel.'

His expression remained deliberately sunny and uncomprehending, but I was always dauntless in pursuit of the truth, and the evening's wine gave my words wings.

'If we're going to be friends, real friends instead of pleasant acquaintances, then you should be able to say what you feel, not what you think I might like to hear. Or else, quite frankly, I could be with anybody, couldn't I?'

'You should have been a barrister,' Dickie said, grinning. 'If I plead guilty will you give me a suspended sentence?'

My own retort was just as swift.

'Yes, if you'll talk seriously.'

'Not tonight, Josephine. Tonight is life as it should be. Let's keep it that way.'

I saw he was serious about this at least.

'All right. We'll talk seriously tomorrow then.'

'Drink your coffee and stop organising me,' Dickie said easily. 'Has anyone ever told you how bossy you are, given half a chance?'

We lay on our stomachs at the top of Tarn How and looked down on the roof and chimneys of the Malt-house. That summer the farmers had cut and garnered two crops of hay. Overhead the drone of a lone biplane sounded like a bee in search of honey.

'Those little aeroplanes used to write advertisements in the sky when I was at Moss Lane School,' I murmured into the grass. 'Miss Todd was always hitting my knuckles with a ruler because I used to stop working and watch them.'

'Halcyon days,' said Dickie. 'Just up there by yourself in the blue. Nearest thing to religion I ever experienced.'

'Music is mostly my religion. But I find it in hundreds of things. Anything beautiful. Coming down in the morning to find the kitchen full of sun . . .' I was afraid of sounding pretentious, and added quickly, '. . . that's when I've tidied it up the night before, of course! And I think Tarn How is beautiful in a wild, harsh way. My favourite place on earth so far, though I do hope there'll be others. There are so many places I want to see.'

Unexpectedly, he asked, 'Did you ever come here with that married bloke you mentioned?'

'Once,' I answered reluctantly. 'I plotted it, so that I could ask him back to tea. That was when he told me he was married.'

'What made you give him up eventually?'

It still hurt me to tell the truth. 'He gave me up, actually. I wasn't important enough to him, and he was too important to me. Why did you give up your Queen Bee?'

He answered, 'Because nothing was important to her except herself. I had to plod through the valley of humiliation before I realised that I was having that affair on my own. Still, I learn. I hope. But the memory of your bloke lingers on, does it?'

I conjured up Christopher Hyde and contemplated him, unstirred.

'Actually,' I said, 'it doesn't.'

And with that knowledge the breeze seemed fresher, the sky bluer, the day hotter and brighter than ever. I gave his memory a little push, and down the hill it tumbled and rolled from Tarn How.

'Good-ho!' said Dickie. He smiled his most engaging smile. 'I say, did you plot this expedition so that I should come to tea?'

I began to laugh.

'The only plotter is Dorothy. She was bartering all yesterday, and she's been baking the proceeds all morning, and if I don't bring you home she'll probably kill me!'

*

Dickie stayed to supper, too, and afterwards we sat by ourselves on the drawing-room sofa in state. Dorothy had established us there, banishing my father to his study, Julian to the cricket club, and herself to the kitchen to cry over *Gone With the Wind* again.

'One more day,' said Dickie.

I could think of nothing to say, and hoped that my silence would seem as sympathetic as it was.

Dickie said, 'And one day at a time. I've been a spendthrift with time the last few months. Chucked hours and days and weeks about as if they were small change. Best part of my enforced idleness. Now I start weighing, counting and measuring it again.'

I put out a hand and he squeezed it.

'Why do you want to know about Mike!' he asked. 'It's not one of your happy-ever-after stories.'

'I loved him,' I said quietly. 'He was one of the people I've loved most. I want to share his death, not have it wrapped up and hidden from me.'

'You're a born bloody martyr.'

'Perhaps. I know that it's my way of dealing with it.'

He said, 'How much do you know about war? I mean, apart from the heartening tones of "March of Time", and the ever-ready chorus of "Britons never, never, never shall be slaves"?'

'I know we're not doing well.'

He said, 'We're doing very badly. We're losing on every front. And the U-boats must be sinking our supply ships at the same rate that the German anti-aircraft guns are bringing down our bombers.'

He looked sideways at me, and squeezed my hand again.

'This information is not calculated to boost morale, Evie, so I don't want you to repeat it to anyone else – except perhaps your father, who also has an unhealthy regard for truth! Scout's honour? Cross your heart and hope to die?'

I nodded and put a finger to my lips, and saw Dickie looking at my mouth as Michael had once looked at Judith's. And instead of being sorry or cross I was interested. I wondered what it would be like if he kissed me. For an instant we paused in mutual knowledge. Then he recovered and kept on course.

'The bombing of Germany has achieved almost nothing and cost us far more than we can afford. We actually broke off the air offensive last November. We couldn't build aircraft or train air crews fast enough to replace the losses. Now we've caught up again, and we're pursuing strategical bombing on a bigger scale – that's the main reason why I'm going back. They need everyone they can get.'

'But you're better?' I said, letting my hand stay in his. 'You really are better?'

'I'm as right as I'll ever be,' he said, as if it were of no consequence. 'To continue my sermon – bombing is purely for the purpose of propaganda. In order to win, the people must believe we are winning. So we need sensational news to keep up morale. Do you know why we bombed Lübeck and Rostock, which are medieval towns built with wood? They burn well! They make a good spectacle.'

I could not believe it.

'Oh yes,' said Dickie, so sadly that he sounded like my father speaking of Michael. 'I travelled in Germany before the war. I know what I'm talking about. Why do a thousand bombers take off in three separate attacks, to smash Cologne and Essen and Bremen? It spells out our power in the air. Sensational stuff. For as long as it lasts.'

Horrified, I cried, 'But that's immoral. Those are wicked things to do. How can you bear to be part of it?'

He said, 'War is about winning, you see, and it never pretended to be nice. I do it because it must be done. I don't want to live in a Fascist world, and I can't stand aside and let the others fight for me. So I'm joining in the dirty work. If it's any comfort to you, the enemy's hands are no cleaner. And we have our moments, you know.'

I asked, subdued, 'Did Micky feel like this?'

'Of course he did. I'm not quoting figures or statistics because I don't know them, but we chaps talk to each other, and we see what happens rather than what civilians are told. A certain number of bombers take off each night, and a very much smaller number comes back the following morning.

I've stopped counting the friends I've lost, the length of time they lasted, and the heavier toll of inexperienced bods who take their places. And it still doesn't make a ha'porth of difference. Even if we knew for certain that none of us was going to get back we'd still be climbing up into that Lancaster at dusk.'

He held my hand, but he had forgotten me.

'You said something about how brave we were. That you'd be sick, or lie down and have to be carried aboard. I've seen that happen. Stage-fright, Mike used to call it. Jolly them round. Cover up for them and carry on. They'll come to, once the chocks are removed and the old girl belts down the runway. Anyway, it's too late to turn back then, and each of us is dependent on the others.

'Yes, we're brave. Not because we're natural heroes but because we're sick-scared of the many deaths we could die, and we go on playing footsie with our penn'orth of luck. And none of us wants to die. We want to live. Some of us just don't make it, that's all.'

Some part of me which had held back, had held him off, now took over. I lifted his hand and kissed it. He blinked and nodded, and hurried on. He had to explain, first.

'I didn't tell Dorothy lies, when I said Mike talked a lot about her and his childhood, but I altered the time sequence. He said all that months before we ditched. Neither of us talked then. We were too damned cold and ill. The sea got rough and was heaving us about all over the place. We couldn't use a paddle. Well, Mike couldn't have paddled anyway. He was pretty helpless. Banged his head when we landed. He was bleeding badly.

'We'd been beaten up by night-fighters. Wings damaged, fuel lost, panels shot up, hydraulics gone, one engine gone. The old girl was a flying colander, and still flying. Well, all Mike's old girls would fly for him. As a pilot he wasn't just good, he was bloody inspired.

'I was the only one who hadn't copped something, and I was the one who had to play the Barber of Seville and run round after everyone else. Figaro come, Figaro go. The three gunners were dead. No use bothering with them. Sparks was badly wounded and I shoved him out over Germany. He stood a chance of being picked up and taken to hospital that way. Saw his brolly open. Don't know what happened. We made it over the coast. The sea was like glass.

'Mike said, "I'm going to ditch her!"

'Bill, the flight sergeant, was wounded too, but I didn't know how badly. He said he was okay. He kept on. Well, we needed him. I stayed with Mike and strapped myself in. Head on knees. Arms over head. Left him and the old girl to it.

'Everything was out of synchrony. The old girl was shaking to bits and we were coming in at a hell of a speed. Must have been a hundred and twenty miles an hour. We ploughed straight in. The impact was a world-shatterer. Smack! Flat on her belly. I still can't bear to see or hear a film where anything crashes. Cover my eyes and ears. God knows how I came to and got the dinghy out and Mike into it. He was unconscious. The old girl slipped under the waves, and then it was all over. Bill never made it. He must have gone down with her. I sat with one arm locked in Mike's, and the other holding on for dear life, and there was nothing but the sea and the freezing cold, and the two of us trying to stay alive. I still go through that sequence of events in my dreams, just to see if there was anything more I could have done.

'The chances of being rescued are about three to one. But the odds against it go up considerably when you're wounded and the weather's bad. Mike came to as it got rough, and we were both sick. Not in a civilised way, leaning over the side and wiping your mouth afterwards, but sick-sick. Sick where we sat, and too clumsy and exhausted to clean ourselves up. Retching in our own stink and misery. And the cold was so cold that it burned. Mike mumbled and moaned for a bit and then he shut up. I think he'd lost consciousness by that time. I hope so, anyway, because it was a bloody nightmare. I didn't want to live then. I wanted to die, only I didn't know how to do it. I've no idea how long we were floating round. They reckon it was only a few hours, but people who haven't ditched use a different form of time. Let's just say it was too long.

'Then mentally I went right down. Full fathom five. And I became two people. A watcher, and the chap in the dinghy. Actually, the watcher was the real part of me. The other part was just a pain, like having a kid brother who hangs around. But as long as he stuck to me I had to put up with him. No thought then of Mike or anyone else. No thought of survival. Just bloody annoyed with the chap in the dinghy, who was still alive and linked to his kid brother. Because I could have floated off quite happily. Better things to do, and a better place to go to than I had ever been, don't you know? But he held on.

'A trawler found us. They had to pull the pair of us out together. I'd gripped Mike so hard, and the weather was so cold, that our arms were locked rigid. He was dead by then. I don't know when he died.

'I haven't told anyone this, except the padre. As I say, I'm not the religious type, but the padre's a good bod and doesn't mind about that. When he came to see me I thought he might cast a light on that experience. I hadn't met the watcher before, but he struck me as being the genuine article. The chap in the dinghy was just the outer casing, and definitely expendable.

'The padre said, as you might expect, that the chap in the dinghy was my body and the watcher was my soul. And the soul, being made of superior stuff and hailing from finer realms than ours, always wanted to return whence it came.

'This I had figured, but I had a couple of questions to ask.

'The first was, why didn't the watcher simply cut and run, instead of hanging about with the chap in the dinghy?

'To which he replied that the soul had a responsibility. In his opinion the powers-that-be had sent a message along the grapevine to say that its work was not yet done. Like those prima donnas who say they want to retire, only the management will keep bringing them back for a farewell performance!

'I am a modest bod. I answered the padre in all humility. Agreed, I said. I have been as flotsam and jetsam on the face of the deep. Good for a party. Good for a laugh. But nothing to write home about. I don't doubt that there's room for improvement. Let's try to make a better job of it this time round. Understood. But what about Mike's responsibilities? He had everything to live for. He'd only been married to Judith for a few weeks. He'd taken on a couple of kids who trusted in him and had already lost one father. And Judith was Mike's sheet anchor, because until he met her he was a bit of a drifter too. So what was up with Mike's watcher? Why wasn't a message passed on to *him*? Or can the celestial grapevine get snarled up?

'That was what I asked the padre. I said, "Who decided that Mike's work was done? And why?" But he said he didn't know.'

We had been holding each other's hands in sympathy. Now we separated self-consciously. Our silence was long as we emerged from the end of one story and stood at the beginning of another. It was as if Michael had come alive again and linked us in a way which had not been possible before. I felt Dickie looking at me and found I could not look back. My momentary interest in the possibility of his kiss had turned into a little frenzy of hope and fear. I wondered how many years we were going to stay frozen on the leather sofa, unable to speak or move.

In my head, a voice said in total disbelief, 'But he's only a friend. Surely people don't fall in love with friends? I mean, he's not even your type!'

But when I did look at him I knew that I had, and he was. And the moment was not of supreme joy as I had expected but of supreme humility. For I had believed love was my right, and discovered it to be a gift beyond my deserving, and judging from Dickie's expression he was feeling the same.

We attempted a smile, drew a quick breath, and looked away again, not knowing how to break the habit of years nor the spell of the last hour's revelations. Then Dickie took the initiative.

He said lightly, seriously, 'I think, if I might suggest it, that a roaming in the gloaming is indicated. Possibly followed by a thoughtful pint at your local Frog and Nightgown.'

I wished, at that moment, I had been a wiser virgin, for I felt that I could not accept his love without confessing my sins. So I came out with it, all in a fluster.

'But, Dickie, before we – Dickie, there's something I must tell you first, about – about Christopher Hyde!'

To which he replied, looking young and old and wise and sorry, 'We left Christopher Hyde at Tarn How, remember? So there's nothing to tell. Now or ever.'

Then he pulled me to my feet, gave me a quick hug, and pushed me gently towards the drawing room door, saying, 'Just get your coat and powder your nose. And let the good Dorothy know where we're going.'

I believed I had removed all signs of the past hour, but my stepmother, emerging from the blazing ruins of Atlanta, focused immediately on my carefully powdered cheekbones.

'You've never been crying, have you?' she said, deflated.

'Tears, idle tears!' I reassured her.

She was so genuinely concerned that I explained, in part.

'Actually, Dickie was talking about Michael, and I got a bit weepy. Although, as Judith says, the tears are a comfort.'

Her own face quivered at the mention of her son, but she wanted to know how I was faring with Dickie. Her tone became jocular.

'You're not supposed to be crying! You're supposed to be enjoying yourself, sitting on the sofa, holding hands with a nice young man!'

The talk had been a catharsis. I was wiser and mellower for it, but not yet ready to confide.

'Oh, we're getting on nicely,' I said, to cheer her up. 'Look, I've just popped in to say that we're going for a stroll. We'll be back when the pub shuts.'

Dorothy looked coy for a moment, and then her expression changed and softened. She was sitting in Grannie's low chair, and she turned away from me and looked into the fire as Grannie used to do.

'Talking about our Michael,' she said quietly, 'do you ever feel ashamed that you're alive and he's dead, Evie?'

She neither expected nor waited for an answer.

'I do,' she said simply. 'Evie, I hope you never lose a child. It's a terrible thing when your child dies first. Even a grown child. I think of my mother at poor Arthur's funeral. I felt for her – make no mistake about that! – but I didn't know then what I do now.

'Evie, if they'd given me a choice, I'd have said to the powers-that-be, "Don't take Micky. Take me instead." And I'd have meant it truly, Evie. I'm not talking like a fourpenny book. I'd have given my life for that lad. Because he had everything to live for, hadn't he? And he was wonderful, wasn't he?

'But, Evie, they never give you the choice.'

33

The world, transformed by moonlight, had become another planet from which all evil was erased. Barrage balloons bobbed overhead in party mood. Tarn Brow steps, steep and grey and uneven in daytime, were a silver staircase leading to silver woods and fields. Mill chimneys took on the majesty of signposts pointing to the stars. A line of pylons in glittering formation seemed ready to tread a stately minuet. Plain stones became precious ones. Mirrors of water shivered and gleamed. Clouds shone. The blackness, the nights of war, had been banished. Clarity, beauty and order had taken their place.

We sauntered hand in hand along Tarn Brow heights, safe and free.

'Fresh start?' Dickie asked, watching me, smiling to himself.

I smiled back. I nodded emphatically. We stopped, and he drew me into the tree shadows at the side of the road and kissed me. The kiss was a question in itself which I answered without hesitation. Our minds made up, we kissed again. Then drew apart, breathless, recreated.

'Like to marry me?' Dickie asked hopefully.

'I'd like to think about it.'

'Favourably?'

'I just need a little time to get used to the idea of us.'

'Understood. Write to me?'

'Every day. And you?'

'Every day. Cross my heart and – promise to live!'

'Oh, Dickie! Don't tempt the gods! And, Dickie, let's not say anything official to anyone yet.'

'No, we'll get used to the idea of us. Eve, apple of my eye. Your wish is my command.'

'Then I'd like another kiss.'

I always took Dickie's letters away to open them, because Dorothy's curiosity could be felt across a table or even across a room. This summer morning it was a registered package containing a brown leather cube of a jewellery box, which I held for a while before I opened it. And though I looked and looked at the ring I did not put it on, because the moment must be perfect. So I ferreted inside the package for my letter, and found it, and also another letter in a sealed envelope formally addressed to my father.

Sitting on the stairs in the warmth of the late summer sun, I read and smiled and sighed, and read again. Finally, slipping the box into the pocket of my cotton skirt I returned to the kitchen where the evening meal was in progress.

My father lowered his paper as I came in, and Dorothy bounced out of the scullery, holding a bowl and a wooden spoon. They had been waiting for my return.

'That packet came by the afternoon post while you were out,' said Dorothy unnecessarily. 'Is it from Dickie?' Knowing that it was.

I nodded and held out the envelope, saying, 'For you, Daddy.'

And held my breath, watching his face.

He took it warily, read it with growing concern, and flushed up.

'The chap wants to be engaged to you!' he said accusingly.

'Engaged?' Dorothy cried, and dropped the spoon into the bowl with disastrous results.

They both talked together, at cross purposes.

'This is a bit sudden isn't it?' said my father. 'You weren't even interested in him a couple of months ago!'

'Well, I couldn't be more pleased, Evie. I couldn't really!'

'And as if an engagement wasn't enough, he wants to marry you on his next leave!'

'Marry her on his next leave? Here, let me see that letter, Gil.'

He handed it over and addressed me sternly.

'An engagement at such short notice is bad enough. Marriage is out of the question. You need much more time to think about that.'

I fingered the little leather box in my pocket. I had hoped for, though not expected, a warmer reaction from him.

'But Daddy, he has asked your permission,' I said stubbornly, 'and he's sent me his grandmother's ring to wear.'

'So that's what it was,' cried Dorothy, instantly diverted from the letter. 'I did wonder! Let's have a look at it, Evie!'

My father and I ignored her. This was between the two of us, just as Michael's engagement had been an emotional tug-of-war with Dorothy.

'Do you give permission for me to wear it?' I persisted.

He evaded the issue.

'Permission? You're twenty-one. You can do what you like!'

'But I need your approval,' I said, and my voice shook.

My father snorted, eyes bright.

'It's all a bit too sudden for me. He's a decent young chap, and I like him, but you don't know each other well enough. . . .'

'They've known each other for years!' Dorothy cried.

He turned on her then, coldly furious.

'I know that you've been pushing him at her for years, but Evelyn always gave the impression that she wasn't interested in him until recently. And very recently at that! Too recently for my liking.'

Now Dorothy and my father dominated the conversation.

'How long does it take to fall in love?' Dorothy demanded of him.

'About the same length of time as it takes to fall out of it, I suppose!' he replied, at his blighting best.

'Just one moment!' I cried, in a turmoil. 'This isn't your personal quarrel, it's our personal decision. Dickie made a point of asking you, Daddy, and you should be pleased about that. Most men don't bother these days. And if we're engaged then obviously we want to marry. And we can't afford to wait, because there might not be much time for us.'

He did not want to give way to Dickie and I was angry with him.

'If you don't like the idea then I'm sorry,' I said, though sorrow had no part in my feelings at that moment, 'but I'm marrying Dickie whatever you say!'

Joy and chagrin, having boiled up, now boiled over.

'And I'm not crying about you! Don't flatter yourself!' I said.

'There!' said Dorothy triumphantly. 'I hope you're satisfied with yourself, Gilbert Fawley. Making your daughter cry and turning her against us.'

He attacked her furiously.

'You're the one who's filled her head with silly romantic notions. God knows why! You've lived long enough to know better! All you can see is a wedding day. But I look further than that. I don't want Evelyn to be a war widow like you and poor Judith, with her life messed up and possibly a child to rear.'

He knew from our faces that he was losing the battle.

He said more quietly, 'If you want to be engaged then I'll go along with that. Otherwise I think you should wait. Six months at least. A year preferably.'

Dorothy said brusquely, 'There's a war on! They haven't time to wait. I wouldn't have thanked my father for stopping my marriage to Harry Harland, even though I was a war widow. And you won't stop Evelyn and Dickie. And quite right too!'

'I am not stopping anything!' he shouted. 'I am taking a sensible and thoughtful attitude which nobody seems to appreciate!'

Ignoring him, Dorothy turned to me and said, 'When do you want to get married, love?'

I wiped my eyes, blew my nose, and gave them the next piece of news with some trepidation.

'Dickie can get a week's special leave at the end of next month. We thought we might be married on my birthday.'

Even Dorothy stalled at this.

'But that's less than four weeks. How are we going to organise a wedding in that time?'

My father gave a snort which conveyed triumph over Dorothy and rage at the present situation.

'I could have told you!' he said. 'Give them an inch and they'll take a yard!'

He strode over to the window and turned his back on us.

I was protesting, hands outspread, 'But we don't expect or want an elaborate wedding. Just something simple like Michael and Judith had. Drinks and snacks. Dickie's talking about a special licence and a registry office.'

'It's too soon!' said my father over his shoulder.

It was evidently too soon for Dorothy as well, but she had committed herself to our cause.

'Now, Gil, don't talk in that tone. You'll only upset her again. They're young. They're in love. There's a war on.'

'If they intend to get married at all costs then I can't stop them,' he said bluntly.

Nobody spoke. I drooped in flesh and spirit. Dorothy glared at his back. Our silence, the atmosphere of hurt disapproval, seeped through to him. He cleared his throat.

'I repeat. I've got nothing against Dickie. Under normal circumstances I would have been pleased. I don't want Evie's heart broken, that's all. Think of poor Judith.'

Neither of us answered, waiting.

He said, 'If you've made up your damned minds then that's that!'

Still it was not enough. Dorothy ignored the sounds of potatoes thudding against the lid of the pan. I held the little leather box like a talisman in the palm of my hand. My father turned round.

'I'm not trying to upset you, lassie,' he said, on a softer note. 'If you're absolutely certain, then good luck to you both.'

I flung my arms round his neck and kissed him fervently. Dorothy smiled at him, and rescued the potatoes.

He protested, through the embrace.

'But you don't know what you're letting yourself in for!'

He reproached his wife.

'And you're old enough to know better, Dorothy!'

We made much of him, and let him grumble himself back to his evening paper. Then I brought out the little box.

'Do you want to see it?' I asked tentatively.

For I wanted the ring to receive all the adulation and delight that was its due. The gold circle was set with a turquoise, surrounded by pearls in the shape of a flower.

My father's interest was aroused.

'That's very pretty. That's a Victorian ring. My mother had a ring something like that.'

Dorothy was momentarily disappointed.

'I thought he'd have sent you a nice big diamond!' she said. 'Connie's got a lovely diamond ring.' And then, superstitiously, 'Pearls are for sorrow!'

To me it was the loveliest betrothal ring in the world. I took it out and smiled at my father.

'Do you give me permission to wear it?' I asked.

'Yes, yes, of course. Do what you want!' he said, pleased and sorry at once. He shook his newspaper out, and added drily, 'You always have done!'

I slipped it on, knowing that it would fit perfectly. Dickie had had it altered for me, but I did not tell them that. They had suffered enough surprises for one day.

And now I could only wait and hope, not knowing towards which holocaust Dickie's Lancaster was heading, nor whether our marriage feast might coldly furnish forth a funeral table. But he scribbled a note each day, and always telephoned after a night raid to reassure me. His voice floated up from Suffolk, light and debonair.

'Germany calling Eden! Germany calling Eden!'

And my apprehension would turn to laughter, as I cried, 'Oh, Dickie! Dickie! What an *idiot* you are!'

Looking back, I am astonished and ashamed to recall how self-centred we were, how totally oblivious of any needs but our own. Accommodation in wartime was hard to find. Near an air base it was at a premium. But Dickie was ruthless and tireless in his hunt for a temporary home. Finally he charmed his way into renting a room on the top floor of a large house, in a village close by.

'All arranged!' he said triumphantly, over the telephone. 'House belongs to parents of an ex-chum of mine. They knew Mike, too. So they were prepared to do us a favour. Tell you about that later. The rest of their place is full of fleeing relatives and evacuees. We're in the attic. Used to be Den's hide-out. Furnished, of course. Just room for us and the wedding photograph. Gas ring and wash-basin already installed. Use of ex-servants' bathroom on floor below, use of cooker downstairs by arrangement, use of telephone in hall whenever necessary. Hey, Evie, we can spend our honeymoon there!

'I've booked the local registry office for Saturday the twenty-fifth at eleven o'clock. Booked your family and mine into the Falcon for Friday night. Local hostelry. Elegant and venerable. Just their style. Wedding lunch at the Falcon. Cake and champers. Kisses all round. And off we go. Oh, if anyone else wants to come – Judith or your Aunt Kate or any of the Blythe contingent – let me know as soon as poss. Falcon's always full up. I reckon I've thought of everything. How about that for organisation?'

'Dickie! You're wonderful!' I cried.

Then we spoke of nothing and meant everything. We hung up. And I floated into the kitchen to deliver the glad tidings.

The atmosphere seemed to be inexplicably cool afterwards but I was too preoccupied to worry about that. Half an hour later, going out to tell Aunt Kate, I surprised Dorothy making a disillusioned telephone call to Connie Blythe.

She was saying, '. . . I thought so, too. We could have done it beautifully between us. Your wine and my food, and plenty of room for relatives and friends . . . Yes, I am, too. But we shall just have to trim our sails, Connie! . . . Yes, people can come if they're willing to make the journey, but they have to let us know now because of staying at this Falcon place . . . Yes, I agree, a big trek and a big expense. . . . Yes, I just hope they understand that our hands are tied . . . Still, if it's what Evie and Dickie want I suppose we must go along with it . . . No, much too late. Dickie's booked everything. Registry office and the lot!' And then, in despair, 'Connie, fancy having to trail all the way to Suffolk and back in a weekend!'

She saw me coming down the stairs and changed her tone to one of bantering affection.

'I shall have to go now, Connie. I see the bride coming down the stairs. Yes. Yes, I will. And take care of yourself, too.'

Their distress must have registered with me, and yet I could run across the hall untroubled, and out into the August evening. Mozart rippled through my head. The climate of my soul was pure Bach. Nor did the music usurp my feelings for Dickie. Rather did it explain and complement them. For Dickie had become the music.

And there was the telephone call from Aaron Feinberg, which caused me some remorse at the time and much more later. He had been my teacher and mentor since the Lilian Lacey affair, six years previously, and she had chosen her successor wisely. For a while, being full of youthful hope and arrogance, I had believed he might achieve what Lilian said was impossible, but apparently her prognosis was correct.

Yes, he said, I was a gifted pupil, I worked hard, I was technically accomplished, and my music should bring pleasure to me and to those who listened, but I was not unique. The concert platform was not for me. And it was a pity, in a way, that I had chosen the piano. Had I played almost any other instrument he would have encouraged me to work in an orchestra, but there was no room for a pianist there.

'You are not the Myra Hess,' he said.

There seemed to be no option but to take a teaching diploma. This fell far short of my original expectations, but my father was delighted. To teach well, he believed, was the most valuable work an intelligent person could do, and a reward in itself. I think that he listened to me with greater enjoyment, knowing that my music would be useful as well as beautiful.

I had taken my finals in June.

'You will do well,' Aaron had prophesied, 'and I will help you. I find you a job plum.'

In August, soon after my engagement, I heard that all was well. This news was eclipsed by preparations for the wedding, but Aaron Feinberg had not forgotten.

His speech was not easy to understand at the best of times. Over the telephone it demanded a careful listener and an inspired interpreter. It took me some minutes to realise that he was endeavouring to open and expand my closed provincial world. He was saying, 'Please to tell parents you live in London for one year with nice good musical family, and you teach. Please to tell parents that you earn money but to live in London is dearest. They help you a small bit, yes....'

I said all in one gasp, 'But Professor Feinberg, I'm getting married next week, and I shall be living in Suffolk, you see. With my new husband. He's in the RAF....'

It took him some time to comprehend that I was refusing his offer. He turned away from the mouthpiece and spoke to his wife in German. His tone registered disappointment, disbelief and anger. He came back.

He said coldly, 'So I do all this trobble for nossing? Why do you not tell me of this husband?'

Now Mrs Feinberg's voice over-rode his, still speaking in German. Her tone was one of counsellor and mediator, soothing, explaining.

He spoke again, stiffly, 'My wife say best of wishes to both. I too. Sometime perhaps we meet lucky man.'

Conscience-stricken, I said, 'I'm sorry. I'm truly sorry, Professor. And I do thank you very much indeed. But I can't leave my husband, you see.'

'Yes,' he said. 'Best luck. Goodbye from both.'

Nor had I thought how inconvenient our wedding date was for my father and Dorothy. He would just have started the autumn term after a six months' absence from Grizedale's, a task requiring undivided attention and all his energy. She was about to take up a new post, as supervisor of two factory canteens. In retrospect, I felt sorry for them both, but of the two I was sorrier for Dorothy because she had the household to organise as well as her work and my wedding.

Martha-like, she struggled through those few turbulent weeks without complaint, and only came to herself on the eve of the wedding, when our party joined a long queue at platform four in Blackstone Central Station.

We had bought our tickets, but that did not guarantee the train would leave on time nor that seats would be available. If troops had to be transported from one place to another they were given priority.

'Stand back!' the ticket-collector commanded, as our family party reached the barrier.

We were tired and breathless, overladen with my trousseau and luggage, their weekend suitcases and a vast and heavy cardboard box.

'You'll have to wait!' he said peremptorily. A very Napoleon of importance. 'This here train's full. You'll have to wait for the relief.' He added grimly, 'If they can get one.'

My world wobbled. I surfaced in a fine panic.

'But what are we going to do . . . ?'

Dorothy thrust me aside and confronted the ticket collector, chin well-advanced. She spoke slowly and emphatically.

'Just let me tell you,' she said, 'that if we have to stand every inch of the way, we must be aboard that train! Our daughter is getting married tomorrow morning.'

With a dramatic flourish of the hand, she introduced me.

'This is the bride!' she said.

With another flourish she introduced the huge cardboard box, under whose weight Julian was swaying manfully.

'This is the wedding cake!'

She delivered a mortal blow.

'Her fiancé,' she said deeply, enunciating every word, 'is the navigator of a Lancaster bomber.'

She let the full force of this statement register before she finally despatched him.

'That brave lad has been shot down time and again, risking his life for the likes of you! Surely you can bend a rule for him?'

The ticket-collector gave ground. He gestured towards the train.

'Go on then,' he said. 'But you'll have to stand in t'guard's van, and if an inspector gets on at Crewe he'll likely turn you off.'

'We'll take our chance on that,' said Dorothy flatly. 'There are other trains from Crewe.'

As we all trailed gratefully after her down the platform my father winked at me, and said, 'I'd like to see the inspector who could tackle your mother in this mood! What's more, if I know her, we shan't stand in the guard's van for long!'

And he was right.

The Falcon had done us proud, and the Fawley-Blythe party was high with joy and wine. Photographs had been taken inside and outside the registry office. Dickie's best man had made a funny speech, and my father a witty one. Julian, as we found out too late, had tied an old shoe, three balloons and a notice saying JUST MARRIED on the back of Dickie's old green Bentley. Dorothy's cake had been cut, eaten and pronounced excellent.

'I've had my doubts about it,' Dorothy confessed to Connie Blythe. 'It's darkened with black treacle and made with dried egg. The fruit's been helped out with grated carrot and chopped prunes, and the marzipan icing's made of anything but almonds! Still, it's surprising what you can do when you try!'

Above and beyond them all, Dickie and I floated hand in hand, mesmerised with love, hearing rather than listening to the conversation.

'Doesn't Evelyn look radiant?'

'Well, it's the bride's occasion, isn't it?'

'Oh yes. I've always felt that the groom was the least important person present!'

'Don't think I'm casting a shadow, Gil, but I'd give anything to have Micky here.'

'Keep your voice down. You don't want to upset Judith.'

'So you're the wonderful Aunt Kate? I've heard all about you!'

'Lord above, I do hope not! I say some awful things!'

Dickie, earnest and pensive for once, fair hair glistening, ears at attention, whispered to me.

'Evie! How long before we can drift politely off?'

I whispered back, 'Soon, I think. Look, your father is in a huddle with my father, probably sorting out your career. And Dorothy is plotting something with Connie at the end of the table.'

I would countenance no interference in our future.

'Dickie! We must never let them run our lives for us!'

He was not listening, looking distractedly at his wrist-watch.

'Evie,' he whispered, 'we've only got six days, six hours and forty-five minutes left.'

I relinquished my passive role as the bride, and took action as the new Mrs Blythe. Charming, I hoped, but determined. I had a momentary vision of my parents' wedding, fourteen years ago, the sudden flurry of excitement in the hall. 'She's going up to change!' Well, I did not have to change, as Dorothy had done, because in these days of clothes coupons my wedding costume was also my going-away outfit. All I needed was a few minutes to set myself to rights.

So I smiled on the little assembly, and said very sweetly, 'Dickie and I are thinking of disappearing now, because time is precious. But please, please don't break up the party on our account.'

'That means they intend to go, and to hell with the rest of us!' my father translated, quite correctly, and everyone laughed.

Alone, in the Ladies Cloakroom, I suffered a momentary eclipse. So much had been forgotten or thrown overboard in the rush. It would have been perfect to come down the staircase of the Malt-house on my father's arm, robed all in misty white, bearing a bouquet of late summer roses. Judith had acted as my matron of honour, but how I should have liked to have Liz as a bridesmaid, Tim as a page.

I was regretting the loss of all the friendly and familiar faces which would have smiled on me at home, and the sound of their voices wishing us well. I had cheated Dorothy of the joy of creating my wedding feast. Her silent acceptance crowned me with thorns. The Blythes, accustomed to making all occasions great ones, had to content themselves with this relatively humble and hurried affair.

I think I was slightly tipsy with love and wine, for I now began to number the beloved dead among my absent guests. Clara smiled an enigmatic smile. Grannie and Grandad stood proudly by me in their Sunday clothes. Uncle Arthur cracked jokes. Even Leo presented himself as a small boy, with bruised knees and fearless blue eyes. And, of course there was Michael. Always Michael.

To the image in the glass, whose eyes were becoming too bright, I said acidly, 'You can't start spilling over now!'

The door opened and Aunt Kate appeared behind me, saying, 'No, for God's sake don't cry. Dorothy and Connie will be following me soon, and you'll start us all off!'

So we took a deep breath, laughed instead, and hugged each other very hard.

I powdered my nose decisively.

Aunt Kate rummaged in her handbag.

'I'm dying for a gasper!' she said.

Our guests had trooped out to the courtyard of the Falcon to see us off. And as we came down the steps arm in arm, Julian, still shielding his wicked handiwork, cried, 'Hurrah!' And threw a precious handful of confetti over my new suit, which was the colour of autumn leaves.

34

Like the Malt-house, our temporary home was a mixture of past splendour and wartime shabbiness. Parquet was scratched, carpets worn, wallpaper faded, white paint aged to a lustreless cream. Once the epitome of gracious middle-class living, it was now noisy and crowded. The daughter of the house, bombed out of London, had taken up residence with her children. An aged grandmother sheltered under its roof. The front drawing room had been given over to WVS work. Yet in the hall a copper bowl of roses endeavoured to keep up appearances.

Dickie and I had been welcomed by our hosts, drunk yet another glass of wine to celebrate, negotiated the main staircase and kept our dignity and patience intact. But at the foot of the servants' stairs, out of sight, we caught hands and ran.

'Home at last!' cried Dickie, and flung open the door.

He skimmed his cap across the room and hoisted me aloft.

'Upsadaisy!' he said.

He carried me over the threshold, kicked the door shut, staggered across the floor and fell with me on the bed. We lay there, laughing.

'There's something infinitely sinful about making love in the afternoon,' said Dickie gleefully. 'Don't you think?'

And he jumped up, pulling off his coat, unknotting his tie, whistling with zest.

'By God, I've been looking forward to this!' he said heartily.

I had tensed momentarily, but this made me laugh again.

My tension vanished. I kicked off my court shoes, and we undressed together quickly, easily, exchanging kisses between the dropping of each garment, with the delight of children about to swim in a long-awaited pool.

We woke at dusk, and lay there for a while in each other's arms. Then Dickie reached across me for his wristwatch and squinted at the luminous dial.

'Time for dinner, Mrs Blythe. Get your glad rags on again. I've booked a table for two at the Knight's Helm. I understand they have their ways of circumventing that five-bob price restriction. Then home again, and the mixture as before. How does that strike you?'

As I turned to kiss him, I heard a sound which made me pause. Not far away, a different kind of orchestra was tuning up. The overture began in a low key, worked up to a crescendo and soared forth.

We lay cheek to cheek, listening in pride and awe.

'Come and look!' Dickie whispered, and caught up his dressing-gown and mine, and drew me to the window.

One by one the Lancasters were taking off into the evening sky. Majestic, powerful, heavy with their cargos of destruction. They were the colour of dusk, a darker dusk, their shapes just discernible. Rising now, they came into formation, heading for the continent and eight hours of noise and cold and mortal danger.

Dickie and I held hands and watched in silence. Both of us were wondering how many were flying out for the last time, and how many would taxi home at dawn, but neither of us said so.

Looking back on that year of our marriage, I have the impression of being borne along on an irresistible tide. Dickie and I lived from day to day, and lived each day to the full, since we never knew what tomorrow would bring. I made a home of our room with flowers and books and small personal possessions. We spent his weekend leaves lying in bed until twelve, frying a meal which served for breakfast and lunch on the gas ring, lazing and loving away the afternoon, joining other young couples at a local pub in the

403

evening. On longer leaves we drove back to the north, dividing our time between the Blythes and the Fawleys, fêted by both families.

The friendships we made then were ephemeral, drawn from a changing population of servicemen, their wives and girlfriends. Sometimes I come across unfamiliar names and telephone numbers in my address book, and remember with difficulty people who were part of that year.

By marrying I relinquished the whole of my former life, including the music. For I could not bring my Broadwood here, and it was too inconvenient to use someone else's piano, even if it had been good enough and in tune. Music at that period of my life was the regular battle-roar of bombers at take-off in early evening, their irregular returns at dawn, and sometimes a heart-stopping explosion and belch of flames as one of them failed to make the runway. Music was Dickie's feet running up the stairs to celebrate a few hours' freedom, the telephone ringing in the hall to say he was safely back. Music was love, and love in wartime demanded so much of me that I let go of all else. Sufficient to dedicate myself to him and the moment.

Lying awake and alone, listening, counting, hoping, I willed him to stay alive. I poured the steel of my will into him. Often during the day I turned pale, I drooped, I took a little nap in the solitary room which was our home, so great was the effort. But afterwards I would gather myself together again, pit myself anew against this emptiness which might swallow him. I had no time or strength for anything but him, while an orchestra of bombers tuned up for destruction.

Dorothy was very good to us. Every week saw the arrival of a badly-packed parcel, trussed with lengths of knotted string and addressed two or three times, back and front, to make sure it reached its destination. Mixed up inside was something to eat, something to read and something to wear, wrapped in the *Hathersall Weekly Advertiser*, with a letter on top.

'. . . and your father reckons that the tide of war – his very words! – has turned in our favour. He's been very busy with that blessed map of his. I think he could do with you here to make him some more flags. He's had to start rationing them since we won El Alamein last November, and now we've invaded Sicily with the Yanks the Union Jacks and Stars and Stripes are running out. Julian inked a few for him last weekend, but he's not artistic like you.

By the way, talking of Yanks, your Aunt Kate put her name down on a list to offer them hospitality at the weekends. Just a cup of tea and a chat. The GIs – that's the name for them – get homesick stationed over here, and it's nice for them to have somewhere friendly to go instead of roaming round the streets. The lads are all very appreciative, and generous to a fault. You'd be surprised at the presents they bring for Kate! Tins of ham, nylon stockings, big boxes of chocolates – I couldn't do better myself.

Oh, and I heard that Mrs Nash – you remember her? – made a point of saying that she would only entertain white American officers! What do you think about that? Well, I never had much time for her, she's very shallow.

Actually, I met a negro soldier at Kate's last Saturday. It's the first time in my life that I've seen one except on the pictures. He was very polite and called me 'ma'am', and we chatted away. I've got nothing against black people. I always liked Paul Robeson.

Your father wants to know if Dickie is in this Battle of the Ruhr, or aren't you allowed to tell us? Anyway, as he's short on Union Jacks he's using black stars to mark the cities we've bombed, and on those three dams we wiped out, and that big canal. There mustn't be anything left of Hamburg by this time, and though I'm glad we're winning I can't help feeling sorry for those poor German women, sitting in cellars with their children and old folks, being bombed night after night. Your father doesn't feel the same way as I do. He can be very aggressive. . . .'

So Dorothy wrote as she talked, and the letter was good to read, with a few lines from my father on the last page and a final postscript from Julian. And on Sunday evenings, when she knew that I would be alone and lonely, Dorothy telephoned to make sure that the parcel had arrived safely and all was still well.

As Berlin's martyrdom began in November 1943, I rang up tremulously to tell them that Dickie's aircraft had failed to return.

The line between Suffolk and Lancashire was bad, and our hall was busy with people passing through. I stood with my back to them, holding the receiver to one ear, covering the other with one hand to shut out the noise.

I heard my father's voice using the same phrases of hope and comfort which he had extended to Dorothy nearly two years ago. He spoke firmly, confidently, as though he had no doubts. He was endeavouring to strengthen me.

I heard Dorothy's voice in the background, saying, 'Does she want to come home, Gil? Tell her to come home to us.'

But my father answered for me tersely, 'Not yet, Dorrie. Not until she's heard about Dickie, one way or the other.'

Then he said very kindly to me, 'Do the Blythes know? Would you like us to tell them?'

'No, thank you, Daddy. I rang them myself. I rang them first of all.' And lest Dorothy object to their precedence, I explained, 'He's their son, you see.'

On the following Saturday Dorothy wrote to say that Flora had died of a heart attack. They had forgotten she was old. Death was merciful to her, a shock to them. One moment she was loping good-naturedly and sedately after a stick, to humour Julian. In the next she was gasping her way out.

She had been given to Michael on his twelfth birthday: the friend and consolation of his boyhood, the chosen companion of his brief exile. She had not regarded his death as a finality, only another departure on a longer trip. Now and again she would ask to inspect his bedroom, and then stand guard outside the door, convinced he was coming home on leave. She had accepted Julian with excellent good grace, but never ceased to be Michael's dog. They buried her under a tree which he had liked to climb.

Three weeks later, I rang up, laughing and crying together, to tell them that Dickie was a prisoner-of-war in Germany.

And he had broken a leg in the fall, but this was mending. And yes, I said, I should love to come back to the Malt-house for Christmas. But afterwards, I warned them, I should be returning to Suffolk, because this room was our home and I felt closest to Dickie there.

At Grizedale's, sitting in his study on the last day of the autumn term, my father discovered that his right hand would not obey him. When he tried to get to his feet he became aware that his right leg was also useless, that indeed the whole of one side did not belong to him any more. He knew, of course, what had happened.

His secretary was in the adjoining room. With some difficulty he stretched out his left hand and pressed the buzzer on his desk. It was fortunate that his appearance evidently told its own tale, for when she came in he found himself quite unable to speak.

I hooked up the receiver and stood in the hall, head bent, arms folded, thinking. The decision was bitter but inevitable. After a while I knocked on the kitchen door to tell them that my father had suffered a severe stroke and I must go home. For I was needed there, whereas there was no longer any reason to stay here, except that I would have preferred it.

They received me with sympathy and understanding. They gave me coffee and comfort. Like them, I was a casualty of the war.

In the end I departed in fine style, having decided to take Dickie's Bentley with me. He had taught me to drive in the past year, and we had squabbled as I learned, but reconciled ourselves afterwards in love-making. Though I shared a little of the driving in our two journeys to the north, I had never driven the whole distance, but some spirit of adventure or desperation possessed me. Besides, the Bentley was part of Dickie, and there was no point in leaving her to rust in a Suffolk garage. So, packing all my worldly goods, and the Christmas presents which would now fall upon a stony occasion, I drove off without looking back.

*

The journey took nine hours over five stages, and remained a memory of perfect freedom. On the road that stretched out before me I was my own mistress, moving at my own behest. No one could reach me, demand or expect anything of me. No one even knew where I was. If I were less responsible, less loving, I could drive wherever I liked, for as long as the petrol lasted, and never be found again. An errant part of me dwelled wistfully on that thought. The other part brought me to Kersley just before nightfall, and parked the Bentley in a side lane at Tarn Brow, only a hundred yards from the Malt-house.

Tomorrow, I thought, I would find her a more permanent home.

Dorothy and Julian gave me a rapturous reception, which changed to astonishment when they heard that I had driven all the way.

'You pisey young cat!' said Dorothy proudly. 'I thought you were coming by train. If I'd known the truth, I'd have worried myself to death!'

Now I was here and safe she gloried in the achievement. Julian, who was now as tall as me, came down the lane with me to collect the luggage and admire the Bentley at close quarters. On a second trip he took three sacks, a piece of cardboard and a length of rope with him, to protect the car against the frost.

Warmed and welcomed, I followed Dorothy upstairs to see the human reason for my return.

'He's inclined to be a bit emotional,' Dorothy said. 'Don't pay too much attention to that. Neville Gould says he's doing quite well. No movement in the arm or leg yet, and his face is all to one side, but it'll do him no end of good to see you. I told him you were coming home and he tried to speak. It came out as a sort of mumble, but I knew what he meant. . . .'

Nevertheless, I was privately shocked to see the god of my childhood brought so low. It was a poor creature who lay helpless and unshaven in the marital bed, lifting his fingers momentarily to greet me, eyes watering with emotion.

I sat by him and held his good hand, smiled and talked

and tried to look as if I understood what he was saying. His situation and appearance filled me with horror and compassion, but Dorothy took everything in her stride. She was at the moment telling him about my drive from Suffolk. Her voice was louder than usual, as if he were deaf as well as paralysed, but he did not seem to mind. He looked from one to the other of us in silent satisfaction. And I saw from the expression in his eyes that though he loved me deeply and dearly, Dorothy had become his sword and buckler.

'I'm taking her away now,' Dorothy said at the top of her voice, 'because she'll want a wash and brush up after the journey, and a hot meal – I've got you a lamb chop, Evie! – but then she'll come back and see you. I'll send Julian up to sit with you.'

My father lifted the fingers of his left hand to acknowledge that he understood, and croaked through the left side of his mouth.

Dorothy leaned over the balustrade and shouted, 'Julian! Julian! Your father wants you!'

Conducting me to my old room, talking all the way, she said, 'He shouldn't be left alone, so we take it in turns. I sleep on the day-couch at the foot of the bed so I can wake at the slightest sound. I've given my job up – well, there's no knowing how long this will take, is there? It could be months. But everyone's been very good to us. Your Aunt Kate comes up every day, and Nellie Crayshaw's a real treasure. I don't know how I'd have managed without them. But you're home now, Evie, and I'd rather have you than any of them.'

In my mind a prison door clanged shut.

Misreading my expression, Dorothy said, 'You're tired out, love. I think there might be enough hot water for a bath. Would you like it now or later?'

'Later,' I said, 'I'll just wash now, thank you.'

'Then I'll leave you to it,' Dorothy said, satisfied.

At the door she turned, 'I've warmed the piano,' she said, as if it were a teapot. 'I thought you might like to run your fingers over the keys again. . . .'

At that moment my sense of loss and exile was most acute. Down in Suffolk the Lancasters were taking off without me to watch and listen for them. Was it the silence where they had been, or the act of coming home which started the music again? Coming downstairs I distinctly heard Schumann's *Kinderscenen* playing in my head, and returned to my former source of freedom and delight.

The drawing room was chilly. Only a small area round the piano had been warmed a few degrees. But the Broadwood awaited me like an old friend, dusted and polished for my return.

I sat down, remembering the feel and shape of the piano stool, and lifted the lid. I wriggled my fingers experimentally, and poised my hands over the keys. I summoned up Schumann.

The jangling cacophony stopped me as if I had been struck. For a moment or so I sat in stunned silence. Then tears of accumulated tension poured down my cheeks.

Dorothy, coming in to tell me that supper was ready, found me bowed over the keyboard sobbing, 'It's out of tune. Completely out of tune. Everything's out of tune.'

35

April 1944

'Darling Dickie,

'Another war winter over – how cold they all have been! And this year spring is full of hope, because whichever way you look at it we're a year nearer to peace, and to being together again.

'I spend my days with you, even though you aren't here, and think of a thousand things to tell you. But as soon as I start to write I become pen-tied, because so much has happened in a month, and I'm afraid of forgetting something important and having to wait another month before I can say it again! It seems hard that our correspondence should be rationed, as well as everything else. We used to write to each other every day before we were married.

'Talking of rations, Dorothy and I are just making up your Red Cross parcel. They advise us to send woolly things, and though it will be summer when you get this, we thought that socks would come in useful at any time of year. I didn't know whether to laugh or cry at your letter, telling us that you had been wearing the scarf and balaclava in bed all winter to keep warm, but Julian thought it was very funny and I enclose his cartoon! The socks are hand-knitted, but not by me, I'm afraid. I bought them at the WVRS Bring and Buy Sale. I wish Grannie was alive to knit socks for you. She was noted for being able to turn a particularly neat heel! The chocolate is from me, and greater love hath no wife than this – that she give up her sweet coupons for her husband! The cigarettes are from Daddy, and Julian gave up six clothing coupons for the handkerchiefs. Dorothy is contributing tea, coffee, sugar and cake – and I just hope it doesn't get mixed up with everything else!

'Daddy has been pronounced fit and well, and will be going back to Grizedale's after Easter. Actually, he isn't one hundred per cent and Dr Gould says he never will be. One foot drags a little when he walks and when he's tired his speech is faintly slurred. But he looks so distinguished, with his silver-grey hair, that any slowness or hesitancy is put down to greater dignity. By the by, he says I am to tell you that progress with the map is good, and he expects it to be even better in future.

'Dorothy is unsinkable. I'm glad you like her and find her funny because if she drove *both* of us mad we'd never speak to her again, and that would be unfair, because (as she so often tells me!) she does her best. She has just started her new job. This time as supervisor of what is called a "British Restaurant", which caters for the general public and public institutions. A very nice place indeed, out in Cheshire. She is already making her mark there – God help her staff!

'Julian is not an angel, I am delighted to report. In fact, in spite of his scholarly talents and his undoubted resemblance to my father, he is every bit as naughty as Michael used to be. The other day he rang Dorothy up, pretending to be the manager of two factories, who wanted to order five hundred dinners a day, to be sent out. Julian said that Dorothy sounded flustered, but was obviously unwilling to lose the order. She was busy chatting him up and working out the costs when he said, "April Fool"! It makes me go cold even to write that!

'Naturally, she was simply furious. I knew nothing about it until Julian crept in at the back door saying, "Mum's not home yet, is she?" Then he grabbed a hunk of bread and jam and disappeared until dark, asking me to listen for three rings on the front doorbell and to make sure that I answered it.

'An hour later Dorothy bounced in, laden with canteen leftovers – we eat what they eat, these days, warmed up! She said, "Find that boy and I'll kill him!" But I made her a cup of tea, and after a while we burst out laughing because it was just the sort of thing Mick used to do. And Dorothy said, "Micky's still with us – the bad lad!"

'Lord, how she loved him! If Dorothy ever dies we'll find the names of Michael and Harry Harland engraved on her heart. Which reminds me, Judith received a proposal last week but turned it down. Do you remember my telling you about that rather nice man who was hanging around her at Christmas? He's several years older than Judith, but immensely likeable, and I should have thought immensely liveable with, too. When I tackled her she said she liked him very much, but hadn't the emotional energy to put into another marriage. Dorothy says a vital spring has been broken. She would!

'So you're going back to school, my dear love? The first time Mick talked about you he said, "His family wanted him to go to Cambridge. He's very bright and they thought he was the college type." Remembered word for word, I do assure you. Well, I'm all for it and so is Daddy – although he says there's a lot less money in learning than in liquor! I think that Dorothy is faintly aggrieved, though she doesn't say so. She had been fancying my chances as the wife of a wine merchant. "Our daughter, you know, married very well!" Meanwhile, the books you need are on their way. Daddy wangled that and is prepared to wangle more. He says have you thought of applying for a place in one of the red-brick universities, because they will be the government's educational darlings after the war. He would recommend Blackstone, of course – I'd call that a black-brick university, wouldn't you?!

'You'll be on the band-wagon when peace breaks out. The past has been swept away – or bombed out! – and we are being promised a new society. No slums. No dole queues. Opportunities for everyone. Oh, brave new world! Since you helped to defend the old régime you may as well take advantage of the new one. How I shall enjoy watching you swot, drinking black coffee with a wet towel tied round your head!

'Now for my personal contribution to our future lives! Daddy and I had a little talk when he was up and about again. Oh, if you had seen and heard him just after the stroke you'd have thought he would never speak or walk again! Anyway, this little talk was about wasting my time and talent, and he fairly pitched into me. You'd have thought that Dorothy and I had been lolling about on satin cushions, instead of nursing him twenty-four hours a day!

'Anyway, at the end of my drubbing I went cap-in-hand to Professor Feinberg. He received me at home and was very cool at first, and gave me yet another lecture. But then darling Mrs Feinberg came in with coffee and strudel, and an exquisite set of underwear which she had embroidered for my trousseau, made out of parachute silk. I'm saving it until you come home.

'Professor Feinberg then received me back into the fold, and organised my future for me. So now I'm working as a music teacher in a private school in Blackstone, and having two lessons a week as his private pupil.

'Blackstone has always had a good reputation in the music world, and people have become much more appreciative of music during the war, so the city fathers are planning a series of lunch-time concerts to be given by students and graduates of our college in St Peter's Hall. They start this summer and I'm taking part in three of them. We don't get paid but the honour is great, and proceeds go to various war charities. Oh, Dickie, I wish you could be there.

'Julian is very clever with engines and says I am to tell you that he is keeping the Bentley in good nick. I drive over to see Connie and Jim once a month, usually when I get your letter, and they are very kind and sweet to me. They don't quite comprehend why we're prepared to be poor, and to put off having their grandchildren for a few years, but they've taken your decision nobly.

'Aunt Kate is busy entertaining American servicemen of both colours! The old guard in Church Street spend Saturday afternoons peering between the folds of their lace curtains. The GIs are mostly very young and always grateful. They turn up with armfuls of flowers and luxuries. Aunt Kate came to supper the other evening and brought me a pair of nylon stockings. I'm saving them for your return.

'Dr Gould once said that the Fawleys incline to apoplexy, and sure enough Uncle Harold has recently been invalided out of the army, also with a stroke. Aunt Kate brought him over with her, still very spruce and military-looking, and parked him in the drawing room with Daddy while she and Dorothy yarned in the kitchen. I went in with sherry for them, and they were glaring into the fire and leaning on their sticks. They're usually at loggerheads with each other, and the conversation went something like this.

'Uncle H. "I thought I was going to be crippled for life, Gil!"

'Daddy, proudly. "But you've only had one go. I've had *two*!"

'Uncle H. "This arm was totally paralysed."

'Daddy, scornfully, "I was paralysed all down my right side. *And* I couldn't speak!"

'It was like two little boys comparing conkers.

'The poor old Malt-house is literally falling apart. Remember Grannie's chiffonier tilting sideways? That was a mere bagatelle! Julian put his foot through a floorboard the other day, and heavy things like hearthcurbs are beginning to sink! Daddy rang the house agent, with no success, and is now writing an official letter.

'It also looks as though the Malt-house will be losing its shine once more. Nellie Crayshaw is expecting another baby! The father is a soldier who was already married, and has not been in touch with her since he heard the news. Dorothy says she will write to his CO! Incidentally, Dorothy's opening comment was priceless. She said, "Well, Nellie, the first baby can be put down to bad luck, but the second is downright careless!"

'Anyway, poor Nellie said that she would work as long as possible, and please could she come back after the baby was born? She needn't have worried about being taken back, I can tell you. Dorothy would employ a female axe-murderess if she could clean the floors!

'Doesn't all this sound jolly and light-hearted? What you might call "the blithe Mrs Blythe"! In fact, despite the work and company I lead only a half-life. The world seems to be full of solitary women: women waiting, women comforting each other in fear and loss and loneliness, women pretending to have a good time. In this manless existence, we roll back the carpet, wind up the gramophone, put a record on, and dance together to the old tunes.

'How glad I shall be, my dearest love, when you come home again.'

June 1944
Stalag etc. (I daresay you know the address by this time!)

'Darling Eve, Apple of my Eye,
'A western wind is blowing, the small rain is down raining, and how I wish we were in our bed again! Still, summer is a-coming in, and perhaps next summer we shall be together. The parcel hasn't arrived yet, but it sounds foot-warming and mouth-watering and I thank you in advance. And I thank you also for sending, into my drab and wholly masculine world, such bright pictures of present and future as make this hut shine. If they weren't so precious, and I didn't want the other chaps to turn grass-green with envy, I would read them aloud.

'How lucky we are to be able to set down our thoughts to each other. Eve on paper is as garrulous as Eve on claret – and I adore them both! So many bods in our hut really are pen-tied. I see them struggling to fill a page with nothing they need to say, and later receiving a letter back which contains nothing they need to hear. There was a time when I would have found this intensely funny. Now I find it sad. The inability to communicate must be totally frustrating and is not always due to lack of education. One Glaswegian from the Gorbals, whose childhood must be heard to be believed – and preferably not heard at all! – is a natural writer and has always been able to express himself savagely well. In fact, style would ruin him, though under my tuition his spelling mistakes become fewer!

'Saddest of all is the ardent lover who left his girl behind him, and lives in constant terror of receiving a *Dear John* letter. He actually offered me a cigarette, which in this place is the equivalent of your nylon stockings, and asked if I would compose a love letter for him. He said, "I keep telling her she's a knock-out, and I love her, but there must be something else I could say, and I thought you'd know what it was." Do I, my love?

'Anyway, I felt that the idea was rather voyeurish, so I refused him reluctantly – and the cigarette even more reluctantly. Since then he has employed the services of another literary Casanova. I hope it works for him, but his girl is only seventeen and her passion is centred on dance halls. I think, in consequence, that she's bound to prefer a dancing partner on the spot rather than in a German prison camp. I hope I'm wrong since he has planned his future round her.

'In contrast, we have the older bods, long and securely married. Pipe-smoking, carpet-slippered types, doing their best to bring up their kids by correspondence. The idea of a steady, purposeful partnership is soothing, but somehow lacks sparkle. I should hate either of us to take the other for granted. I'm not talking about trust and loyalty, but about a quality of surprise. I like to relive you, to keep the image of you coming up fresh. So if I ever refer to you as "a good old girl" you have my permission to strike me with the nearest frying-pan.

'Eve, Eve, your young tyke of a brother may not be an angel, but you are. Your father and the prof should have blamed me about the music, not you. They should have come over and dragged me round the compound by both big ears and bounced me off the barbed wire. I am ashamed, looking back, that I never once considered that part of you. Our fourteen months together was a prolonged honeymoon. That is my only excuse. But I will improve, and you must keep me up to the mark. I'm glad that you and music are together again. Let me know the dates on which you are playing, and what you are playing, and I'll think of you and pretend I'm there.

'My thanks to your father for the books he's sending. My class is growing daily, not because I'm a brilliant teacher but because there's nothing much to do here. Scholastically speaking, it's small beer, because I'm dealing with illiterates, of which there are a surprising number. Still, they enjoy it, and I enjoy it, and there's an enormous amount of satisfaction in opening a whole new world for them.

'Eve, this war has made me look and think and feel, and I've literally and metaphorically suffered a sea-change. The car-racing and the flying and the general bumming around were part of my youthful zest. I'm not regretting anything, but I know that I *would* regret falling idly into the same comfortable old rut. The reason I shall be reading History is partly because I must find out why the world got itself into this mess, and partly to see how another and bigger mess can be prevented. Then what? With any Arts degree you mostly teach. I'm not the ambitious type. Never was. I don't expect to become anything as fine as the headmaster of Grizedale's, but if I'm a good teacher that would be all right by me. Is that all right by you?

'And what about you? Because this changes our position (as the actress said to the bishop). No posh modern house in Cheshire with a little car for you and a large one for me. No faithful servants to do all the nasty chores. No coffee mornings and tea parties and arranging the flowers. Just temporary accommodation and the need to postpone the babies – unless they can be tucked under each arm while you play the piano! But if you will bear with me (as the bishop said to the actress) I promise to do the same for you some-time. In lieu of which, and with apologies to John Stuart Mill – and just about every married man I've ever met – I have set down the beginnings of a Blythe Magna Carta. You might call it our new marriage contract.

1. That we share all household chores. (I promise always to clean my own shoes!)
2. That whoever comes home first cooks the evening

meal. (I promise not to make tea only for myself, and then sit in the débris waiting to be rescued!)

3. That all money is declared and general expenses pooled, except for a spot of pocket money each. (I will not regard your wages as mine, and mine as my own!)

4. That nothing, but nothing, is ever taken for granted – as in, God bless and help them, your family and mine.

'You'll think of lots more, my dearest girl, and can kick these around as much as you like, so over to you.

'Do I really convey how much I love you? Do I . . . ?'

36

September 1944

'That surveyor from the agent's was out to find fault from the moment he walked in!' said Dorothy. 'I thought we'd have had a cup of tea and a bit of a chat, but no. What's more, he didn't want me around. He said if I could show him where the damage was he would manage by himself, thank you. . . .'

Running his penknife through butter-soft boards, slicing off flakes of wood and crumbling them between his fingers. Examining the little pools of sawdust beneath the floor.

'Finally he borrowed a ladder to look at the attic. I explained that we only used it to store things, but he never answered. . . .'

Shining his torch into recesses which had not seen light for years while she stood at the foot of the ladder talking.

'Poker-faced thing! Still, he made a thorough job of it. He was covered in dirt and cobwebs by the time he'd finished. So I offered him a wash and a clothes' brush and asked him if it was serious.'

'Dry rot,' he said, busy writing up his notes.

'Will it be a big job? We're out all day, you see. It'll be difficult if we have to have workmen in for any length of time.'

'I take it that you rent this place, madam?' he said, putting his notebook away.

'Yes, we do. And apart from the fact that it takes a lot of

heating we haven't any complaints. Mind you, with the shortage of coal we've had to burn anything we could get, even peat – sweet-smelling but very slow burning. And when you think what dreadful winters we've had all through the war. . . .'

'I was meaning,' he said, 'that you were very lucky *not* to be the owner.'

'Oh. It's an expensive job, is it?'

'One of the worst cases of dry rot I've seen. Must have been going on quietly for years. Right through the house. I'm surprised you didn't notice it earlier. . . .'

'Now you mention it we noticed the first hole in the floorboards when we were moving the drawing-room sofa, three years ago – or was it four? But we didn't think anything of it. . . .'

'Most of the beams and floors are affected and the rest will follow unless the landlord acts sharpish. It's only a question of time before it becomes uninhabitable.'

'Uninhabitable? When? What will they have to do to put it right?' He stalked to the front door and stood there waiting for it to be opened.

'Oh, pull up all the floors and replace the boards and joists. Strip off the roof slates and put in new beams. Take down the porch. And while they're at it they might as well rebuild that back wall. It's bulging badly. They're looking at a fortune in major repairs. Might not be worth their while.'

He was settling his bowler hat down on his forehead.

'Not worth their while?'

'Still, that's not your problem, is it, madam? I shall send in my report and it's up to the owner to sort it out.'

'But the owner lives in Australia!'

He spoke over his shoulder, walking away.

'As I say, be thankful it's not your problem. Good day, madam!'

'And then I couldn't help myself,' said Dorothy, 'I fairly shouted after him, "But it *is* our problem! We live here. We've lived here for sixteen years. This is our home!"'

*

The letter from the house agent said little and meant much more. He pointed out that there would be an unavoidable delay in contacting Miss Hartley, that builders and materials were hard to find and the job would involve considerable inconvenience over a long period. Mindful of our plight, he suggested that Dr Fawley might like to consult him with a view to inspecting other properties. He added that rented properties were difficult to find nowadays. Had Dr Fawley perhaps thought of buying one?

We held a family council.

'I don't believe it,' said Dorothy, up in arms with the surveyor. 'I told you that man was trouble. Still, the problem remained. She said, 'Whatever shall we do, Gil?'

He was slower both mentally and physically since his second stroke. We waited several seconds before he replied.

He said, 'I think we should have a second opinion, and I'll pay for it this time. It's worth the fee to know where we stand.'

Dorothy evidently liked the next surveyor who was friendly and talkative and drank two cups of tea, but her hospitality did not alter his professional verdict.

'I should leave, if I were you, Mrs Fawley,' he said. 'The condition of the house will only get worse, and if the owner decides to put workmen in then you can reckon on twelve to eighteen months' really rough living. There's something else to consider. The place won't fall down but these floors are none too safe, and in your husband's present state of health a minor accident might turn into a major one. He shouldn't be put at risk, now should he?'

We held another family council. We read the agent's letter again.

My father said, 'We can obviously forget about renting anything. In fact, I think we should consider buying a place with a view to my retirement. Something smaller and more convenient this time.'

Dorothy was unwilling to lower her sights.

'But you're not due to retire for some years yet, Gil!'

'I've been given two warnings. A third stroke will either cripple me – in which case I shall have to retire early – or wipe me out. In both cases you'll need your own roof over your head.'

When Dorothy spoke next she was subdued, head bent, fingers picking at the hem of her dress.

'Don't talk like that, Gil. Besides, there are the children to think of. If Julian's going to be a doctor, as he says, then he'll be living with us for another ten years. And when Dickie comes home he and Evelyn will need somewhere to stay while they look round.'

Now I spoke up, thanking God that I had been given an opening instead of springing the news on them.

'Look, it's very good of you to offer, and I appreciate it – and I know that Dickie would, too – but you can count us out. I'm going to rent a flat in Blackstone.'

My father looked sad but unsurprised. He had parted with me when I married. But Dorothy, who never knew when to let go, was planning to live with and through us.

'Rent a flat?' she cried, aghast. 'I'd think twice, if I were you, about leaving a good home. Does Dickie know about this? What will Connie think? Does *she* know about this? Why don't you answer?'

'She will, if you let her speak,' said my father drily.

'Connie has also offered to house us while we look round,' I said, 'but Dickie and I have discussed the matter thoroughly, and we want to start off by ourselves in our own place, however humble.'

'You'll never find one! And you wouldn't be able to afford it if you did! Mark my words.'

'I have already found one,' I said deliberately. 'I've been hunting round for months. One of those old cotton-merchants' houses at the end of Ducie Grove is being turned into flats by the owner. She can't keep it up any longer. She's offered me a ground-floor flat. Large living room, decent-sized bedroom, a minute kitchen and a sliver of a bathroom. Two pounds a week. And I can afford it. But I shan't have enough money to buy furniture and carpet, so if you could spare us any old thing we'd be grateful.'

'Well,' said Dorothy, deflated. 'Well.'

There was a short silence. My parents exchanged looks,

each worried about the effect of this statement on the other.

Then my father said slowly, clearing his throat, 'I'm sure I speak for both of us when I say that we'll help in any way we can.'

Dorothy nodded, but her lips were compressed.

Julian, ever-optimistic, said, 'I say, Evie, I can drop in and see you on my way home. The old crammer's only a mile away.'

Dorothy was recovering, coming up for battle.

'Well, I shouldn't be in too much of a hurry, if I were you,' she remarked, chin to the fore. 'I expect the Blythes will have something to say about this. Two rooms in a house in Ducie Grove doesn't sound the sort of thing they're used to!'

'It isn't the Blythes who'll be living there,' I replied with some asperity. 'It's us.'

'Well, Dickie's only used to the best, you know!'

'Dickie's used to an air-force base and a prison camp,' I reminded her. I brought out one of my big guns to answer hers. 'And he wants what I want. Independence.'

'That's right, be hurtful!' said Dorothy, thwarted.

'No, Evie's right,' said my father. 'They're both right. I told you they wouldn't be bossed about! They're not children any longer. They're adults.' He chuckled, obscurely pleased by his wife's disappointment. 'And if you don't watch your Ps and Qs, Evie won't invite us to tea!'

Julian forestalled a sharp retort by saying, 'Oh well, if Evie's going to live somewhere else that leaves the three of us. So where shall *we* live?'

My father glanced slyly at Dorothy's face.

'I fancy one of those newish bungalows at Werneth on the other side of Tarn Fell,' he said. 'What do you think, Dorrie?'

The suggestion took away her breath, but only for a moment.

'What? A man in your position live in a tatty bungalow, out at Werneth? It's miles from Grizedale's. Much too far for you to travel.'

'Neville Gould said I could still drive.'

'Not in bad weather you can't! I won't have it!'

'Surely there's a direct bus and tram route?'

'There isn't! I'll get the map out and show you. Just wait a minute while I find it. Evie, put the kettle on. Werneth, indeed! We'd never see that girl again! It'd take us all day to get to the other side of Blackstone from Werneth.'

She bustled into the hall, talking partly to us, partly to herself, her voice growing fainter as she hurried away.

'Which reminds me. Evelyn can take all the furniture out of her bedroom, and I've got a lot of Mother's things from Parbold House stored in the attic. There might be a carpet or two, I can't remember, but I do know there's cutlery and china. She can have what she wants out of that lot. The piano's hers anyway, and I'd be most surprised if Connie Blythe didn't come up with a few offers.

'Oh yes, Evie and Dickie will be like the couple who came to the picnic without any sandwiches and every member of the party gave them one. They'll end up with more to eat than anyone else! Oh, and she can have some of our silver – I'm fed up with cleaning it and she's fond of a bit of a silver. Which reminds me. Didn't Kate say that she could have Grandma Fawley's silver tea service? I must ring Kate up and ask her. Besides, we must put up a good show, give her a good start. I'm not having anybody looking down their noses at my daughter. . . .'

I went over to my father, put my arms round his neck and kissed him in memory of all the love that had ever been between us. But since he hated shows of sentiment, and was nowadays too easily moved to tears, I kept my tone light and offhand.

'Who's a clever old Machiavelli, then?' I said, and laughed as he gave his dry chuckle.

'Where *do* you want to live, Dad?' Julian asked.

Quiet and temperate, they had an understanding, these two.

'I really want to live in the Lake District,' said my father. 'I'd always planned to retire there. But that's likely to be a pipe dream, I'm afraid. The best place here would be the district round Dowson-under-Fell. Small and countrified without being isolated. It means a longer journey for you and me, Julian, but we can manage that. And I'm sure your mother will find something there that needs organising! But, of course, it depends what's on the housing market.'

Dorothy's voice was returning jubilantly.

'I knew it! Werneth's fifteen miles from Grizedale's, and right off the beaten track. So that's out. I think we ought to go down to see the agent this afternoon, Gil. Put it entirely in his hands, and tell him that time is of the essence. I'll take some sugar with me. Perhaps a quarter-pound of tea. The sooner we start house-hunting, the better. Gil, talking about a town which *is* on the Kersley bus route, Dowson-under-Fell's a nice little place. . . .'

Decisions had been made. Removals are not so easily accomplished. Dickie's father and mine insisted that I should have a legal contract before I rented the flat, but this proved difficult. My future landlady was a novice in the business, already encountering official obstacles which had never occurred to her. At one point she nearly gave up the idea altogether.

Then, there was no house suitable for my parents at the price they could afford, though Dorothy took her little bribes of tea and sugar to every agent in Kersley. My father's life's savings amounted to no more than the price of a remote country cottage.

'It's not fair!' Dorothy cried. 'A man of your abilities, and can't afford to live.'

He said ironically, 'I can less afford to die!'

Dorothy's usual way of coping with a crisis was to talk about it to anyone who would listen, without resolving anything, but this time she went to ground and kept her counsel to herself.

A fortnight later, the governors of Grizedale's, in recognition of their headmaster's long and valuable services and his state of health, offered him the Old Lodge at a nominal rent.

My father was astonished, moved, delighted. He confronted us with this news, lording a space on the drawing-room hearth-rug, since the hearth-curb was sinking gradually into the floor.

'Funny thing,' he said, 'I've been so busy rebuilding the school that I left the Lodge to one side. Mind you, we've had no porter since the war began. We've been using it for storage purposes. Apparently, the head governor heard that we were house-hunting without success, and called an informal meeting to see how best they could help us. And they decided that as the Lodge was intended to be a home it should be used as one.'

He gave a little humph of appreciation, and rocked on his heels, hands in pockets.

'Of course,' he said judiciously, 'the Old Lodge is a building of some architectural value, so it should be kept up.'

Then the wonder of it overcame him again.

'But I promise you that I'd said nothing to anyone about our problems! I knew nothing about this meeting! Nothing at all. They did this behind my back, and without my knowledge.'

His eyes begged us to believe him.

'And old Maylie has been most kind in his tribute to my work. He writes . . . wait a minute, where are my reading glasses? Ah, thank you, Evie . . . he writes, "We cannot afford to have you worried. Grizedale's needs you. Over the years you have become identified with the school. To many of us you are Grizedale's itself." I really am most touched. Most touched.'

'Yes, it's very good of them,' said Dorothy, 'though no more than you deserve.'

'We can live there for as long or short a time as we like,' he continued. 'That means that we can still retire to a cottage in the Lake District when the time comes. But if I die before I retire then you'll have a home, Dorrie, and Julian's education won't be interrupted. However, the privilege doesn't extend beyond your lifetime and mine. They're drawing up a contract to cover us.'

At which point I sighed, for I had almost lost the Ducie Grove flat through his fussing over contracts.

'They're going to do the Lodge up, decorate it, and make sure that that everything is in good working order,' my father went on. 'It should be ready for us by the beginning of

September, just in time to move in and settle down before the autumn term begins.'

'You lucky old things!' I cried, relieved and glad for them. 'Imagine living in a Georgian lodge!'

Yet I did not envy them. I had left their home in my mind long since. I had a home of my own.

'It shows how much they value your father!' said Dorothy.

He gave a derisive chuckle.

'They're just making sure that I last as long as possible,' he remarked. 'Placing me in a superior alms' house!'

But Dorothy refused to let him darken this triumph.

She simply said, 'Rubbish!' and went into action.

'Now, Gil, write to the agent and give him notice, and we can start packing! Evelyn, you'll have to supervise most of it because *I'm* the only one who won't be on holiday. Some of us,' she added, 'have to work *all* the time!'

That evening, as she and I were making up Dickie's parcel in the kitchen, she said, 'Evie, I've got something to tell you.'

Amazingly, she stopped organising the parcel, sat down and began tracing an uncertain pattern of thought on the tablecloth.

She said, 'I know I can trust you not to let it go any further, because it must never leak out. Evie, I went behind your father's back. I spoke – in the strictest confidence, of course – to Mrs Maylie, the head governor's wife. I told her we were at our wits' end and I didn't know where to turn. And she was lovely, Evie, she really was. She put me at my ease straight away. And she said she'd speak to her husband, but she didn't doubt that the governors would do everything in their power to help us.

'But I didn't expect them to go as far as this, I must say. I thought they might lend him some money at a low interest rate, or offer to pay his pension in a lump sum. Something like that. And I did say that he must never find out, because he'd never forgive me.'

She was pleased with herself, and yet afraid. Since she could not have my father's approval she needed mine.

She said, 'And they did approach him very diplomatically,

didn't they? And your father is pleased, isn't he? And it is a good idea, isn't it?' Then she asked humbly, 'But did I do right, Evie?'

In that moment I truly loved her.

'Yes,' I answered, and gave her the sort of hug reserved for Aunt Kate. 'Yes, Dorothy, you did absolutely right.'

It was time for us to go. Even before we began packing, one leg of the hallstand fell through the floor of the vestibule. Yet so much living had gone into the Malt-house that we could not part from it easily or quickly, and the past confronted us at every turn.

'What do we with this lot?' my father asked, hovering on the threshold of Michael's room. 'I don't like to say anything to your mother, but there isn't space for it at the Lodge.'

And the long attic was alive with ghosts.

At the bottom of a trunk, still in their Barber's brown and gold shoebox, were the carpet slippers Grannie had never worn.

Packed with my father's army uniform, reeking of moth-balls, I found a cardboard shoebox full of faded sepia photographs, held by a rubber band which burst when I touched it. And there inside were a young Gilbert and a younger Clara at various stages of their courtship: feeding squirrels at New Mills, on honeymoon in the Isle of Wight, standing on the threshold of their new home. Then they became three, and I appeared, yelling at Grandma Fawley in my christening robe; sitting up proudly by myself in a photographer's chair, all smile and satin hair-bow; digging a sand-castle with their help; wading into the sea clutching both their hands. On the back of these last two snapshots was written, probably by Clara, *Conway. August 1923*. The last summer together. We had never been to North Wales since.

Should I say nothing and keep them? Dorothy would have hidden or destroyed them rather than worry my father. I preferred not to treat him like a sick child, and this was a piece of unfinished business which had happened long ago. I gave him a choice, or took a risk, whichever way you look at it.

'I found some photographs with your old army kit which you seem to have forgotten,' I said. And lest he toss them on the fire in a fit of pique I added, 'If you don't want them, I'd rather like to have them, myself.'

Then I left him with his Pandora's box of memories, and made a pot of coffee and prayed.

When I came back he was still alive and his tone was normal, though he cleared his throat once or twice before speaking.

'You're very like her,' he said quietly. 'In appearance, that is. Not in character. You resemble your Aunt Jane in character. My favourite sister. Yes, very like Jane in character.'

I could hardly bring up the question of Clara's infidelity, whether real or Dorothy-supposed.

I said, 'I should have liked to know more about my mother, but Grandma Fawley put a ban of silence on the subject and you never mentioned her yourself, so I was always afraid to ask. What sort of person was she, Daddy?'

He stirred sugar into his coffee, pondering.

'Funny, how time passes. Clara was only nineteen when we married. She was only twenty-four when she died. . . .'

He looked at me quickly, disturbed, astonished.

'How old are you, Evie?'

'Nearly twenty-four.'

'A girl!' he said of me. And then of Clara, 'Only a girl.'

He was answering some other and deeper interrogator than myself.

'I think she was too young to be tied down as early as that. I may have been too hard on her. May have expected too much. She was a bit of a butterfly. Oh, I don't mean frivolous or silly. Not a Dora Spenlow. Just – light-hearted. When you chatter on, sometimes, you remind me of Clara. Something airy about it. Paradoxically, the very thing which drew me to her in the first place was what annoyed me most about her later on. Ah well, marriage is like that, I've noticed.'

He did not sound bitter or betrayed, simply regretful.

'I've learned a lot since then,' he remarked 'Unfortunately, I seem to learn some things too late.'

I dared to ask him. 'How much did you love her?'

He made a sound of affectionate impatience, as if to say, 'How on earth do I tackle a question of that magnitude?' He was picking up a thought here, a remembrance there, setting them down again gently, seeking the essence of her. Then his face cleared. I saw the young man in him, dark and swift and bright. Clara was with him again, in the fire and passion of their youth. Clara, the butterfly, had alighted for a while.

'How much did I love her?' he repeated.

He mused upon her evanescent shade. Paused to watch her flight. Cleared his throat.

'I thought she was . . . simply . . . wonderful,' he said.

I felt the spirit of her flying free. As long as I lived she would live in me. That brief and vivid life, haunting my own for so long, had today become one with it.

My father and I sat in smiling silence together. Complete.

And then Julian burst in, covered with dust.

Crying, 'Oh, Evie! Look what I've found. Flora's first collar, when she was a little puppy, with Mick's name and address on it.'

The removal vans were due to arrive after breakfast. The Malt-house, denuded, now revealed the full extent of its decay. Faded wallpaper round the shapes of pictures, scratched parquet round the shapes of furniture, and everywhere the spreading cancer of dry rot. Only the uncarpeted staircase was still splendid, showered by a confetti of coloured light from the stained-glass window in the hall.

We ate our last meal under its roof.

Julian was excited, longing for the new life to begin. But my father spread marmalade on his toast in leisurely fashion, and read his *Manchester Guardian* as usual. He was immaculately shaven, his shirt was white and crisp, his suit brushed, his shoes well-polished.

'And how much use are you going to be, dressed up like that?' Dorothy observed critically, clearing the table.

She was wearing her old navy blue polka-dot dress and a shapeless brown cardigan.

He folded his paper and replied, 'I'm coming to help you now.'

'With what? Evelyn, this crockery is going in our basket, so that we can make tea when we get to the Lodge. Yours is already packed.'

'I'm going to take down my map,' said my father.

Dorothy followed me into the scullery, saying, 'That's all I needed. Now he'll get in our way and start asking us to do things!'

'Evie,' my father said, hovering in the doorway. 'Can you find me some small boxes for the different flags?'

'Do what he says,' said Dorothy, 'before he drives me mad!'

The map was now a splendid sight for British eyes. All over Europe the lines of Allied flags marched forward and the enemy flags shrank back. The black spots on German targets resembled a tragic case of measles. And only the other week the four of us had stood round the wireless as Paris was liberated, and sung the Marseillaise.

'Nearly finished,' my father said with deep satisfaction. 'The war's virtually over. The only question is when. This year or next.'

'You said that in June, when we landed in Normandy,' Dorothy called from the scullery, 'and a week later the first flying bomb fell on London, and they had to evacuate people all over again. . . .'

She came to the doorway to argue with him.

'. . . and I don't know how many were killed, but it was as bad as the blitz. Worse, in fact. Nasty things. It's the silence when the engine stops that gets me. I know it's coming down then.'

My father considered her over his reading glasses.

'But that's practically over now,' he said. 'They're destroying most of the bombs in the air. And we had very few up here, anyway.'

'Very few?' cried Dorothy indignantly, dishmop in hand. 'You only need one to kill you! One came buzzing over the restaurant the other week. I heard the engine cut out when I was in the store room, and threw myself behind a sack of potatoes!'

Julian mimed this incident wickedly, and grinned at us, just as Michael would have done.

To stop myself from laughing, I said quickly, 'I wish you'd mentioned the boxes earlier, Daddy. There aren't any. The flags will just have to go all together in a big envelope.'

My father absorbed this information gradually.

'I don't want that,' he said at length. 'Julian, could you sit in the back of the car with the map spread out on your knees, and the flags still sticking into it? It's mounted on a cork board.'

Dorothy bounced back into the scullery saying, 'Of course he can't! I never heard of such a thing.'

'Okay, Dad,' said Julian, winking at me, 'but it might be a bit of a squash.'

The front doorbell rang peremptorily.

'I knew it!' Dorothy cried. 'I knew they'd come before I had time to wash up! It's your fault for keeping me talking!'

Our voices echoed in the empty house. Only two broad wicker shopping baskets remained, one for the Lodge and the other for Ducie Grove, each containing provisions for tea-making on the new premises, and a clean drying-up cloth.

'You can keep that basket, Evie,' said Dorothy. 'It belonged to Grannie Annie, and it's still got a lot of wear in it. You'll find it useful for shopping. Now, before we go, is that communal telephone of yours connected?'

And she stressed the word *communal* most bitterly.

'Not as far as I know, but when it is I'll use it.'

'Then we can't ring you, so you'll have to go out and ring us tonight. You've got our number, haven't you?'

I nodded, and touched my handbag.

'And it's your birthday and your second wedding anniversary at the end of the month,' said Dorothy. 'Will you come over to us, or shall we come over to you? I'll make the cake.'

'Dorrie,' said my father patiently. 'First things first. We've all got to settle in. Besides, Evie probably wants to make her

433

own cake, and may well have other plans. Let the girl run her own life.'

Dorothy said, 'Oh, it's easy for you men. You can just walk off. Hail and farewell and don't give twopence. But this has been my home for sixteen years and Evie's my daughter. . . .'

Julian, who had been sent round the house to check that nothing was left behind, called, 'Mum! You left the dining-room clock on the mantelshelf!'

And came out with a handsome mahogany timepiece in his arms. It was chiming in little protesting jolts.

'Give that clock to me at once!' Dorothy commanded, grabbing it from him. 'That's extremely valuable!'

She paused and turned to me.

In quite a different tone she said, 'Have you got a nice clock, Evie?' And as I shook my head, 'Here you are then, love. Take this one. There's room in your basket. Wrap the tea-towel round it.'

We trooped out to the front porch, and my father shut the front door very carefully lest the Malt-house fall down around our ears.

In silence we walked down the gravel path between the trees. In silence we closed the gate on a family's lifetime, and stood in the lane dispossessed.

Dorothy said, 'I wish. . . .'

Then shook her head and said no more.

The sound of an engine caused us to turn our heads in the direction of Tarn How. And over the scrolled wave of rock, which had been arrested in mid-motion some millions of years ago, flew a solitary biplane.

'De Havilland Tiger Moth two-seater!' Julian shouted, knowing them all. 'Probably training a pilot.'

He reminded us, 'Mick trained in a Tiger Moth.'

The plane flew over our heads and came back again, describing a graceful circle round the Malt-house and Tarn How and our little group standing in the lane.

We could see the helmet and goggles of the solitary occupant. And though we did not know who he was or why he was there, we waved and cried, 'Good luck! Good Luck!'

And as he came low, almost within touch of us it seemed, we saw him raised one gloved hand in greeting.

He was heading back now, gaining height, would soon be no bigger than a bird in the sky, and then invisible, leaving only the sound to linger behind him for a while longer.

Above Tarn How, as if he knew we were still standing there in watchful smiling silence, he waggled his wings in a final salute. And sped away.

I was too early, and now he is late. The sun dazzles my eyes so that I cannot see who opens Peeble's door. The bell gives a brisk ting of introduction, and the door closes emphatically, as it has done so often during the last hour. Before he emerges through the haze I know he is there.

Neither of us says a word. He puts one long thin hand questioningly on the back of the chair opposite. We stare at each other in silence, thinking, 'Is this really you?'

The genteel conventions of an English tea-shop close round us, tight and strait-laced as a corset. We should have met at Blackstone Central Station where tears and emotional embraces are regarded as part of the homecoming, and the crowds hide both. Only extreme politeness will do here.

I rise halfway from my seat and hold out my own hand, as to a stranger. My smile is a mere tremor of the lips.

His clasp is cold and tentative, his expression unusually grave. He is no longer immaculate, wearing a demob suit which must have been the best of a limited choice. He does not know what to do with the raincoat he carries over one arm, or that terrible trilby hat.

I lean forward to move my own coat from the chair.

'This is in the way!' I say.

My first words to him in eighteen months.

It is difficult for him to speak. He swallows and is distressed. So thin, so remote, with his tired grey face and guarded eyes.

The waitress, who cannot or will not see that we are in deep shock, comes up to ask us if we would like to order now.

He says, 'This is the wrong place.'

His first words to me in eighteen months.

The waitress looks offended. Like all women I strive to harmonise the situation. I explain how long she has allowed me to keep the table, how sweet she has been, and just look at those gorgeous cakes! But I know that we cannot pick up where we left off because we are not the same people, just as Peeble's is not the same place.

He is struggling to get through, as I am. It is a difficult birth, as difficult as Grannie Annie's death. The waitress is tired and elderly, and this is her busiest time of day. She poises a pencil over her notebook and looks questioningly from one to the other of us.

Then Dickie emerges, recognisably, saying, 'No, we shan't be wanting anything, thank you.' And gives the waitress half-a-crown to pay for my shilling pot of tea, adding, 'Thank you *so* much.'

I move gingerly towards him. He holds my arm firmly and begins to steer me out of the café, while I babble over my shoulder, 'So kind! So very kind!' Then we are out in sunny St Anne's Gate, turning to face each other for the second time, now knowing that this is real, holding out our hands and coming together in a public embrace. At which spectacle the people smile, hurrying by.

For this is not the end of the story but our beginning.